MORTAL END

MORTAL END

An Opera of Cursed and Fated Vampires

MADDIE ROSE ANDRY

Published by Pleiades Publishing

ISBN: 979-8-9915748-0-8

CONTENT GUIDANCE

I want to express my appreciation to every person who chooses to embark on this journey with me. It's important to explain that the potential triggers/content within my writing are not simply for shock value, and please remember this is a work of fiction.

I create fiction to reflect experiences I have either personally lived through and can identify with or have helped patients and clients recover from. The situations in my books are not to be taken literally, but are meant to reflect the grief, pain, love, and long list of emotions experienced during our journey through this vast human experience. In my twenty-plus years within the medical world, I have worked with people from many walks of life and the one constant is—that we all suffer in some form or another; it is inevitable. Yet I have seen people overcome time and time again.

My life's mission since late childhood has been to give a voice to the things that hide within the darkness, the things no one wants to look at or talk about because they cause discomfort. I believe writing is one place we can pour out our "blood," turning it into a healing "ink" for ourselves and others. Our imaginations can be an amazing place to allow healing and the completion of the trauma response.

Reading fiction makes room for the growth of empathy and compassion, not just for others but also for ourselves.

I hope as you turn the pages of anything I have written (or works by other authors), you feel inspired to look into the darkness and know you are not alone—you are loved, and you can overcome; for where there are shadows, there must be light.

Wishing You Love in All Things,

For full content guidance pertaining to *Mortal End* and a list of resources if you need them, please visit https://www.maddieroseandry.com/resources-contentguidance.

"Only those who will risk going too far can
possibly find out how far one can go."
T. S. Eliot

CURSED

EGYPT, ELEVENTH DYNASTY

Sadeh stood staring out at the sandy horizon as the sun rose, kissing the beautiful landscape of her home. Peace filled her, as she knew that her lands were no longer at war for the first time in ages. There had been so much fighting between her people, for so long, and to see it end at a time like this gave her hope.

Hope was dangerous, she knew. The past taught her not to hope, for it had always led to nothing but grief and heartbreak. She glanced down, making her coal-black hair fall forward, and though she fought to stop the sensation, dread seeped into her heart.

She placed her creamy brown hand on her motherly belly, losing the fight with her conflicting emotions. Tears traced down her face very slowly and dropped one by one on her linen dress adorned with green beading. With one hand she brushed her tears away while wrapping the other around the amulet that hung from her neck.

"Taweret, hear me, for today is the day." She looked at the floor and saw the puddle of liquid she was standing in. "Let my child have breath. Protect him." It had begun. She prayed this time would be different.

The heat of the day was starting. She turned and walked toward the papyrus stalk pavilion, the reeds that grew like wildfire along the Nile River. She was holding onto the amulet around her neck so tightly that a small drop of blood landed on her chest and rolled in a fine line down to her gown, leaving behind a red stain on the purity of her clothing.

Inside the pavilion were gorgeous vine-wrapped pillars. Placed in the middle of them was a birthing seat for Sadeh, along with a bolster, pad, and pillow. She walked slowly to the center of the room and toward her female servants and midwives. They all had an extreme look of terror on their faces, but this didn't stop them from preparing the pavilion for their queen.

Hot water was waiting, along with the statue of Taweret, the protector of women and children. She was a fierce demoness, for she is the union of three deadly man-eaters, with the paws of a lion, the back of a crocodile, and the standing body and head of a pregnant hippopotamus with large breasts. Taweret's job was to scare off any evil that may hurt the unborn infant or the mother. Not only was her statue present, but her wand, also used as a knife, was placed next to Sadeh's seat to rest upon her belly during labor. Made of hippopotamus ivory, the wand was believed to have the magic to ward off any evil.

"Servants, come to me now! It is time. He is coming!" With this more tears came, and the kohl ran from under her eyes, staining Sadeh's face and dress with black streaks.

Sadeh's servants and midwives ran around the room. Two came to help her to the seat. One placed the water under the seat before she could sit down, but they all managed to chant in unison the same words over and over: "Maintain life where life already exists, and give life where life is coming." This prayer was to Amun, the god of breath, the creator of the gods.

Sadeh called on the gods and goddesses, demons and demonesses alike. She called on all the heavenly beings to make this time different. To make it a success in creating an heir. She longed for nothing more than to be a mother.

She asked Thoth for help. She called on Hathor, the known protector of all women and their family bliss. Then she prayed to Amun for his breath. She wanted him to blow the northern wind to her, to ease her pain, and most importantly to give this son, her fourth son, the breath of life. For none other had been alive. Three times had Sadeh carried, three times had she prepared, and three times had they given her death.

Today she prayed for heart, for breath, for a voice to cry, and for life.

"I beg of thee to give this child life!" And with this the labor continued along with the prayers.

Sadeh chanted over and over between her panting, screams, and cries: "Give him life! Heart. Breath. A voice to cry!" She yelled around her tears and pains.

The servants chanted, "Maintain life where life already exists, and give life where life is coming," while they wiped away her sweat and made sure the magical wand didn't slip from Sadeh's belly. They were wonderfully attentive and scared out of their minds. They all shook, waiting with great anticipation to see if all the prayers would be answered.

On the final push, all was silent. The tension in the room was stifling, and with the dense void, all hope was strangled.

The tiny baby boy was in the hands of one of the servants. Her cream dress was covered in blood and fluids from Sadeh's labor. One of the other attending midwives continued to work with Sadeh to make sure the placenta was expelled. It was then placed in a bowl and removed.

The silence was deafening. There was no crying.

"Where is he?" the queen questioned.

The servant turned toward Sadeh. She had him cleaned and bundled in linen. With tears racing down her cheeks, she responded weakly, "My queen. He is like the rest…beautiful, but he has no breath…no heart."

"Lay him on the pad," Sadeh monotoned. Her voice was flat and devoid of emotion. Her eyes were vacant and hollow, as if life had fled from her as well. She had no more tears. Her prayers were not heard. They were not answered.

The servant did as she was told. She placed the clean, neatly wrapped boy dressed in sun-bleached linen on the pad. He was gorgeous, beautiful. If only he were alive, he would be perfect.

The women were crying and praying frantically. Another unnamed child had been brought to the queen. What would happen to his shadow, his soul, and his life force? He would not gain his afterlife.

Sadeh was the only noncrying, silent one in the room. "Leave me." It was a whisper, but audible.

"No, my queen." A servant ran to her and kneeled, covered in Sadeh's blood and crying.

"*I said leave me at once!*" Sadeh was no longer quiet or unaffected. Her rage was filling the room, and no one would want to be near it.

At one point in time, the queen had been kind and full of life, but with each dead child, part of her soul died too. All the kingdom's servants had experienced her wrath over the years as the number of dead children passed through her body and she was robbed of her chance of motherhood. The knowledge that the kingdom remained without an heir made her wrath only grow more heavy and violent.

The women, bloodstained and covered in their own tears, felt the all-consuming rage bubbling within the queen. All fled at once. All but one brave woman.

"Please, let me take him away." She was a young, pretty girl, strong and brave for her age.

Sadeh stood from her seat, allowing blood to run down both of her legs. "*No!*"

Covered in blood, her once-white dress was now pink and red, with green beading glowing through like the eyes of a cat. She no longer looked human. Rage had taken over, and her face was stained with black lines from all her worthless tears and sweat.

"It is not a *him*! It is not my child. It's a *thing*! It is a curse delivered to me from the deities. *Leave me now!*" She screamed. Her body shook and trembled from the volcanic rage about to burst forth.

Sadeh grabbed the magical knife of Taweret from beside the seat and raced toward the servant. "*Leave!*"

At this threat, all courage fled the servant. She ran from the pavilion, wrecked with sobs and fearing for her life.

In her madness, Sadeh walked back into the center of the pavilion, knife still in hand. She dropped to her knees beside her stillborn son and screamed, "Oh, I have prayed before all! Before all the deities of childbirth and of motherhood every day that I carried. I have adorned myself with amulets and worn the colors of fertility. Yet you deliver me a fourth child of no breath! I curse you all! I curse you, Taweret and Hathor. I curse you, Thoth! I curse you, Mut! I curse you, Amun! I curse all the deities. Why deliver such decay from my womb? Not once, which I could forgive, but four times. This is a crime of evil, the purest evil. There is no goodness in all of Egypt! No good in any of her deities! You have no afterlife to offer, no heavens to visit, no universe to command. You have nothing! I will end all of this. You will no longer plague me with your cruelty. I will prove that this creature is no child but an abomination you have sent."

Sadeh raised the knife of Taweret into the air and plunged it into the heart of the baby boy. Though the boy's heart did not beat, a small amount of crimson blood poured from the wound as she pulled the ivory out.

"I don't believe this! It is evil trickery. This isn't a child! There is no life and should have no blood, for he has…*no* heart! *No* breath! *No* voice to cry!" Her screams sounded like she recited yet another prayer as she raised the knife and stabbed the corpse of her son again. More blood poured from the tiny body.

As grief began to replace her rage, Sadeh realized what she was doing. She screamed out in painful agony. Tears began to flow freely down her face once again. She raised the knife in the air once more and swept it down into her own womb and ripped it out. Her blood gushed out of her belly, down her kneeling body, and onto the ground.

"How dare you never let me be a mother, for this is all I have ever wanted!" Sadeh's appearance changed. Her pallor paled and grew sallow.

Yet she was determined to make the deities and the universe pay for her losses, for her agony. It could be heard in her deep, rumbling voice and seen in the madness that was stretching across her face.

"Your heavens shall fall for this. I will make your universe collapse. You shall be damned! All the gods and goddesses, you will all be damned!" Sadeh swung the knife of Taweret toward the sky throughout her rant. The mixed blood, from her and her son, began to run down her arm with each violent swing.

The earth started shaking, and blood began to pour from the papyrus stalk walls. All went dark as the sun was eclipsed. None of this forced Sadeh to ask for forgiveness. It proved they were listening.

"Let the heavens fall!" she bellowed.

Already quickly dying from her abdominal wound, Sadeh raised the knife for the last time and pierced her heart with it. As she pulled the ivory out, she fell atop her baby boy, face down, and spoke her last words. "If only you had life."

From the whispered words against his dead chest, the blood of her son pasted her lips. The taste of his blood flooded her mouth.

A voice from the heavens spoke as Sadeh finished bleeding to death. "You were never meant to be a mother. Your bloodline was fated to die with you. Until this moment we had not cursed you. Now you have cursed yourself. You are plagued to walk the earth for all eternity, *alone*, with the taste of your son rotting upon your tongue. May this be your eternal *hell*."

Sadeh used the last of her strength to push back from her son, noticing the moon was bright in the sky. All her self-inflicted wounds were gone, but she could still feel the pain of motherhood. There was no trace of blood anywhere. Not on the walls, not on the pad, not on her, and not on her son. She believed it was all a dream.

Sadeh stood and caught her breath. Stepping very slowly over to her son, scared to death that he was dead like all the rest. Then he began to cry!

"Oh, thank the gods and goddesses. Thank all the deities!" Sadeh cried, kneeling to lift him from the pad. She was so overwhelmed to be a mother finally. "I promise, my boy, I will be the best mother ever. My breath of life, my Nifé-en-Ankh. I had the worst dream, my Nifé-en-Ankh."

It had all felt so real. Him being born dead. The pain and agony of yet another dead child to mourn. Sadeh stared into his glorious, blinking black eyes, amazed by the tiny life nestled in her arms.

As she cradled him to her chest, she began to murmur to him. "My boy, it was so real! So vivid! I could feel my heart breaking with the knowledge of never getting to meet you. I felt my soul fracture and break with the longing to know you, my love. And here you are now…with breath to cry! With a strong heart beating so loudly, it is the only thing I can hear!"

She found the sound and feeling of his heart beating, pounding against her chest, mesmerizing. She became lost in the rhythm of each tiny, rapid thump.

Lup-dup. Dup-lup. Lup-dup.

The sound was so alluring, enticing even. She blinked rapidly, trying to shake the odd sensations coming over her. His heartbeat only grew louder, like it was taunting her, calling her in.

Hypnotized by the thumping of Nifé-en-Ankh's heartbeats, Sadeh noticed the room spinning. She was overwhelmed with dizziness and hunger. Obviously, the labor had taken its toll on her. She glanced around the room, looking for someone to help her. Someone to bring her a seat, some food and water. None of her midwives or servants were nearby. She attempted to shake off the growing physical sensations.

The beating of his heart grew louder and louder. So loud in fact, a deep longing appeared within her to make the sound stop. It was becoming a shrill, shrieking noise that she could no longer tolerate. Along with the rapidly growing need for silence, her hunger became so ravenous her throat dried up, as her stomach burned with thirst.

Without any awareness Sadeh picked up the ivory knife and stabbed Nifé-en-Ankh right in the heart, lifted him to her mouth, and began to drink her son's life away.

Once every drop of blood was gone and the room was dead silent because there was no longer the *lub-dub* lullaby reverberating around the space, the voice returned.

"This is your eternal *hell*." As soon as it came, it was gone. Sadeh was left holding her murdered son, Nifé-en-Ankh. Sadeh opened her bloodstained mouth, and a wretched howl escaped.

Chapter 1

AWAKENING

"N*o*!" I awoke screaming, covered in sweat, and grappling with the blankets and pillows. My breath was raspy as I gasped for air. I slammed my eyes closed, trying to shake the agony ripping through my body.

It was the same nightmare again. For months this woman had haunted my dreams nightly. Ever since these nightmares started, my sense of control over my emotions kept slipping with each occurrence. With each haunting, a part of me gets sucked into *her* world, *her* chaos, and *her* curse. Almost to the point I have started to feel cursed myself.

My world continued to slip and crumble out from under me. I had started to feel like she was following me, even in my waking hours. It had been years since I felt this out of control. Years since I had experienced such debilitating panic and paranoia, to the point I was almost terrified to go out into the world.

I started therapy young. I was diagnosed with post-traumatic stress disorder, or PTSD, by the time I was eighteen. The diagnosis was obvious to my therapist. I had no control over the symptoms, and the condition went beyond just a onetime event haunting me. I'd suffered uncountable reoccurring traumas, making the PTSD condition complex; it had literally changed the physical structure of my brain. In situations like mine, it was common for the amygdala to grow larger and overreact to stimuli.

Basically, I had a version of someone in a bell tower who would constantly ring the alarm notifying me I was in danger. My hippocampus had filed away every bad thing in my life, creating an intense state of hyperawareness; and thanks to the brain's negativity basis, my younger self saw five-alarm fires everywhere.

This meant I had my work cut out for me in therapy. I could be taken over by an amygdala hijack instantly and fly into an uncontrollable rage because in my brain I was fighting for my life even when there was no danger present. It made me feel *crazy*. There really wasn't any better way to describe the sensation of being a victim to the reactions of your body and getting no say over what it did. I still had moments when I felt *crazy*; being a prisoner to such a condition could be so debilitating and maddening that at times I would lose sight of who I really was. I would lose myself to it. The resulting rage was like nothing I could ever explain.

I used to be plagued with nightmares of the abuse. I would have flashbacks in public if some aspect of a past event crossed my path. It could be as simple as a sound or smell, or if someone stood too close to me; I could lose my grip on reality and slip into a flashback causing me to lose time. These were some of the most embarrassing moments of my life. It was mortifying to wake up with a group of strangers gawking at me, not knowing where I was and needing time to come to terms with what had just happened.

The work I'd done to overcome my past and learn to live a life with some peace was what inspired me to help others. Don't get me wrong; I wasn't in denial about the ways the PTSD was still in control. I did my best to be emotionally unavailable. I was avoidant with people. I lived alone and always had. I had exactly one best friend and no boyfriend. I isolated myself and had a strong need to control my environment. I was a workaholic, which was simply a coping mechanism. I was so hard on myself, and the committee of inner critics, who resided in my brain, were, honestly, harsh and shitty. Sadly, the list of how PTSD still haunted me was long, and I was aware of all these things. But the victory had laid in conquering the flashbacks and nightmares. To feel like I had a say over my body and mind meant the world to me. Then she came into my dreams!

With each nightmare this bitch stole a part of my soul! Yesterday morning, when I looked in the mirror, I almost didn't recognize the haunted, pale woman staring back at me. This woman's curse had been literally unmaking me slowly, night after night. I felt pieces of myself dying, cell by cell. Almost as if I had been sucked back into my life when I lived with my father. All the progress and healing therapy helped me achieve was destroyed every time that boy died. They have begun to feel real, so real in fact, it was like my life was the dream, and this bitch was as real as the sun!

Trying to shake the all-consuming panic, and the fear of regressively sliding back into a world of flashbacks, I opened my eyes, letting the light flood in. All the colors around me were more vibrant. The red of my bedroom walls reached out to embrace me in their rich, dark tones, as if I had never noticed them before. Each hue had a life of its own. The pounding of my heart wouldn't stop; the red walls looked like blood. The more I focused, all I saw was thick blood pouring down. I closed my eyes tight and ran my fingers through my hair. I gasped for air again, not finding enough.

I prayed for the walls to change colors, even though my rational mind told me neither a prayer nor a wish could change the paint color. It was just fucking paint, Phenice. Get a grip! The color of my walls was one I had loved so much before I started having nightmares about the walls bleeding; now it made my skin scream in pain. I desperately needed to paint my bedroom.

I made myself open my eyes and look at the walls. My heart sped up again, but this time the walls were not moving, not dripping; they were just red. I pulled it together, slowing my breath, and with that my heart slowed, almost becoming steady. The panic eased slightly.

I looked down at the blankets and bed linens I was tangled up in. I let the gold hues pull me in. I was looking for something to calm me, but they reminded me of the sands of Egypt. She loved Egypt. She felt so fucking real! I couldn't help but wonder if she was real. If so, what did she have to do with me? Why did I dream of her, over and over?

My flesh prickled with goosebumps. I could still feel the heat of Egypt, as if I were literally there. It pressed in on my body, scorching my skin, instead of Sadeh's, as if it were inviting me into hell and not her. Like I was meant to take her place. To suffer her eternal torment. The panic flared back to life. I was fucking panting. I hadn't felt this pathetic since before I left my dad, deciding life had to be easier on my own, away from his abuse. I grew up quickly.

I noticed my mouth watering too. I didn't dare swallow. I held my breath, trying to get a grip. I didn't want to taste blood. Not again. Something about the horror was unavoidable. The walls began to pour blood again. I heard the cries of the women, followed by the sound of Sadeh drinking her son's blood. The gulping vibrated off my eardrums, making nausea shoot through me quickly. I threw the covers back, letting them fall with great hazard to the floor.

I scurried out of my bedroom, making my way to the bathroom and the toilet. I desperately attempted to hold down the vomit. With every step I took, Sadeh clawed deeper, crawling underneath my skin. The T-shirt I had worn to bed was weighing me down, setting fire to my flesh. I ripped it over my head, throwing it in my wake. The vomit tried to free itself from my mouth, but I fought to hold it in a few more steps. I pleaded with my stomach to wait. I began to shake from head to toe, making me stumble over the bathroom rug, and the vomit ripped from my gut. I lunged for the toilet, barely making it. My whole body convulsed with the need to expel the darkness that had made its way in. Tears rolled down my face from the force of my retching as I clung onto the commode, sweat pouring over me. After all the contents of my stomach were gone, and the bile had left my nose burning, I continued to heave, over and over.

My heart was broken and bleeding. I could feel his fragile body in my hands and on my lips. I heaved again, and again, and again. Like I said, the bitch had transferred her curse to me.

Finally, the vomiting stopped, though the nausea lingered. I dropped back to my ass and scooted to the wall, needing the support, something to lean on. I grabbed the washcloth from the edge of my four-claw tub and wiped my mouth. Sweat still poured down my forehead. I wished I could blame this bodily reaction on food poisoning. Anything more physical to explain the violent response tearing through me. I had never, in all these months, woken from the nightmare so physically consumed by it. This nightmare was literally breaking me; sucking me back into an older version of who I once was, and I was sick with terror because of it.

For the first time in my life, I considered taking a day off and not going to work. The thought lingered for about half a second before I jumped up, shook off the dizziness, and climbed in the shower. I was going to stick to the coping strategies I had for now. As the water poured over my body, I pleaded with my mind to release the images, the scents, and the sounds of the brutality I kept living through every night. I prayed I wasn't regressing. I didn't know if I could live like that again.

⸙

An hour later I pulled into the parking lot of my building and killed the engine on my Jeep. I still felt shaky, but when I focused on my hands, they were steady and motionless. That was good enough for me.

I climbed out of my truck and walked up to my office. A smile crossed my lips at the sight of my name on the door, followed by a slight chuckle. I still felt like a kid in a candy store when I saw my achievements spelled out. As I opened the door, I glanced at my watch. I would have a patient waiting for me. I was ten minutes late. I was never late. The chaos of this nightmare was ripping my world apart. In truth, it was really starting to piss me off. The most irritating part was I felt helpless, not knowing how to stop the nightmare and get back to the life I had worked my ass off to achieve while this figment of my imagination or psyche was undoing everything with rapid efficiency.

I entered my office and nodded a hello to Alina as I walked by her. A sudden warmth grew inside of me. Her presence always helped bring me back to reality. She helped ground me, creating a deep sense of gratitude. After everything I had been through, having her steady and consistent friendship felt like an anchor in my life. And now, with this plaguing nightmare on repeat, I needed her more than ever.

I went straight to my office to put my things away. As I walked the distance of the hall, the small lifelong, ever-lurking sadness inched up my gut. Alina was my only friend, my only family. Admitting this fact opened a chasm within my heart, filled with all the people who were absent in my life. Proof of just how far I still had to go on my road of recovery. I wasn't willing to trust anyone with my heart. It was evidence of the lingering PTSD. The ghosts and demons that haunted my heart tried to claw their way up from the deep, dark pit. I quickly slammed a steel door over that chasm. Today was not the time to sink back into that particular pain; not with the queen stalking me every night. I had plenty going on without feeling sorry for myself and reawakening the stream of negative, self-destructive emotions, like shame, guilt, and the never-ending rage deep inside. Instead, I chose to hold on to the knowledge, no matter the sadness my past held. Without Alina, I would truly be alone, and my estrangement would be complete. Accepting her friendship and love had been progress. An accomplishment I need to acknowledge today more than any other.

"I don't know what I would do without her," I muttered aloud, not realizing it.

"Good morning, Dr. Jones." Alina's engaging voice rang out and filled my ears as she entered my office.

I prayed she hadn't heard my ramblings. I couldn't tell her how much she meant to me. I had never been able to tell anyone how I truly felt. It felt like a type of exposure I was not willing to offer. Again, evidence of the PTSD, the need to keep people at a safe distance. I could feel the fear of that vulnerability pounding in my heart. The truth was that being open with anyone simply felt like weakness, and it made me feel like a caged animal, desperate to escape. Just thinking about it made the person holding the cord to the bell in my tower, known as the amygdala, ring with reckless abandon, sending me straight into fight or flight.

Nope, I would not share my heart in that way with anyone, anytime soon. I took a deep breath and let out an audible sigh. It was a technique I reverted to frequently when I needed to signal my vagus nerve to soothe my amygdala to release the fight or flight response. All the neuroplasticity work and reconditioning I had done with my therapists over the years to learn how to not react in the face of a trigger was slipping.

"Good morning, Alina. We are in *my* office. Could you please call me Phenice?" I managed a smile. I wish she wouldn't call me Dr. Jones. I hated the sound of it.

Even though it had been four years since I finished my residency and opened my own office, I still couldn't get the image of Harrison Ford in a dusty fedora out of my mind at the mention of "Dr. Jones." Maybe I should start sporting a whip, just for kicks. Honestly, the automatic flashes of his face and the scenes from the movies running through my brain were enough to make me want to change my name. The internal flinch came from the images of watching the movies with my dad. It brought up the smell of stale beer and smoke, of seeing him drunk and passed out while I listened to the dialogue in the background. How horrible was it that the sound of someone speaking my own name was a trigger for me? It was something that didn't even occur to me until people started calling me Dr. Jones and I'd black out during a shift. The heartbreak of that moment lingered still. But whenever we were in the office, I could not convince her to call me by my first name. She insisted it was professional for patients to hear her address me with the title I had worked my ass off to earn. I didn't disagree. I needed a different connotation in my brain at the sound of it. Regardless, I let her have her way because I wasn't willing to tell her the truth; I found the truth embarrassing. I was hopeful one day she would give in and just call me Phenice. After four years it didn't seem likely though, but I was nothing if not tenacious. The true test was seeing if my tenacity would win over her stubbornness.

"Here's your usual, Dr. Jones," she said my name through a smile with the slightest hint of sarcasm as she handed me my tea. It was her way of letting me know she was sticking to her choice of being *professional*. I grimaced internally.

"Your first patient is waiting in suite one." She turned and left my office, closing the door behind her.

I went to my bathroom for a quick glance in the mirror to make sure I was presentable after the morning I'd had. I was scared to look. I took a deep, agonizing breath as I slowly faced the mirror. What I saw shocked the hell out of me. Staring back at me was a beautiful woman with long, wavy blond hair, green-gold eyes, and a creamy-cool complexion. I had this mask of peace fixed on my face. There was no trace of the panic that had my brain wrapped up in a chaotic maze and my stomach tied in knots. None of the internal struggle reflected back at me.

I mouthed, "What the fuck?" to myself in the mirror and shrugged. Years of practice apparently paying off. I was grateful how I felt inside was not reflecting outwardly, and I was emoting calm energy. What kind of psychiatrist would I be otherwise?

I walked out of my office and up to Alina. "Who is my first client?"

"Emil Gannon," she replied. I began to walk away with a nod. "I don't know how you do it," she said in a low voice.

"What?"

"Work with him, with the way he stares at you. You can't pretend like you haven't noticed." She laughed softly. I forced a small laugh in reply. The truth was I had noticed Emil more than I should considering the dynamic of our professional relationship.

I couldn't help but question all my internal thoughts; being haunted by an Egyptian queen every night while I slept was throwing my world into chaos.

I continued to suite one.

"Oh, Dr. Jones." I stopped and turned back toward Alina. "Your last patient canceled, by the way. Sorry." She seemed worried.

"Don't be sorry." I waved my hand in dismissal. "Can you set up a call with Dr. Postmere for me? Then if you're free, let's have lunch. If you want." I managed a weak smile, even though the thought of food made the nausea crawl back up my throat with the lovely taste of bile. I took a sip of my tea, trying desperately to wash it down. Alina gave a sweet nod in agreement.

Chapter 2

ADMISSION

I found myself sitting at my desk, staring into space with my mind running a million miles an hour. I had finished the session with Emil, and I couldn't be more grateful for the foresight to have Alina schedule a meeting with Dr. Postmere. He had been my mentor all through my psychiatric residency. For good or bad, his presence in my life had filled the void my father left behind.

My early attachment bonds were nonexistent; my mother was dead, and I didn't know what having a mom felt like. I didn't have a bond with my father either, due to his substance abuse. All of this left me with a blend between avoidant-dismissive and disorganized attachment styles. Meaning my modus operandi was being overly independent, to push people away, to seek short-term casual relationships with men who didn't want to settle down, and to be untrusting of love because inside I didn't feel like I deserved it. In a nutshell, I didn't feel worthy of being loved and I never wanted to go through the hurt and rejection like I had as a child.

I lied to myself; believing all I wanted was to be left alone to care for myself. Really it was just a deep-rooted terror of intimacy. Alina was safe for now because it was just friendship, a sisterhood of sorts.

Rationally, thanks to my years of therapy and education, I knew all humans needed to feel connected with other humans. We were hardwired to crave love and acceptance. We desire a community, a group of people we can belong to. It's important to feel like you matter through feeling accepted, cared for, receiving kindness and empathy; knowing when you express your authentic self that community will see and hear the real you. Humans long for companionship and a life that is meaningful.

I've deprived myself of all these things, cutting myself off from the true purpose of living, all because of fear. The nightmare may have reawakened the intense aspects of the PTSD, but if I really looked at how I had been living, it was clear I wasn't living at all.

I was simply surviving and enduring day in and day out with no heart and soul driving me. I had fallen into some coping mechanisms that may have been functional five years ago, but now they were dysfunctional; I was using them to avoid life altogether by staying busy. I was avoiding everything and everyone.

I needed Dr. Postmere's help with finding a new therapist. It was time to be brave and take the next step. I had to figure out how to heal my heart so I might one day let love in. I had to ask him about how to proceed with Emil as a patient. This was the first time I had ever experienced anything like this in my professional career, and I needed help. I despised asking for help.

My phone vibrated on my desk, snapping me out of my thoughts.

With a glance at the screen, I answered. "Hello, Dr. Postmere."

"Hello, Phenice." I sighed, happy he at least would call me by my first name. "Alina reached out to my assistant to let me know you wanted to chat."

"Yes. Thank you for your time."

"Phenice, as you know I will always make time for you. What do you need, dear?" The tone of his voice sounded as a father should, open and loving. My heart squeezed with an intense sense of longing, my loneliness rising to the surface.

I took a deep breath trying to find the courage to expose my heart to this man. He knew about my past. He had been there for me the day I blacked out during my residency. I almost quit; the embarrassment almost won, over my desire to succeed. He was the one to help me see through that humiliation and move on. This was nothing compared to that, and if I continued down this road, I would have even more work to do.

"Well, I have two issues for you. One is personal and one is professional, about a patient." I felt the weight lift from my shoulders as soon as the words left my mouth. It felt good to let it go.

"I'm happy to help with both if I can, as always," he replied.

"The personal issue is the easy of the two. Not that it has been easy for me but will take less of your time," I rambled.

"Okay, let's start with what it is I can do for you personally then," he motivated me to proceed.

"I am having a reoccurring nightmare. It is not a traumatic event I'm reliving or anything, but it is still terrifying. It's causing the same symptomatic manifestations during my waking hours like past PTSD flashbacks and nightmares. I haven't been in therapy for about two years at this point. I wanted to see if you could refer me to someone who isn't local and doesn't know me." I wiped my mouth. The nausea was coming back. This time it was because I was anxious.

"Oh, Phenice, I'm terribly sorry to hear this. Is there a reason you don't want someone local?" he wondered.

"I would feel more comfortable with a sense of anonymity, even if it's an illusion." I chuckled.

"Yes, okay. This I completely understand. May I think on some colleagues I feel would be a good fit for you and get back to you within a few days?"

"Of course. A week or however long you need is perfect. Thank you for your help." I placed a hand atop my leg under the desk, in an attempt to stop the frantic bouncing from my nerves. I needed help like yesterday, but I wasn't going to pressure this man.

"Okay, now that your personal issue is out of the way, how may I help you professionally?" he inquired.

"Okay, it's actually two-fold now I've thought on it more; it is partly personal as well, I'm afraid," I began.

"Okay, let this old man have it." He let out his throaty laugh, making me smile. My first real smile of the day.

I opened the clinical notes I had made about Emil on my desktop. "Okay. It is about a patient I haven't been seeing long. Not long enough to have an official diagnosis I am comfortable with, but long enough to have some theories."

"You've got me on the edge of my seat, Phenice." I loved talking shop with him. It lit a fire inside of me to bounce ideas off him like I once did. There was a familiar comfort in it. The tension started to drain from my shoulders; an involuntary sigh fell from my lips.

"So the patient is a thirty-year-old single heterosexual male. He stated he was feeling emotionally overwhelmed through the first few sessions. As he grew more comfortable with me, I began to dig a little deeper into his past trying to find the root of his emotional upheaval. Primarily, he seemed worried, stressed, and paranoid. I asked about his relationships with his family, his friends, and intimate partners," I started.

"Those are all good places to start to build a healthy professional trust between the patient and the provider. Did things go astray?" Dr. Postmere questioned.

"Yes, after about two and half months of sessions, he confessed to me there was a woman in his life. A woman who was his *soulmate*, his exact words. He proceeded to tell me how he had to protect her from some extreme danger he wouldn't reveal to me. I asked him how well he knew this woman, and he confessed to following her but that she had no clue who he was. He followed that by letting me know he had always known her, since the beginning of time." I paused there to let Dr. Postmere feel the impact of that statement.

"Since the beginning of time?" he asked.

"Yeah. Since the beginning of time."

"Did you ask him to clarify what that meant to him? Did he mean she felt familiar?" Dr. Postmere asked.

"I did ask. He told me they had spent many lifetimes together, but it always ended tragically. That was the statement that made me worry. I'm worried for this woman. He is clearly having some signs of delusions and is fantasying about past lives with her. He seems to be stalking her, though he comes across as harmless to her; I turned my attention to any psychological conditions that would lead to this type of behavior." I explained my thought process.

"There isn't much research on stalkers or what causes this type of behavior. This falls more into the field of forensic psychology because when this behavior is severe enough, the legal system gets involved. Most stalkers do not seek therapy, Phenice," Dr. Postmere interjected.

"That's partially why I'm stuck. He doesn't fit any axis I condition. He is not schizophrenic or bipolar, nor does he seem to have major depression. I started to dig to see if he fits any of the axis II personality disorders, and nothing fits," I informed Dr. Postmere.

I stuck with the DSM-IV criteria versus the newer DSM-V (*Diagnostic and Statistical Manual of Mental Disorders-Five*) when he and I had any discussions because he trained and practiced under the previous version, as had most of my educators. The updated system eliminated the multiaxial system of diagnosis. It reorganized personality disorders into three clusters: Cluster A, Cluster B, and Cluster C. It was something that frustrated the man, and my goal was to receive his guidance, not his tangency and resistance to change.

"So, he's empathetic?" he asked.

"Yes, very much so, almost to an extreme. He feels deeply. He blames himself for what he says is going to happen to this woman. He doesn't sound like he is the one who is going to hurt her. He seems to think someone else is after her," I told him.

"Then he doesn't seem to fit the criteria for antisocial personality disorder. He sounds like he cares about the rules of society too much to fall into that classification," he was thinking aloud. "He also doesn't seem shy or withdrawn if he came to you for help. Therefore, that rules out avoidant personality disorder as well. Unless he has had a hard time with anything critical you have said."

"No, not at all. He seems extremely receptive," I told him.

"We can also rule out dependent personality disorder, for he doesn't seem to have a problem with making decisions or leading in life," he thought aloud; I knew he wanted my confirmation.

"Yes, we can mark that one off. He runs his own business with three business partners," I informed him.

Dr. Postmere taught me to be systematic and complete, so I continued. "We can, unfortunately, rule out the rest of the personality disorders, I believe. He doesn't meet criteria for schizoid or schizotypal. No OCD signs either. Just the fact that he came to see me nixes paranoid type. He can be paranoid at times, but it's more of an emotional state versus a condition because it seems to only apply to this woman. He has no histrionic signs, no excessive emotional outbursts or attention-seeking behavior. I kind of wondered about narcissistic, but he's far too empathetic and takes responsibility to a fault. Honestly, I'm stumped." I rattled it fast because I wanted to get it out, and that was how he liked a report on a patient. It was like being back in class with him.

I was holding my breath as I hoped Dr. Postmere would agree with me. That was a problem all its own and the second part of this conversation regarding Emil.

"I would have to agree with you. Maybe the simplest diagnosis is erotomania—a delusional belief that this woman is passionately in love with him. So he has concocted a fantasy where she is in danger and needs him to save her. As if he must rescue this damsel in distress," Dr. Postmere stated.

"I thought about that, but I hesitated because most studies show it is predominantly diagnosed in women. Therefore, I dug deeper, thinking there had to be some deeper causation." I sighed.

I had racked my brain trying to figure out why Emil was doing what he was, and it had been staring me in the face the whole time. My first thought was he had erotomania because it was the simplest answer, and Dr. Postmere seemed to agree.

"In this situation the only hope for improvement is for him to realize the delusion exists?" I uttered; it was a question, not a statement.

"Yes, that is the course of action," he responded.

"Dr. Postmere, this condition and behavior is outside my scope of practice. I don't feel comfortable treating him," I confessed.

"I can ask around and see if there is someone who specializes in this or something similar. I have a few colleagues in the forensic science department I can reach out to."

"Thank you. I would be grateful," I responded, ready to be done hashing over this situation, grateful I didn't have to reveal the *feels* under it all.

"So tell me the personal part of the issue with this patient, Phenice," he prompted.

Shit. I could've solved both issues without ever having to expose myself to my mentor. Warmth flooded my face as shame crawled into my gut like liquid heat. He agreed he needed to transfer care, but I'd opened my big mouth at the start of this conversation. I hadn't been thinking clearly for months now. If my head had been on straight, I would've referred Emil to someone else a while ago. Damn it.

"Honestly, Dr. Postmere, I'm experiencing countertransference with this patient. I don't know when or how, but somewhere along the way, I developed feelings for him. He is attractive, more attractive than any man has the right to be. With the nightmares coming back for the last few months, I'm slipping. The isolation I have created to feel safe has obviously backfired." My heart was racing.

I verbally vomited all over the man through the phone. Sweat started to pop up across my brow as cold chills ran down my back. Emil made me feel things I didn't want to feel, yet unless I wanted to live in complete denial, the feelings were there screaming loud and clear, attempting to get my attention.

"Phenice, it's okay," he stated firmly.

"It really isn't, Bruce." A tear fell from my right eye as I called the man by his first name—something I only did when I needed him to be a friend, not an educator. When did that tear creep up on me? I wiped it away quickly and shook out my hands, blowing out a quick breath.

"Phenice, you are being hard on yourself, like always. We are still human. We do the best we can to take care of the people who cross our paths, the patients who ask for our help. But if you are not honest with yourself, kind and loving, you're not only doing yourself a disservice, but you're also going to end up letting all of them down too. You must take care of your feelings and your heart first," he spoke gently yet firmly.

"But..."

"Nope. It happens sometimes, Phenice. It's why we educate students about countertransference. So when it does, they know how to do the right thing for themselves and the patient. You have wonderful reasons to refer him to someone else. His needs fall outside your expertise. That is what's best for him." His voice was kind and gentle but held a tone not to be argued with.

He wasn't done. "Caring for your heart, instead of hating yourself for feelings you cannot help, can be solved by sending him elsewhere. There is no fault. Do you hear me?" he finished.

"Okay. You're right. I know you are right. Thank you, truly," I whispered. It was almost too vulnerable for me.

"Anytime, Phenice. You know that. Now I need to get to my next lecture. Stop by and see me when you are on campus next."

"I will," I said as we both hung up.

Chapter 3

SOULMATES

We sat at a patio table at one of my favorite cafés. I always took advantage of outdoor dining any chance I got. It was too beautiful not to, with the clear skies and cool breeze. This was one of the many things that brought me to Oregon when I was younger. I loved it here. After all these years, I couldn't imagine living anywhere else.

The waiter was a tall and rugged-looking young man, most likely a student at the University of Oregon where I taught. He brought us water, took our drink orders as he placed the menus on the table, and finished by rattling off the daily specials.

Once he left, Alina started in. "So how did your session with Emil go? It had to be intense, sitting there, staring into his deep, mesmerizing eyes. They're like gazing into the ocean, so vast. And my god, his voice, with that formal-yet-husky British accent. Not even Barry White holds a candle to what he can do to you. That is a panty-dropping voice if I have ever heard one. I swear, just the sound of him speaking could cure infertility! There is no way even you, the great fortress you are, can withstand his powers!"

I don't think she took a single breath throughout her rant, while she batted her dainty sky-blue eyes, trying to lure me in to her fairy tale of lust. Her blatant excitement lifted a weight from my shoulders. Her lightheartedness helped me relax in a way I didn't realize I needed until after it happened. Her playful energy was just what I required following the heart-to-heart I just finished with Dr. Postmere.

"Firstly, my dear, breathe, and secondly, you know even if you were right about a single syllable"—which, holy shit, she was—"being the most wonderful and utmost respectable professional, I cannot breathe a word to you that isn't absolutely necessary to my patient's health, due to his confidentiality rights. So, my love, you will have to have your daydream fantasies about some other people. I will not feed that lovesick brain of yours!"

Her face started to turn red in frustration and possibly something more.

I loved driving her mad, and it was blissful that in that moment, the oath of my profession was helping me. It was one thing to talk with Bruce. It was another to give in to these fantasies with Alina. I needed to get her off the topic of Emil. He made me sweat, among other things.

"So…why don't you tell me some of your intriguing love stories? Maybe you can inspire me. You keep telling me that I need to go out. I need to meet someone. Arouse me, Alina, wet my taste buds to how astonishing men can be." I was being sarcastic in my tone, but really…I was lonely. I had made my career everything and ignored all the fun things in life. I knew letting people get close was my greatest fear. My heart was closed for business. Part of me lived vicariously through Alina's exploits. Definitely something to bring up in therapy once I found someone.

"Oh, come on, Phenice. I mean, *Dr. Jones*." She couldn't help but roll her eyes and snicker at me.

"Shit. Alina, how long have we been friends? I'll give you the doctor bullshit in the office, but nowhere else, you brat." She started giggling. "You stopped calling me Dr. Jones after you passed my class. You can cut the sarcasm. I mean it: dazzle me, let me in. I wanna be in the club; I'll pay the fees, oh please!" I was having more fun than I'd had in a long time. The conversation with Dr. Postmere had lifted a weight from my heart, making it easy to tap into her playful, childlike nature. I had always wished I could be more like her in that way. Carefree and deeply loving what life had to offer.

"It can be a lot of fun. There's so much to experience. Men are so different. They're like candy, so many flavors and textures. The hard part is finding your favorite!" And with this I could've sworn all appearance of innocence vanished and actual horns grew from the top of Alina's pretty head, right out from between her wavy brown ringlets. The most gorgeous, breathtaking smile lit up her heart-shaped face as she fantasized about, I'm sure, some *candy* she must've had in the not-so-distant past.

I found myself jealous and not a bit judgmental. Who could judge such happiness that clearly illuminated her delicate face? She looked almost like a fairy. No, a sexy nymph. Yes, a lustful, sexy nymph with horns.

I couldn't help but laugh at the mental image. Good thing Alina thought I was laughing at her candy analogy. "See? You could totally do this. You could go out and meet some nice, yummy guy. Who knows? You may actually enjoy life for once."

"Ouch! That was below the belt, Alina. I enjoy life." I was surprised she felt this way about me, or should I say that I was shocked that she saw through the mask I wore for everyone. I wanted love badly, but all I could remember was how everyone left, and I kept collecting baggage. The storage closet in my heart was filled with enough brokenhearted moments that I truly didn't think I could close the door anymore. That made it difficult to keep trying.

"Yeah, which part exactly? Seeing patients most mornings, followed by a quick-yet-healthy lunch, then straight to the university for either a lecture, a discussion session, or office hours? Followed by stopping by the grocery store a few times a week just to go home for yoga or a run, followed by a bath? Then you cook a sensible and healthy meal, only to curl up in bed *alone*, every night, unless you count the book you fall asleep reading. *Boring*." She accompanied the word with an eye roll. She wasn't done either. She needed a breath. "You're way too intelligent to let your life pass you by like this. Don't you want more? Don't you need more, crave more?" Alina's happy-go-lucky temperament disappeared, as did mine.

Shocked by her brutal honesty and having the illusion of my life shattered so completely, I involuntarily dropped my head into my hands and the tears started to flow. Not a few single tears, but a full-on raging sob. I had never cried in front of her. Truth was, I don't remember ever crying in front of anyone. As expected, I hated it! I would rather be pissed and screaming. I knew anger and rage; those sensations were comfortable. It was why I ran—*daily*. Everything was crashing down; the last few months of nightmares had revived the PTSD symptoms. I was having feelings for a freaking patient. My world was unraveling. Now I was losing my shit in front of Alina and in public. I was officially a mess.

All the times my dad hit me, I'd never let him see me cry, and here I was, dining outside at a café, bawling like an infant for all to see. It was too similar to the times I blacked out in public when I was younger. I started to panic. I willed myself to stop. I pleaded with my eyes to dry up and quit this nonsense. I tried my hardest to will the water back behind the internal dam I once constructed as a child. Fuck. The dam was broken. I could not get it to stop. I was done for. The tears just kept coming. The harder I tried, the faster they came.

I felt Alina's hand on the nape of my neck and vaguely heard her tell me that she was sorry, but I wasn't upset by her frankness. I was devastated by how right she was. My life had no meaning. I wasn't living at all. Hatred bubbled up out of my gut. I was a coward. I hated myself for it. At some point in my life, I had given up.

I had run away from my father with a dream to have a life, to find happiness. Once, I had been so determined to not simply survive but to forge a way of life that allowed me to thrive, and here I sat, a grown-ass woman hiding from the world. Hiding behind my achievements and routines. I had prided myself on strength, on courage, and what was I now? A fucking coward! Fuck that. I needed to fix it. I wasn't going to let PTSD or anything beat me.

"Phenice…Phenice, please, sweetie. Say something! I'm sorry, so sorry. I didn't mean to be so curt. I'm an ass. I'm the worst friend ever. Please, say something, anything. Let me be selfish. I need to make it better so I can feel better about me…*okay*? Take care of me; you're wonderful at taking care of others. *Please*!" I looked up at her, tears staining my face. And like magic I stopped crying.

She was right. All I'd ever done was take care of everyone around me. My needs be damned. It was all I knew how to do. I mean, shit, I had made a career out of it. I hid behind taking care of the people around me, so my problems remained buried along with the pain. Leaving me in the cold to die. If I looked closely, I was dying a slow, lonely, miserable death.

I fell into the fawning trauma response. Her words spoken so directly made me see all the ways I sacrificed my needs to please the people around me. I had done it for years with my father in hopes he wouldn't hit me or be cruel.

I was still waiting for the next attack, the next slap, or beatdown. I withheld my opinions in groups; no wonder I isolated myself. I starved myself of my desires, believing someone else's needs held more value than mine. They came first so I could feel safe. I had been conditioned for years to keep my abuser happy and appeased to stop the beatings and harsh words.

No one had ever taken care of me. Your parents are meant to, in theory, but my mother was dead. So she never got the chance. I never got to call anyone Mom, or Mommy. My heart broke, as I sat with the grief her absence still invoked, how deeply the lack of her was etched in my bones. I knew her absence hurt, but in truth, it hurt so badly my bones felt like they could snap under the weight of craving the love of a mother. In that moment, I wished I had a *mommy*. It had taken twenty-nine years for me to admit that to myself.

I ached for the opportunity to call my mother and ask her how to find love. To have the support of someone like that to help me navigate the intimacy of relationships so I could stop screwing up so badly every time.

As for my father, what could I say? He never counted. He was the person who taught me my needs didn't matter, and he was one more person to take care of. He might be dead and gone right now, and frankly the world would be better off. He was nothing but an abusive bastard. A man who never loved me. A man I hadn't seen in thirteen years. I got my driver's license, and I left.

I reached for the napkin lying in my lap and used it to wipe my face. "I'm okay, Alina. You're right, that's all. Your honesty proves you care. You're my best friend. What I want is love. Real love. And how do you find that?" The question was so honest it hurt to even say the words.

I made eye contact with her. She looked almost as sad as I was because tears started to form in the bottom of her eyelids.

"Don't you start too." I tried to laugh. "They're likely to kick us out if we're both howling fools." I let the silence linger for a few minutes. "So, I take it the candy is just a distraction?" I used her metaphor for men to see if she had ever been in love.

"Yes and no. I'm hoping that one of the flavors will be true love." This brought slight smiles back to both of our faces and provided safe passage for the rugged, tattooed waiter to come and try to take our order.

As we both ordered, I studied her face. She wasn't as happy as she wanted people to believe. Apparently, we had that in common. I wanted to tell her how important she was to me. I wanted to tell her about my parents because outside of therapy I had never spoken about it to anyone. Yeah, I had trust issues, clearly. She knew my mom had died during childbirth. She also knew I didn't speak to my father, but she had no idea why. She didn't push either. If I was going to ever tell someone, it would be her. Instead of opening up to my best friend, I bit my tongue, holding back my past. The dread of her pity was what held my words.

"Phenice, I have to tell you something."

Here, I wanted to confess to her, and she was going to spill *her* guts. She was braver than me.

"What is it?"

"I know I should mind my own business, *obviously*, but I just can't help it. He seems perfect for you." She started, and all I could think was, *Shit!*

"Alina, what the hell did you do?" Now I was scared—correction, embarrassed. I could feel the redness pooling in my cheeks. I had let her set me up on a few blind dates in the past; they all ended horribly. I wasn't ready for whatever was about to come out of her mouth.

"After you went in with your second patient, I read through your notes on Emil Gannon." She hung her head. I sighed. It could've been so much worse. Alina was a sweet person, but she could be very aggressive at times. I feared she would say something to him.

"And what did you think?" I knew she was waiting for me to yell because I could lose my temper, but with her it would've been more of a stern *what were you thinking?* But my curiosity outweighed any anger I had toward her. I already knew I was going to find him someone else to work with after my conversation with Dr. Postmere. I was curious about Emil, and I wanted to hear her thoughts on the matter.

She gazed at me as if I had slapped her right in the face. "Phenice, are you okay?" Clearly, she might've been more accepting of the smack over my calmness. It threw her.

I wondered if she was questioning my objectivity, because when it came to Emil, I was.

I thought about her question—*Was I okay?* I didn't think I was. Clearly the reoccurring nightmare had rattled me to my core. It was breaking old parts of me back open. Parts I never wanted to look at again or be honest about. I was bored with my life. I wanted something new and exciting. I don't think that made me *not okay* per se, just in transition maybe. I had so much to work through in therapy. I had to remind myself I wasn't starting over, just taking the next step.

"I think I'm okay, or maybe I'm not. I'm starting to realize I need my life to evolve or change. And I'm interested in your opinion. I would like your advice and support. When it comes to Emil, you have a degree. What do you see?"

"Why ask? Do you feel like your judgment is *clouded*?" She smiled brightly. I knew she was hoping my answer was yes.

"Yes, Alina, I have developed a soft spot for Mr. Gannon. Maybe even a small *crush*. That was what my conversation with Dr. Postmere was all about. I'm going to transfer him to a colleague once Dr. Postmere gives me a list of names." She was about to pounce out of her chair due to her overwhelming excitement.

"Holy shit! That's fuckin' awesome." She attempted to gain some composure but failed miserably. "I mean, completely the most professional thing to do." She was laughing so hard she could barely get the last part out.

"But if you read the file, you know he has a *soulmate*, and that means I have no chance. If you're fantasizing about him and me together." I would in no way ever follow through on these thoughts. I had to admit, it was nice to think about finding someone I could call mine. The thought of being so connected and close to someone made my heart race and my breath catch.

Our food came. A hamburger and fries for Alina, a large spring mix green salad and hummus with pita for me. We sat silently as if we had nothing interesting to say. We both thanked our waiter. I told him everything looked amazing. Alina and I both assured him we were fine. He turned to leave, and before he was out of earshot, we returned to our gossip. I had turned into a lovestruck girl in the last few minutes. How did that happen?

"I did read the file. Only three times! His soulmate has no idea he's alive, and he wants it that way. Which frankly I don't understand. You must've left a lot out. It was very confusing. I felt like there were gaps to his story." She was eating her hamburger and fries and trying to talk through them. She was doing well. After many lunches with her, I knew all too well that practice made perfect.

I left my food alone and decided to explain the best I could.

"He says that every one of us has a soulmate, and it's the same one for all eternity, but the problem is we are not always in the same *place* or even alive at the same time. He said the sad part is we may pass through many lifetimes and never get to spend one with our mates, but we can always feel them, and their absence causes us great pain." Alina was staring at me with so much passion, and I believed at that moment, she had as much faith in the concept as Emil had when he was explaining it to me.

Emil had treated it as sacred, as having faith in a higher power or a god. While I sat across from him this morning, staring into his silvery-purple eyes, I felt like the world's biggest cynic. I didn't want to be. I wanted to be a carefree optimist. I wanted love, and he made me want to risk everything to have it. This morning he had made me feel like the Grinch whose heart had grown three sizes listening to his love and passion for this woman. I longed to be loved the way he loved her.

I sat with my lunch as I tried to recite the theory as best I could, while all the feelings came rushing back to me.

"But can't you fall in love and get married? Can't you still be happy?" Alina intriguingly questioned.

"He said you could be with whomever you wanted if your soulmate was elsewhere. 'On another *plane*' was the phase he used. But you would be settling, and it wouldn't be love. It couldn't be love. It's more like companionship or a deep friendship." When he had talked to me in the office this morning, it had been romantic, but now that I was repeating it out loud to Alina, I felt depressed and hopeless. My well of loneliness grew deeper as despair lit up my gut. If I had a soulmate, I was damn sure I had never met them.

"So, if this cosmic love is so rare, why is he not chasing it down and holding on to it with everything he has? I read in your notes he is avoiding her as much as possible. All he wants to do is protect her. Protect her from what?" She asked the same questions I wanted answered.

"You've got me. All he would say was—and I left this out of my notes because I didn't understand it—'for we are not of the same nor do I want us to be, and we must be the same to unite.'"

She stared at me. "Sounds…medieval," she replied, confused, which I completely understood. I didn't get it either.

"Yeah. That's what I thought. It's why I didn't put it in my notes. It was too weird. He went on to say, 'This doesn't stop me from watching her, from wanting to protect her.' I asked him what he was protecting her from, and he told me I wouldn't understand."

Alina's eyes widened.

"He's stalking her?" It was a question, not a statement.

"Yes, I believe so."

"Do you think he is going to hurt her? Should we report him?" A bit of fear crept into her voice. I bet she didn't think he was perfect anymore.

"No, I don't believe him dangerous, not to her. He believes the protection is necessary because she is special. He said she was more special than she even knew. What he actually said was, 'She doesn't even know what she is, and those hunting her don't know just how unique she is. If they did, they would leave her be.' I spoke to Dr. Postmere about him. We both agreed he doesn't have a personality disorder. He most likely has erotomania. I am going to try and find him someone who specializes in forensic psychology and takes clients." Alina had stopped eating, even though she was only halfway done. She was peering at me with her jaw hinged open like a deer caught in a set of headlights.

"Phenice, he is talking about people hunting other people. So you think he has made up some fantasy, a story in his mind, to have a reason to follow this poor woman around? Do you think he may end up hurting her?" The passion that had filled her eyes moments before while talking about love and soulmates was now replaced with fear for a woman neither of us knew.

Oddly, I felt a sense of safety and deep longing. Longing to be desired and loved by someone so completely. Deep in my gut, something told me I could trust Emil—like he wouldn't lie about anything.

"Yes, that was the conclusion Dr. Postmere and I came to during our conversation. His behavior is outside of my expertise." It was all I could say. I didn't believe he was dangerous to this woman.

"I think you need to report him," she urged.

"If Dr. Postmere doesn't get me in contact with someone soon, I'll think about it. It may be challenging not knowing the woman's name. Hopefully I'll have someone to guide me through the next best steps soon." I withheld the part about my issues with countertransference. That was private and embarrassing.

"Thank you." She seemed relieved.

She started eating again, and I finally got to start my meal. We ate in silence. She was clearly in shock and most likely judging herself because she felt like she had misread someone. I was quiet because many things lately left me evaluating my whole life. My emotional outburst just being one more event to add to the ever-growing list.

Her bringing up Emil made me realize how strongly I felt for him. Now that I was going to dismiss him as a patient, my mind and heart began to wander. I really had no clue how blinded I might have been over the past few months due to my desire for him.

I saw now, I was extremely attracted to Emil. So much so, it was overwhelming during our sessions. Today, whenever he would smile, my heart would start to pound in my chest, stealing my breath.

He was upset this morning when I walked into the room. He seemed anxious to the point he was on the verge of lashing out with rage. I wanted to kneel in front of him and take his pain away. My heart wept at his discomfort. I didn't understand. I watched patients cry, scream, and break open all the time. It was in my job description to hold space for them while they shifted through some of the hardest feelings life had to offer. I always felt sympathy for them. Never had I been moved in such an empathetic way. I wanted to carry his burden, share his pain. It was like I felt it too. As I ran over it again in my head, a sudden shock slapped me in the face. The truth was I wanted to kiss him this morning. I had been in denial all these months. Talking with Dr. Postmere had cleared so much up.

Emil had been occupying my thoughts a lot lately. I felt invaded by wanting him. I was desperate to touch his creamy skin, and it went beyond lust. I had always been a person of great willpower, but one look into his rich amethyst eyes and all willpower had been stripped from me, leaving me naked and helpless. Deep down I had been blaming it on loneliness, but my gut now told me it was much, much more.

Just add this to the ways my life was falling apart at the seams.

We finished our meals wrapped in our own internal meditations. I paid the check, even though Alina felt bad because I broke down and cried. She blamed herself. I didn't blame her at all, and I knew it bothered her to see me weak. Shit, it scared me.

Today had been so fucked up. A complete mess from the time I woke up this morning covered in sweat and vomiting. I decided not to judge anything too hard yet. It was obvious I was feeling vulnerable and not thinking clearly. I would do my best to ignore it. See no evil, right? That became my brilliant plan. Somewhere I heard an internal voice chuckle at this plan. It told me I was full of shit, and it wasn't going to work. Crap!

I told Alina it was no big deal. I was planning to get a life as soon as possible, thanks to her. This brought a forced smile to her face. She was such a beautiful woman. I didn't think she realized it. If she had the confidence to go along with the face and the body, I didn't think she would have a problem finding the *flavor* of true love. I gave her a huge hug, not knowing which of us needed it more. I left the café, walking toward my truck as I waved goodbye.

Chapter 4

STRANGER

I watched as Alina walked in the opposite direction toward her car, and thanks to my complete lack of focus, I ran straight into another pedestrian. I stumbled, almost falling until I was caught by the person I collided with.

"Oh my god, I'm so sorry." I managed to mumble out my apology before I even made eye contact with the stranger. I straightened myself while pulling my hair out of my face.

Surprise slammed right into my core. I had run over Emil.

"It's okay, Dr. Jones. I was staring at the sidewalk instead of watching where I was going. Completely my fault." His smooth accent slid through me like honey.

He smiled at me. And there it was, that heart-stopping, luminous grin showing perfect white teeth encased in his soft, berry-colored lips. I had an instant urge to lick them. Followed by immediate embarrassment and shame, which must have left me flushed because my face was set ablaze. The list from Dr. Postmere couldn't come fast enough. I couldn't live with these contradicting urges and wanted to refer him to someone else immediately.

It felt like forever before I could speak. I had parted my lips a few times in the attempt, and I failed horribly. Amateur.

I finally managed a "Hello, Emil." From there, it got easier to behave as if I had a brain in my skull. "It's good to see you again and not in the office. I would love it if you would call me Phenice, please. I specifically remember discussing this in our sessions."

He laughed lightly as he ran his hand through his wavy mahogany hair. As the sunlight reflected through it, I could see strands of gold mixed in with the deep, rich reddish-brown. The color was captivating. It was long and fell well past his shoulders. I ached to touch it so I could see how soft it was. I clinched my hands into fists to stop the twitching need of my fingers.

My eyes traveled back to his lips and over the thick, well-groomed beard highlighting his buttery, light bronze skin. I again wondered if his facial hair was soft too. What would it feel like against my skin? Oh my, he was stunning. I couldn't help it—I wanted to reach out and pet him.

"Okay…Phenice it is. I will try. That is all I can promise." As the words fell from his lips, it was like a slap in the face. Shit. I was staring, possibly drooling. I had to get it together.

"That is better than nothing." Just the sound of my name slipping over his lips made my knees weak. It took all my strength not to crumble where I stood. I would beg this man to break me in the best of ways.

I needed to focus on something, but all I could see was Emil standing there in front of me. He was glorious, in his six-foot-four, well-chiseled frame, wearing dark-blue jeans and a deep clover cashmere sweater that didn't hide any of his strength. I yearned to be that sweater. I wanted to wrap myself around him. Shit. I needed to sleep with someone. This was ridiculous.

He was staring intensely at me, making my heart thunder in my chest and my palms instantly clammy. I inhaled, and as the breath entered my lungs, I shuddered from head to toe as if someone had passed their fingers lightly down my spine. It made me wet. I couldn't believe it. Looking at him, standing next to him, had made my body cry out.

"Phenice, are you okay? You seem cold? You're shivering." Great, he noticed, *and* he was moving closer.

"Yeah, I'm a little cold." Great, now I'm a liar. Who was I today? My world and composure were most definitely falling apart. "But I'll be all right. I really need to get going. I would love to stay and talk, but I have a lecture."

Okay, so either I slammed a door in his face, or I opened one. I suck at this. Not to mention he is still a patient—a patient I was intensely lusting after on a public sidewalk. If he made a move on me, would I stop him? Nope, most definitely not. My cool, composed nature was failing me.

"May I walk you to your car?" Okay, so maybe an open door. Possibly. What the hell was I doing?

"Truck, actually. And yes, that would be nice, thank you."

He laughed.

"What?"

"Sorry, but I didn't see you as a truck person," he replied with his laughter sliding into a light, breathy chuckle. The sound of it rocked my body in all the right ways. Yet my mind was yelling at me, *This is so wrong.* These involuntary reactions were most definitely going to get me into trouble.

"Why is that?" I turned and started to walk in the direction of my mom's old 1969 Jeep Gladiator J3000 Thriftside 4x4 with Emil following right beside me.

It was the only thing I had left of her. The only thing I owned that once belonged to her. It was the real reason I drove a truck. I could see why Emil didn't see me as a truck person. I wasn't really, but to feel close to her, I would drive it as long as I could.

I had it towed from my father's place years ago as soon as I had the money to restore it. It was now pristine with its custom silver metallic paint, white leather interior, and chrome details. I even had the engine, power steering, brakes, and all the sound equipment upgraded. It was pretty much a brand-new truck with an exterior body from 1969.

I loved everything about my truck, but mainly I loved knowing once upon a time, she drove it. It was my one physical connection to who she was, and every time I looked at it, I thought of her.

Drifting back to the present and leaving thoughts of the mom I never got to meet behind, I noticed Emil walked so close to my side I could feel the warmth of his body kissing my skin. It took everything within me not to reach over and touch him. I sucked in a quick breath, desperate to gain a small amount of my dignity back.

"Well, for one, you weigh about what, 120 pounds or so? And at five foot eight, that's tiny." He was laughing again, and it was the most beautiful sound. It didn't stop me from wanting to slap him while also wanting to slam my lips to his.

"I weigh more than that, thank you, but I will never tell. And I'm not tiny!

Tiny implies weak, and I'm not weak." I wasn't yelling at him, not really, but he had hit a nerve. I didn't want to ever be helpless again, and the thought of being overpowered by anyone made the hair on the nape of my neck rise.

"Hold on, Phenice." His hands were in the air as if he was going to surrender, but the smirk on his face said he found me extremely entertaining.

I might have overreacted, but his delight pissed me off more, even if compared to him, I was tiny.

"I know you're not weak. It's written all over you in how you carry yourself," he stated, placing his hands in his pockets.

"You're beautiful, long, and lean. I can see that. It's not what I meant by tiny. By 'tiny' I was implying you are the type of woman a man could toss around and do the most devious and delicious things to." He paused and looked up at me from under his lashes. I was fucking speechless. That was not what I expected him to say.

"You're the kind of woman I would love to ravish in all the best ways. That's what I meant by tiny. I could have my way with you…but only if you begged me, that is." He was devouring every inch of me with his dark-purple eyes.

I wanted to feel uncomfortable, invaded. I should've felt that way given our professional relationship, but I wanted everything he had offered. My core was throbbing with need. I had images pop in my head of him pinning me to a wall and having his way with me. I could imagine the sounds this man could make pour from my lips. My knees felt weak. I realized I had stopped walking, and I was simply staring. I closed my mouth, because yeah, it was hanging open, like an idiot. I really hoped I hadn't drooled.

I must admit I loved his eyes caressing my body. He said I was beautiful, and he was talking about ravishing me. He said it so casually, as if it were obvious he wanted me. Then it hit me hard. He had a soulmate. Why was he hitting on me? Was he hitting on me? I blinked rapidly trying to rediscover the ability to speak again.

"Um…ah. Well, okay." Oh, my goodness, I'm a bumbling moron.

I lowered my head as I smiled because today my emotions were kicking my ass, and now I had apparently lost all coherent thought. It had been years since I felt this out of control.

"So what, Emil, fuck-able and tiny women can't drive trucks?" WTF? I have lost my freaking mind. I wanted to find a corner and hide. Instead, I lifted my head and looked right at him like I was unfazed. I could see my truck up ahead. Was that good or bad? Good, I could make a getaway. Bad, this conversation would be over.

He laughed hard. "No, Phenice, not at all. I think it's great you drive a truck. To be honest, I find I like talking to you outside your office. I am finding I like this form of dialogue much better. You're different from what I imagined. I am, however, going to make sure to stay out of your way." He was still smiling, and it was a smile that would stop a girl's heart, among other things.

"What does that mean?" His laughter was contagious. The desire to laugh with him caught in my throat. Being near him made me lighthearted. It was easier to smile. Not something I experienced often. *Uptight* would be a word I would use to describe myself, restricted, on-guard, closed off, and unaffected. This man was breaking me in so many unexpected ways. I hadn't decided if I liked or hated it, and I couldn't stop my mind from drifting to the images of how he could *break* my body in all of the most enticing ways.

"I have the feeling if you were mad enough, you would run over just about anything or anyone." He cheered at me.

"I really am a nice person, Emil." I smiled at him.

Damn, he was reading me like an open book. He was right though; anger was my go-to emotion. I hoped he could also read my bitchiness for what it was, a tool I used to protect my heart. I wouldn't let anyone near my heart ever again but my body—he could invade it.

"Oh, I know you are. I have no doubts, but I also believe if you were angry enough, you would act, and that's good too. I like that. I love a fiery woman. It speaks to me in ways nothing else does." His face was so sincere, all humor gone. I thought I saw a dark, lusty desire in his eyes as he gazed at me. It was probably my wishful thinking; again, he was obsessed with a woman he called his soulmate, who wasn't me.

We had finally reached my Jeep. I didn't even realize we had started walking again. I had been so lost in him. I unlocked it and began to climb in.

He reached out and took my hand. It was the first time we touched, if you didn't count the collision on the sidewalk. His skin was soft and warm. I loved the feel of his touch way too much. I shouldn't though; he was still a patient for now.

I was nervous and excited, but all he did was hold my hand briefly. I think I might have felt a slight brushing of his thumb rubbing little circles across my flesh, but I was so breathless and lost in his eyes I could have imagined it. He let go way too soon for me. I didn't want him to ever let go. The nervousness left and was replaced by disappointment.

"Not only do you drive a truck but a vintage one. You are most definitely full of wonderful surprises, Phenice. Have a safe trip to your lecture. I'll see you at my next appointment." He turned and walked away.

My heart was broken by the thought of not seeing him sooner and with the knowledge there wasn't going to be a next appointment. I found myself speechless from a deep longing for him I couldn't explain. I felt hollow inside due to his absence. I had to change something with my life, like getting one. I watched him walk away for far too long before I drove off, realizing I didn't even tell him goodbye. I would probably never see him again. Darkness started to seep through me. I didn't understand the hold he had on me, but he had sunk his hooks in, catching me in his snare. I was enraptured by him, and I had no idea what to do about it.

Chapter 5

CRIMSON LIGHT

For the most part, it had been a shit day. From the hell dream waking me screaming to the tear-filled nervous breakdown at lunch with Alina and the serious consideration of throwing my career away for a man. Yeah, I had decided to mark this day as one from hell. It truly had been one of the worst days of my adult life, and that was saying a lot.

After wrapping up my class, it dawned on me it was probably the worst lecture I had ever given. My thoughts would not leave Emil throughout its entirety. There he was, looming in the corner of my brain, patiently waiting for my complete attention, and some part of me wanted to give all of myself to him. These feelings and thoughts were morphing into a downright fixation, as if he had cast an enchantment over me.

I was home, sitting in my parked truck, frozen in place because I was having an internal war. I needed to be honest with myself even if it was ugly and something I had been in denial about. The truth was I hadn't been able to stop thinking about Emil since the first session with him. He had been ever present in everything I did. He even filled most of my dreams that didn't star the hellacious Egyptian queen.

I was mad at myself for getting lost in the impossible. For allowing myself to fantasize even a little bit about this man. My patient! Yes, I wanted love, but I'd worked too hard to throw everything away on a man I shouldn't want, and he clearly wanted someone else. And no matter how sexy he was, I was pretty sure he had erotomania; he had created a fantasy about some woman out there he was stalking. He had not been a patient long, but after speaking with Dr. Postmere I felt more positive with this diagnosis. I was letting how I felt for him get in the way of my intellect. It might have been why I dragged out settling on a diagnosis; did I just want to keep seeing him?

What did that say about me? It was clear I'd completely fallen for him, head over heels. Was I possibly even in love with him? If not love, it was totally clear I was infatuated. With everything I had been going through, I was clearly falling back into old patterns of making shitty decisions. Not for the first time in my life I was questioning if I was emotionally broken. Did my childhood truly break something I could not repair? Was I doomed to be forever wounded?

Well shit. I'd prided myself on being a woman determined to never fear anything again in my life, and now I discovered I was petrified of love, even the possibility of it. What I might be willing to do for it left me bewildered. How did I go from keeping everyone at a distance to lusting after someone I couldn't have? Is that why I was aching for this particular man? He was untouchable, so did that leave my heart safe? He was emotionally unavailable because he loved someone else. Damn I was fucked. That much was clear.

Over the past several months, my handle on my internal emotional state had slipped; the PTSD symptoms were coming back with a vengeance. The panic of losing control was making me fear everything, and battling this ridiculous state of affairs between my heart and brain was getting me nowhere. I needed to stop psychoanalyzing myself and go inside before one of my nosey neighbors came to see if there was anything wrong.

As I stepped out of my truck, the balmy evening embraced me. It was probably sixty-five degrees with a fresh breeze. Typical for this time of year, and it meant tonight was going to be cold. The sky was overcast but not raining, leaving a gray sheen over everything. The landscape looked fake, almost surreal, matching my mood perfectly. As if today were designed for the melancholy state I found myself in. It made me smile. Even though I knew how insignificant I was in the great scheme of life, I enjoyed pretending someone cared about how I felt.

As I walked in the house, the first thing to grab my attention was the huge three-wicked candle Alina had given me, probably with the hopes of bringing some sense of romance to my world. It sat on the end table by the cream sofa. I walked over and lit it. It made thoughts of Alina more potent and helped clear my head of Emil. With a nod to myself, I decided to stop obsessing and to stop beating myself up for things I couldn't control or change in that moment.

Today had made it clear I was a slave to my routines. Obviously longing for control. So in the spirit of a new way of life, I did exactly what my long, exhausting day left me the energy for. I ordered a pizza. Something I hadn't done since I was an undergraduate.

I showered away the day, changed into sweatpants and a tank, and by the time I was finished, the pizza arrived. I sat on the sofa, flipping through all my streaming options, aching for something hilarious to provide a distraction. I had my remote in one hand and a pizza slice in the other. After I was done eating, the anxiety and unease was completely gone. I laid back, pulling my blanket from the back of the sofa and snuggled in, thrilled by the comfort of junk food and junk TV.

It didn't take long for me to drift off. It had been a long night and day. Sleep found me quick. In moments, I was taken over by a flourish of emotions. Emotions no one should ever experience at the same time: fear, peace, sadness, panic, anguish, pain, a great overwhelming sense to laugh, and then the desire to plead. There were so many. Some I couldn't even describe. I was lost in a raging tidal wave of sensation, leaving me nauseous. I had lost the ability to sort anything out.

Out of nowhere, I found sweet clarity. I was floating in a body of water, lost at sea with the current licking my skin. I struggled to open my eyes, to breathe. I was fighting for my life, but against whom or what? I didn't know.

I couldn't see, smell, hear, taste, or feel anything. All senses were stripped, as I laid unprotected and helpless against a ghost of an enemy. With an explosion of crimson light, everything flooded back. Smack!

My eyes popped open, frantically taking in my surroundings. My breath rushed out of my lungs. Apparently, I had been holding my breath. I was still on my sofa. I worked hard to calm my racing heart. I clearly had some kind of PTSD nightmare again, but I didn't remember anything other than the intense emotional sensations. It wasn't a past memory haunting me. What was happening? I sat up, running my hands through my hair. The TV was still on, playing the next episode in the series I had picked, but I couldn't absorb anything other than the raging emotions consuming me.

Stupid pizza. That's what I get for ordering junky delivery.

Though I told myself it was the shitty food, deep in my gut, it felt like a warning. The water around me had been real; it's why I was holding my breath—I didn't want to drown, and in that moment, I knew I was dying, and I couldn't do a damn thing to stop it.

With the stream of emotions still running like ice water through my veins, I reverted to what I knew, to my hard-tested coping mechanisms. I craved movement. A run was exactly what I needed to work through the raging emotional invasion. I didn't know what was happening to me, but that wouldn't stop me from doing my damnedest to run away.

Chapter 6

THE END

I was ready to run away from my life. So much for changing my ways. With self-critical thoughts smashing through my brain, I climbed the stairs to change into my running gear. I dressed as fast as I could, went straight to the door, and grabbed my Sauconys out from under the bench. I directly turned and sat down, slipped on my sneakers, and laced them up. Throughout all of it, I continued to be flooded with warring emotions, leaving me panicked and chaotic. I was ready to literally try and run from everything. Especially from how I was feeling.

I told myself, after *this run*, I would start over. Tomorrow is a new day, and I would begin living my life right. This run was going leave the past behind me, and I was going to run straight into a new and brighter future.

The air slapped me in the face, stealing my breath as I walked out into the cold night. I didn't even know how late it was, never having taken the time to look at a clock. Once adjusted to it, I loved the steely night air. I loved the freedom of not caring about the time or anything else for that matter. It reminded me I was alive, and I needed that now more than ever. After locking the door, I placed the house key in my fleece pocket.

With a quick glance around, I took off for Skinner Butte Park. I started at a gentle pace, taking in the cold air. Within moments I began to feel rejuvenated. The rhythmic sound of my feet hitting the pavement filled me.

Letting my feet lead the way, I was pulled toward the Owen Rose Garden. I felt compelled to see the rose bushes before they were deadheaded for the season. Roses, without a doubt, were my favorite flower. This route would be longer but worth it. Letting the scent embrace me and seeing all the flowers in the moonlight would be amazing. I planned to let go of all my worries.

On the way back, I could do my cooldown by strolling through the paths within the garden. It would be a sweet escape lit by the stars. This thought alone elevated my heart with joy. I picked up the pace.

Lost in meditative daydreams created by the steady tempo of my falling feet, I found myself thinking of what a new life could mean. I reactively glanced down at my left wrist. I stared at the menacing scar. For the first time in my life, it didn't make me want to cry; my heart didn't ache. Instead, I smiled, knowing there had to be a better way out of the pain. I knew my father no longer had a hold on me, and he would never break anything again. My joy made me run faster.

I was stunned by all the colors as I entered the gardens, the brilliant reds, crimsons, pinks, yellows, and my goodness, the white roses seem to glow in the night from the full moon's light. It was a pleasant sensory overload. I wanted to stop, to stay here forever, but I needed to finish my run. I decided tonight I was going to take my time wandering through the rose bushes on my way back home.

I made my way to the loop, picking up the pace yet again. It brought me to a full-out sprint. I was running as hard as I could. I could feel parts of myself falling away and the excitement of a new life lighting a fire in my core. I was ready for an adventure. Maybe even love. I was so elated that it felt like wings were morphing out of my back and I was about to take flight. I was ready to take risks to find happiness, no matter what that meant. I was running headfirst, eyes wide open, into my new future. I turned onto the bridge to cross the Willamette River and—*wham*.

I slammed right into what felt like a mountainside. I fell backward, flat on my ass, and the breath was ripped from my lungs. I gasped, and water ran from my eyes, making it damn near impossible to see. I frantically wiped at them with the back of my hands, but the sweat on my skin made them sting and water more. I couldn't see through the burning. I felt hands grab me.

"Let go of me, damn it!" I fought and struggled while I screamed to be released. I heard a cynical laugh.

My vision slowly returned. I saw two strange faces glaring down at me.

I could vaguely hear more footsteps behind me. I panicked and wiggled; to my surprise, I broke free. I think it also surprised the two men holding me. I ran as hard as I could away from them. Unfortunately, that led me to the Willamette River.

In being grabbed and temporarily blinded, I lost my sense of direction. As I ran in fear, I didn't pay attention to where I was headed. Now I was in the damn woods, where no one would see or hear me. Shit!

Panic seized my heart.

At the river's edge, I turned because I had nowhere else to go. Right behind me I saw…one…three…no *six* of them. They didn't even look tired, as if they had simply walked to this point while I panted. They also looked determined to tear me apart. I didn't know what else to do, so I did what I knew best. I got angry.

"What the fuck do you want?" My hands balled into fists, ready to defend myself.

As I studied their faces, it was clear what they wanted. It was obvious they wanted to hurt me. Probably murder me. They were going to do whatever they desired to me. Shit! As my eyes passed over all six of them, the hard truth slammed home: I didn't get a new start; all I got was a tragic end!

Chapter 7

BEASTS

My eyes darted across the four men and two women trapping me against the water's edge. To be honest, I found the women stranger and more terrifying than the men at first glance. They all looked deadly, yet somehow mesmerizingly beautiful. I imprinted the pictures of their faces in my mind, hoping I would get the chance to report them. That hope lingered in my heart. Maybe I would make it out of this alive. Holding on to that hope, I tried reasoning with them.

"Just let me go. You don't have to do this. We can walk away, and I won't say anything. Okay?" Every word was met with silence.

"What do you want?" I yelled, wanting something, some answer for why they had trapped me like this. Was it me personally they were after, or was I in the wrong place at the right time for them?

I continued to grasp for hope in my heart, but that didn't stop fear from radiating throughout me as I witnessed the longing for my death in their eyes. What I needed was the deep-rooted fury I desperately tried to hide from everyone to fuel my fight.

Reaching deep inside for that burning volcanic anger, alarm ripped through me when I found nothing. My old emotional companion had abandoned me. Without the comfort of my rage, I didn't know how to feel. I didn't know what to do. How could I survive this without that hate? Without my fury from all the old pain? I was lost and terrified. Instantly a wash of confusing emotions rushed over me. Emotions I had never felt.

"We can't let you go, and what we want is you, sweet pet. We are here for our queen, who we lovingly serve," one of the women said.

She had a low, roaring voice that sent shivers down my spine. Her eyes were jet black and empty, like two bottomless pits calling me in. I wanted to look away from her, but I couldn't. Her hair, the color of coal, hung to her waist. I imagined it was as soft as silk. Her skin was glowing, and her beauty was unmatchable.

"Some queen wants me dead?" My voice was flat and unaffected, as if I were discussing a beverage choice, not my life. So it was me they wanted. This wasn't a wrong place–wrong time situation.

"In a way, no, but life as you know it is over." This time a man with hair the color of fire answered. Though he didn't speak loudly, his voice boomed off the water behind me, causing me to jump and leaving me shaking.

Lost in his voice and captured by his caramel eyes, I could see his corrupted lust burn like a roaring inferno straight from hell. Not carnal lust. No, this was dark and wicked. He would take great pleasure in my suffering.

My body started to tremble harder. I hated the betrayal of my body, but I could see he was going to enjoy breaking me. His immense enjoyment meant a tremendous amount of pain for me. Looking into his eyes made me wish for a quick death.

By the time I tore my eyes from him, I realized the others were crouching. The hope in my heart flickered out like a candle in the wind. The two females lunged. I felt my body try to run, but they were simply there, in the blink of an eye. As fast as thought, and I didn't even see them move before I was lost in a sea of black and chestnut hair. One of them latched on to my ponytail and pulled me down so hard it felt like my scalp was being ripped from my skull.

The next sensation was the tearing of flesh. Skin from my neck was ripped away by teeth in a flash, and blood ran down my chest. It all happened so quickly I didn't even feel the pain. At least, not at first. I tried to fight. I wanted to scream, not out of fear, but pure frustration at my weakness. Nothing and no one could save me.

I was only a feast for them when the four men joined. I thought the pain would be the worst part of dying, but it was the sound of the skin being torn from my bones that got me. Something in my mind broke; like a tidal wave, everything slammed into me. The combination of hearing flesh rip, feeling the blood pour down my skin and drip to the ground beneath me, and the radiating pain caused the vomit to erupt from my gut.

When the retching stopped. I sensed they had vanished; the feeding frenzy had stopped. I peered up at the moon through the canopy of trees and tried to let my eyes adjust, but everything had a pink wash of color. It was difficult to see. I blinked my eyes rapidly with no benefit. I listened, and all I heard was a static resonating in my ears.

Mostly blind and unable to hear, I rolled over to all fours and scanned the area the best I could, but I saw nothing. There was no one near me. I wobbled and surprisingly had the strength to push up to my feet.

I was up, unsteady and weak, but I was on my feet. It felt like a victory. I didn't care how small; I would take it. I felt blood covering my body, and from how my clothing clung to my skin, I knew it was a lot. I didn't dare look. The fear of completely breaking prevented me from taking an assessment of how badly I was hurt.

I took a step, and the skin hanging from my neck to my chest flapped with the movement. A bright light seared through my vision, and that was it. The vomiting started again, bile burning my throat and nose as my body seized over and over again. The desire to give up blasted through me. I could simply lay down and die right here, and it would all be over. Wouldn't that be easier anyway?

My vision cleared slightly. I thought I saw them. They seemed to be talking in whispers, but I couldn't hear what they were discussing. Fight or flight must have kicked in because I took off running as fast as I could. I was lost in one of those terrifying dreams of being chased. You run away with everything you have, but there is some unseeable force holding you back, freezing you in slow motion and all-consuming fear. I was slow, as if running through water.

I was barely moving. No matter how hard I wished for this to be a nightmare I could wake from, I knew this wasn't a fucking dream. I was so screwed. Finally, anger roared to life throughout my body, setting me on fire. Sadly, those flames didn't propel me any faster or any farther away. Too little, too late. I kept moving anyway.

I was running for my life, but with how badly I was injured, it was hopeless. My heart cracked wide open because I knew this was it. I kept running anyway because I was too stubborn to lie down and die easy. Death may have finally come for me, but I wasn't going to quit, and I wouldn't go easy.

I made it back to the paved track. I saw the sign for the rose garden. I turned, praying there was a way to save myself.

As I entered the garden, I could smell the sweet scent of roses mixing with the rust and copper smell of blood. It was sweet and metallic, topped off with the salty scent of my sweat. Nausea tore through my gut yet again. Pushing it down, I focused on getting away. I pushed harder, trying to shut everything out. The fastest way was straight ahead, but as I took my first step, the dark-haired lady was standing in front of me. Where the fuck did she come from? She didn't pass me. I didn't hear her. The urge to fall to my knees and cry was overwhelming. The nausea was so strong, and giving up was so enticing. I wasn't ready to die. So I dug deep into my soul and turned right and kept running. I was going to run through the next break in the rose bushes for the parking lot and toward the street. At every break there was someone waiting for me. I came to the old cherry tree in the garden, and there they all stood, like they had manifested out of thin air.

"How the hell?" passed my lips, barely audible. I finished in my head— *were they everywhere all at once?*

The running had sped my pulse. I could feel the blood pouring faster down my neck and drenching my clothes. I was growing weaker by the second. I was faint, dizzy, and nauseous. The world around me began to spin. I had nothing left, and no one to save me. I dropped to my knees on the gravel path. The tiny rocks cut through my thin running pants, embedding into my skin. What did it matter now? I wanted to sleep. I cursed myself for giving up as I wondered, if I had something or someone to live for, would I have fought harder? *Maybe* was all I could think before everything went black.

Chapter 8

CHERRY TREE

I awoke to the sound of someone bellowing. Searing pain ripped apart every fiber of me as rods were slammed through my forearms and calves, pinning me to the earth below my broken body. Stars danced across my vision from the searing pain.

I heard screaming, continuous, gut-wrenching wailing. The sounds were distant and growing farther away with every howl of agony. My ears started to ring, blocking out the sounds of some creature's torment. The feeling of my mouth opening and closing was barely noticeable, but with it came the knowledge that I was the one bellowing in pain.

At some point the searing anguish of my wails broke my voice. The screams died on the wind. Tears rolled down my face and into my ears. When I opened my eyes again, I saw the old cherry tree looming over me with its distorted, arthritic branches, a canopy from the night's sky in their creepy glory, only allowing a glimpse of the full moon to peak through.

The tree was so old it needed help to stay standing. I laid there helpless and gazed up at the mess of wiry webs stringing the tree together. Tears silently rolled down my face and salted the earth. I turned my head slightly and saw the iron stilts supporting the heaviest of the branches, trying to maintain the tree's life. I almost laughed at the ironic sight. I was pinned by metal rods, having my life stolen, as the massive tangles of metal attempted to keep the tree alive. We were being tortured. One to provide and sustain life, and one to be deprived and robbed of it. As I continued to look up at the cherry tree, I strangely felt better knowing I had something to share my torment with.

I was ripped back from my connection to the tree when the beasts gathered around and leered down at me. Tears continued to leak from my eyes. I cursed myself. I wished I could make them stop. I didn't want these savages to have the satisfaction of seeing my pain and fear. I wanted to be brave. I wanted to at least die with dignity. I wanted to speak, but what could I say that wouldn't sound as if I were begging for mercy? No, they could have my fucking tears, but I would not beg them. They would never have that! They could all go to hell. Instead, I watched them as each tear slid down the side of my face and watered the earth.

One by one, they bit into the radial artery of their wrists. With blurry vision, I gazed at the blood cascading down to the earth. I watched as they walked in a circle around my body until they reached their starting positions. They were chanting something, so quiet, whispers I was unable to hear.

One at a time, they walked forward and held their wrists over my face, letting their blood flow over me and into my mouth. When the first rusty tang hit my tongue, I began turning my head side to side in an attempt to avoid the blood cascading toward me. There was too much. It came at me too fast. From shaking my head back and forth, the blood poured into my mouth, eyes, and hair. It covered my face. I had no choice but to swallow to keep from drowning. I gagged and spat as much as I could, but I had to swallow so much of it. My stomach rolled.

Once I was covered in their blood, the flow slowed, then finally stopped. I couldn't see past the blood in my eyes, and because I turned my head to avoid drinking it, I got it in my ears. What little sound had returned was gone. Completely deprived of sight and sound, I waited. I couldn't brace for what was about to happen. Terror radiated through my body. My heart was beating wildly, as if it were a caged animal demanding to be set free. I took a deep breath, smelling sweet roses, musty earth, metallic blood, and decay. I let out an involuntary sigh.

They attacked. I gasped. I held my breath in an attempt not to scream. The pain of flesh being torn away seared through me. I was on fire as they ate me alive, flesh burning where their lips touched me. The need to fight and flee took over. I struggled, fighting for my life. A whole new pain tore through my body. The bones in my arms and legs snapped against the forgotten rods.

The sound of the snapping bones followed by the intense blinding pain tore another scream from my lips.

As the scream died, I went limp. I held as still as I could. I was dying in the most horrible way. I needed this to end now. I laid there, limp and broken in unspeakable ways, as I prayed for death.

More sound started to return. I wished it hadn't. I could hear the feeding frenzy. The sucking and slurping of their hungry cannibal mouths. Ripping, popping, and crunching filled the air as tendons and ligaments snapped between their teeth. Having the sounds to go with the pain only made it hurt worse. The smell of blood filled the air, overpowering even the roses nearby. When I didn't think it was possible, the pain intensified. I longed to die. I needed the suffering to cease.

Through a reddish haze, I stared up at the cherry tree, catching a hint of the blood-tinted moon watching my demise. Out of nowhere, a laugh bubbled up. I had lost my mind. I was officially broken, mind and body. I did the only thing I had any control over.

I lost myself in the cherry tree with the moon as the only witness to my death. I watched as the limbs and branches tried to move in the night's breeze. It was sad and comforting seeing the forced stillness. The same type of stillness forced upon me. Peace started to fuse into my heart, knowing I was not alone in my restraints. Neither one of us had any control over our painful situations. The breeze also brought the sweet smell of roses back to me, helping to clear away the rusty smell of the blood. I inhaled deeply, and the blissful aroma cleansed the stench of pennies and salt from my nose.

I felt the soft grass under my back, cool and comforting. I focused on only that section of greenness, as it helped clear away the sensation of my sticky, coagulating blood pooling by my sides. The breeze picked up, blowing harder, allowing the smell of the river's fresh wet earth and rock scent to fill my nose.

I began to cry for a new reason. I knew in that moment I would never feel or smell any of this again. I was sad. I had taken life for granted. Regret slammed into my heart for a life unlived because of fear.

As redefined tears streamed down my face, a laugh startled me out of my trance. I blinked a few times to clear away the numbness and the world my mind had created for me to ease my suffering. A tall man with rust-colored hair and amber eyes, like the embers of a fire, was looking down at me. Uncontrollable shivers racked my body, reawakening all the pain. I needed it to stop. I wanted to die, not with fear, but with a sense of honor for the life I had lived. Regrets and all. Even those regrets were mine and mine alone. I didn't care if it made any sense, but at least I could have that, and this bastard was stripping it away from me with a stupid laugh.

He kneeled next to my ear and, with a soft voice, purred, "Don't worry. In no time it will all be over, and you won't feel a thing."

His horrible laugh filled my ear as he bit into my neck again and tore away more of my flesh this time. The sound of him drinking caused the nausea to roar back with a vengeance. I wanted control over my reactions, but control was a fucking illusion. I couldn't stop my cries this time as they ripped from me, ravaging my throat in their intensity. He enjoyed my pain. My anguish encouraged him to bite down harder. I knew my screams were making it worse, but the pain was excruciating. I sobbed and bellowed. My will snapped. I begged him. I hated myself for it, but I would have done anything to make it stop. He finally broke my will. The rage in my heart at that moment was indescribable.

The others began drinking again too. The sound vibrated throughout my bones causing a soul-crushing ache. Pain flared up, agonizing, but the sound was still worse. They were draining me, and I could feel every bit of it, like being turned inside out. I wanted to crawl away from them. I tried to move again, but misery shot through my entire body. Not only was I pinned to the ground by my broken arms and legs but also by their teeth, drinking from six points of my body.

Finally, the pain started to subside, as did my strength to cry. Blissful numbness descended upon me. My body seemed to float away. Considering the state I was in, the loss of sensation made me giddy, but no laughter would come. This death wasn't something to laugh about.

I silently begged for it to end. I was barely breathing. My life was slipping away. It was wonderful. I couldn't smell death riding the air any longer. In fact, I couldn't smell anything. I tried to swallow, but there was nothing, no blood, no vomit, and no saliva left. I couldn't taste anything.

I tried to look around to see how much longer I had and realized I couldn't see anything other than a cerise haze, the color of blood filling my eyes. I was dying, and after what I had just gone through, I was grateful it was almost over.

It was like my vision today—all loss of bodily functions and senses, and my vision clouded with the color of crimson. Somehow I had been foretold of my upcoming death. Where was the sea, the water, to lick my wounds? I wanted it to carry me away from here, from my murderous beasts, from the pain, and from my life. I could finally be free. I found peace.

Some muffled sound floated into my conscious mind as I drifted in and out.

"She is going to kill us," a female voice said with complete panic.

"We failed. We drank too much. She's dead." It was a familiar voice. It was the rusty-haired man with the amber eyes who pinned me to the ground. "Our queen will not be pleased. She wanted this one more than any other."

"What is there to do? What's done is done," stated a calm and bored male voice I had never heard. It was clear he was ready to move on.

"Throw her body in the river, and let's leave." It was the black-headed female with the voice of a lion.

I never felt anything. I only heard the splash.

Chapter 9

NOX NOCTIS MUTATIO

The icy, dark water ran down the bank of the Willamette River. Misty swirls of silvery-sapphire clouds filled the morning sky, making the water appear sinister to my freshly opened eyes. I stared off into the distance. I didn't know for sure where I was. I sat up and paused, allowing myself to take in the scene around me. The trees were sharply green and dense. I could see everything within each individual leaf. Each tiny vein was visible. In fact, I could see clearly for miles. I even saw the path back to the Owen Rose Garden across the river. I blinked a few times because the amount of input flooding my brain was overstimulating.

I looked down at myself. I was covered in dried, crusted blood. A scream attempted to bubble up over my lips as rapid images flowed into my mind, reminding me what happened the night before. I apparently survived. The images of terror and unrelenting horror played like a movie reel, over and over. I waited for the panic to seize my heart and gut, but nothing came. It made me wonder if I was truly still alive.

Passively, I did the only thing I could think of: I felt for a pulse. It was there, but it was almost nonexistent. Possibly ten beats a minute. I had to be in shock because that couldn't be right.

The lower half of my body was still in the water with the current tugging on my legs. I slowly and gently pulled myself out. Numbly, I glanced around. I found myself on a small northern bank behind the mall only about half a mile from where they probably threw me in. I simply wanted to get home. Dazed, I decided to try and pull my beaten body up and out of the water. I was surprised by how easily I moved. I slid right up to standing without a single shake or stumble.

Numb to everything, I started walking. I didn't look at anything as I placed one foot in front of the other. With my mind absent and my body on autopilot, I found myself unlocking the front door to my home roughly thirty minutes later. I didn't even recall grabbing the hide-a-key to let myself in, but I must have because I no longer had the fleece on. At some point it was taken off me or torn from my body.

With the door locked tight at my back, I looked at the clock. It was 8:18 a.m. I hadn't even paid attention to the sun in the sky. I had only seen the clouds floating overhead. My first patient was always at nine. I needed to call Alina to cancel my day, maybe even my week. I wanted a shower and my bed. I felt like I needed to stay in bed forever. Falling asleep and never getting up sounded really nice.

I should probably see a doctor. That seemed like the right thing to do. I wondered about calling the police. What would I say to them though? Anything about what actually happened would sound crazy, like an extremely traumatized victim. I knew all about that. The missing bits of information and how the brain loved to fill in the gaps with a story it felt was more manageable. We lied to ourselves at times like this so we could survive the extreme trauma. Our brains loved to hunt for control. I could hunt for ways it was my fault. For how I could have stopped it or prevented it. I could tell myself the story that I would have been safe had I never went on that run, but what am I supposed to do? Never leave my house again? In reality, there hadn't been a damn thing to do differently, and none of what happened was *manageable*.

I was tired. Too tired to think about doctors and police reports. I would revisit all of that after I woke up. At some point, I made my way to the coffee table where I had abandoned my phone last night before my run. What an idiot. I went for a run, after dark, alone, without a phone, and almost died. What was I thinking? The weird dream had unnerved me, and I had carelessly run away in true Phenice fashion. Always running away—or fighting.

I picked up the phone noticing the date and time again. How was it only Wednesday? The last twenty-four hours felt like a never-ending, life-altering nightmare. I numbly dialed Alina's number half hoping she wouldn't pick up.

"Hello?" She must not have looked at the contact information. She usually answered with some wisecrack remark.

"Alina, I need to ask a favor," I whispered.

"Who is this?" she replied. She was right; it barely sounded like me. I'm sure it was from all the water I must've swallowed while floating down the river.

Then I remembered the screams, cries, and sobs my throat and vocal cords had suffered. I slammed my eyelids closed, trying desperately to block it all out. I wasn't ready to relive any of it.

"Alina, it's Phenice. I'm sick, and I need to cancel my day. Possibly my whole week. Whatever it is, it's bad, as you can tell. Plus, can you call my teaching assistant and let him know he will need to fill in as well?" It was a lot to ask, but I have never taken any time off or called in sick in my life. I figured a near-death experience—well, let's call it what it was, almost being murdered—was a very good fucking reason!

"Sure I will, Phenice, but you don't sound sick; you sound…different. Not like you. Do you need me to come over afterward? I can bring you anything you need. Soup?" She sounded worried. I couldn't let her see me like this.

"No, Alina, I'll be fine. Please don't worry. I'll call later to check in. Thank you so much. You're wonderful as always. I love you. You're the only family I have." It was true, all of it, and it slipped right out of my mouth without a single thought. I had never been so honest or vulnerable with my feelings for her. At least not out loud.

My confession was met with a long and ghastly pause, followed by, "I love you too, Phenice. Do you want me to go ahead and reschedule or wait until we know for sure about your health?" She was concerned. I must have sounded like death. Not far from the truth, I guess.

"I think we should wait. Thanks again. Talk to you soon." I hung up without even waiting for her to respond.

I didn't want to be on the phone any longer. I felt so strange. I didn't want to give her any reason to come running over here. I headed to the shower lost in all-consuming numbness. I was clearly in shock.

As I walked into the bathroom, a strange woman in the floor-length mirror confronted me. The dazed feeling I had felt since I woke by the river was chased away. I hated crying, but the tears started as I stared at myself. Part of me felt like I was making up for all the unshed tears of my past. I'd cried more in the last twenty-four hours than I had in the past fifteen years or longer.

I examined the woman. Her tears slowly rolled down her perfect alabaster face. I was able to see the cool, creamy complexion peeking out from under the patches of blood and through the tracks her tears were making. Her eyes were a rich sage with molten gold spiraling out from the pupils, creating a hypnotic vortex. I blinked, thinking that couldn't be right. I hoped if I looked again my eyes would change, but they stayed the same. My eyes drifted to the tangled and bloodstained hair showing multiple hues of gold, wheat, and honey as it shimmered in the overhead light. I desperately tried to take it all in.

I knew I was looking at myself in all my flawless fictitious glory, but I was having a hard time believing my eyes. It had to be the trauma. I decided to focus on the other facts in the mirror. I was caked in sheets of reddish-brown from head to toe. The blood was so dried, what remained of my clothing was pasted to my skin like scales. The river water hadn't been able to wash it away; there was so much.

I turned from the mirror, not wanting to see any more at the moment. I was hot, burning up, but I still wanted a hot shower, as hot as my flesh could stand. I opened the bathroom window overlooking my personal rose garden to let in the cool morning air. The sweet smell wafted in, and I felt my panic ease away. I then turned the shower on.

I kept waiting for the searing pain to kick in. The only reason to be pain-free was shock. I peeled what was left of my running pants away from my battered legs, followed by the once-white and now reddish-brown tattered Under Armour I'd had on under my absent running fleece. Next to come off were my sports bra and socks. I begged myself not to look in the mirror, but I couldn't help it. My body looked as though the bloodstained clothing had taken off a layer of skin as I pried it away from my should-be corpse. Even as I stared at my blood-covered and beaten remains, which only had a few bruises and absolutely no torn flesh, no open wounds, and no broken bones...*nothing*. I couldn't help but feel like a shell. A hollow and bottomless mass of existence, but the beauty was glaring back at me within my reflection. I didn't know this stranger. I didn't want to know her. Hatred filled my heart. I stepped into the shower.

I welcomed the familiar escape of the water pouring down over my head in a hot embrace. I stared at my feet and watched as the water turned shades of ruby and morphed into pasty pink hues. I slid down the shower wall and wrapped my arms around my legs, letting the water beat off my body. I became lost in the warmth.

"*No, no! Oh my god, no!*" I woke screaming. I had blacked out.

My eyes flashed wide. I looked down at my forearms, remembering the metal rods being rammed through them mere hours before. I felt the pain as if it were happening all over again, but to my amazement, all that were present were slight pink marks. No open wounds, no broken bones. I remember feeling them break, feeling them shatter as I fought to get away, but I walked home. How? What the hell? How does someone suffer shattered bones then get up and walk away from a crime scene a few hours later? My medical training nagged at me, telling me what I was seeing was impossible.

These marks looked months old, not hours. My eyes roamed down my body to the sites on my calves, and as I hoped (*feared* was more accurate), they were the same as the ones on my arms. The doctor in me found this intriguing. The person in me was disturbed, terrified, perplexed, and seriously confused as hell. *What the fuck happened to me?* How am I actually alive?

Exhaustion slammed into me hard. I needed to sleep so badly. I couldn't remember a time I had ever been this fatigued. I turned off the water, grabbed my towel, barely dried off, and went straight to bed naked. Within minutes, I was out.

Chapter 10

OBDORMIO

Tall blades of grass swiped against the sides of my low-crouching body. The sweetest breeze blew past my face and around the body of a lioness. This was not the body I knew, not in my current life, but it was familiar. It felt like home. The warm wind made the grass caress my pelt like a million fingers humming across the delicate fields of flowers on a sunny day.

I was in my element. Eyes sharp, mouth watering, muscles firing, all senses fixed on the target—a gazelle about thirty yards away. In an instant I was gone, running so fast everything in my peripheral vision was a complete haze, shapeless shadows with no meaning, no purpose. My paws pounded soundlessly on the ground as the thrill of the hunt coursed through my body.

As I made the kill, I was filled with pride and satisfaction. The taste of the blood in my mouth was inviting, the most delectable substance ever! It was heavenly as it washed over my lips and teeth. I tore flesh from the bone. I swallowed, and the flavor was mouthwatering as it coated my throat, thick and warm. I wanted more and more. It would never be enough. I became entranced. Lost in the richness of the flavor filling my belly, I drank and ate my fill.

A sound rang out, parting the air. Sudden pain radiated throughout my body. My body dropped down atop the dead gazelle. There was nothing to be done. My heart raced erratically. Trying to hold on to life. My breathing became ragged and difficult. Then as my last breath huffed out of my nose, peace embraced my essence. That time and body was over, long past.

I found myself floating through space, pulled back through time. My vision swept up to a statue of a goddess with a head of a lioness and the body of a woman dressed in red. Without knowing where the information came from, her name crept into my mind: she was Sekhmet.

She was the Egyptian goddess born from the fire of the sun god Ra's eye as he gazed down upon the earth. She was a warrior goddess. A goddess of medicine, with the power to heal and protect, yet she could also bring about plagues, war, chaos, and destruction.

She was overwhelmingly powerful, and her gift was to create harmony through any means necessary. Sekhmet was a goddess of balance and the avenger of wrongs. If balance required healing, she would create it, and if it required destruction, so should it be. This was simply the way of the universe.

I floated around her statue, basking in her beauty, while noticing I had no form, no physical body. Soft murmuring voices in my head whispered stories of how Sekhmet and I were one. She was part of my eternal existence. We were one and the same and had been since the beginning of time.

The many voices speaking at the same time and filling my mind with stories and knowledge became overwhelming. Anxiety rose within me. In my panic I took in a breath and let it out quickly, but instead of air, I exhaled fire. I burned everything before me in a wash of beautiful chaos. As the flames died, instead of finding ash, everything turned to sand.

With absolute terror and raging spasms, I woke up, looking all around for something familiar. I was in my bedroom, in my bed. The red walls and golden-hued comforter triggered my memories. I remembered when I had crawled into bed, but I didn't know how long ago. I looked at the clock and my stomach jumped.

"Twelve hours?" fell from my lips in an exasperated hush.

A voice reverberated off the walls. "The gift of the lioness and her goddess passes on."

"What the actual fuck? Who's here?" I yelled.

I frantically looked around, jumping out of bed. I forgot I was naked and still weak from nearly dying. The dizziness overtook me, and down I went. I got one last fuzzy view of my carpet before all went black again.

I floated out of the clouds, soaring down toward a huge river. Once again existing but not part of this reality and having no physical form. The river looked like the Columbia, but not, at the same time. It was familiar and foreign. It was massive and powerful like the Columbia, but it was so much older and so much more. I felt small in comparison. I had always loved that feeling. The feeling of being reminded of how small our problems really were.

Trees towered over the banks along the raging waters, greener than any color I had ever seen. The pine needles were rich and bright. The tree trunks were covered with muted green and magenta-colored moss, making them look soft and cozy. Everything was ripe with life. I felt like I had discovered a new planet.

Pulled by an unseeable guide, I glided down just off the shore to an old woman chanting. She was beautiful, with age lines marking her face with wisdom. There was evidence of many smiles etching out from her vibrant lavender eyes. She had long, silky white hair, the color of a full moon. It hung down her back in perfectly woven braids. She radiated power and tranquility. The same type of ancient power as the river, the trees, and the wind carrying me to her. Her voice was soothing, mesmerizing. I didn't understand the language she hummed as it flowed from her lips in purrs and pops. The words, however, felt familiar, safe, and knowledge filled me as she spoke.

She sat close to the water, calling to it, asking for guidance, and a cool breeze blew around her. She smiled and chanted louder. As time passed all became quiet and still. She stood in the center of a sacred circle she had created using plants, herbs, timber, and stones.

I watched for hours as she sat and smiled, motionless but happy. She was filled with peace. I wanted to walk up to her, to speak with her, but I knew I was from a different time and place. I no more existed in this reality than she existed in mine. This knowledge didn't stop me from feeling a longing, an eternal bond to her. I wasn't an intruder. I belonged here with her and to this time, somehow. I could feel her energy swirling in the air, dissipating, becoming one with all the elements that surrounded her, including me. She belonged to everything as everything belonged to her. In that moment, I was one with everything too.

The sun fell to the earth, and the moon peaked high in the night's sky, full and luminous. Everything was aglow, radiant, much like the woman, who seemed to get younger as I continued to gaze at her. In the middle of the circle, she picked up the different types of timber one at a time—there were seven in all—and built a fire. She began to sprinkle the fire with herbs and water as she sang. Her voice carried up the great peaks that surrounded the river. Her ritual was beautiful.

I didn't even know where or when this was in the past. I didn't know when this woman had existed or why I got to share in her sacred ceremony, but I was filled with overwhelming joy because of it.

She continued singing and gazing at the fire. She reached toward the fire and pulled the swirling smoke toward her. I watched as her essence pulled away from her body in a misty shimmer and intertwined with the smoke from the fire. Rain began to fall, and the flames seemed impervious to the water from the sky. With extreme elation, she laughed and danced. She kneeled beside the fire and unrolled a sparse mat to use as her bedding. She laid back as if to go to sleep. When she exhaled, a vaporous form in the shape of a large bird escaped her lips and flew away. The woman laid motionless, with a smile upon her lips. I watched her, waiting to see her take a breath, but it never came. The fire began to dance along the ground, making its way to her, and in moments, she went up in flames.

I wanted to do something, but I knew I couldn't and shouldn't. This was meant to happen. It was what she wanted, it was the purpose of her ritual, and this had already come to pass. As soon as her body was burned to ash, the fire snuffed out in an instant as if someone had poured water on it. It was clear she had been wielding the flames. The rain stopped.

I looked up toward the moon, and there sat the bird. It was no longer simply vapor, it was flesh and bone. In its physical form, it looked like a mystical phoenix.

It turned its head to stare at me. Overwhelmed by its beauty, I sucked in a sharp breath. The phoenix took flight, headed straight for me. I was alarmed and scared, but I couldn't move. Within moments the hard body of the phoenix slammed into my misty form. Flames danced over my incorporeal body, burning with hot intensity. Pain seared hot and fast. The fire and pain died as quickly as they came.

Stunned, I blinked. The phoenix was gone, and my shadowy, misty self now glowed with a golden-red hue so bright it was blinding. I slammed my eyes closed.

Rattled with disbelief, I found myself back in my house, lying on the floor, still naked as the day I was born, with someone frantically pounding on my front door.

"The gifts of the elements, ash, life, and rebirth, pass on," the voice sounded again.

"What the hell is happening to me?" I wondered aloud, completely dazed and bewildered.

Chapter 11

⸺❧⸺

DIFFERENT

I climbed up the side of the bed, needing to sit for a moment. I was beyond disoriented. Whatever was going on with my head was leaving me foggy and discombobulated. I took a deep breath, looking around the room. My vision was drastically different. Everything was so clear and sharp, like I could visualize every molecule. It was making it impossible to focus. I blinked multiple times, but nothing changed. This was seriously freaking me out. I couldn't keep from focusing on the tiny particles I had never seen before. It was like when you catch the sun rays coming through the window shining on dust particles, but so much more intense. Were those freaking air molecules?

Then the demanding beating on my door captured my attention again. I grabbed a pair of yoga pants and a tank, throwing them on as I made my way out the door and down the stairs. The knock had turned chaotic within the time it took me to get there.

As I opened the door, I shouted, "What the hell?"

Immediately I felt remorse as I saw the look on Alina's face. She had been crying. The whites of her eyes were bloodshot. She had dark circles under them too. Her face was the perfect image of worry and despair.

"Oh my, Alina, I'm sorry. Come in. What's wrong?"

"What do you mean 'What's wrong?' What's wrong with you? Fuck, Phenice, I have been calling you for two days. You haven't answered or returned my calls. I didn't know what to do." She marched through my door and straight for the kitchen without a backward glance. I stood there stunned, trying to process what she had just said. I had slept for two days?

Once I had made my way into the kitchen, she was putting on the kettle for tea. She hadn't even looked to see if I had followed her. As I stood in the doorway, she threw herself down in one of my brown upholstered dining room chairs just off the massive kitchen.

She wiped her eyes, and with a sniffle she stated, "Please, Phenice, tell me what is going on. You have never done anything like this. You're scaring the shit out of me."

I stood frozen. I tried to wrap my brain around what she'd said. I felt so weak and tired. I looked around the room and then back to her. I was able to sense everything so keenly, yet I had no energy. I felt half-dead, and all I wanted to do was go back to sleep, which, if Alina was telling the truth, made absolutely no sense. Where did the past two days go?

The first thing I managed to say was "What day is it?" It made me feel like an idiot.

"It's Friday evening, Phenice! I tried to call Wednesday evening to see if you needed anything and to ask about Thursday, but you didn't answer. Then I called Thursday morning. Never mind all that—what's going on?" I could sense she was scared even though she sounded pissed.

How could I know she was scared and not mad? Then it hit me—I could smell her fear. That was weird. Why was I smelling emotions coming off Alina? Fear shouldn't have a smell, and yet I could smell a moldy musk wafting off her skin. The strangest thing was I could identify what the smell meant. I simply knew moldy musk meant fear of some kind. The stronger the odor, the more intense the emotion.

I came out of my mental reverie, realizing she was waiting for an answer. I didn't know how much to tell her, if anything, but she had to know some-thing. She wasn't going to swallow my lie about being sick, not anymore.

In trying to decide what to say, I realized I really didn't know what was happening to me. How exactly was I alive? How could I answer her when I didn't have the answers she needed? The answers I needed. I needed to figure out how much to tell her. I was never telling her, or anyone for that matter, about hearing voices or the weird dreams I'd had since the attack. It was not on my agenda to be forced into an involuntary seventy-two-hour hold because I was having a mental breakdown. I went through that when I was younger and having flashbacks regularly. I wouldn't do it again. I had to tell her something, a partial truth at least. I didn't want to lie to her, even though omission was still a lie in my book.

I sighed. "Alina, something really horrible happened to me Tuesday night." My voice was low, barely a whisper. I cleared my throat, needing a moment of delay. "I went for a run and was attacked."

Her jaw dropped open, and the tears started again. "Oh my god, Phenice. Did you call the police?" As soon as I saw her reaction, I knew I should have been gentler in sharing this information, but I didn't have my usual faculties about me.

"No." I paused, trying to think how I could fix this. "I didn't. It didn't seem like the right thing to do. Plus it all happened so fast, and it was so dark I wouldn't have been able to tell them anything."

I kind of lied. I said the words just right to make it a truth, and the truth was I wouldn't be able to tell the police anything. They would never believe my story. I remembered everything, every detail of their faces, and I could recall every bit of pain they caused me. I didn't want her to suffer at my expense. If I shared my truth with her, it would break her precious heart. I was never going to do that. She could never know all the details of what I'd suffered. So I'd give her enough. Enough for her to understand, so she would stop asking. Then we could move on.

I continued. "I had gone for my run, and before I knew it, they had me. I'm lucky to be alive." I hesitated and ran my hands through my hair. "I'm simply grateful to be alive. I don't want any doctors doing tests or examining me, and I don't want the police playing twenty-one questions when I can't answer them. I've been through enough. Now I want to rest and heal…okay?" I paused momentarily and saw her about to make an objection. "Please, Alina, this is what I really need." I preyed on her generosity and prayed this was enough for her to back off.

"Phenice, I'm so sorry. Is there anything I can do for you?" She had walked up to me while I was talking then placed her hand on my shoulder. She felt so warm.

I could feel and hear her heart beating loudly. It sounded amazing. It was *appetizing*. What the hell? I pulled away. She looked confused and mostly hurt because I wouldn't allow her to be there for me.

I immediately tried to fix it. "Sorry, being touched is…well, not good. It was all very brutal. I'm not ready to talk about it. Someday, maybe, I'll tell you more. I hope that's okay. For now, what I need is time and patience."

She backed away and nodded.

"Thank you, you're a great friend."

I knew I needed to get her out of here. I had this strong feeling being this close right now could end badly for her. She smelled so good and not in a well-groomed, awesome perfume way, but in a mouthwatering way.

"Can I make you some tea or something to eat?" she asked.

I realized I hadn't eaten anything since being attacked, and the thought of food made me nauseous. I clearly wasn't ready.

"No thank you, but you can stay for a cup of tea. Then I would love to go back to sleep, if you don't mind." I felt rude, but it was honest.

"You look different, Phenice, and not the kind of different that almost dying can cause, but different physically, almost unrecognizable. Your hair and eyes, even your body, are different. You don't look like you. Are you sure you told me everything?" She paused. Taking a few deep breaths. I could tell she was desperate not to leave. She was worried. "You know whatever happened, you can tell me anything. You're my only family, and I'm yours. Please don't exclude me if you need me." Tears welled up in her lower eyelids.

I could tell she was fighting them back. She sprang on me, giving me a big hug. I tensed. The hug was a big mistake. I wanted to drink her the way the beasts had drunk me. The way the lioness had drunk the gazelle in my dream. I held my breath until she let go and backed away. I could see hurt in her eyes as she peered at me. I felt bad to see it there, but somehow I knew it was better to hurt her feelings. She wasn't physically safe with me, not now. I was thankful when the desire departed.

"I don't need the tea." She walked back into the kitchen and turned the kettle off. I tailed behind. She turned to look at me again. "You get some rest, but promise you'll call me soon, very soon. Please." She smiled as she wiped the almost tears from her eyes.

I couldn't help but promise as I looked at the pain etched in her expression. "I promise, Alina, I will call you as soon as I wake up. You'll be the first one I call. I love you, sweetie. Don't worry. Everything will be fine."

Alina turned to the door and walked slowly. Somehow I knew that was her normal pace, but now it seemed sluggish. She turned to wave bye as she closed the door behind her, and I gave her a pathetic smile. As soon as the door clicked closed, the fake grin fell from my lips.

I stood there for a moment. My body felt weighted, and every movement cost me energy I no longer had. I knew I wasn't making it back to the bedroom, so I meandered around the furniture to the sofa, grabbing the blanket from the lounge as I passed. I was gone instantaneously.

Chapter 12

—⚬⚬⚬—

EUDORA

S he paced back and forth over the cobblestones while gazing at the vast mountains behind the temple. Her feet were adorned with sandals snaking up her slender tan legs and held in place with a simple bow. She was dressed in Greek fashion, a deep-violet Peplos. The violet was so vibrant it reminded me of the skin of a ripe plum. Tiny gold starlets danced across the fabric in mini-explosions. It was a great work of artistry and a true masterpiece. Her left shoulder was exposed with the cloth drawn up and tied over the right one. It was belted at the waist and hung long with slits to allow her legs to move freely. Her long, wavy hair was dark, almost black, with traces of auburn. Her skin was a deep, warm shade of nutmeg.

I watched as the wind blew her hair and the linen about her body; I knew that she and I were one. This felt the same as it did with the lioness, Sekhmet, the wise woman, and the phoenix.

Once again, I found myself in an incorporeal form watching what I now assumed was a past life play out. This dream felt a bit different. Instead of simply watching and being given bits of knowledge along the way, I was one with her. I was able to hear her thoughts and feel her emotions. It was disorienting. I was literally experiencing what it meant to have two conscious minds running inside my thoughts at the same time. I felt me, Phenice, and her, Eudora, as well. Separate but one. This life was once mine, and I was simply remembering. I wondered if this was like having amnesia, then in an instant, having your memories come back to you.

Knowing this life had been mine and had belonged to me in one of my incarnations, I surrendered to the experience. I let this life lead its course, eager to remember my history before I became Phenice.

The air felt ancient, pure, and undiluted. Eudora felt young, but wise, gifted with knowledge that she didn't want. I could feel resentment for her gift. Her gift had left her imprisoned. Not in the traditional way, her cage was gilded. She was respected and provided for. She never wanted for anything material or for food, but she didn't get to have choice in her life. Everything was chosen for her. Her heart ached with the longing to live freely, and my heart ached right along with her.

She closed her eyes and inhaled the sweet smell of the earth, allowing it to enfold her. The warm, moist spring breeze wrapped her delicate skin in a caressing embrace while it toyed with her hair, causing it to tickle her shoulders and back. She envisioned love and peace. She let the images of life with a family dance through her mind. She wanted freedom, and she knew what that meant for a woman with her talent. She knew the price. She would not be free until she was dead. This is the life of an oracle, of the Pythia. To be blessed with the sight of past and future was to be cursed to chains. Not visible ones but chains all the same. To serve for all time on this mortal plane, never to have any simple pleasures, like love or children.

A single tear slid down her soft, beautiful face and found its way to the violet cloth she wore. She didn't even bother to wipe it away. At that moment she kneeled on the stones of the temple and began to water them with her salted tears, and only one word escaped her full plum lips as she raised her dark-chocolate-brown eyes toward the sky: *"Please."*

I felt her pain. The need to be liberated. Her agony radiated from her body like fire. Ready to burn anyone who would dare get close enough. She filled all the space around her, creating a vortex filled with emotional suffering, her despair a hundred times the size of her delicate body. As she wept, my heart broke.

Suddenly she pulled the turbulence back within her and swallowed her despair. She slowly wiped her tears away and stood. Seconds later, a man appeared behind her.

"Eudora, our Pythia, you have fasted. It is time for you to cleanse yourself in the spring to make way for the descent into the chamber." He appeared to be a priest, but no more was said. His name was left unspoken.

She turned and walked in his direction, never looking back at the beauty of the massive mountains surrounding the temple. The world was lost to her. Her pain was hers, never to leave. He bowed his head as she passed.

She undressed once she reached the spring and stepped in. It felt as if she were washing away her mortal existence and becoming something more, a gateway. She could always sense the future and see the past of people around her, but this ritual opened her up even more. She felt invaded, not cleansed as the priest had said. It made her feel dirty, tired, and used. She didn't belong to herself, not like others did. I could feel her hatred rising within her. She felt cursed.

She walked deeper into the water. The moment the current touched her torso, I felt intoxicated. The feeling was disorienting. As the vertigo slammed into her body, it made me want to vomit.

She walked to the middle of the spring and kneeled, letting the coolness surround her. Then she laid back and completely submerged herself. All at once her body started to spin around in the water involuntarily, as if something had taken her over. A woman possessed. She started to convulse. I felt her conscious mind slip away. I was terrified we would drown. I wanted to save her, to help her out of the spring, but I was trapped within her body. It was amazing to be her and witness from afar at the same time. It was like nothing I had ever known.

I continued to watch and experience her body in the water. The spring had a soft current when she stepped in, but now it was perfectly still except for the hurricane effects around her body. I watched in disbelief, knowing she should be dead by now. She hadn't had a breath in over ten minutes, and yet she remained under the water seizing and spinning.

Feeling into her body and tapping into the many times she had lived through this torture, it was clear this was expected. None of the surrounding priests showed any alarm. Her mind, heart, and soul broke down, opening to something mystical. Something not human but still alive. She was transforming into some kind of celestial being. There was no need to breathe, for there was air enough in her lungs, and no need for a heartbeat, even though I could hear and feel it under the crashing water. There was no panic, no fear.

Without warning, the water stilled. The water became peaceful as the ripples vanished, leaving the spring liquid glass. Eudora was motionless under the water, lying on the bottom atop the smooth and silky stone. Without effort, her body levitated to the surface. The water parted to let her pass. Her eyes opened, and she inhaled through parted lips, not a gasp as expected, but a gentle sweet wisp of air moved into her lungs. Her chest barely rose.

The water ran off her body in tiny beads, passing over her breasts and stomach. As she floated higher into the air, above the body of water, the beads slowly rolled down her arms and legs ever so sweetly, like the morning dew sliding down a blade of grass.

You could see the tiny muscles in her body, well defined and sculpted. She was beautiful. Her body rotated in the air, bringing her feet back toward the ground. Not a drop of water decorating her skin. She was as dry as she was before she stepped in the spring. Eudora drifted, without her feet touching the water's surface, over to her clothing. With a dazed glance toward her garment, it lifted from the ground into the air and began to wrap itself around her as if an invisible person was dressing her.

Eudora didn't look like the same woman, nor did she feel the same. The few movements she made were robotic, completely controlled by an outside power. She didn't walk. She glided, levitating above the ground. She didn't look around as she floated. She was being guided, led to her intended destination. The longing for freedom had disappeared. The extreme despair for something more no longer radiated from her. In truth, Eudora was gone. Replaced by something else inhuman and wrong. The only part of her that remained after the transformation was her physical body. What made Eudora had been eradicated. There was a voice present in her head, but it was not her voice. Her pain no longer saturated all her thoughts as before. She was only a vessel now, lost to herself. I wondered where her essence went during these invasions.

Eudora's body was drawn to a chamber under the earth. It appeared to be a space roughly nine by twelve feet, not large by any means, but the room held power. The power vibrated off the walls with immense intensity. The hum of it was slowly unhinging my mind. I felt like some force was picking me apart one piece at a time.

I watched as she floated to a tripod. Eerily, her body spun and sat down. A priest appeared. He handed her a bowl full of water and a bouquet of laurel leaves. She opened her mouth, and he placed three leaves on her tongue. She chewed and swallowed without expression. With the bowl in one hand and the bouquet in the other, her head dropped. With glassy eyes she peered into the water, never to look up again.

Within moments men began to come in and ask questions of her. It was time for her to predict the future for these men who paid a fee to hear what she had to say.

I tried to sense Eudora's being within her body, but all I could feel was the entity who had taken over. I dug as deep as I could within her, floating within her mind, wanting to gain understanding of the unnatural takeover. I found an answer while sweeping through the haziness of her mind.

Deep in the recesses I found a set of huge platinum-sculpted gates. They appeared to be physical doors, and they were swung wide open. When I approached, knowledge hit me so hard I was thrown back and out of her mind. The doors were a gateway to the Fates, and when the doors were open, she was suppressed so deeply no part of her was left.

I didn't understand why the Fates would use her this way. What did it matter if the humans on earth knew their destinies or not? As if I had asked the question aloud, the answer was given. It wasn't the Fates; it was the priests. They did it to gain riches. It was sacrilegious.

The Fates would never use one of their most cherished children in such an evil way. I understood then why the process felt wrong and sickening. Eudora wouldn't feel like a prisoner if this was the way divinity intended her gift to be used. She was to be worshipped and cherished, not used and tainted for the wealth of worthless men. Her gift was supposed to heal the world. This realization caused anger and fury to rise within me. The priest had twisted this beautiful healing gift and robbed her of life, love, and freedom.

Now locked out of her mind, I was left with only the ability to watch. She didn't speak in any known language to the men in front of her; it was gibberish. The priest stood beside her, stoic, as he translated her ramblings. Even locked out of her mind, I had no need for a translator. I knew what she was saying. I knew what she was telling them was fact, not a vague prediction. Before that moment I had always believed no one could tell the future or see the past. I didn't even believe in the concept of a person having a destiny. Yet here I was having it presented to me, and I could feel it. I could feel and see what she was telling these men. The humorous part was the priest was only getting the translations about half-right.

All the questions had been mostly benign, until one man approached Eudora. He was handsome with his smooth, unblemished skin and illuminating crystalline-blue eyes as deep as the oceans.

"I am Xenres. I come seeking guidance for my king." His voice sent shivers down my spine.

Until this point Eudora had stared very intently into the cauldron of water that she held, never even glancing up, but at the sound of his voice, she raised her head and Xenres gasped. The hair on his arms stood on end. He felt it too. She very slowly lowered her head back to the water as if nothing had happened.

In the brief connection of their eyes, Eudora had returned for a moment. I felt her, and I knew who he was. He was her soulmate, a connection so deep not even the tainted magic of the priest could block her from feeling him.

He felt so familiar. So safe, and not just in Eudora's lifetime, but in my own. I had met that soul before. The truth was I had probably met that soul in many lifetimes. Yet I couldn't place who he was in my present life. What I did know was now that I had felt him with the knowledge of who he was to me, I would never forget him.

Xenres spoke his master's request of the Pythia. "My king would like to know of what the gods say to the attacks against Greece from Persia."

A wind blew through Eudora, same as it had with each question asked of her. An internal tornado swelled from her tailbone up to the crown of her head and erupted out. It was a funnel from the heavens down into her body. I was amazed that no one could see it and that she didn't move. I could feel it and see it, but I was linked to her completely. Her ramblings were thrown like debris from the raging wind. Eudora opened her mouth, and out came the answer.

Xenres was lost, but like all the others he walked over to the priest for his translation. I knew what was said: his king would fall in Thermopylae. It would be a good death for the king and good for Greece, but he would not be happy with Eudora for making such a prediction. The king knew the priests were jaded, but his counsel required him to seek guidance from the Pythia before going to war.

This question was different from the others because the fate of Xenres, his king, and Eudora intersected. I saw what was to come. In her trance she could not react, but I knew Eudora would receive the freedom she longed for. Sadly, it would come at a price she would not want to pay.

Xenres stayed stoic as he got his jumbled translation from the priest. Even though his king would be angry, Xenres didn't even flinch at the devastating news. The only emotion he showed was in his inability to take his eyes from the Pythia as he left the chamber.

Chapter 13

FREEDOM

Eudora woke in a cream sleeping gown, frantically looking around. She quickly realized it was all over. She let her head fall back, grabbed her pillow, and slammed it over her mouth. A blood-curdling scream of frustration tore up her throat and over her lips, muffled by the soft pad.

Once she couldn't scream any more, her hoarse and abused voice whispered to no one. "Why would you curse me so? I've done everything you've wished. I have obeyed even though I did not want to. I have served you with my gift. Allowing you to take over my mind, body, and soul." She sounded broken.

"Now that I have found the one thing I have longed for, ached for, and prayed for, this is the path? How could you be so cruel?" Tears slowly rolled down her cheeks.

"I wanted love but have been denied. I wished for freedom, even knowing it will only be granted through my death. I have been willing to die to end this suffering." The tears came faster.

"Now it has been written in my destiny to be granted both in such a cruel and horrible way. Freedom through death, as a gift, from the hands of my soulmate. What have I ever done to deserve such torture?" Another ragged grunt raged from her lips as she slammed her fists over and over into the bedding at her sides.

After a few short moments, Eudora reached up and wiped the tears from her face. She took slow and steady breaths. I felt the rage dissipate from her heart. Her heart was broken, but she knew there was no way to change what the Fates had written for her. The only choice left was to accept this fate. To devour every moment of happiness in the days she had left.

She closed her eyes to journey back to what she'd seen of the future while in the chamber. She had to accept her fate. She had to see it again so she could find the joy, the love, and any other moments to make it worth it.

Eudora took in a long, steadying breath. She could smell the richness of lavender from her linens and room. Lavender had always been her favorite scent. It soothed her soul.

When her muscles finally relaxed, she was able to travel back to the vision she received. The vision Xenres's presence invoked when he broke the hold the Fates had over her in the chamber.

⸏⸏⸏

Delphi, Greece: The near future

It was winter in Delphi. Snow covered the ground and mountains. In the winter months, Eudora belonged to herself as much as a Pythia ever could, for in the winter, no one came to ask questions of her. This was her only break during the year.

What little freedom was allowed consisted of reading and writing, and because of this, Eudora was well educated. Her education was part of the gilded cage, but it was a part she could find peace and contentment in. Her joy was palpable. She loved getting lost in the words she read and the ones she wrote.

She loved to write stories about love and happily ever afters. The kind of loving endings she knew she could never have, but creating them in her mind and on the page soothed her in a way nothing else could. Her stories felt real to her and met a longing deep inside. Since the spring, all her stories had featured only one man.

As the sun set and the day ended, she went to bed knowing what was to come. Though she had made peace with her fate, it didn't stop her from trying to find ways to enjoy what she had left. She had to find a way to tell Xenres who they were to each other. This was the only hope she had. They had a few short moments together before the end. They would have to squeeze a lifetime of love into mere days.

No mortal could change what the heavens had put in place. So as she laid her head on the pillow, she accepted her future with grace and fell asleep quickly.

She was woken by a band of men. They gagged her while tying her hands and feet, even though she didn't scream or fight. The man holding her head close to his chest was nervous or scared. She could feel his heart pounding against her cheek. What they were doing, if caught, would lead to instant death. She was ready to be free though. She looked around her quarters one last time as they rushed her out.

She was carried to a chariot led by two mules. The men placed her inside. The back of the chariot dipped as a few men climbed on. Then the front rocked forward slightly as the rest of the men clambered up to take the reins to drive the mules to their destination. One Eudora knew she would never see.

Once again, I found myself able to observe and be one with Eudora, like the day of the chamber. The gift of witnessing this past life of mine unfold must have some meaning. Though I didn't know what it was, I found it fascinating and terrifying. I could see it wasn't going to end well, and there was a high likelihood it would break something precious. I realized this had to be why humans didn't remember their past lives. It was staggering—watching, knowing, and feeling it play out. I prayed the next memories would not break me in irreparable ways.

She looked around the chariot. Her eyes landed on Xenres. He was sitting very still in the back of the chariot, staring into her eyes. I felt her heart speed up. She longed to tell him everything. She wanted to explain what was happening and what they were feeling. Why he shouldn't go through with what he was about to do, because it would cost him his heart and his own life.

Again, nothing she said could prevent their shared destiny, but she wanted to live to the fullest with him during the short, precious moments. She needed to convince him, but at the moment, her tongue was tied. He was the most stunning creature she had ever seen.

She drank him in with her eyes, starting at his buttery walnut skin. She longed to touch him. It made her heart quicken. He had the body of a warrior.

She wanted to see every inch of him and hear all the stories of how he got every scar. She knew a warrior like him would have them. Spartans always had scars.

Staring at his bare feet, her eyes slowly swept up his body. With every inch, her breath quickened slightly. His dark, blood-red cloak was trapped beneath his body, creating a surreal backdrop for the richness of his flesh. Around his lower legs he wore bronze greaves that hugged his strength. Eudora envisioned how the metal would feel in her hands as she took them off to expose the muscles beneath. Shivers danced across her skin with the thought.

Daring to go farther up his body, she found he wore the traditional *pteruges* low around his abdomen. The layers of hardened chocolate-brown leather wrapped around his thick, yet trim waist and rested over his thighs. It would be so easy to run her hands under it, to touch his flesh. Beads of sweat broke out along her skin as flesh bumps rose all along her body.

Making her way to his chest, she found his cuirass. It looked like liquid bronze had been poured over his chiseled body and molded to highlight his strength. She wondered what his chest would look like naked. She had never seen a male naked. She had never touched a man nor been touched by one. She felt a flush of heat prickle over her chest and crawl up her neck.

Next to his hip on the seat, his left hand lazily caressed the bright red hair atop the Corinthian helmet. His fingers looked strong and powerful. Her eyes cascaded up the length of the bracer covering his forearm, catching sight of his dark hair. It was long and fashioned in dreadlocks, common for a warrior. She followed the dreadlocks up to the crown of his head. He had the locks swept back from his face. A face so breathtaking, she stopped breathing momentarily.

His strong jaw was covered with a dark, well-groomed beard, which drew attention to his full, luscious lips. Involuntarily, her tongue darted out to her lower lip, sucking it back between her teeth. In that moment she was grateful for the gag over her mouth. It saved her from the embarrassment of him seeing her react so strongly to him. Raking her glance up the strong bridge of his nose, she finally landed on his eyes.

They were the most unusual color for a Spartan. They were intoxicating and mesmerizing. The cerulean color danced and sparkled with the power of the waves crashing to the shore. Lost in her amazement, a reflexive gasp slipped through her gag. She was staring at her kidnapper, her death, her soulmate, and she was in wonderment. He didn't seem real. How could he be? He was everything she had fantasized he could be and more. She was gazing at a man her imagination would never have been able to create in her stories of love and romance. She finally found her voice when she became lost in his eyes. She longed to speak to him. She nodded her head and tried to speak.

The chariot took off with barely a sound.

Xenres leaned forward and whispered, "I wish to untie you and remove your gag." He ran his eyes over her body much like she had done to him.

"Sadly, I am afraid you would try to escape…or scream. I hope you understand; I cannot have this. I don't fail, and my mission is to deliver you to my king." He leaned back and continued to run his fingers through the hairs atop his helmet.

The sound of his voice rattled her bones and made her thighs clinch, forcing her to briefly bow her head to break the enchantment. When she lifted her eyes to meet his again, she shook her head side to side. Gesturing to him she had no plan to escape or yell.

"Are you telling me that you go willingly?" He tipped his head to the side, slightly looking puzzled. Eudora knew it was fate, and she had no choice, so yes, willingly she would go.

She nodded.

"I will remove the gag, but I am sorry. I must content myself on leaving you bound." With a predator's grace, he slid forward and removed the gag. Relief blossomed quickly within her.

He slid back, leering at Eudora in fascination or shocked at how calm she was. It was clear from his expression she perplexed him. A slight sheen of perspiration decorated his bronzed skin, betraying his exhilaration. He must have been having the same emotional and physical reaction as Eudora. After all, she was his soulmate too. He probably felt a pull toward her.

Nearly ten minutes passed, and neither one had muttered a single word. Eudora sat quietly observing him as she tried to figure out how to tell him what she had seen, what they meant to each other. She desperately needed him to know. Her motivation was not to save her life. She knew better than anyone the Fates could not be deceived, but for the chance to experience love; that opportunity alone was all the motivation she needed.

She wouldn't die before exploring the gift of a man sitting before her. Not when the Fates had so boldly presented him to her. Everything she had ever wanted now sat across from her. She planned to take a leap of faith because she had nothing to lose. She may only experience love for a few days, but that was better than never at all. Her courage grew. She had been preparing for this very moment since the day he walked into the chamber.

"May I speak if I do not scream out for help?" she asked in a small, yet solid voice.

"Yes, you may. We have roughly a four-day journey by land to Athens. We would grow very bored if we had no conversation." The corners of his mouth lifted slightly. He seemed to have some compassion for her situation.

"I remember you from your journey in the spring to Delphi. You came to see me in the Temple of Apollo. Is this why you come for me now? To complete what the Fates showed me on that day?" Eudora lowered her head to look at the floor of the chariot due to the anxiety creeping up within her. Her courage slipped briefly. There was no going back now. She sucked in a slow, deep breath, forcing her brown eyes to glance up at him through her lashes.

No man would stand a chance against her beauty. The seduction was natural and unintentional. Her goal wasn't to seduce him. She hunted for a way that allowed him to let her in, so she could tell him everything and have him believe her. Eudora needed his trust, not his lust.

Her anxiety hadn't left her. The tension in her body belonged to me as well. As her emotions raged within, I found myself drawn to living this lifetime again with her. I wondered why I was here. Why this time? This place? And with this gorgeous man I wouldn't be able to keep. Why do I have to remember any of this?

From everything I felt and saw in the chamber, I knew this life was filled with pain and heartache. Anger flowed through me. Had I not already suffered enough as Phenice? Apparently, the heavens didn't think so. This felt like a sick game, a mockery of human existence. Were the Fates trying to break me completely?

I tried to wash the resentment away, but a small amount crept in, making itself at home right in the center of my heart. I was running out of room in there. One day I would wake up and this would be too much to bear, leaving me with only one choice: giving up.

Xenres's voice brought me back to the chariot and Eudora and out of my thoughts.

Xenres looked shocked. "I was under the impression the Pythia does not remember the predictions she makes while in the chamber." It rushed out wrapped in a tone of betrayal. It was the most emotion he had shown since she had been dumped in the chariot with him.

"Usually I don't remember anything. As the Pythia, my everyday consciousness is asleep or absent during the readings in the chamber, only to return the next morning. My body is simply a vessel. I have the gift to see the future and the past, but I can't always channel it clearly. Nothing like what happens in the chamber. I am used by the priests. I am put to sleep through a ritual, and only my gift and body remain to answer the questions asked." Eudora's voice was calm and factual.

"Then how do you know me? How do you know of my question? And most importantly of my quest at hand?" He lifted his hand from his helmet and began to rub his fingers along his beard.

"Normally the water of the spring within the cauldron keeps me asleep. I stare into it, and the water is all I can recall. As you approached me, a sudden warmth started to spread throughout my body and woke me from my slumber. Do you remember our glance?" Eudora was hopeful and tense as she questioned him.

"I do." He paused for a moment, continuing to rub his fingers along his chin and through his beard.

"I remember a chill rushing over me when our eyes met. I felt captivated. My breath froze in my lungs as if someone had stolen my existence. It seemed as if I had met you before. As if I had always known you. Then nothing, you were gone." Xenres closed his eyes, lost in thought for a moment. Eudora remained silent.

"What happened? Do you know?" he questioned, meeting her gaze once more. It seemed he had spent many moments thinking about that small glance they shared.

"I don't know how I woke, but I do know what you felt. And I believe you still feel it now, sitting here with me, talking with me." Eudora smiled as she said this to Xenres. He needed her as badly as she needed him. He wanted answers. Hope blossomed in her heart.

"If you know what came over me, I would like for you to tell me. I have never felt so much…pleasure and passion…such longing for another in my life. I need to know what happened in that chamber between the two of us." His eyes became turbulent.

"It is the only reason I volunteered to complete the king's quest. To come and take you. I am a warrior not an errand boy, but I needed answers about the way you have affected me," he completed.

Tears slowly started to fall down Eudora's cheeks. She wasn't upset by his tone or being kidnapped. It was because their love would only last moments this lifetime. Their souls were bound for all eternity, and her heart was breaking at the thought of having to wait until another lifetime to find him again.

Even as pain filled her heart, she couldn't help but bask in the joy of being near him. She gave Xenres a small smile as she wiped the tears away with her bound hands. She grabbed the length of her hair and pulled it in front of her as a distraction, a way to collect her thoughts. It was hard to move around while tied up, but she managed to still look graceful.

While staring into his bottomless midnight-blue eyes, she inhaled deeply. On the exhale her fear left her. Her sadness dissipated. Her anxiety melted away. Determination took over, and she decided to tell him all she knew.

"I will tell you. More than you may want to know, but you must trust that I am telling you what I have seen through my gift, no lies. What I have seen has been foretold by the Fates and cannot be altered. I believe this with all my soul. Can you trust that?" Her confidence radiated from her with each word.

"I believe that you are pure and that you will be honest. That is the code of the Pythia. I know when someone is lying to me. My life depends on this ability." His eyes were truly the bluest Eudora had ever seen.

With a sigh, she spoke again. "Both of our lives will be greatly altered by what I have seen. I apologize in advance for being the messenger of our joined fates."

Eudora closed her eyes and focused on the near future that awaited both her and Xenres. "I will now tell you everything if you are ready and willing to listen without interruption."

"I am ready, but how will I understand you without a translator?" he questioned.

"You will understand. Even though I trust you will not like everything you hear." Eudora glanced up at him and whispered, "May I be unbound?"

Xenres pulled a blade and sliced through the ropes that had Eudora tied at both wrists and ankles.

"Thank you." She rubbed her wrists, took a breath, and closed her eyes. She took us all back to the vision she received that spring night in the chamber.

It was the height of winter in Delphi, cold and dark. Eudora was awoken by her kidnappers as they stole her from her place of slumber. They carried her to a chariot and placed her inside. Her mind whipped through an obvious conversation; although the Fates hadn't graced her with its context, it was clearly the conversation between her and Xenres. Eudora stopped here, like pausing a movie. She rewound the vision back to the voice she heard on that spring evening in the chamber, the voice telling her Xenres was and had always been her soulmate. This was where she had to start.

"As you approached me in the chamber, my body became warm as if dipped in a hot spring. It's the feeling that awoke me, mind and spirit. I was brought back to my body. Then the Fates spoke to me, not through me, like they do when I am in the chamber. The voice told me that you were my one soulmate. For your body housed the soul mine was bound to for all eternity. My expression of love rests within you, always.

"Once the voice stopped speaking to me, the vision started. I saw the winter's night bring forth the men to steal me from my slumber and the chariot to carry me from Delphi. I knew that you would be waiting for me inside. I even saw the conversation you had with your king, which led you back to me.

"He was angry about his fate. Angry he will fall at Thermopylae. He wants to make the Fates pay. He is hoping I may be able to bribe the Fates. It cannot be done. Once it is written, so it shall be. This act will end my life.

"Death does not bother me, for I am not free. I am a prisoner of my gift, the chamber, and the people who know of my gift. I am used as they deem fit. I have long prayed for my ending in this life. Death will be a blessing. The pain of death only came once you were known to me. The only thing I have ever wanted other than death was love."

At this proclamation Xenres could no longer hold his tongue. "I have not come here to kill you nor will I," he whispered. "If what you say is true, and I am your soulmate, and you're mine, I will protect you. I know what I felt, what I feel now, and I believe what you say is true. I know that your gift is pure and honest. How else could you have known the intent of my king? I have no other choice but to believe every word you say." Xenres held a stoic expression and a calm voice, though it was clear he was anything but. If you looked closely, you could see the muscles along his jaw twitch. The thought of finding his love only to lose her so quickly was something he seemed not ready to deal with.

Eudora held her eyes tightly shut as if physically holding her place within the vision as she responded to his words. "I have not finished telling you all that I have been shown, Xenres. I fear that the rest will not please you. It will most likely make you angry and go against who you are as a man…but it is the path."

Xenres sat motionless within the chariot. The only sign of his distress was the slight increase in his breathing and the rigid way he sat. So still he could have been carved of stone.

Eudora remained still and patient, waiting. Wondering if he would have another reaction to what she shared. She'd had her whole life to learn to cope with the pain and sometimes pleasures of being able to see the future. As in the case between Eudora and Xenres, the Fates seemed to take pleasure in inflicting contradicting emotions on humans. They gave all the joys anyone could ever want while pulling the rug out from under their feet. It made life bittersweet. No one should ever take a moment for granted.

With her eyes still closed, she relaxed at the sound of his voice. "Please tell me. I wish to prevent it, to save you and our love." Her eyes popped open, allowing her to stare into his eyes. She felt as if she were being washed away from shore, floating adrift, peaceful and free. A smile played across her lips as she gazed into the vast deep blues. She wondered who would ever want to come back? Nonetheless, she had to come back from his depths and explain to him there was nothing he could do to change the course their lives were about to take.

Eudora closed her eyes again. It was the only way she could escape his stare. She pulled in a deep breath and responded. "Poor Xenres, you do not understand. Fate has spoken…it has been told. There is nothing to change. I will die."

"No," he growled in a low and brutal whisper. "I will not hear this." Xenres was a warrior, and if that rage had been directed toward her instead of for her, it would have made her tremble.

Opening her eyes again, Eudora reached out to him and took his hands in both of hers. When they touched, electricity passed between them. Energy swirled, and light flared around their bodies within the chariot. It wasn't a physical light, but I could see it. I assumed it was because my soul was in Eudora. I was witnessing the connection of my soul to its mate.

It was euphoric being Eudora and feeling such great power and love. The universe wanted them to be together always. It was sad this power was only going to last a few days. The world would be darker without it. I felt my heart break and a fissure crack down my core.

With Xenres's hands still in hers, Eudora continued. "I can tell you what is going to happen, or you could go through the next four days blind to the experience." She offered him the choice to continue living as he always had. It was difficult to live as she did, and most could not handle it.

"Are there any good parts?" he murmured.

"Oh yes, there are." She squeezed his hands. "Then there is the end." Eudora smiled a very brave smile. Unlike Xenres, she'd had months with this knowledge to prepare for her destruction. He was getting blindsided.

"Okay, tell me. But will you sit with me as you tell me our future?" He moved his helmet from the seat and slid over. He held out his arms to her.

Tears began to build in her lower lids as she climbed over to him. She leaned over and kissed his lips sweetly. Their first kiss. She closed her eyes, forcing a single tear to slide down her cheek as she reentered the vision. She shared everything she saw.

Since this was my life as well, I saw and felt everything too.

The trip to Athens was spent with them talking and getting to know one another. They discussed literature, philosophy, and the stars. She learned of the battles he fought. It sounded like she was lucky Xenres was still alive for her to meet him. He was strong and brave. He had fought his way up through the ranks of the Spartan forces and was now close to the king. He had a sharp mind. He was calm and thoughtful. He was not a reactive person. Even in the moments Eudora could tell he was struggling with what was to come, he didn't say anything. He was strong for her sake, and she was grateful.

During the five to six hours while the mules fed and rested, they stayed tucked away in his tent, tight in each other's arms. Eudora decided this was her favorite place to be. With her head resting on his chest, hearing his heartbeat and feeling the rise and fall of his breaths made her feel complete in ways nothing ever had.

On the last night before they were to meet up with the king's messenger, Eudora mustered up the courage to ask Xenres to make love to her. She knew the next day would be their last. They would find themselves on a ship instead of finishing the trip to Sparta. Xenres was hesitant. They were not married, and he respected her greatly. He wanted to give her everything. When she confessed this was their last opportunity, it was clear he would deny her nothing.

Eudora found herself in his tent, still dressed in her cream sleeping gown. Days before, Xenres had given her a cloak to keep her warm, but she had discarded it once they were alone together. Xenres stared into her eyes, frozen in place. He was still dressed in his full warrior attire. She slowly walked up to him, determined to feel the weight of his armor as she finally got the chance to strip it from his handsome body.

Eudora placed her hands on his cheeks, pulling his face down to her, allowing their lips to meet. As soon as the heat of their flesh touched, Xenres lost all uncertainty. The heat of their kiss invoked roaming hands. Xenres grabbed her body and pulled her to him. Eudora worked hard, trying to figure out how to free him from the confines of his bronze protection. He didn't need armor with her. He would be safe in her hands, as she was in his.

Unable to find all the latches and hinges, she pulled back from his lips in a huff that sent her hair flying out of her face. She laughed. "Are you going to free yourself from these contraptions, so I may finally see you? And touch you?"

The biggest smile Xenres had ever given her lit up his face. "As my lady desires."

Xenres took a step back from her and began to unfasten the many buckles and ties holding on his greaves, bracers, cuirass, and *pteruges*. He carefully laid each piece down. Showing respect for what his armor meant to him. Once free of the armor, he was left in nothing but a simple linen undershirt.

His naturally dark skin was radiant. He looked as soft as velvet, and Eudora couldn't wait to touch him. A few locks fell forward as he stepped toward Eudora. All his muscles were well defined.

Once he was in reach, Eudora grabbed the hem of his tunic, rubbing the fabric between her thin, delicate fingers.

"May I?" she asked.

"Of course." He smiled.

With slightly shaking fingers, she grabbed ahold of the soft linen with both hands and pulled it up and over his head, throwing it to the ground behind him. She inhaled sharply as she took all of him in for the first time.

I must admit, he was the most amazing man I had ever seen naked in my whole life. He definitely had scars from battle, as Eudora had expected, but they made him more real, more touchable. I couldn't wait until Eudora touched him because that meant I would get to feel him, even if only in her vision and only in my dreams.

"I feel a bit exposed here, Eudora. May I remove your gown? I would love to see you," Xenres said.

Lost for words, Eudora nodded. He took both of his hands and bunched up the fabric around her waist, slowly working the length of her gown up her body. A chill rushed over her skin as more and more of her became exposed. The slightest of shivers danced up her spine with the brush of the linen. Then as the gown pulled up and over her breasts, neck, and head, her whole body let out an involuntary shake. She closed her eyes.

Eudora had undressed many times in front of the priests of Delphi as she prepared to immerse herself in the spring for the ritual, but never with the intention to be touched by a man. For the first time, she felt shy and timid to be standing there nude. This meant so much more than it ever had. She heard the soft whisper as the gown fell from his fingers and landed at her feet.

"Eudora, my love. Will you open your eyes and look at me?" Xenres whispered.

She felt his breath brush her earlobe and his hair tickle her shoulder. She sucked in a breath of excitement. She opened her eyes.

He stood in front of her, looking at her like she was the meaning of life. Before she could stop herself, she leaped up, wrapped her legs around his waist, her arms around his neck, and slammed her lips to his. He immediately opened for her, slipping his tongue inside to dance with hers. He swallowed her gasp as it passed her lips.

She felt him start to walk backward. He kneeled with her still tightly wrapped around him and kissing her. Placing her on the bedroll he had prepared on the ground inside the tent, she found herself flat on her back with him over her, holding all his weight. She loosened her hold, letting her legs fall wide and open to the sides of his hips. She allowed her hands to roam over his hard, warm flesh. One hand rested over his heart. She could feel it pounding inside his chest. The rhythm seemed to match her own excited pace.

Xenres sat back on his heels, kneeling between her open legs. He allowed his eyes to take her in completely. He began to run his fingertips over her cheekbones, across her lips, down the center of her neck, and brushed them delicately over her collarbones. Eudora's back arched as she pushed her feet deeper into the bedroll, needing to squeeze her thighs together but unable to because he was between them.

He leaned forward, placing both hands beside her head as he whispered into her ear. "I love you more than life itself. I am grateful for the gift of you, no matter how long or short. You have made it all worth it."

He placed gentle kisses along her ear and down the column of her neck. Between every few kisses, his tongue would dart out to taste her skin, causing him to groan deep in his chest. The sound created a vibration throughout Eudora's entire body from the contact of his chest against her breasts. Her skin flushed in anticipation.

Working his way with kisses and licks across her chest, just above her breasts, he stopped at her other ear. "I promise not to hurt you, my love. You must tell me to slow down if I get too excited and become too rough. Please, promise me," he whispered.

Shaking with need, Eudora nodded.

"Not good enough, my dove." He breathed into her ear then gently bit down on her earlobe.

Eudora whimpered, causing him to let out a soft masculine chuckle. "Please use words, beautiful. I need to hear your voice. I long for your approval. Do you accept me and all I am offering you?"

His body was resting flat atop hers, with his weight held on his elbow and his other hand creating slow, torturous circles on the outside of her hip. It was blissfully excruciating. She felt his lips gently nibbling on her earlobe while he waited so patiently for her to give him the go-ahead. She was so ready, but finding her voice was hard. All the sensations flooding her skin and mind were like flames dancing over her flesh, devouring her alive. She didn't have a single coherent thought in her head, but she needed to say something, or he wouldn't give her what she wanted, what she needed.

With her hands exploring his back, Eudora took in a deep breath helping her to slow her mind enough to speak. "I trust you will not hurt me. You have my word. I will tell you if it is too much…and Xenres…"

"Yes, love?"

"I love you as well. I have since before I saw your face. I will always love you," she murmured into his ear.

With her declaration, he kissed her long, deep, and slowly. Both of their hearts quickened. With great urgency their hands found each other. As she lost herself in the cool, minty taste of his mouth, she ran her hands down his shoulders, along the sides of his waist, until she found his backside. Reflexively, she pulled his pelvis closer to her. He deepened the kiss with a groan. The pressure of his hardness pressed into her was nearly her undoing.

To feel him so close, so powerful, it created a vortex of energy within them. Eudora felt on fire and not warm enough at the same time. The contrast made it almost unbearable, but to be truthful, it was perfect. She felt so alive. So hungry for him. She had never felt passion like that. She was aching for him. The wetness between her legs was new to her. She could feel it flowing faster with each thrust of his tongue, each roaming touch of his hand. She moaned into his mouth, and as if he couldn't take another second of it, he pulled away and began his decent down her body.

Working his way down from her neck to her collarbone, he slowly explored her delicate frame with his lips and tongue. Eudora softly moaned again as the pleasure filled her. With the first pull of her nipple into his mouth, her back popped up off the bedroll. Quick as lightning, Xenres snaked his arm under her, pulling her closer, giving him more leverage to feast upon her.

With a guttural groan and a popping sound, he moved to her other breast and savored it as well. Sweet sounds escaped the lips of both lovers. Eudora was panting and so heated her skin pricked with beads of dewy sweat. Xenres eagerly licked them up as he trailed farther down to her navel with his hot, wet mouth. Scorching passion burned into her core with each kiss and lick. She had ahold of his hair as he kneaded her body and tasted everything she was offering.

His head dipped farther, forcing her hands to slip from his hair onto his face as he looked up at her. Those amazing cerulean eyes captured her, making it impossible to look away. While gazing into her eyes, Xenres reached down with both hands and pulled her legs farther apart. Eudora gasped.

Xenres's eyes swept down her body and back up. He was lost in her. "Damn, woman…I must taste you."

Without any more of a warning, he dove straight in with no hesitation to taste her. With the first brush of his soft, warm lips, the tickle of his beard, and the wet flick of his tongue, Eudora cried out, and her body began to quake. He moaned into her folds, which brought out another cry from her. He ran his hands up and down her thighs and back up to her breasts, but he never took his eyes away from her face. He held eye contact with her as he made her scream over and over with pleasure. She bucked and struggled from the pleasure. It was almost too much. She would reach a peak and then fall limp and quivering. He caught her every time. He would ease up, placing soft gentle kisses along her wetness briefly before diving in again. He didn't miss a single expression and seemed hungry for every bit of ecstasy he could wring out of her.

Weak with pleasure, Eudora begged for him. She wanted all of him. She needed him. In response, he rose up on his knees between her legs. He wiped the glistening wetness from his beard and lumbered over the top of her with the power of a lion. He placed a chaste kiss on her lips while delicately laying his weight against her body. Eudora could smell herself on his face and breath. Her low belly ached.

"Please, my love. I need you…all of you." Her voice quivered. A moan fell from her lips from the light pressure of his body pinning her down.

"As I need you, my dove. This is the part that may hurt…please, keep your vow to me. I will stop or slow if you need me to." He kissed her more fully as he reached between their bodies taking a hold of himself to line up with her opening.

Slowly he slid in. She sucked in a breath from the pleasure tinged with a slight pinch. He paused briefly, halfway in, to allow her body a moment to adjust. It was like nothing she had ever felt.

The entire world was for them at that moment. Her body relaxed, and unable to wait a second more, she grabbed him, pulling him in the rest of the way. He moaned as his body slapped into hers. He brought his lips to hers. She kissed him hard and deep with reckless abandon, tasting herself on him. He started to move faster with deep, long strokes. Her breath quickened. She loved it. She wondered how could love like this ever hurt. It was the most amazing experience she had ever had.

Their rhythm together was like no piece of music ever written or heard, so perfectly timed. They laughed a few times together from the pleasure. As the laughter died on her lips, Eudora shed a few tears, knowing they would only have a few moments like this, at least in this lifetime.

"I know, my love. This is perfect. Our love is perfect. You are perfect. I am so sorry we have been cheated of time. You have all of me. You always will…" He placed sweet kisses all over her face between each statement, kissing away each tear.

Then he picked up his pace; deeper and faster he went. She screamed with so much pleasure, and as they came to the end, they cried out together. He wrapped her up, pulling her over to lay halfway on top of him as he fell to his back. He held her as if she were life itself.

He didn't ever let go, not even when he fell asleep.

Before she fell asleep in his arms, Eudora whispered in his ear. "I will die a happy woman tomorrow. I love you. Thank you."

They woke only after a few hours of sleep and made love again. Eudora watched Xenres get dressed. She was saddened as she watched his clothing steal the wonderment of his nakedness. With a heavy heart, she stood. He watched her in awe as she walked over and picked up her gown. Xenres was frozen. He didn't even blink until she slid her clothing back on and belted it at her waist.

Moments later, irritation filled him as two of his men came in to gather their bedding. Once they were done, Xenres walked over to Eudora and wrapped her in his arms, placing a kiss atop her head. Without a word, they walked out to the awaiting chariot. They would arrive at the meeting point today.

Once alone in the chariot, Eudora kissed Xenres and told him, "Once we get to the meeting point, there will be a messenger there with a letter from your king." Xenres was not happy about this news. He seemed still lost in last night's passion.

Her statement made the reality of their situation roar back to life. All he could do was stare. The pain was clear in his eyes. His eyes grew slightly glassy, but within a moment they dried, and all emotion vanished. He straightened up in his seat.

They rode the rest of the way to the meeting point in Athens in silence. Though they didn't speak, they never once slipped from each other's embrace.

"Eudora…please stop. I do not want to hear any more." Xenres shook her gently. His face remained stoic, but it was clear a part of him was breaking, hearing what was to come.

Eudora looked at him, blinking slowly. The vision had left her because he had broken her concentration. It was disorienting to be pulled out of the vision and yanked back to the chariot, days earlier, back to the night Eudora had been taken. I had let my mind merge with Eudora's. The vision had taken me completely. To the point I forgot none of it had happened yet. Eudora was telling the story, and I was lost in my/her love for Xenres.

"I am sorry, Xenres, but if I don't share the vision, if you do not understand, I fear I will lose my freedom and you. I agreed to tell you everything, and though it is hard to hear, it is necessary." Eudora looked at him. Her heart broke seeing the pain he hid so well.

"But you whispered you would die. You said it in my ear after we made love, while I was sleeping. I cannot bear the thought of your death." He was a powerful man used to being able to control any situation. To use his brilliant mind to navigate the world and create desired outcomes in the face of impossibilities. This time he wouldn't be able to use strategy to change things.

"There is good reason for my death. You will see. Let me tell you the rest. Please, be still and have peace. This is the way of the Fates, our destiny. I am sorry it cannot be more, but I am not sorry that I have you." She kissed him again and ran her hands over his hair.

He surrendered. "Okay. Please, forgive me." He kissed her sweetly on the lips and pulled her back into his lap.

Nestled into the strength of his chest, Eudora closed her eyes, pulling herself back to the future as if watching a movie in fast-forward until she reached the part she wanted.

She stopped when she found them in Athens. A messenger was waiting for Xenres. Eudora began to speak to Xenres, telling him what she was witnessing.

"The messenger is waiting for you with a letter. You ask to tie me up again in case he gets word back to the king. I agree. You step out once we stop and walk up to him. I can't help but watch you." Eudora smiled. "Do you know how handsome you are?" A small giggle passed her lips while Xenres pulled her tighter to his chest.

"You take the letter from his outstretched hand and dismiss him. You turn abruptly and come back to me without reading the letter. Once we are back in the chariot, you hold me as you read the letter."

Xenres's heart rate picked up, pounding against her back. She didn't open her eyes. If she did, the vision would be lost again, and Eudora didn't think she would have the courage to finish telling him what happens next.

"In the letter, the king explains his plan for me has changed. Through further counsel he now understands there is no way to change the minds of the Fates. So to harm the Fates, his plan is to imprison me for the rest of my life. He will not offer me death. That would be too simple. He believes by making me, a vessel of the Fates, suffer, he will make the Fates themselves suffer."

Back within the vision:

Once Xenres finished reading the letter, he tore it into unrecognizable scraps of confetti, as if this could change his king's plans. Every bit of anger was reflected in the tiny bits of parchment as he tossed them into the wind. They scattered, finding their way to the sea.

Xenres turned and knelt at Eudora's feet. He wrapped his arms around her legs, dragging himself close to her. He lay his head in her lap. His breath was ragged and irregular.

After a few moments, he lifted his head to gaze into her eyes. "Please, forgive me, Eudora. I would never have come for you had I known. I am sorry, my love. This is my fault. Had I not come in the spring, you would be safe. I am…so…sorry." His plea was barely audible.

Eudora braced his face between her hands, while he stayed kneeling at her feet. "Oh, my love. This is not your doing. You have not set this fate upon me, nor can you undo it. You are the only blessing in this cruel life. I have been nothing more than a slave. You gave me freedom. Please, understand…please, Xenres. I love you…There is nothing to forgive, my sweet. Thank you for loving me, for saving me. For the first time in my life, I am free of all chains, and I will never be chained again. Please, understand. I will never be caged again. Not even to save my life."

Eudora's attention was pulled outside the vision as Xenres interrupted her. "Let us leave now. We can run. I can keep us safe and take you to a place he will never find us. Tell me we can change this future. Please, tell me it is possible."

With her lids tightly locked and holding onto the vision, Eudora managed to whisper a reply. "No, my love. Fate will always find us. I have begged the Fates to change it. The Fates have shown me many possible avenues, and sadly they all end exactly the same. This one is the one to bring us the most time and the most happiness. We have no choice how it ends, but we do get a choice in how we live our last few moments."

"I cannot take the story of your death. It seems I will soon experience it. For you, I will accept there is no other choice, but I am not ready to hear it. I will not be able to think of anything else. If you keep this part from me, I will commit to enjoying our time together," he whispered next to her ear. Xenres paused in thought. He touched her face, then asked, "How many years have you blessed this world?"

"Twenty-two, my love, too young to die and too wise to think there is any other way." Eudora remained calm with her eyes still closed.

"How cruel to not have happened upon you sooner," he murmured while pulling her head to his shoulder, breathing in her scent and snuggling into her hair.

Eudora stayed silent for a while, enjoying his embrace. "I can tell you this much: after you read the letter, you charter a boat to sea, away from Athens and the men we are with. We sneak away while everyone is asleep, departing at night. We spend the night wrapped in each other's arms, making love, talking…and well, making love." She finished with a giggle.

A passionate smile played upon Eudora's face. She had never known such passion was possible, and as much as she wanted to hate her fate, to be angry with the Fates for cursing her so, she could not. There was too much happiness in her last days to be bitter about anything. After all she could have lived a life never knowing love like she had with Xenres.

Not in control of my incorporeal self, I floated off, leaving them in the chariot, forced to watch the last few moments of their lives.

During their last night, Eudora and Xenres never left their sleeping quarters on the ship. Between sessions of lovemaking, they shared laughter, smiles, and pain too. A few hours before dawn, knowing the men will wake and find them missing, Xenres finally asked her for the solution. He was as ready as he would ever be, simply because they were out of time. Lying next to each other, Eudora wrapped him up in her arms, placing his head on her chest, exposing his ear to her lips.

With a slow intake of breath, she allowed herself to speak her request of him. "I want you to end my life and prevent my suffering."

For the first time, she witnessed Xenres lose control. Wrath poured from his body as he bounded up from the bed. Eudora was immediately on her feet, throwing her arms around him with all the strength she had. This calmed him in an instant; he clearly wouldn't hurt her, making her request all the harder.

Taking advantage of his chivalry, Eudora began to explain her demand. "I want to be free. I have always known my freedom would cost me my life. I have, many times, considered doing the deed myself." She paused with a labored inhale.

"It's not in my destiny to die such a death. The Fates would not allow it. Honestly my will would not allow it. So I remained caged by my circumstances, awaiting the day the Fates would grant my wish…and they sent you to me."

She caged his stressed, handsome face between her hands, forcing him to look at her.

"I never thought they would answer both my prayers. I prayed for love and for freedom. I didn't know this was how it would end. I beg you, my love, please free me. Release me from my prison. Gift me the end of this life. So I may one day be reborn to find you again in a time and place where we may have what we are meant to have." Tears rolled down her cheeks. He was all she had ever wanted, and he was hers, *always*.

He pulled her tight to him, petting her hair as her sobs tore out of her body. Knowing they had only a few short hours left was breaking her completely.

Dropping his lips to her ear, Xenres spoke. "I will give you what you ask, but only if you will give me the same in return. I want you to take my life as I take yours. I cannot live a day in this world without you." His voice cracked. "Now I have found you, knowing you are no longer in this world will leave me in chains. I refuse to be caged either, my love. Will you free me?"

He clung to Eudora for dear life.

"Yes, I will. That is how I have seen it from the beginning," she replied, closing her eyes.

Xenres picked her up. Eudora wrapped her legs around him as he found her mouth with his. They fell back into bed for their last chance to feel their love in this life.

The sky barely had any stars left as dawn approached. They stood on the outside of the ship's railing, holding each other tightly. Xenres had bound them in rope, from their legs to their waists, fastening their bodies together. They each held a blade. The endless sea was in front of them, but they only had eyes for each other.

As the sun grew higher in the sky, they knew time had run out.

Xenres kissed Eudora on her forehead and whispered, "A gut wound is a painful way to die, but it is a slow way to die. I want to spend as much time with you, no matter how much it costs me." He placed his free hand over hers, holding the knife, and turned it toward his stomach, indicating where he wanted her to pierce his flesh.

Eudora took her free hand and pinched his chin, pulling his attention back to her face. She smiled when his eyes found hers. "There will be no pain for me as long as I am in your embrace and lost in your eyes." Even with her death imminent, it was amazing to see her aglow with true happiness and peace.

They stood for a moment, taking each other in, with the blades positioned to cause death yet give them as much time as possible. They leaned in to kiss each other, allowing the blades to pierce the other's belly. Their kiss swallowed the other's gasp of pain. They dragged the knives across the other's gut, slicing it open. Blood began to flow. They never broke the kiss as the knives were ripped out and dropped into the sea with a splash.

With their hands free, they wrapped each other up in an embrace, deepening the kiss. Their blood mingled and flowed freely, staining the ship's deck.

They were lost in each other, kissing and refusing to blink as they stared into one another's eyes. Stepping as close as they could, Xenres tightened the rope, binding them together. They would forever be together in the depths of the sea.

As life poured from them, their kiss intensified. They both knew this would be the last kiss they would share until their next lifetime. Weakness overtook them. Life began to fade from their eyes.

Eudora passed first, her eyes no longer seeing anything. Xenres finally let his tears fall with no one present to witness his weakness. With the last of his strength, he closed both of her eyes, placing a kiss atop each eyelid.

He kissed her forehead, brushed his hand down her cheek and cupped her face. With his eyes looking over her beautiful face one last time, he whispered, "You have my whole heart, all my love. You will always be the key to unlock my soul. Until our next life, my dove." He placed a last kiss on her lips and tipped over the side of the ship.

I saw the light leave his eyes as they hit the water. I couldn't look away as their corpses sank into the deep, dark sea. There was nothing left behind but their pooled blood and a feeling of emptiness in the world.

With the death of Eudora, I felt something snap in my core. Like something coming back to me. I didn't know what that meant. I didn't care.

Unable to blink, I watched their bodies sink farther down in the eerie midnight water with the reflection of the last few stars dancing on the surface. I blinked back the last of my tears I didn't know I could cry.

In their absence, my attention was drawn to the blood pooled on the deck. Though there was an aching wound tearing its way through my heart, caused by the loss of their love, a new sensation ripped through me from the sight of the deep, rich crimson blood. I was ravenously hungry.

Chapter 14

CRUENTUS

"The gift of past, present, and future passes on. For now, you are done."

I whipped up gasping for air. With frantic need, I spun all around trying to figure out where I was, *when* it was. What was happening to me? It felt like I had left for weeks. As much as I tried, I couldn't focus on a single thing or get an idea of space or time. I felt pulled from my body. Was I in hell? Did I die, and now I was being forever tortured? Was I a bad person? I had to get a grip.

"What the hell is wrong with me?" I wondered aloud, not expecting an answer, and what I heard was definitely not anticipated.

A voice stated in a matter-of-fact tone, "Nothing is wrong with you. You are just not what you were."

"What the hell is that supposed to mean?" I screamed, expecting a reply this time. I waited and got nothing. I jumped up. "Fuck! Fuck! *Fuck!*"

I started pacing around. I am losing my fucking mind! In my confusion and panic, I hadn't realized someone was in my house. I had passed out on the sofa, and I wasn't alone.

Sitting across from me in the chair, watching me pace and freak the hell out, was Emil. He leaned forward and slowly stood, his hands outstretched in a calming motion with an extreme look of concern etched on his face. His mouth was moving. He was speaking to me. Panic rose even higher than it had at the sight of him when I realized I couldn't hear him. Why was he here, him of all people? How did he get in? My world was spinning. I was disoriented. A slow, constant sea of nausea climbed up from my gut, leaving me drowning in bile.

I frantically looked around again. I was a caged animal. I needed to escape. All the rapid whips of my head left the room swaying. I lost my balance. As I fell backward, I gripped the arm of the sofa to steady myself. Waves of consuming chaos crashed down on me. I couldn't stop trying to get a handle on the melee of emotions pouring through me and the pain rushing through my body.

No matter where I looked, no matter how desperate I felt, I was unable to get control. I needed control. I craved control above everything else. I closed my eyes and begged for it to stop. As an answer to my silent prayers, I heard someone familiar.

Flying around the couch involuntarily, confused how I got to her so quickly, I was standing before Alina with her kind and gentle sky-blue eyes. She looked at me with tenderness, so full of compassion and something more, something hollow and broken. She looked grieved, like someone had died.

Her mouth was moving. I heard whispers of noise, I heard her voice, but I had no comprehension. Her voice was familiar, a soothing lullaby. Yet all I heard was a loud ringing cased in static.

It was clear Emil and Alina were speaking to me, but nothing was making its way to me. I had no understanding of anything they said. All I could hear was low, whirling gibberish and static. Nothing else. All this did was make the panic worse.

They both started approaching. The need to escape soared once again. I took a few rapid steps back, retreating. More anxiety rose within me. I was trapped and cornered by predators. My eyes darted back and forth between the two of them. Flashes of the beasts in the rose garden darted across my mind, a flashback slammed into me. The room disappeared. It was replaced with blood and pain. Oh, the sounds…the sounds of my bones shattering and breaking. The sounds of flesh tearing, tendons and ligaments popping. The sounds of them swallowing as they drank my life away. It was too much.

Suddenly, the room rushed back as the PTSD flashback dissolved. My internal struggle only increased. I was suffering from some intense mental whiplash. Should I fight or flee? Instincts took over. A low growl rose from my belly, forcing itself from my lips in a low vibrating roar. The sound startled me. I ran.

I could hear them following, but without effort I made it into my bedroom, slamming the door behind me and locking it reflexively. My solitude calmed me slightly. I looked around the room, noticing everything felt strange and unknown but oddly familiar at the same time.

My room was a mess, which was never the case. Even as a child, it was spotless. Always tidy and clean with a place for everything. It gave me control because the world outside was determined to get me. To eat me whole. I had no control in the outside world. At least that's how I felt as a small girl, cowering in her immaculate temple. Images of my father sprang to my mind. He was my first monster. I shook my head. I didn't have the strength to deal with him right now.

Look at me now, a grown woman running scared, seeking her safe place and finding it in ruin. Terror tore through me. I shot like a rocket to the bed and curled up in my blankets, letting the warmth take me in. I was freaking hiding, a complete fraidy-cat. Nothing more than a scared animal looking to her nest for protection, seeking safety. It was an odd realization, and yet it felt completely naturally and normal.

I settled in, letting the warmth of the bedding embrace me. I tried to relax, but I could still hear Alina and Emil outside my door. I blocked them out by counting in my head. As each number passed, I felt myself becoming more centered, a fraction at a time. I needed to get control of my warring emotions.

I was having a panic attack. I hadn't had one in years. It would pass if I allowed it. I had to stop freaking out. Ten…eleven…twelve…my muscles began to relax. Twenty…twenty-one…twenty-two…I slowly unwound myself from the fetal position. Thirty-one…thirty-two…thirty-three. I took a deep breath in and let it out with an audible sigh. Forty-eight…forty-nine…fifty. I opened my eyes to stare at my ceiling, realizing the panic was almost gone. I could feel the rational person peeking out from deep within me, beginning to govern my thoughts. The nausea disappeared. I gently pulled myself into a sitting position. I was happy to have the world no longer spinning.

I pushed back to my headboard, pulling myself into a crossed-legged position, and rested my hands on my knees. "I need to separate facts from feelings," I spoke aloud allowing myself to physically hear the words. I stated this mantra multiple times.

I decided to start simply. What day is it? I turned my head and glanced at the clock on my bedside table. I was stunned. I blinked a couple times, making sure I was reading the display correctly. It was 11:43 p.m. on Tuesday.

"Holy shit," I murmured as comprehension hit me. It had been a full week since I was attacked. I hadn't eaten or drank a single thing. I hadn't gone to the bathroom. These were the facts, and yet I wasn't hungry or thirsty, and I didn't feel the need to urinate. I should feel weak, but I felt stronger than I ever had.

I felt some panic rising as I wondered yet again what happened to me.

"No. Focus on the facts, not how you feel about them," I told myself.

My eyes traveled to my forearms, looking for the reminder of what had happened last Tuesday. I turned my palms up, allowing myself the best vantage point, but all I saw was perfectly flawless pale flesh. I turned my hands down, still gazing at my flesh in awe. There was not a single imperfection to be found. Not a trace was left of what had happened to me. Not a mark, no scar, no pink memory etched on my skin leaving a tattoo of that night. Gone, erased completely. It was incredible. Yet painful. How could something so horrific leave absolutely no mark? No physical memory. No proof of what I survived.

My mind then jumped to the last coherent words I remembered: *Nothing is wrong with you. You are just not what you were.*

I knew something colossal and life changing had happened to me, and it was triggered by the attack. I tried to think back further. I also remember hearing, *The gift of the past, present, and future passes on.*

"I'm Eudora…or I was Eudora in a past life. What does that mean?" I breathed, remembering the dream or vision, whichever. I was she, and she was me—one and the same really. So, do I now have the abilities of the oracle?

I decided to ask. Maybe the voice that spoke to me was the voice of the Fates. Was that the voice I had been hearing over the last week? Was it my life as Eudora tying me to them? They might commune with me now, like they did in my past. Or maybe the attack took the last of my sanity.

Here goes nothing, I thought before I spoke aloud. "At one point, was I Eudora?"

I waited.

The same voice as before returned, and I knew no one else could hear it. *You have always been Eudora. As you are the lioness and her goddess. The wise woman and the phoenix…one soul for many lives. You have had many lives since your first incarnation. All powers are for the present and future, for you, Phenice, to wield for all eternity.*

I wanted to know more. "What am I? Please, tell me what happened." The words choked me as I spoke them because part of me knew I didn't want to hear the answer.

For now you are a vampire, a very special vampire. One meant to bring change to your kind. She created you, but it was our will that led her to you.

"Who created me? Who made me a vampire?" I had to be in shock because I wasn't really processing what I was hearing. At that moment, I was gathering the information and trying to avoid any emotional reactivity. If I allowed myself to feel any of this, I would find myself back in the fetal position counting for the rest of my life.

The Damned One. She was the first vampire. The Original. We sent you a dream of her creation, to foreshadow what was to become of you and by whom.

Visions of my dream rushed forward. The Egyptian queen who damned the heavens and drank her son filled my eyes. Quickly, her face was washed away by blood, sand, and death. I could hardly speak.

I swallowed back the tidal wave of death to ask, "Sadeh, she was the first vampire? She did this to me?"

Yes, but always remember this has been your fate since before your first human incarnation…for many lifetimes. She was simply the means to get you here. That's all.

"I don't want this," I said slowly in a hushed voice. "I wanted a new life, a new beginning, a chance to live right. This is a dead end. Please," I pleaded. "Please, undo this."

Nothing. All I got back from the Fates was nothing. A big, gaping wad of nothing. Shit!

I knew in that second no amount of begging would change what the Fates had in store for me. The lesson was clear from my vision and lifetime as Eudora. Once it was written, so shall it be. Damn it!

I could do nothing but make the best of my new situation. The stubbornness within me had to ask one more time regardless of how pointless my efforts were.

"Undo this, please," I whispered my plea.

But as expected, the voice stayed silent, and all I could do was sigh as my heart broke. Each new transition or revelation created another fissure through my core.

I sat there forever, staring at my red walls. Despair wasn't a strong enough word for what I was feeling. I don't think language had a word to describe my anguish. I racked my brain for a more rational answer to what I was going through, and I kept coming up empty. I prided myself on finding a logical answer for everything, but this didn't have one, no matter how badly I wanted it.

I hoped I really had gone batshit, but in my gut, a deep knowing reverberated. Insanity and brokenness would be easier, simple. Ultimately, I knew this was going to be so much more painful. I knew I would prefer the bliss of insanity over what was waiting for me outside these red walls. I had to admit, I kept questioning my sanity because part of me wanted the easy way out. I wanted the ability to check out and not care. I had fought my whole life. I was so tired…so tired I could feel it in my bone marrow, that deep ache throughout your whole being.

The longer I leaned against my headboard, the deeper the hollowness burrowed. The raging uncertainty was carving me up. The longer I did nothing, the more dead I felt.

How am I a vampire? What alternate dimension did I slip in to? Hell? Purgatory?

I no longer felt any gratitude for surviving last Tuesday. Now I wished I had died. I should've drowned or bled to death; that would've been peaceful, easy. Anything would be better than this. How did anyone venture into an unknown this vast? A whole new world I never knew existed.

That answer would have to wait. At that moment my guests had ran out of patience. There was a knock on my door. Okay, a "knock" was stating it kindly. It was a loud pounding, an "open the fucking door or we will open it for you" kind of knock.

"Phenice, please let one of us talk to you." It was Alina. Her words were clear and easily understood. Clearly, my earlier panic prevented understanding my unwanted guests. Grateful as I was to understand the spoken word again, I couldn't help the desire in my heart for the whole world to vanish.

I waited to respond. Questioning whether I should answer, and if I did, what would I say to her? She would want to know what happened to me, and I couldn't tell her. I didn't want to lose her. I needed her desperately. That thought sent bone-aching fear radiating through me. I didn't want to need anyone because ultimately my heart would break because of it. Every relationship I had ever known ended with my heart shattered in pieces so rigid and sharp, so irreparable, I still didn't know how to put the pieces back together.

I climbed from my bed, advancing toward the door for two reasons: One, they weren't going away. They sounded determined to stay forever perched outside the door. Two, I didn't want to be a coward. A fire burned inside of me in response to my fear. I hated being scared of anything, and I wasn't going to run. My mind was back under control, at least for now, which meant I would walk tall toward what was waiting for me.

As I opened the door, I asked, "What are you two doing here?"

My eyes were all for Alina. My voice was different, forceful and harsh with a strong ringing undercurrent of power. It wasn't the voice I was used to, but obviously I was no longer that woman. She was lost to me. Who I was now was a mystery, and I hated surprises. Part of me hated this new woman too.

"Please, trust me. I know what has happened to you. So does Emil. We're here to help, Phenice." Alina's voice was soft and inviting, but her words made me furious.

Before I could stop myself, a response flew from my mouth, tainted with my hostility. "How do either of you know what has happened? I am still figuring this shit out."

I turned my glare to Emil who was standing at attention, gazing at me with an air of sadness. I immediately felt guilty. I swallowed my consuming fury. I turned my attention back to Alina. She started to answer my question while confusion filled me. Why did I have an instinctual urge not to hurt Emil?

"I knew something was different with you. I could tell by looking at you when I was here on Friday night. When I was leaving, I ran into Emil. He was able to fill in the pieces because...well, because he is like you." Her voice had dropped to a whisper.

I slowly turned my eyes back to Emil, trying to understand Alina's words. He wouldn't look at me; his gaze was just over my shoulder. I didn't say anything. Instead, I walked past them and motioned for them to follow me to the living room. I glided down the stairs, knowing from the sounds of footsteps behind me they were obedient with my command. I passed through the entry and made my way into the living room.

I sat down in my favorite chair, partly out of habit and partly to seek comfort. How many times had I curled up in this chair with a book? I let the inanimate object hug me. It was a false sense of security, but with everything I had been through, I needed some self-indulgence. The comfort this gave me allowed my fear and anger to drift away, if only slightly.

I watched as they entered the room. Emil sat apprehensively on the edge of the lounge, leaving the sofa for Alina. She sat down absentmindedly. It pleased me seeing them sit far from each other, giving me the sense they were not planning to gang up on me. I relaxed a bit more, shifting in the chair to sink in a bit deeper.

I stole a glance at Emil, and in that moment, I noticed, not for the first time, he was the handsomest man I had ever seen. In forcing myself to look away, my eyes landed on Alina. The sight of her made me uncomfortable for some unknown reason, but I didn't have long to analyze why. Magnetically my gaze slid back to Emil. I was lost in his face, forced into a kind of trance, as I tried to navigate the labyrinth of his beauty. I was completely distracted by him. As desire filled my whole body, I shuddered from the intense pull toward him, forcing a gasp to pass my lips. I closed my eyes to remove the temptation.

"Explain to me how you two crossed paths within the last week and what that has to do with what happened to me." I waited for one of them to speak, but that wasn't what happened.

The air around me thickened as if I were instantly submerged in a viscous fluid. A slight panic rose from my gut, then swiftly vanished as a sense of calm shrouded me. A vortex tugged at my navel from behind, pulling me back. I surrendered, as the whirlpool yanked me back through time and into a vision.

Chapter 15

ANSWERS

I opened my eyes. It didn't seem as if much time had passed. I was back in the present. I blinked multiple times as I listened to Emil and Alina. I tried to pick the conversation back up.

"Phenice, it is going to take some time to explain it all," Emil was saying as I embraced the present moment again. He was trying to answer my question, the question the vision had answered.

My gaze dropped to my lap. I raised my hand to stop him as I whispered, "It's okay, Emil."

"No, I want to explain, to help you," he protested.

"You don't have to. When I asked you about your encounter on Friday, I had a vision. The Fates showed me what I needed. So I know everything. All of it." As I spoke, I was still processing the vision. I was stagnantly numb from what I had seen.

"The Fates just tugged you into the past by you simply asking a question?" Alina asked.

Emil stared at me.

"Yeah, I guess so." My tone was flat, lifeless.

"What did you see, Phenice?" Emil leaned forward as he spoke. He seemed nervous, or eager. I couldn't tell, or maybe I didn't care.

I stared at him, dazed a little as everything started to click into place. Emil was Xenres. He was my soulmate. He remembered her. He remembered their life together. He must have gone through a transition period just like me. This was freaking crazy shit.

"Well, I guess to start, I know you are my soulmate. You figured it out five months ago when you walked past Alina and me on Broadway. *And* in true Fate-fashion, they crammed my destiny into your brain because we are connected. You decided to get close by becoming a patient in an attempt to change my future. You told me all about this *woman* you loved and longed for, but had to protect…and all along, that woman was me. Sound about right?" My voice was still unaffected. It was only the facts, and nothing I could change.

Emil stared at me. He looked lost for words.

"It sucks having someone else seeing shit you don't want them to, huh?" Okay, that was bitchy.

"Phenice, please. It wasn't like that. I didn't want this life for you. Even if it meant we could never be together." He looked so sad.

"That is shit, Emil. You weren't even going to give me a choice. What if I didn't want to live another lifetime like I did as Eudora? That fucking sucked. As you very well know because you must have relived it, too, as Xenres. After you knew the pain I had suffered not having a choice, you would make this decision for me? What if I don't want another life without you?"

It was all true. Was it fair to be angry with him? I don't know, but the Fates were already making big-ass decisions for me, and they weren't here. He was. So he got my wrath. I was done with my choices being taken from me.

I glanced over at Alina because I needed a break from his sexy-as-hell face. If I kept looking at him, my anger was going to drift away like a leaf on a fall day. She seemed so confused. Then I realized she didn't know who Eudora or Xenres were.

"Alina, I will fill you in when we get the opportunity. I'll tell you all about these past lives I apparently lived that have now created my power source as a vampire. Did I get that part right, too, Emil?"

Yep. I was a huge ass.

"I just went through a seven-day transformation. During these seven days, I slept and relived some of my past lives. *And* during this reliving, reawakening process, the gifts from each lifetime merged with my human body, which is now immortal by the way, because our souls are immortal. This union of body and soul creates our power source as vampires. It's this union that is the true definition of what a vampire really is."

My eyes had shifted right back to Emil, piercing him like a sword.

Alina sat quietly, not knowing what to say or do. She understood my anger. She was letting me get it out. I usually got angry instead of crying. Emil didn't know me on a personal level. He was frozen, clearly not wanting to say the wrong thing.

"Have I gotten most of it? I mean, most of it except the part that involves Alina staying in my life and putting herself in danger now that I'm a vampire." I paused. He needed to answer.

"Yes, Phenice, you pretty much got all of it. The situation with Alina will make her stronger. Gifting her with a lot of the benefits of being a vampire without the hang-ups," Emil encouraged.

"Yeah, well I don't know about the statement of…no hang-ups. Not if I understand the Fates correctly. They told you, and I quote: 'For this human creature who has gifted herself as an apple of life will be exceptional. By no means will she ever be unwell. To be graced ever so slightly as the vampire without the curse.'" Those were the exact words from the Fates to Emil about Alina's role in my *new* paranormal world.

She wasn't my friend anymore. She was a freaking snack! I'm assuming that was what they meant by "apple of life." I was a vampire, and we needed blood. In the vision, Alina asked Emil how much blood he needed. He stated he and his caste, the vampires he ruled, only needed two pints every few weeks. He ruled a group of vampires, a group that owned therapeutic blood banks in Oregon and other locations. I couldn't even go there right now. I couldn't think about vampire politics and how they ran their business practices.

The Fates made it clear the caste's way of life wouldn't be enough for me. Apparently, I was going to be too powerful. Blood bags were not in my future, but feeding directly from a human was…and *Alina* was the lucky winner.

In the vision, I listened to them debate about vampires being like humans. Both could be good and/or bad. It was our choices that defined us, no matter what we were. I agreed with that, but I still only wanted to be human. To have a simple life. No blood or cursed queens. I didn't want any powers or past incarnations to weigh me down.

Now my best friend and only family was going to be in danger because vampires are dangerous. When anyone gained the knowledge of their past incarnations and immortality, life had a way of becoming overwhelming. The bad could quickly outweigh the good and break your soul, eating up your goodness. It was how Emil explained it in the vision, and it made perfect sense. I felt the fissure cracking deep in my core. It didn't feel fixable. It made me dangerous, possibly deadly to Alina. I remember wanting to drink from her when she hugged me the last time she was here. I could kill her in an instant. Her life was being flipped upside down because of me. To help me survive. Even part of Emil's caste didn't want her around.

"Phenice, it's okay. I know what you need from me, and I am okay with it." Alina broke the internal storm of thoughts.

"Look, I know you are both worried about me. Emil, you haven't left me since I was turned. Your caste has even helped guard me. Thank you for that. And Alina, I know you're worried about me, too, but I will not have you doing this simply because the Fates told Emil I won't survive without you. This isn't fair to you." I was so over this freaking conversation.

"Now you wait a second, Phenice…" Alina was glaring at me now with an intensity that could've burned me to ash with the power of her eyes.

"I believe my connection to you is part of my path in life. It's why we met and became friends. I may not know all the details, but I do choose this, and I do choose you. Not because I have to…because I want to," she finished.

I was about to respond, but Emil started. "Look, Phenice, I should have done this differently. I was blinded by wanting to keep you from this life. I didn't see it as taking a choice away from you. I'm sorry. That was not something I wanted to do. We just need to figure this out. I cannot go back and do it better, but I am here for you, as is Alina." His eyes were pleading. He was trying so hard to reach me, and I was numb. The only emotion I could feel was anger, rage, fury. What was new?

Chapter 16

WEAKNESS

"Can we talk about it?" Alina asked.

"Sure." My voice was monotone. "I'm a vampire. No longer human. I'm a deadly abomination. Let's talk about it." Okay, so maybe there was some sarcasm in my tone as well.

It was so hard to pull together a coherent thought, to verbalize any single emotion I was feeling beyond my go-to. I knew, under my blind rage, a part of me was broken. I was blind in this new world of mine, and the truth was I wasn't feeling much of anything other than profound loneliness and fury. I looked up from my lap, trying to focus on what surrounded me, but it took a moment. My eyes took in Emil. He was patient with me.

Once I made eye contact, Emil slightly nodded his head then began to speak. "Yes, Phenice you are a vampire, but it's important you understand, you're still very much alive. You are a living vampire who has been tied to all five elements. During the ritual, which started your transformation, your body became bound to the earth, same as your soul became bound to your body. You will never age or die unless you are murdered, and trust me, it takes a lot to kill a vampire. It's nothing like the fiction novels littering the shelves at the local bookstore. You can walk in the sun, go to church if you wish, and beheading and wooden stakes mean nothing." Emil paused.

I had no idea what to say. I sat staring right through him at nothing and everything, which made my vision blurry. I could hear what he was saying, and part of me was listening, but none of it seemed to matter. It did not penetrate any part of me. The numbness was so profound and all consuming. I sat there, suspended in a vast hollow mockery that was now my life.

"Phenice, I know it is a lot to take in. The transformation is hard on everyone as they go through it. I want to help make this as easy on you as I can," Emil stated with so much compassion it should have moved me to feel something, but alas the coldness hung on, digging deeply into my bones.

I managed to mutter a reply. "Thanks." It was truly pathetic.

Alina couldn't take it anymore. She clearly wanted me to accept this new life. "You're his soulmate, Phenice. The woman he has been protecting. His vision of you led him to inject himself into your life to try and stop this from happening. He wanted to keep you safe. He didn't want this life for you. You know that from your sessions with him and from the vision you just had." She restated the facts, pleading with me to take it in, to forgive Emil. It wasn't necessary. I didn't blame Emil for what I was and never would.

I didn't respond. I could tell Alina was showing great restraint. It was obvious she wanted to dash over to me, reach out, and shake me out of it, but she didn't. I needed time to process the mountainous pile of shit, which kept growing. Before this had happened, I would've given anything to have a soulmate the way Emil had described it in our sessions, but now it was overwhelming, and it came with a world-shattering transformation. It could leave my soul damned for eternity. The coldness in my core grew as the fissure cracked and deepened. I was going to split in two.

I studied Emil. I didn't have any doubts about him. He was part of me, a vital part of my soul, a part I had been missing, apparently for lifetimes. He could help me feel whole if I let him. That was the true question, really. Would I ever really let anyone in? And would this end tragically, like it did with Eudora?

There was a knowing. He could warm the constant, growing coldness. He could repair the gaping wound in my core, but I wasn't ready. The truth was I wasn't ready to feel anything.

With the way he looked at me, I could tell he was ready. He was excited and eager to have a more meaningful reason to live. I could see the hope in his eyes. Why would he not be excited? Our souls had been separated countless times, and in this life, we were immortal. There was a possibility of never being separated again.

I understood his longing. As a human I had longed for love. Right before the attack, I was determined to commit to finding real, lasting love, but now everything was different.

Oh, I loved him. I could feel my love for him deep within. It was an essential part of me. No matter how distant or buried it was. I knew he was a key part of who I was. He was a part of my soul. He was Eudora's Xenres, the same souls from a different time, meeting again. Here we were in Eugene, Oregon, centuries later, and I wasn't ready.

I had nothing but grief blossoming in my heart. I didn't think I had any room for love. Especially with the grotesque chasm splitting me down the middle. With everything I had learned and been through over the last week, it seemed like nothing good would come from any of this. I felt forever stuck, doomed, never changing. *For all eternity.* The numbing cold began to crack and splinter. The pain wasn't physical, but it was encasing me. I could feel pieces of my heart and soul crumbling with each new discovery.

Emil and I remained silent, staring at each other. We were both lost in our separate worlds, obviously thinking of each other, though the context probably varied greatly from his mind to mine.

"Did you hear me?" Alina was almost frantic as she lost all patience with me. "He is the *one!*" she exclaimed, pausing between each word for emphasis.

I turned my attention to Alina. "Yes, I heard." My voice was still flat and unaffected. Nothing in my tone reflected the mass destruction occurring inside.

Too much had happened. Joy and love were concepts I couldn't even begin to wrap my mind around, but maybe soon, I hoped. I wondered, was there still room for hope?

I looked at Emil, and he looked away. Probably trying to hide the hurt he felt; my indifference had to hurt him. I hated hurting him. Seeing his pain caused something inside me to stir, besides the ever-growing coldness. It made the wall of ice crack. I began to crumble. I felt the dam holding all my pieces together start to rage like an avalanche. I took a deep breath, trying to reinforce the fortress of numbness holding me together, but the empathy for Emil brought it right the fuck down.

A feeling of sickness slammed into me. Dizziness rocked my world. The room began to spin. I leaned back, trying to abate the vertigo.

"I don't feel right," I said while rubbing my forehead. "Something's wrong. The room is spinning." I pulled my knees to my chest, huddling in on myself. I continued to rub my head, hoping to stop the dizzying feeling, but the only change was a slight dew springing up on my flesh.

Emil turned to Alina. I watched as they stared desperately at each other.

"We must hurry. Time is running out." Alina nodded at his request. I tried to brace myself. I had a terrible feeling that I wasn't going to like this next part.

"Phenice, you haven't fed since the change, and it is time." Emil was very serious as he maintained eye contact. I noticed his eyes were more silver now, with highlights of violet. I guessed as a situation intensified, his eyes grew lighter in color and the silvery hue consumed them.

Their anxious energy was making everything worse. I tried to ignore their panic.

"Yes, I guess I should. I haven't had anything since I was attacked." I wasn't thinking clearly at all. The dizziness was growing, and I felt so strange, almost incoherent.

"You must eat, Phenice. What you are feeling is known as the *cruentus*; all vampires experience it during the *nox noctis mutatio*. It is the bloodthirst that follows the nocturnal transformation, and you haven't had anything to sustain the change. It is time. It's why you feel strange," Emil rattled in rapid fire.

"Okay," I mumbled, disoriented. I wasn't grasping shit.

Then it hit me like a freaking train. I loved reliving my life as a lioness, getting to kill the gazelle. I remembered the vivid sensation of drinking the life of the helpless animal. I remembered wanting more. It had been intoxicating. Never had I tasted anything so delicious, so appetizing. I was enthralled as its warmth passed into my mouth and ensnared all my senses.

Flashbacks of my life as Eudora hit me. As she and Xenres sank into the dark water, I was left enraptured by the pool of crimson blood on the ship's deck. I had felt ravenous. I knew why now. I wanted blood. I needed it to sustain this cursed life.

The latest vision slapped me in the face. I physically jerked back. It was Alina's blood that would give me life. It was her blood that would sustain this cursed life. With that final insight sinking in, the all-consuming numbness abandoned me. I cracked and shattered into a million irreparable pieces.

Shit! Fuck! I wouldn't do it. *No fucking way!*

Alina began to speak even though I wasn't listening. I was spiraling out of control. I was disgusted with myself. Hatred started to fill that ever-growing chasm at my core.

"Sweetie, my destiny is tied to yours. I want you to have my blood. It is how it is meant to be," she stated as she stood up and began to walk toward me.

"*No!* No fucking way, Alina!" I stood up. The room went black for a second, but I managed.

She didn't move.

"Phenice, you are too strong to have it any other way. It must come from a person. You won't kill me. It will make me stronger. He has seen it. You saw it." Alina was pleading with me to drink her blood. My freak out reached a new height.

Anger surged within me. Faster than was possible, I was on him.

"You lie! There is no way draining her life will make her stronger. All I offer is death! I can feel it growing within me, consuming me. I'm a corpse inside, rotting in the darkness of a coffin in the cold, dank ground. I have nothing but death to give, and I will not share it with her! I would rather die," I screamed, inches from his face as I pointed my hand in Alina's direction. I stumbled back a step as the vertigo increased.

Emil reached for me. I ran, grabbing my keys as I flew out the front door.

Chapter 17

———⊛———

SANCTUARY

I didn't know where I was going, but I knew I had to leave. I had to get as far away from Alina as possible. The look in her eyes when she offered me her blood was disgusting. Yet at the same time, knowing she wanted me to drink from her made her more appetizing. Admitting her desire made it sound even better, which made everything worse.

I drove as I muttered to myself. "I won't hurt her. I can't...I can't let her be that for me. I won't rely on anyone so completely. If I crossed that line, I would have to depend on her more completely than I ever have depended on anyone besides my father. No, absolutely not! I won't do it! To open up and be that vulnerable with anyone is not possible for me."

Lost in the haze of my denial and ramblings, I found myself back at the Owen Rose Garden parking my Jeep. The oddest sensation came over me. I felt safe. It reminded me of what it might feel like to go home if your home was filled with love. Some unseen force had pulled me here. There was a powerful connection calling out for me.

I climbed out of the Jeep while looking around. Since the transformation the degree of details my eyes could comprehend was amazing. Under different circumstances I might've been able to rejoice in the gift of seeing how beautiful the roses truly were. As a human I found them stunning, but as they were now, it was like peering into a new universe. Each petal its own unique *fingerprint*, a special *snowflake*, one of a kind.

I glanced at the clock noticing it was 4:01 in the morning. I hadn't realized the flashback, panic attack, and argument with Emil and Alina had consumed most of the night. It was still pitch-black outside, but the sun would rise soon.

Even in the darkness, I was able to observe the park as if the sun were at its peak. I could see all the way to the river, make out every tiny leaf still dangling on the branches of the trees, see every single petal that made up all the roses in the garden. It was a lot to take in. It was also amazing to see something beautiful after the pain and suffering from the last week.

I made my way through the garden, realizing I was heading straight for the place my human self died. It was strange that this was the place where I felt a connection. I was fleeing right to the spot where my life ended. With each step the chasm in my gut split and cracked further along my body. I was in mourning; it hit me hard as I approached the cherry tree. I was grieving my death—I needed to say goodbye. There was a catharsis in knowing this place belonged to me. It may have been morbid, but this tree had become my sanctuary and my tombstone.

My eyes zoomed in on the distorted cherry tree. I still had a good distance to walk, but I could see the combination of bark and wire. I could see the leaves floating off the branches and into the breeze. We had so much in common. Some force was holding me together, while pieces of me blew away from the pain. We both wanted to die, but no one would let us. Suspended in a morbid mockery of life outside our control.

A light, misty rain began to fall from the cloud-filled sky and kissed my flesh. It was cold outside, but it didn't affect me. Not anymore. I was still wearing a tank and yoga pants with no shoes. I found myself aching for the goosebumps I should've had etched on my skin. I wanted them to keep me company, to take me back to my old world, where things made sense, but here I was abandoned, alone, and completely warm and cozy. I hated it!

I made it to my cherry tree quickly with my new and improved walking pace. The blood that had been offered here was still strong in the air. Not visible, but if I inhaled, I could smell my former self sinking into the earth along with the water that fell from the sky. My heart ached as I noticed it was barely beating, and my lungs stung as I realized I didn't need to breathe anymore. Tears started to fall silently as I became more aware of exactly how different I had become.

Trying to forget about my freak-of-nature status, I gazed at the tree. I could feel it watching me. I stood there lost in its malignant beauty, and a thought struck me: I may not be dead, but I wasn't alive either.

I inhaled only to smell. My heart beat only to circulate the blood I drank. Blood was a source of life, but now I had to steal it from another to maintain the abomination of this existence. It's why the six of them made me drink their blood here under the tree. They had to give me part of their life force so I could create my own. Then they stole my blood, my human blood. It was a trade, one life for the other. One I didn't want and didn't ask for, but apparently it was my destiny.

Well, I say fuck destiny!

I walked around the tree, drinking in its decrepit form. As I came to the metal stilts that supported its life, I ran my hands over them. I felt the strength the metal possessed, but the tree did not. I completed a full circle around the tree, making sure to pet all four stilts. I peered up to the branches and into the webbing of metal cable. The webbing kept the tree from lying down in defeat. The tears had not stopped. In witnessing this torture, even more tears raced down my cheeks. I could tell the difference between my tears and the rain as they both hit my chest. The tears felt like boiling water scalding my skin. I wondered why the tree and I weren't allowed to die in peace. I could hear the tree screaming in agony, the sheer pain its continued life was causing. I recognized it. It was the same cry I had raging inside me.

I felt my soul ache, forging a oneness with the cherry tree. It, too, wanted to die but was kept alive by someone else's hand. It was cruel and wicked. My soul was still present within me. I could feel its power. My soul was the key to my vampiric strength. Yet I wondered, how could a creature like me, who only offers death, have a soul?

I stood right next to the tree. I reached out and touched it. I traced my hand down the lumpy and knotted bark all the way to the ground. I turned and sat down, leaning back against its trunk. I hoped I didn't knock it over. Praying I would not cause it any more pain.

As I sat, leaning against the cherry tree, I closed my eyes, and in doing so, I realized I didn't only feel my soul, I could see it glowing brightly within me. It was beautiful, like a clear night sky glittering with diamonds. I had never felt so torn and confused. How could a monster also be beautiful?

The mist continued to fall from the darkened sky and hit my body, and all I could do was cry. I wanted to set my glowing and simmering soul free. I wanted peace, not eternal torment and confusion. I didn't want some great destiny forced upon me.

Suddenly the air around me changed. I didn't understand how I knew, but someone was coming. My eyes snapped open.

I turned and kissed the tree goodbye. I vanished through the west side path of the garden, finding myself climbing inside my Jeep instantly. As I drove away, I noticed an Aston Martin in the parking lot.

Chapter 18

DEVIL'S CHURN

I didn't know where to go, but before I could pull myself together enough to decide, I was on OR-126 west, heading for the coast. There was no one on the road, considering how early it was. I was grateful for the vast emptiness of the road, for it was about a sixty-mile drive to the Pacific Ocean, and I didn't want any distractions. I needed to focus on the pain growing inside of me. I needed nothing more than to feel it, to understand it. With a deep breath in and out, I embraced the agony icing my veins.

Flashes of my life popped up in my mind. I've had to learn to deal with hurt, with pain, both physical and mental. My past gave me no choice in the matter.

Any time life got hard, it was a challenge to keep the monsters locked away, one monster in particular. Thoughts of my father bled into my mind. His cruelness came storming back, as if he were sitting right next to me. In reality, I had no idea where he was. I left when I was sixteen and never looked back. All the symptoms of PTSD came rushing back; no matter how hard I tried, I couldn't keep the past locked away. The new traumas of the last week had fully reawakened all my demons.

Memories rushed across my vision faster than the tears sliding down my cheeks. The hateful words and insults. The broken bones, black eyes, and busted lips. The smell of stale alcohol filling my nostrils as the morning light poured in through our dingy kitchen window. The nights and days without enough food.

The power and water being turned off because he was too high or too drunk to work and pay the bills. And the teasing of the other kids at school for so many reasons. My clothes were too big or too small. I smelled because I couldn't shower, or I was too thin due to the lack of food. It was a barrage of torment and chaos flooding my mind and heart.

I hadn't thought of any of this in years, but having my life stolen and the grief from everything broke whatever dam held it all back. No matter what anyone else said, I fucking died that night. My whole body shivered with an involuntary shudder.

And now, now I am a vampire.

"A fucking vampire." I breathed. "Shit." I sighed. "I'm supposed to feed from Alina, my best friend, my only family now. How do I do that? Can I?" I whispered through the tears.

Rapidly I shifted subjects as Emil's face popped into my mind. *Can I trust him?*

He seemed to have the most to gain from my transformation. He acted as if this wasn't the life he wanted for me, but people don't sacrifice their wants and hearts for others. He had everything to gain while I had everything to lose.

Is he lying to me?

Quickly a sensation came over me, telling me to trust him. It permeated through my mind as the air turned to water, and I was pulled back in time into another vision.

In a blink, I was back in my Jeep driving the OR-126, and it was clear no time had passed. The vision came rapidly, like watching a flipbook and slamming knowledge of conversations and images inside my brain. It was disorienting. It was something I didn't think I could ever get used to.

My question had been answered as I watched Emil struggle over my situation. I received glimpses of him agonizing over whether he and his caste should turn me instead, with the goal to save me from the queen and her Hunters. Apparently, my beasts were referred to as the Hunters; they had all been handpicked by her, changed by her, tortured by her. She had molded them into the most grotesque monsters history had ever known. That was quite an accomplishment. Emil ultimately refused to harm me or decide for me. He couldn't bring himself to change me.

Guilt filled me from lashing out at him, from accusing him of robbing me of my right to choose. I witnessed his heart breaking. He knew there was no saving me. He hated what he was. I saw him watching and protecting me, and I had shamelessly blamed him for the blight of my destiny.

He watched Alina and I have lunch last Tuesday after his appointment. He saw my meltdown. My desire for a love connection. The one he knew I could only find with him. He realized he was stealing my last chance at love by not turning me. When I collided with him that day on the street, it wasn't clumsiness or my lack of attention. He wanted to have an encounter with me. He changed his mind that day. He was going to let me decide what I wanted. He was going to tell me everything.

He watched me that evening when I completely fucked my routine. He believed I was going to stay in. He left to make plans to save me, and I went and ran away from my life, not truly knowing what I was leaving behind. I could've avoided all the suffering of that night if I would've stayed home. The night was my fault, in its entirety.

He came back Wednesday morning. I saw his phone as he walked up to my door at 7:44 a.m. to knock. The vulnerability it took to risk my rejection when he already hated what he was only reflected his courage.

Immediately he smelled familiar vampires. He knew the Hunters had come for me. He knew I wasn't home, and the house was empty. He called the caste to search for me immediately. Determined to save me from the queen, even if it meant her finding out they were all still alive. When they escaped her, they did it in such a way she believed them dead.

I watched as they tracked me. They found my murder scene, and the look on Emil's face was heartbreaking. He blamed himself for not acting sooner. He saw all my blood on the ground under the tree as a stain marking how he'd failed me. His face reinforced my own shame for blaming him.

The team worked efficiently, realizing I had been dumped in the river. The Hunters believed me dead. I, frankly, agreed with them. The woman I had been was truly dead and gone from this world. Members of his caste found my vampire scent and tracked me back to the house. That was where the vision faded, with Emil standing guard outside my home, determined to be there for me when I woke. He was emotionally torn—relieved I was *alive* and not in the hands of the queen and devastated I was like him now. I could feel how much he hated what he was. He carried a darkness latched to his soul, and he believed no amount of goodness could lift its weight.

I blinked the tears away. How could he ever expect me to accept this life when he couldn't accept it either?

"Thanks," I whispered, grateful for the vision no matter how disorienting it was to get ripped through time and space and have a bunch of crap shoved into my head.

I didn't really know who I was thanking or how the visions came on. Regardless I was glad to have peace about Emil. I could trust him at least. The vision proved he would sacrifice himself for eternity, if needed, to save me.

Regardless of what the vision showed me, I pushed the thought of Emil's love away in exchange for the more familiar pain I had inside. I focused instead on how much he hated being a vampire. That hatred resonated with how I felt about becoming a monster as well. Masochistic of me I knew, but I wasn't about to change one more thing about me. Pain was familiar, whereas love was not. What I wanted more than anything was for everything to stop. I wanted to wake up from my nightmare and laugh at its absurdity.

"I can't be a vampire. I can't feed on Alina. I just cannot." I pushed everything down so I could shut my mind off and stop thinking.

When I shut my mind down, I was able to sense the world around me in ways that shouldn't be possible. The air around me was electrically alive with a soft whispering *om* sound. I could hear the water as it fell from the sky, crooning a soft lullaby. The ground beneath me omitted a palpable percussion. The rhythm of all the elements was loud. It made my bones ache with annoyance as it invaded every part of me. I placed a hand to my head and rubbed while I wondered if this was normal.

A flash of raging hunger came tearing through my gut, followed by an ear-piercing scream pouring from my lips. As the hunger grew within my body, the only emotion left was complete and pure self-loathing. I hated myself for who I had become.

"I won't live this life. Taking life so I may continue. I cannot be a murderer!" I screamed to the Fates while pounding my hands against the steering wheel. Was anyone even listening?

My anger increased as more tears started to stream down my face, and even this form of water had a vibration, a life of its own. The tears that ran one by one down my cheeks carried with them agony, pain, despair, grief, longing, and so much more. Every single warm, salty drop had a purpose, and I could sense it. It was eerie. All I wanted was to be human again, but that wasn't an option.

A true death seemed to be my only way out. My death could really end all of this. I wouldn't have to bear this life or hurt Alina. A small part of me paused, pondering. It wasn't wise to be overreactive after severe trauma. My professional brain knew this. I should stop and think. I needed to calm myself and not give in to the panic tearing me down piece by piece.

Fuck it! I was done with all of it. This was the thing that finally broke me. I could accept that. Any chance of a peaceful life was gone, and being normal was over—that had been taken from me. At least in death, I felt like I got to choose. So death it was.

Phenice, our child, you were never normal, only extraordinary.

"Damn it! Leave me alone!" I was shouting at the voice in my head. I might be losing my mind, but a deep part of me knew that voice belonged to the Fates. It sounded like a choir of singing angels talking, and I had learned very quickly to hate the harmony, no matter how tranquil they may sound. Nothing good had come from them so far!

We cannot leave you, our child. We have always been with you and will always be.

"Fine! Tell me why I am sensing everything!" I pleaded.

It is your power, child, for you are gifted with all the elements—air, water, earth, fire, and spirit.

"What does that mean?" I muttered, losing my will to fight but still desperate to understand.

You can feel them greatly and use them at your will. You must learn to embrace all your powers, Phenice. Embrace all that you are.

I knew they were gone. I felt them leave. I was starting to notice a physical pressure in my head when they spoke to me, then the absence of it when they left. I didn't ask any more questions.

The rain stopped as I turned north on I-101. I got to the interstate too fast. I glanced down at the speedometer and that answered how I had made it here so impossibly quick. A part of me knew I should slow down, but most of me wanted to get this over with. Consequently, my right foot pressed the accelerator down even farther.

I kept driving north without a plan. I guess I was waiting for a sign or possibly merely procrastinating what I knew was inevitable. I had to die one way or another. How? I did not care. The hunger continued to burn within me. It was an all-consuming fire, and in its wake, it left behind nothing but heartache, self-loathing, and the ash of who I once was.

Lost in my suffering, I hadn't noticed the sun coming up to my right. The sight of its impending brightness made a deep sadness bloom in my heart. The sun, for some reason, didn't hold me the same way the darkness had, as if I no longer belonged to the land of the living or light. I truly had become a creature of the night. I was even more determined to end this torment.

Then I saw it—a sign. An *actual sign* marked Devil's Churn. It seemed exceptionally fitting. I slammed on the brakes, making my Jeep fishtail across the oncoming lane of traffic and off the side of the road into the grass. There was no parking where I had stopped. This was not the public entrance to the cove, which made it more perfect for what I was about to do. I shifted into four-wheel drive and drove into the rough terrain, parking out of sight.

Before I had barely put the vehicle in park, I jumped out. Running was exhilarating. I felt as if I took flight, but no matter how freeing my run was, it didn't change my plan. It only meant I made it to the cliff of Devil's Churn in seconds instead of about half an hour. Amazing really but not amazing enough.

I sat down on the rocky ledge and gazed at the ocean. It was fitting, sitting there at Devil's Churn, being what I was, a vampire, a would-be killer, but the devil couldn't have me. No, not today or any other. It would end here. The only life I would take would be my own.

I watched the ocean waves rage as they crashed to shore; another storm was coming. I had seen a storm dance on the ocean before as a human, but never like this. Today I could relate to the fury of the water as the waves rose and crashed so violently, capable of obliterating anything within their path. The envy grew within me. The desire to destroy and maim crept into every molecule of my being. I observed the power of the water grow, and then from the sky with a thundering crack, rain poured down in sheets, showering the earth.

The sky moaned in relief to release its fullness, and the earth was happy to receive it, but the ocean continued to cry out in agony, protesting the extra drink the clouds were providing.

My skin was crawling as I took witness. The air whipped around me, throwing my hair into my face. Sand from the white shore came up to bite at my skin, but nothing hurt. Oh, how I wanted it to. Damn it, it should burn as it tore my flesh! However, I sat, pounded by the elements, and I was left flawless. I stood from my rocky seat, drenched through and not feeling for a second the bitter cold that should make my bones rattle. Standing at the edge of Devil's Churn, I finally glanced down.

Looking up at me from the sandy earth were jagged, razor-sharp slices of stone, like the earth had teeth, ready to devour me. These teeth praised the sky. For the first time since the attack, I felt truly awake. A real smile played across my lips. It was the evilest smile, even if no one was present to witness it. I felt it reach all the way to my eyes, making them shine with glory.

With my smile in place, I looked up to the sky and screamed, "I am meant to die!"

I simply fell forward.

I heard a faint "*No!*" from behind me, but mainly I was elated as the air flew past my body on my descent to Devil's Churn.

I felt a sharp, piercing pain through most of my chest and belly. I knew the rocky teeth had devoured most, if not all, of my body. I had thought it would hurt more, make me cry out, but I remained silent. I didn't even shed a single tear. My blood poured out of me and down to the earth. An offering, much like the rain from the heavens. I could feel the rhythm of the earth change once it tasted my blood, but before I could understand if it was happy or sad about my passing, the darkness took me. I welcomed my sweet death with such an embrace I might have been laughing. I was happy. I was at peace.

Chapter 19

⚬⚬⚬

ELEMENTS

"N o. No! Phenice, my love, what the hell have you done? Please, goddess, no! For all the gods and goddesses in the heavens, please!" he screamed.

I opened my eyes and found Emil screaming and covered in my blood. His beautiful eyes were stormy and had turned the darkest midnight plum with flashes of silver dancing across his irises. They were unreal. He had followed me, had found his way to Devil's Churn, and now he held me tightly while I stained his beauty with my tainted blood.

I loved him so deeply. I knew it looking up at him while I watched his agony over my limp body. He hadn't noticed my eyes were open—his pain was too intense, too overwhelming. I could feel his heart shattering, and I wanted to comfort him.

All I could manage was a croaked, "Why did you save me? I want to die." I wanted to yell, but physically I was unable. My self-hatred grew as the desire to hurt him rose within me. His pain was clearly displayed across his face—in the lines between his brows, and the tight pull of his lips—and I wanted to hurt him even more. I didn't want to be the only one suffering. I truly had become a monster.

Once he heard my voice, his appearance morphed immediately, becoming more guarded. Although I could tell he didn't want to shut down, he did it all the same. I knew he did it for me. He didn't want to put any pressure on me. He was willing to wait for me to find my way to him, however long that took. It was clear in his expression.

He spoke softly, sweetly, in his slightly accented and eloquent voice. "Phenice, you don't understand. You can't die like this. Vampires can live in coma states just as humans do, if we lose enough blood. You haven't eaten since the change, and now you have lost almost all the blood you have. Please, understand you won't die." He paused. "I'll just lose you," he whispered, trying to control himself. "Again." He exhaled with a deep look of capitulation overwhelming his eyes. He continued, trying to make me understand. "You'll lose yourself."

Emil still held me in his powerful embrace. I knew he wasn't going to let go, and I could feel that he had begun to shake. Was it from fear? Rage?

Lying there in his arms, feeling him shake from the deep-seated worry of losing me again made my anger toward him vanish. The sight of his pain pulled deeply buried compassion out of me. At this point all I could do was try to explain myself.

"I only wanted to be free, Emil," I whispered while gazing into his eyes. I could feel his devastating sorrow.

He was staring at me, and if it were possible, he appeared graver than moments before.

"My love, there is no heaven for you or me. Death doesn't offer us freedom," he crooned woefully.

Realization hit me: my death would have kept me from an afterlife. This was all I had now. This was my last chance of any kind of existence; cursed or not, it was all I had. Gratitude for Emil saving me filled my heart. He saved me from whatever hell I might have sent myself to. Or was there simply nothing after this? A vast void? If I died a true and final death, would I simply cease to exist?

"Why? You said we weren't evil." I couldn't take any more bad news. Had he lied to me? Am I evil? I felt evil. I felt the desire to destroy as I watched the storm. To cause the same kind of mayhem. Didn't that make me a monster?

A deluge of emotions slammed into me, making me forget I had asked Emil a question. I brought my attention back to his face, noticing him posed to answer it. He could tell I was lost in thought. I looked at him so he would know I was ready, and he gave me a slight yet painful smile as he began to speak.

"It is not because we are evil. During the change, the ritual merges our soul with our body. Therefore, they're no longer separate because the soul has found a permanent home. If the body dies, the soul dissipates. We are living our eternity; there is no afterlife for vampires. You must live, don't you see?" Emil asked with devastating agony in his voice.

I did understand. If I died, we would never have another chance to find each other. I would not be reincarnated. I would cease to exist. So a vast void was all that awaited me if death came for me, leaving him alone for all eternity. The thought of that caused more pain than was endurable. I may not be ready for him because of what I had been through, but that didn't mean I didn't ever want to be with him.

I swallowed my apprehension and stayed on subject. "So we have no afterlife, no heaven, no hell. Then what is there to look forward to, to live for?" I felt my hatred slipping away as I began to ponder my future once again.

"I have spent so many years hating my existence, wishing that I could perish. To be honest, even as a human I wished for death. Life never seemed to offer me anything, nothing close to joy. Only pain and despair. I asked the same questions you do now, while you lie here in my arms covered in your own blood after an attempt to end your suffering. All I can tell you is it hasn't been long since I have found something worth living for. Now my answer is… love. Now, it's you," he confessed.

Emil's eyes had lightened back to the silvery amethyst I associated with him, and the wind coming off the ocean was blowing his wavy brown-mahogany hair around his handsome face. I reached up and ran my fingers over his closely trimmed beard. The hair was soft, like running a rose petal between your fingertips. How was that even possible?

"Please, kiss me, Emil." It came out before I could stop myself, but as soon as I heard it aloud, I knew I wanted it more than anything else.

He pulled me gently to him, still holding me in a tight embrace. He moved slowly, drawing out the moment our lips would meet for the first time. I was surprised when my slow heart quickened in anticipation. This made his mouth quirk into a sly smile immediately before his full lips met mine. As our lips touched, an instant fire burned throughout me. It was almost intolerable as it coursed throughout my body. When I thought I couldn't take any more, he gently separated my lips with his tongue and entered my mouth.

Passion erupted, giving me the strength to throw my arms around him and pull him closer. Our kiss managed to stay soft and gentle even though I had an intense need to consume as much of him as I could. He ran his hand through my hair, calming me with his touch. I knew I could spend eternity with him. He was enough to make me want to learn how to deal with what had happened to me. He could and would teach me. In that moment, I knew I was going to let him. I knew I would completely surrender to this man in time.

He gently explored my mouth with his tongue. Soft, wet caresses along my tongue, teeth, and cheeks made my body tremble with lust and need. He tasted like mint and citrus. A low rumble purred deep in his chest, spreading heat through the core of my body. It invoked a light moan of my own in response. His hand tightened in my hair, slightly painful, but more blissful than anything, giving him leverage to pull my head back farther to grant him more access to the depths of my mouth.

All too quickly, he broke our kiss. I gazed up at him, lust filling my body so completely while he stared lovingly into my eyes.

"Phenice, my love, please feed so you can heal. You're still in danger. I cannot lose you again." His gentle, smooth British accent was commanding. I found myself wanting to give him anything he asked. His intense need to see me well was not lost in his tone or his physical posturing.

The word "heal" sparked something inside me. A sense of knowing, of knowledge. I remembered what the Fates had said to me. I had the power of the elements. I could use them at my will. I had to embrace my power. I opened myself to the elements and instead of letting them terrorize me, I called them to me with purpose.

I summoned the water of the ocean, the air around me, the sandy earth beneath me, the fire of the sun, and of course the spirit simmering within my core. As the elements lit within me, the words poured out. It was clear to me now; the transformation imbued me with knowledge of how to use the power from my past lives as well.

"Water, come! Bathe all wounds, cleanse me, and make me pure, fill me up where I have had losses. Earth, enfold me as your child. Caress my wounds and leave me mended where I am broken. Air, breathe into the vessel. Give life where it has been taken and leave it at peace. Fire, warm the heart to beat again. Give it strength to carry on. Spirit, embrace me and make me whole!"

As I spoke the last word, an invisible wetness swirled around me. I kept my eyes locked on Emil as he stared at me in amazement, neither of us blinking. The blood was washed away and carried into the sky. I could feel my veins full again. The sand whirled around us like a sandstorm, and I could feel all my wounds closing, knitting together. Air rushed into my lungs, making me gasp, and I felt alive and energized. As I exhaled the air, a great warmth started at my toes and worked its way up my body. Once it reached my chest, my heart began to pound loud and fast for the first time in days. The feeling was wonderful. A raging laughter spilled from my mouth. I felt happy, alive. As the laughter quieted and the warmth settled down, I began to glow from within, a bright silver shimmering light emanated from my body. My flesh and bones didn't cage it; the light radiated out beyond me. Emil looked shocked as it reached for him, stroking his skin in a familiar and loving way. I smiled at him, and he returned it. I felt whole, more whole than I ever did when I was human.

Emil stared in astonishment. All my internal organs were mending. My heart continued to pound, sending blood racing throughout my entire body, feeding it. I kept breathing in and out involuntarily, as a human would. All of this was necessary so I could heal. Energy was pouring out of me and into Emil. I knew he could feel it too. The bright silvery shine withdrew back to me, sealing all that had been done.

I was whole again. It had taken less than a minute to complete.

"How?" Emil purred.

"I have power over all five elements. I guess that gives me the ability to give life," I countered, not really understanding what I had done, but I knew it was part of me.

"I saw your power of the elements—but how?" he inquired again, disbelief written all over his features.

"In one of my transformation dreams, I was a wise woman. When it was over, I woke and heard a voice say, 'the gift of the elements, ash, and life passes on.' That must be it." I thought this would help him, but if it were possible, he looked more confused.

"A voice? I haven't ever heard of anyone hearing a voice during the transformation," he retorted.

"I still hear voices. It's the Fates, I believe. They answer some of my questions but not all. Sometimes they talk to me when I don't want them to."

He blinked, knowledge filling his eyes. "I forgot you communed with the Fates as Eudora," he mused, allowing what I had said to sink in.

"So, you recall Eudora then?" I wondered what it was like to relive that time as him.

"Of course I do. I am your soulmate, Phenice. I am Xenres, as you are Eudora. When I went through my transformation, I lived through that lifetime as well." He confirmed my suspicions.

His confirmation cemented it even more just how connected he and I were, how tied we would always be.

"So much has happened. Honestly, I have been so consumed with pain and anger, I pushed the concept of love away. I wasn't willing to hope," I confessed. I wanted him to know I wasn't rejecting him, only the institution of love.

We had been so in love in that lifetime. I remembered how badly Eudora had wanted love and how badly I wanted it before the attack. Could I have it now? In this life? With these circumstances? I thought about it, but only for a second. In that moment, I did find hope. Maybe I could have love. As soon as the hope surfaced, a nagging voice popped up whispering dark, venomous words into my brain. It told me I wasn't good enough for that kind of love. If I were, wouldn't my father have loved me?

With the darkness of my past yet again creeping in, I needed to change the subject before that cynical voice in my head forced me down a pessimistic path of self-destruction. I couldn't let it end so quickly or let my brain find some rational reason why it wouldn't work or why I shouldn't have it.

"Where's Alina? You said I needed to feed. I know you're right. It's making me emotionally irrational, almost manic. It's probably why I tried to kill myself. I wasn't thinking clearly. I felt as if I was being driven mad." Even though I was still worried I would kill her, it was clear I truly didn't have another choice.

As if he could read my mind, he said, "I saw her destiny, Phenice. She will be stronger for it, and so will you. You'll be happier with her in your life. If you don't believe me, ask the Fates yourself." He was very sure I could sense his honesty.

I could tell he was telling the truth, but I asked anyway, not aloud, of course. After closing my eyes and sending my question out to them, I got the same answer he had given me. They answered this time with a quick and brief confirmation, letting me know I would not hurt Alina.

I opened my eyes and nodded in agreement. I told Emil I was fine, but he wouldn't let me climb the cliff. Instead, he went and got Alina and brought her to me.

Chapter 20

—⚬⚬⚬—

INFINITY

I watched Emil as he climbed up the side of Devil's Churn. He was incredibly fast and agile. I was able to track every step he took. I knew it would take him only seconds to reach Alina, but I wondered how long it would take for the two of them to return. I hoped it would take a few moments so I could have some time to myself to prepare for what was about to happen.

I stood from the sandy spot where Emil had left me sitting. I paced over to the protruding rocks, which had been my skewers not so long ago. I reached out and touched the largest piece of upturned earth, and it was tacky with blood, sticky with my life. I prayed as I petted the sharpness, prayed for the strength to live this life. I wanted to have the courage to accept myself and others like me.

A feeling of regret came as I took in the evidence of my almost suicide. Regret that I had given up. I had given up and quit. I wanted to be stronger than that; I needed to be stronger. As I stood and stared at my should-be death scene (the second one in the last week), I decided this wasn't good enough. I could do so much better. I declared to myself and anyone listening I would be strong enough to overcome anything this life threw my way. I was truly done running.

Apparently, someone wanted me alive. Even if I wasn't human anymore, I was alive. As I made the commitment to myself, a fire began to roar deep inside me. I would conquer this new world. Being a vampire was going to be one more challenge to add to my list.

Unwanted, a bit of my past came funneling in again. I grew up without a mother. I never had a protector or someone to pick me up after I fell. I never had anyone to talk to or explain life to me. There was no one to show me how to use makeup, take me shopping, or tell me about boys. That's probably why, at twenty-nine, I had times when I felt so lost.

When I started my period, I thought I was dying because I didn't even know it was a normal part of growing up. I hated her for not being there, but it's not like she had a choice. I killed her. She had to sacrifice herself to give me life. She passed within a few hours of my birth. I knew how irrational my thoughts were regarding her death, but my father didn't think so. He made sure I knew exactly how he felt on the subject. He had hated me since I entered this world. He wasn't shy about letting me know he was in a hurry for me to leave it. I knew if left to him my tombstone would read, "Good riddance."

Growing up, I had heard how wonderful my father was, how kind and giving. He had the biggest heart, apparently. I heard stories of how generous he was. I think they felt sorry for me, for how he treated me. They tried to convince me he was a good man, somewhere deep down inside. Maybe he was, once upon a time, but that man died with my mother. I never got to meet him.

All I got was a raging, abusive alcoholic ass for a father. As far as I knew, he could be dead at this very moment, and frankly, I didn't care. He hurt me badly. Part of me knew all the years of torment at his hands was why I had tried to end my life today. It was why I pushed the thought of loving Emil away. He taught me love was not to be trusted.

I wondered, how long am I going to give him this much power over me? Can I ever let this go and forgive him so I may move on without the shadow of him hanging over me?

With that huge question looming over me, I came back to my present, leaving the ghosts of my father and mother where they belonged—in my past. I'd been through therapy, and just a week ago I was planning to start going again. What do I do about that now? I had worked so hard to cope, to let all this pain go, but it still hurts. It might always hurt; I didn't know. Regardless, I was okay, safe for now. If I could raise myself as a child, alone with no help, I could do this. I had Emil and Alina, and that was more than most people would ever have. They were more than I had then.

I took one last look at the rocks so I could always remember how desperate I had been, how I had completely given up. I never wanted to get to that point again. My eyes traveled down the rocks, following the blood lines as they fell to the stained sand. I kneeled, reaching out to grab a handful of the grainy red earth, and it gave me the answer I was searching for before the darkness had taken me. The earth was sad at my passing. Not because it didn't want me, but because it wasn't my time. It was amazing to hear the earth whisper to me, to hear its love for me and its desire for me to live. The universe wanted me to fulfill my destiny. Whatever that may be.

I smiled. "Thank you for your kindness." I put the bloody sand back in place. The woman who came here desperate to end her suffering no longer existed. This was where I would bury her. I lightly patted the bloody sand, leaving it where it belonged as I silently told her goodbye. It was time to let it all go, even the ghosts of my parents.

I could hear the water calling me. I turned and walked to the shore. The storm had passed. The water was calm with gentle waves dancing toward my bare feet. I loved the salty aroma swirling into my nose and the light mist of seawater kissing my skin.

I wandered, letting the atmosphere nurture me until I found the perfect piece of driftwood. I took a seat to wait on my friends. The elements played with me, but unlike before they weren't an overstimulating melee of noise. In embracing them to heal myself, I recognized I have the same rhythms as all the surrounding elements. I found their songs, rhythms, and beats soothing and peaceful.

I closed my eyes and listened. I was taken in by all of it. I knew when Alina and Emil were close, for they had their own rhythms and musk. The air made way for them, but this time I didn't flee. I simply sat and waited. I would run no more.

My instincts told me I knew what to do with Alina, and through my love for her, I knew I would keep her safe. As a vampire, my instincts were stronger, easier to read and understand. I knew I needed to trust myself and trust the vampire inside me as well as the part that was still human (though this body was now immortal, I was still human). All the parts of me would work together if I would let them. I needed to get out of my own way. The mirth of that realization made a small laugh roll past my lips.

Emil placed his hand on my shoulder, but I didn't open my eyes. His hand was warm on my bare skin. He had always felt warm to me, but would vampires feel slightly cool to the touch for a human? To me, he felt like a warm bath, waters I wanted to slide into and soak up. I sat and scented him. He smelled of rosewood and musk with the smallest hint of lavender. It was masculine and sexy. I also found that his scent soothed a deep part of my soul. Then it clicked: lavender was the scent Eudora found peace in. Now the light, camphor scent of his essence felt like home to my soul. I wanted to roll around in it. He was so inviting. His smell was appetizing and sensual. It made me want to throw him on the ground and climb on top of him, ripping his clothes off as I went. Was it that he was a vampire? Was it because I was a vampire now? My body seemed to understand more than before what it wanted, what I needed. I was determined to figure out my new senses, but I needed to feed first.

Turning my attention to Alina, I noticed she didn't quite smell like herself. She had the aroma of dying roses. She was scared. Why wouldn't she be? She was about to offer herself up as food to her best friend, the vampire. If the situation were reversed, would I do it for her? I opened my eyes and turned to Alina.

"You don't have to do this." She started to protest. I raised my hand to silence her. "I say this because I don't think I would do it for you. Matter of fact, I *know* I wouldn't. Don't get me wrong, I love you dearly. I love you more than I have anyone in all my life, but I still wouldn't offer you what you are willing to sacrifice for me."

I gazed at her for what felt like forever. I expected her to be hurt by what I said. I had never told Alina no. During our entire relationship, I had always bent over backward and gone out of my way to do anything and everything for her. Now we were in a situation where, if the tables were turned, I would tell her no for the first time ever. I knew it would crush her.

Instead of hurt, her eyes began to shine with victory. Her scent changed. Now she smelled of roses and fresh rain, what I assumed was her normal scent. All fear was gone, and she was delighted. A smile crept across her lips, and she began to giggle. At first it was faint, and then it grew to a roaring laughter, making her brown ringlets bounce with great enthusiasm.

"Phenice, just for that, I want to do it even more. You have always done more for me, and I've never had the chance to pay you back. Now it's my turn. I'm happy you wouldn't do this for me. Damn it, I'm downright deliriously euphoric about it. It makes the offer mean more to me. Selfish, isn't it?" Her hasty rant was broken here and there with giggles.

"Alina, you don't have to," I stated again, not completely understanding why my unwillingness encouraged her even more.

She sat down beside me.

"No, I don't, but I really want to," she replied, all laughter gone and replaced with a serious and compassionate expression.

"Would you like me to leave?" Emil still had his hand on my shoulder. I looked up at him. I still couldn't get used to how lovely he was.

"No. I feel like I can trust my instincts, and myself, but I would love it if you would stay just in case. Please, stay." Deep down I knew I didn't need the safety net.

I knew I would never hurt her. I also knew feeding from Alina was the way it was meant to be, no matter how much I wished it were different. It was right. Not only for me, but for her too. I knew from my vision of them, Emil was worried about a human surviving in our world. I also learned feeding from Alina will make her stronger. Maybe this was the only way she could live in my new world. This way I could keep her, and she could keep me. Our chosen family would remain intact.

Emil drew my attention as he removed his hand from my shoulder. He reached into his pocket. When he extracted his hand, he held a necklace. He then reached out and hung it around my neck. I looked down at the gleaming soft-yellow gold now resting on my skin. It was a thick chain made of delicate circular loops. A gold pendant hung between my breasts and near my heart. I lifted the pendant into my hand to admire it. It was an infinity symbol sized about two-and-a-half inches long by one-and-a-half inches wide. It was the most beautiful piece of jewelry I had ever seen in my entire life, and it was mine. I didn't want to seem ungrateful, but I didn't understand why he had given it to me.

I looked up at him. "What is this for, besides the fact that it is absolutely stunning?"

"It is an infinity symbol, and you are now infinite, immortal." Emotion was apparent in his eyes as he called me immortal. It looked like speaking it out loud made it finally sink in for him. He was happy. I guessed his happiness was from the thought of never having to be without me again.

"It also serves a purpose." He reached down, grabbed the pendant, and gave it a slight tug. It separated in the middle, and out slid a small gleaming blade. He handed it to me.

"What is this for, Emil?" I asked.

"We don't have fangs, Phenice, contrary to popular myths and fiction. Our teeth work wonderfully if we intend to kill what we are eating, but that is not the case for you. So I had this made." He seemed anxious as he spoke. Probably worried I would lose it again as he talked about me piercing Alina's flesh. I hadn't been very receptive to anything, making his hesitancy justified.

"Thank you. It's gorgeous, and…well, thoughtful." I didn't know what else to say. It was beautiful and deadly. I needed to feed now because the thought of killing things with my teeth sounded really, well, amazing!

"Thanks, Emil. I personally don't want to be eaten." Alina started to giggle again, and I couldn't help but smile at her. I felt better too. It was one of the many reasons I loved her. She could always make things easier with her humor.

Emil took a seat in the sand facing us, but he wasn't staring. He almost blended into the landscape with his statuesque stillness, but he was more beautiful, more handsome.

I managed to pull my attention from Emil, not an easy feat, and gave it all to Alina. I didn't know what to say. How do you ask your friend to let you drink them? I stared at her, lost, and as always Alina made my life easier. She extended her arms giving me a choice.

I took Alina's right arm in my grasp because she was left-handed. I didn't what to cripple her any more than necessary. I looked at Alina. She smiled at me with complete confidence. I spoke a silent prayer to myself: *please don't let me hurt her.*

With her arm grasped by my left hand, I rested the tiny knife over the antecubital vein in the bend of her elbow. I could feel her pulse in my palm. Every beat of her heart passed through my hand and radiated throughout my entire body. My hunger grew.

I looked into her eyes and knew I wouldn't be able to go through with feeding from her if she watched me.

"Alina, please close your eyes."

She did without a single word.

I watched her close her eyes. I glanced down at the thin knife and slid it into her arm, puncturing the vein under her creamy, tan skin. A small pool of blood appeared on her skin around where the knife was still in place. I knew as soon as I removed the tiny blade, her life would pour out from the wound. I would have to move very quickly not to spill a single drop. I hesitated, worried again about not knowing how to stop once I started. I let my eyes roam over Alina and realized my spirit was shimmering around her, protecting her. I must have sent it to her when I prayed not to hurt her. She was still smiling. She seemed peaceful. I relaxed at seeing this. I lowered my head, pulled out the knife, and placed my lips over the wound within fractions of a second. I didn't waste a single drop of Alina's blood.

The blood began to gush into my mouth as heat began to flow throughout my body. I drank deeply. I could hear Alina sighing. She sounded happy, content even. Knowing she was not in pain, I relaxed, allowing myself to enjoy the experience.

The balminess of her blood filled me. It was heavenly, blissful. So sweet and creamy as it ran over my lips and swirled around my tongue, screaming to be swallowed. As I did, it pulsed down my throat in waves of euphoric delight like nothing I had ever tasted. I had never wanted to taste anything so badly in my life. Electricity ran through all my bones, shooting lightning bolts out to all my muscles, making me throb with so much intensity it felt as if I may split open. Still I wanted more. I was happy, at peace. I felt alive.

The wind blowing off the ocean felt cool. Immediately I felt goosebumps rise on my skin because I was cold. My mind laughed and screamed with joy. I loved it! My heart pounded, thrumming to circulate her blood, to fill me up. I felt human, or as close as I would ever feel again. My heart ached with happiness. I couldn't swallow another drop as much as I wanted to. It was time to stop. I pulled away. Alina was unconscious but alive.

I put my hand over her wound calling earth to me to heal her wound. "Earth, come and mend flesh, leave it untainted." Within a second, the only proof of what I had done was a faint white scar from the puncture of the knife. Pleased with this evidence, I continued to heal her.

I called water to me to replace her blood. "Water, come. Pour substance and life in the form of blood from where it was taken. Leave it replenished."

Alina opened her eyes, and she was glowing. She smiled brightly. "Did you feel that, Phenice? It was amazing!" she said in a soft, raspy voice.

She looked younger, as I was told she would. Seeing her like this made me wonder what powers she might've just gained. The Fates had said she would gain some power, not like a true vampire but something similar.

"Yes, sweetie, I felt it. Are you okay?" I asked. She looked amazing, but I still had a small amount of guilt over feeding from her.

"Perfect. I felt you heal me! I feel like I could do anything. This is wonderful. I have no doubts or worries. Thank you!" She gave me a huge hug and kissed me on the cheek.

I looked over at Emil, and he couldn't help but smile as well.

With the success of my first feeding, we decided to head back to my house in Eugene. After feeding I had much more control. My mind was able to control the elements instead of them making my thoughts erratic with their overwhelming whispers. I could think clearly. My emotions had settled down, and I was starting to feel like myself again. I realized being a vampire might not be so bad. Not if it was like this. I was in touch with the world around me. Everything had life, a heartbeat. It was invigorating feeling the pulse of the world, even as I felt my pulse start to slow again. Knowing I was still connected to so much life made it easier to hear my heart nearly stop. The silence within my body wasn't the damning I thought it to be. The silence within made it easier to pay attention to the universe around me. I marveled at its beauty in a way I had never been able to before.

Emil captured my attention as he spoke. "The ritual is complete, Phenice. You should feel different."

A small laugh escaped my lips because he was right; I did. That was what I'd noticed. My mind skipped over all the events from the past week. I wanted to understand the process I underwent to become a vampire. I had no problem remembering the events. I just didn't understand their significance. I asked Emil to explain the process, and he promised he would soon, but he felt I had already been through enough today. I knew he was telling me the truth. I could smell his excitement. He was eager to share everything with me.

As I drove back, the elements filled my truck. I was figuring them out. I was learning quickly how to use them and call them. I still didn't know anything about the rest of my powers. I knew there were more. I could feel them bubbling deep down inside of me. The past, present, and future held power over me. I felt it all around me, but I had no clue what to do with it other than the rare conversations I had with the Fates or when the random visions would take over. The lioness and her goddess were circling within my gut, ready to spring forward and be of use, but again the how of doing so escaped me. There was even more, more I didn't know about, but still I felt peaceful. For now, I was finally calm enough to accept this new reality. Hopefully the acceptance would last.

Chapter 21

───⦵───

NEW GIFTS

As I took a shower, I noticed how alive my skin felt from Alina's blood. I could hear the water singing to me. It danced along my skin as it cascaded down my body on its way to the drain at my feet. It was probably the longest shower I had ever taken in my lifetime. I wanted to capture every sensation and catalog them away, to remember this ecstasy. If everything was going to be this intense as a vampire, I thought I could get used to it, even learn to love it. Daydreaming of the new possibilities brought a smile to my lips.

After I reluctantly turned off the shower, I dressed in real clothing, not the rain- and blood-drenched yoga gear that had been torn to shreds. Those went straight into the bathroom trash bin as soon as I could strip them off. I had stood in front of the mirror for a while, admiring my body, not because of its curves but because I didn't have a single mark on me. The healing had been so complete it left my skin flawless, and I meant flawless. The scars I had prior to the transformation were now gone as well. This new ability would require some adjustment.

I dressed in my favorite jeans, which had been worn to ultimate comfort. They were as comfortable as a pair of sweatpants. I tossed on a lightweight raspberry sweater and reached inside the neckline to grab my now-cleaned necklace. I had cleaned the necklace Emil gave me while in the shower. I had thought about taking it off before I entered the water, but I couldn't part with it. I held the pendant in my hand, admiring its beauty. It was, without question, astonishing. The light made it shimmer exactly like my soul. That made it feel more like a part of me. Plus it was my first gift from Emil. It was thoughtful and kind. I loved it.

I walked out of the bathroom with my hair slightly damp and the pendant still gripped in my hand. I couldn't seem to let go of it. Something about the feel of it grounded me.

I walked downstairs and followed the sound of Alina's heartbeat. I found her sitting at the dining room table eating. I paused, watching her. She hadn't heard me enter the large open room because I no longer made any sound when I moved. I couldn't help but smile because she seemed happier than I had ever seen her. I wanted to let her enjoy her meal and leave her to whatever internal joy was putting that look on her face.

I turned my attention toward the living room. Emil sat on the sofa, where he had been waiting for me. He looked up from his contemplation when I stepped from the bottom stair. Unlike Alina, he could hear the slight groaning of the wood beneath my feet from my weight. I walked into the room, bringing a smile to his face. I thought about sitting in the chair at first, but I changed my mind quickly once I saw the look in his eyes. I sat down on the sofa next to him.

I'm glad I did because I felt the tension slide from his body.

"So," I started as I turned to face him tucking my leg under me, "what's next? Do I just carry on with my life? You know, work, seeing patients, the university?"

His expression changed within an instant.

"Phenice, I don't think you can. Under different circumstances I would say yes, but the queen thinks you're dead. Even with this she may send a reconnaissance team to make sure. Your normal routine could put you and others in a lot of danger." Somewhere in the middle of his speech, he had lowered his eyes, no longer looking directly at me.

"So I really did die then." I sighed. With a hint of resentment, I asked, "I can't even try to be normal?"

"You could take a sabbatical," Alina stated, trying to help. She had finished eating and was now entering the living room. Clearly she had overheard us.

"Honestly that's a good idea. You wouldn't have to quit, and you could take a year off. That will give us time to figure out how to deceive the queen," he spoke quickly as he gave Alina a pleased look.

"Okay…maybe." My reply was monotone. "What do you mean by 'deceive the queen'?" I leered at him. I tried not to appear upset, but from his stiffening, I knew there was some scorn in my gaze.

"We can hide from her. Make sure she doesn't find you. Plus you need to train. A year without interruption would be great." He faced me and looked into my eyes again.

"Training?" I questioned calmly even though what I said in my head was, *What the hell? Is he serious? Training for what?*

"Once you become an immortal, we go through training to learn to track, hunt, and control our powers. I would like you to come and meet the caste."

I sat for a moment, staring at a painting on the wall, not noticing anything about the brushstrokes or colors the artist used but instead trying to understand what Emil had said to me. A caste of what, vampires? In the same thought, I answered my own question. Of course, what else would he be talking about? I realized I knew nothing of Emil's life. The truth was I knew nothing about Emil at all. I only knew of our connection. Emil didn't scare me because we had always been linked together, and my soul knew that. All I felt around Emil was peace, joy, and love. Wholeness really. That was, if I allowed myself to feel it. But the thought of meeting other vampires made me hesitate.

"Phenice?" Emil asked, checking to see if I was all right or maybe to see if I was paying attention.

"Sorry. My mind wandered off. Tell me of this caste of yours." I knew I didn't have a choice.

I was now a vampire, no longer human, and I knew I didn't fit in the human world anymore. So the only place left for me was in the vampire world, his world. Whatever that meant. Instead of being in denial about how my world had changed, I surrendered to it and decided to gain as much knowledge as I could.

"They are the other vampires who fled the queen's rule with me. They followed and trusted me to keep them alive." It was clear he was passionate about his caste and protective.

It was apparent in the power his voice emanated as he spoke. He was excited for me to meet them. I, on the other hand, was not. I had never been good at making friends or meeting new people. I felt awkward at parties or social events, but I had promised myself I would try. Meeting his caste was trying, and I would make the best of it.

"They know of you, Phenice. They helped me watch over you while you were in transition. They helped me track your scent to the rose garden, and then back here." I knew he had picked up on my hesitation even though I had tried hard to hide it.

"Emil, it's okay. I'll go," I said, trying to make up for causing him to worry by being reluctant. I followed it with a request. I needed something to help me feel connected to the only life I knew. "But I want Alina to come with me." He stiffened slightly then relaxed immediately. "Is that going to be a problem?" I asked.

"No," his reply was short. The request made him uncomfortable even if he wouldn't admit it. I decided not to pry; it was his problem, not mine.

I didn't take my eyes off him for a while. In that time Alina had gone back to the kitchen and cleaned up. She rejoined us in the living room, sitting down on the lounge. She looked so different since the shore, but I couldn't place what it was. I knew she looked younger, even a bit more beautiful, if that was possible. She had always been beautiful, but now she seemed to glow, and that was new.

Alina spoke. "Emil, you're lying." He looked at her sharply and started to object, but she carried on speaking right over his attempt. "It is a problem. They don't want me anywhere near Phenice. They don't want me to be a part of her new world and ultimately part of their lives because of it. Two of them are supportive, but the rest are decidedly against me." She paused, leaning back on the arm of the lounge and crossing her arms as she stared Emil down.

"This is not acceptable, Emil. You are their leader, so lead them. Phenice will soon be something more than that, and you will not have to anymore, but until then you must make this right. It is your duty," she finished, her voice full of indignation.

Emil was stunned. I was totally blown away. I was going to be some kind of leader? Though we were both shocked, I was the first to speak.

"How do you know all this?"

"I believe it is the power you gave me. I don't hear voices or anything; I just know. One minute there is nothing, and then the next, like the blink of an eye, knowledge, and I know without a doubt it is truth." She looked at Emil. I knew she wanted him to confirm what she had said. When he didn't take the nonverbal cues, she spoke again. "Come on, tell us. Am I right?"

He was silent. He continued to look at me, not once glancing away to peer at her. At some point during Alina's speech, he had taken my hand in his. I could tell this made him uncomfortable, which was proof enough for me. She was right.

"Please, answer her," I whispered, my voice light and gentle. His hesitation left as soon as I spoke.

"She is correct. Aidan and Dante are fine with Alina. They can see the bigger picture. They are older and understand the need for change and evolution among our kind. Avery, Amora, and Eden are not happy with involving a human in our affairs. She is also correct about my being the leader. I will make them fall in line with this. I promise." Emil stroked small circles on my hand with his thumb as he spoke.

I was still absorbing everything Alina had said. The one proclamation I didn't understand was the same one I didn't want to be true.

"What is this about me becoming more than a leader?" I hesitated. "I don't want to lead, Emil. I don't." My look to him was pleading, and he returned it with a sad smile. He knew I was having a hard time adjusting, no matter how much I displayed a confident air about me now. He wanted me to be happy. It was easy to sense his love for me. Yet he was worried I would snap under the weight of all the changes. Who could blame him after what I put him through? But I'm stronger than what my recent actions reflected, even if the last few weeks or months showed differently. I would get a handle over the PTSD symptoms again, just like I had in the past. I may not have wanted this life, but I would not be conquered by it.

He answered me. "Phenice, it is your fate. I saw it. You are not only a vampire. You are different, something more, special. I don't understand all of it, not yet, but you are. I wish I could tell you more, but the Fates have left me in the dark about this. I only get the pieces they want me to have, when they want me to have them. I may get more with time."

As I looked into his silvery amethyst eyes, I felt nothing but love and trust. I also knew he and Alina were right. I was different. I could feel it in my spirit. I think it had always been there, and the vampiric transformation simply awoke it. I slightly chuckled thinking about it. I died and was reborn to some higher purpose. Under the humor I still had a strong desire to live a simple life, but I didn't think that was in the cards for me. If it had ever been. When I really thought about it, my life had never been simple.

"I feel it too," I admitted with a sigh. After a pause, I continued, "I see it. The Pythia part of me can see what I am supposed to be, but until I accept it, I won't live up to it, and my heart knows something important is at stake—it scares me. I don't want this." My heart sank as I spoke. Admitting it aloud brought the fears to the surface. I was scared I would never be good enough. A voice inside told me I wasn't capable of being enough for anyone. I was terrified of failing.

What would happen if I failed at this higher purpose? What was truly at stake? Who was at risk if I failed?

Emil's eyes changed. They became silvery clouds without a trace of purple, like a metallic storm. He stared into space like he was somewhere else, like he was watching something. I sensed he was watching my destiny as normal people watch a movie. I wanted to ask what he saw, but with all I had been through, I decided it was best not to ask. I kept my mouth shut because I was not ready to know.

"You're right, Phenice, you will change the world." Alina was so matter of fact.

"More knowledge out of nowhere?" I said, my voice soft. An attempt to hide the stress I felt.

"Yes, but I know it's true." She smiled at me. "You can ask Emil. He knows more now. He just got more of your destiny. That's if you want to know."

I turned to Emil, hoping he would keep my destiny to himself. Sometimes things were best left in the dark.

"I'll tell you if you're ready." He picked up on my hesitation as he leaned forward and kissed my cheek.

"I'm not, but I want to be. Will you help me?" I asked, smiling because of his tender affection.

"Of course, my love. I'll let you know this: what I saw gave me more peace and happiness than I have ever known. If that helps." I was conflicted because it did, and yet it didn't.

Alina went into the kitchen and pretended to clean the already-clean room, while Emil and I continued to sit on the couch in silence.

I was enjoying soaking in the happy and peaceful mood he radiated. His skin was humming. He laid his head back and scented me. After a while he opened his eyes to look at me. They were a creamy shade of lilac with a few flakes of silver falling in his irises, like snowflakes falling on a beautiful winter's day. I couldn't help but lean down and kiss him. His beard felt like cashmere against my face, and his sweet lips parted and invited me in with his soft, wet tongue. I grabbed a handful of his wavy hair as I began to involuntarily inhale. His scent poured through me, making me delightfully dizzy. The lavender was like an aftertaste that caressed my skin, leaving me warm and cozy. I drank deeply from his mouth as we continued to explore each other. His minty, citrus taste was intoxicating. The feel of his mouth on mine, his tongue dancing with mine, set a fire low in my navel. I clenched my thighs as I slid closer to him, trying to trap the sudden release of wetness in my panties.

I didn't want to stop. My soul was meant to be right here, entangled with this man forever. A knock on the front door was like someone throwing ice water on us. We both startled, mainly because we should've heard whoever had approached. The energy swirling around us fell away. All sensations of him vanished. Damn, I wanted it back. I craved drowning in him. As the longing to touch him again increased, I laughed to myself. I thought, *I guess I am ready after all.*

Alina, who had been trying to ignore our make-out session, walked to the door with a grin on her face. I knew she was pleased to see me tangled up with Emil on the sofa. It made me love her even more, if that was even possible. She looked through the peephole, turned to Emil, and motioned for him to come see if he knew who it was.

He pulled away from me and scented, which caused a smile to grow on his lips. He made his way to the door. Before I could see our guest, I was taken somewhere else, somewhere in the past, pulled into another vision.

Chapter 22

DANTE

As he walked, he glanced down at the ground littered with dead bodies. He had to step over the screaming men while he attempted to tune out their cries for help. They were dying, and he knew there was no saving them. They would perish this day and be taken from this world. The earth had been painted in blood and death. The ones crying out for help were outnumbered by so many already dead. He felt sorrow growing in his heart. He had been the cause for many of the dead. He had followed orders, but somewhere inside, he felt today was the day he had damned himself.

The air was incensed with death, the smell of burning hair and rust so strong it would make most sick. So much smoke filled the skies he could hardly see. He feared not even the breeze from the coast would carry the taint of death away from this land. Today they had won. To him, this didn't look like victory.

Dante knew the victory should make him happy; it had been the goal, but he had no happiness inside of him. It was November 25, 1177, what would be known as the Battle of Montgisard, the day that King Baldwin IV had beaten Saladin, even though he was greatly outnumbered. Saladin and his army suffered huge casualties, but Dante could not feel glad about winning this day. He only felt numbness crawling up from deep inside as he made his way across the massacre and to the king. Dante, a Knight Templar, found his warhorse Valente and rode him proudly, even though there was no pride within him, not anymore. This battle had broken Dante, had broken something vital to his soul.

As a man, Dante was lithe and svelte, but power emanated from all around him. He had been a warrior fighting for his cause, and this day he had helped the young and dying king to his victory. Whatever that meant after so much death. The cost of so many lives didn't feel like a triumph.

After he made his way to the king, Dante climbed from the back of Valente and kneeled before his sovereign. His white mantle was stained with the blood of the men he had killed, but he appeared to be unharmed. All he wanted was to go home.

"My king, I hope that I have survived you well. I pray you will let me take my leave to go to my wife and son."

"Sir Dante, I had hoped you would stay with us for some time. Our victory gives us the city. We could send for your family." The king was covered from head to toe, not showing a single inch of skin due to leprosy, but he still sounded like a king, proud and happy for the success.

"I am full of gratitude for your offer, my king, but I long for my home as well as my family. If you grant me my leave, I vow I will return if you call for me." Dante meant every word, but pain ran through his veins at the thought of ever having to kill another human again for any cause.

He prayed his killing days were over. He wanted peace. He wanted to finish out his days in tranquility because he knew someday he would pay for his sins, either in this life or the next.

"That is fair, Sir Dante. I give you my leave to return to your family on your word that you will return to me if I request it."

"Yes, my lord, my king. You have my word. I will return upon your summons. Thank you." Dante bowed deeper and stood so very gracefully. He turned so quickly it would take a trained eye to catch every movement.

Dante was back on Valente, and without another word to anyone, he was gone.

Genoa, Italy, was Dante's home. Where he had been born, met his wife, and where his son had been born. This was all he wanted to know of life from now on. He planned to live out the rest of his days here and to die here.

Dante had begun to forget that November in 1177, for it had been over two years. He had drunk in the love of his family and the familiar sights of home. He admired the beautiful coast surrounding his land. He allowed the warm southeast wind blowing from the ocean's depths to the rich green lands to caress his skin. He lost himself in all that belonged to him. As time passed, the unseen wounds of battle slowly began to fade. Dante had begun to heal his heart. The nightmares had decreased, though they still haunted him from time to time.

In the year 1180, a woman came knocking on the door in the early evening. Dante felt cold as he opened the door and was greeted by a lovely dark woman. Her hair was long and coal black, and her skin was the color of cinnamon. He couldn't help but notice she was beautiful. No matter her beauty, Dante felt the darkness radiating from her. Nonetheless, she had said she was there by order of the king. Duty bound to his king, Dante invited her in.

Once the two were seated in his family's seating area, the lady spoke: "It has been requested, Sir Dante, for you to pick up your sword and return to the Knights Templar."

He felt the wrongness within her. She was cold and wicked. Dante knew she hadn't taken the same oath he had. There was something about her. He sat studying her, trying to place the wrongness he felt. He had never felt anything like it.

All focus was lost when his wife and son began to scream. Masculine laughter erupted, bouncing off the walls of his home, alerting him to the knowledge the woman was not alone.

With inhuman speed the woman made her way through his home. Quickly, he stood, with no chance of stopping her; he had never seen anyone move with such lethal grace and speed. She was like smoke on the wind. As his eyes caught up to her, fear tore through him. His wife was caught in her iron grip. Some man had delivered his wife to the woman while the man still held his son. The dark lady stared down at him, eyes glowing with midnight fire.

What happened next happened so quickly he was left defenseless and frozen in place. She lowered her mouth and tore out his wife's throat with her teeth. He watched helplessly as her blood sprayed across the room. The metallic smell was overwhelming. Dante could smell all the men he had murdered throughout his life in the name of god and king. As the images of his past caught up with him, he fell to his knees, a roar ripping from his throat. He deserved this. This was his punishment for all the blood he had spilled, all the lives he had ended.

The dark beauty dropped his wife. She was dead before her body hit the floor. Her clothing covered in what little blood the creature had managed not to spray the room with. She glanced at Dante on his knees, howling with laughter. It was evil and daunting. The hair on the back of his neck stood as his skin crawled. He remained motionless, frozen in shock, as she reached for his screaming son, taking him from the arms of the man holding him.

He wanted to cry out, to tell her to stop, to leave his baby boy alone, but no words left his mouth. He simply watched, for this was his punishment; murder was a sin, and it was time for him to pay. He didn't blink. He sat on his knees, tears rolling down his face, each one stinging like acid as he watched this demon cradle his five-year-old boy in her arms.

She petted him and told him, "All is well. Your daddy wants me to have you because you have been a very bad boy, just as he has."

As Dante was about to cry out, he readied himself to attack and fight for his son. She bent down and tore out his throat as well. His son didn't even have time to whimper.

His body shifted into movement finally, snapping out of his traumatic state of terror and shock.

"No!" He ran and grabbed his dead son from her. His eyes had gone black instead of their normal chestnut brown, staring at nothing. Dante pulled his baby to his chest and rocked him over and over. He didn't even notice when four more people walked in, joining the woman and the man who had delivered his wife and son to the devil woman.

They had come for him. She had chosen him. She tore his son's corpse from his arms, tossing it to the floor with a reverberating thud. No more important than a piece of trash. Slowly she leaned down and sunk her teeth into Dante's neck. He didn't fight. He welcomed death, as he had always known he would when the day finally came. With his family gone, he had nothing left to live for. He was ready to face his final judgment. Dante didn't understand it wasn't death she was offering him.

And so began the ritual.

Chapter 23

PERSPECTIVE

Like waking from a dream, I found myself back in my living room, sitting on the sofa right where I had been before the vision. No one seemed to notice I had checked out. Emil hadn't even made it to the door. Though it felt like I had been gone for hours. It was obvious no time had passed. Almost as if time froze when a vision took over. I would bet anything that Dante would be the one standing on the other side of the closed door.

"Wait!" As soon as I thought it, I was standing next to Emil. I placed my hand on his arm, stopping him from answering the door. He stood frozen, waiting for me to explain my alarm.

"The man standing on the other side of my front door is named Dante. Right?" I inquired.

"Yes, from the scent I know for a fact it is Dante standing outside waiting for us to allow him admittance," Emil replied, confused by my inquiry.

"He was made in 1180," I stated the fact. It wasn't a question because I knew he had.

"Dante is mine, love," he said as he placed his hands on my shoulders. He thought I was scared.

"I know he is. I saw him help you find me. That isn't my concern. I'm only trying to understand why I get the visions I do. I want to learn how to control them, to summon them. Instead of always being sucked in randomly," I informed him.

"You had a vision?" Emil inquired.

"Yes, I did. A vision of Dante. Let him in, and I will try to ascertain why the Fates showed me what happened to him." I released Emil's arm, and he dropped his hands from my shoulders with a nod. He leaned down and kissed my forehead before walking the rest of the way to the door.

Emil turned the knob, then pulled the door open. There stood Dante. The same man from my vision minus the white mantle with the red cross covered in blood. Instead, he was dressed in designer clothing that left him dark and sleek. His creamy olive skin gave away his Italian heritage. He stood roughly five foot ten inches. He was slim, but well sculpted, like a swimmer. You could see every muscle fiber even through his clothing. He was, without a doubt, gorgeous. He was strong and fierce. That was obvious in the severity of his eyes, which were a deep amber gold. He had been a warrior as a human, and I could only imagine what being a vampire for almost a millennium could do to anyone.

He looked past Alina and Emil to peer straight at me.

"Dante, you may come in," I stated.

He bowed and entered.

I knew vampires didn't require an invitation, but I knew he wanted one. He had stood poised right outside my threshold, determined not to enter without permission. He was a gentleman, without a doubt, but something told me it was also some vampire code of etiquette.

He walked into the living room without taking his eyes from me. We stared at one another. I waited for him to speak, wanting to hear his voice. Even though I knew what it would sound like, I needed to hear it out loud, instead of in my head. A primal animalistic instinct took over, telling me not to look away or back down. Therefore, I stood my ground, anticipating his movements. We walked in a tight circle as we sized one another up. I could feel Dante's power rolling off him. It smacked me down as if I were caught in a tidal wave. In response I called the elements to me, instinctually forming a barrier around me and slamming his power back at him. Emil and Alina watched.

After a protracted time, Dante finally bowed without losing eye contact. "I will accept you, Phenice."

The statement was odd, but it felt right, so I nodded slightly without taking my eyes from him either. He sat down gracefully, the picture of perfect ease. All sense of power tightly sealed away. As if the power display hadn't taken place. Emil followed and sat next. I was the last to sit, a little confused about what just happened.

"I came to see her progress." It was obvious he was speaking to Emil, but he continued to stare at me with a blank expression. I was annoyed by his rudeness. He was treating me as if I wasn't sitting there perfectly capable of answering his questions.

I decided since he wasn't going to speak to me directly, I would return the favor. "Emil, why will Dante not look away from me?" It felt childish, but I had a thing about being treated like an inferior, and honestly, I had been through enough lately. This, I wasn't willing to tolerate.

"He accepted you, Phenice. He would be a fool to take his eyes from you without you doing the same. Accepting a vampire is the same as offering each other peace during your interactions. This is how vampires greet one another. We either accept or deny. If you deny him, it is a fight to the death unless the winner offers mercy," Emil stated in a matter-of-fact manner as if greeting someone like this was normal.

"Barbaric, isn't it?" All I could see were animals fighting for alpha position, yet here we were, still human in a way, humans that had moved up on the food chain, apparently, and down in basic social functions. In truth I didn't want any part of it, but I had the feeling if I wanted to survive, I needed to learn the customs of this society.

"Phenice, our society is power driven. Therefore, we fight for our place. It isn't much different from the human world. Just more honest." Emil was calm, and I was intrigued by his words.

He has had centuries to observe human behavior, and I had dedicated my current life to the understanding of human nature. I had to admit, the nerd in me was excited to see how alike the two species were. The idea made learning vampire customs seem more appealing. At least from an academic standpoint.

I thought about his words. It made me think about the power struggles humans have at work, with their peers, in their intimate relationships, and within their families. The daily manipulations they suffer as a society. I'll be damned. He was right. The human world was power driven, if not downright obsessed. Before I became a vampire, I had made it my life's work to help people cope with all the pain and suffering society could inflict, yet here I was thinking vampires were barbaric. What else could they be? They were once human, born of human characteristics. All they could be was a shadow of what they once were—damaged, ego-driven people wanting to control their lives any way they could. Then a thought occurred to me: I might be projecting. Maybe it was only me who felt that way.

At least in the world of vampires, I knew what the rules were. There was a code of conduct. With humans, anything was game. I could get used to this. The concept seemed simple, black and white really. I would have to become a warrior to survive, but life could be simpler. Something deep down in my gut told me, I was only half-right. Vampire society was going to be way more difficult than that, but maybe still easier than being wholly human.

"Dante accepts you, Phenice. Though you are new, he sees that your powers are strong. He doesn't want a challenge," Emil stated, seeing I was having an internal debate. It was a polite way of getting my attention.

"Nor do I." I was still staring at Dante, for he had not stopped looking at me. I thought looking away would be a bad thing before we had determined dominance and settled on peace. "Is that good enough for you since I don't know proper vampire dueling etiquette?"

"Yes, Phenice. Thank you." Dante chuckled. He was powerful. I could feel his essence pushing into me, but along with great power, I sensed intense kindness and tenderness. He would choose peace over war if he could. I am sure that was why he wanted acceptance on both sides, for now we could coexist in peace.

The tension dissipated. I could sense ease embracing Dante, but Emil's power began to creep up the walls of the room like smoke swirling off a fire.

"Dante, you can see Phenice's progress. Why come to me instead of call? Were you sent to check up on your master?" I was taken by his forceful tone. I hadn't seen him so agitated before. Toward me, he was gentle and vulnerable, but none of that remained as he was offended by his caste's actions.

"You may calm yourself, brother. I am not a spy. I came of my own accord. I want to be of assistance, if I may," Dante replied softly, offering Emil a tight smile, emanating kindness instead of humor.

Obviously, satisfied by Dante's reply and informal reference to him, Emil's power quieted. "We have been discussing the plan. I feel it would be best if Phenice comes back to the house to live among us."

"What? Wait a freaking second. No one said anything about that. I agreed to training and leaving the university. I know I will have to close my practice. You have no idea how hard sending my patients to another psychiatrist is going to be, but leaving my home? I haven't agreed to that." Anger bubbled up at Emil's presumption.

This was my home. The only real home I had ever had. I had done so much to the house. I restored it when I bought it. I planted and babied the rose garden in the backyard. This house was my therapy, my counseling. How could I move? This house was my first and only safe place in my life.

"You could rent it out for a while. You don't have to sell it. They could find you here. Please, Phenice, understand if they come looking for you, sweetie, this will be their first stop. No house is worth that," Alina responded quickly, so practical, but of course she could be. She wasn't having her life torn to shreds and being uprooted.

I would have nothing left to remind me of who I was. How would I hold onto myself? Everything I was, I put into my career and my home, and now it was all falling apart.

The room was silently waiting on me. Dante spoke before I could gather my thoughts.

"Phenice, she is right. The queen would easily find you here. The safest place is with us. I know how you must be feeling."

Of course, he knew how I felt. Shame filled my heart. I was the one who couldn't understand how he must've felt. Here I was, upset over a career and a house, when she came for him personally. She came and not only stole his life but murdered everyone he loved right in front of him. He knew what it was to lose everything so precious in life.

The sad part was I didn't have anything that precious. How cruel was I? Sitting there bitching about the material in life, about the nothing, about the things I could replace, all because I hated change. When Dante had watched his whole world bleed and die.

I wanted to drop to my knees and apologize for his loss. To hug him and tell him I was sorry for my selfishness. I wanted his forgiveness. He was offering me empathy, but I couldn't sympathize with him.

I understood now why the Fates gave me the vision of Dante and his last human days. They wished to make the transition easier for me. To show me my suffering could have been worse—so much worse—and they were right. We forget, when we are in the thick of it, buried in our pain, it could be worse. It could always be worse. The reminder of this did make everything easier.

The vision gave me the ability to see my new life in a much brighter light, looking at it through his eyes. Knowing what he had lost when he was in my place. Probably for the first time in my whole life, I was grateful I had no family left to me. In the vision I had felt his pain and suffering. It had been a gift from the Fates, one to help me move on and leave this world behind me.

Dante was still talking. I felt a little bad missing what he said, but I didn't need convincing. He had already persuaded me; he just didn't know it.

I raised my hand to silence him.

"Thank you, Dante, but it's not necessary. You are right, all of you. My work and my house are small compared to what the queen could've done to me. They are insignificant losses. I think it best if Alina rents out the house." I turned to her. She was sitting on the sofa beside me now. "This way, it will look like you have taken over my affairs because I'm gone. I will get my lawyer to take care of everything. The lease for both the office and the house. Once they are leased, the checks will go to my business account, which I will grant you access to. This way you can deposit the checks and make withdrawals if I need them. I will manage as much as I can online. Does that work for you? I know it is a lot to ask when you are already doing so much for me."

Alina smiled and gently hugged me, offering comfort and reassurance that I was doing the right thing.

"Of course, I am. Whatever you need to survive. I want to help you disappear. We will take care of everything tomorrow so you can go into hiding soon." My submission made everyone in the room happy. I felt the mood lift, and the air became lighter. The elements surrounding everyone seemed more peaceful and moved more freely. I was still trying to figure out my powers and all their sensations. How was I able to feel emotions through the air?

"I will go meet with the head of the psychology department to request my sabbatical. If I can get all my meetings done tomorrow, I can be ready to leave by Friday." I quickly ran my to-do list through my head: the bank to start the paperwork to make Alina a signer on my accounts, meet with Jeffery, my law-yer, to draw up leases for both the house and the office, making Alina property manager at both sites, meet with Dr. Postmere. It was manageable.

"I will make all the calls you need first thing in the morning. Hopefully we can get appointments. I will put them all in my name, that way your name will never show up on a schedule just in case someone comes looking." Alina was on top of everything, as always.

I wanted to be sad about moving, but my mind went back to Dante hold-ing his dead son as he cried, mourning his loss, and with that image in my mind, everything in my life was no longer painful, simply necessary.

"Phenice, you are handling this all extremely well. What changed?" Emil was cautiously happy. I could feel a fiery warmth that was his joy waiting to burn from him, but he lassoed it tightly around him like a second skin.

"It was my vision. It left me with a great perspective." I smiled in Emil's direction and then carried my kindness to Dante, but he was watching Alina.

She had run to the dining room table and pulled open the laptop I kept downstairs. I knew she was doing as much as she could to prepare for tomor-row. I hadn't asked. I've never had to ask her for anything. She's always just done the thing I needed her to do when I needed it done. I had a feeling with her feeding me, and me passing power to her, she would only get more percep-tive. I didn't know if this increase in her perceptivity would be restricted to only me or if it would extend to others. Only time would tell. As I watched her, it hit me: she was my *precious* person, and I would do anything to prevent losing her.

"Emil, you know Alina will be coming with me. Without her, I will not go. I will stay here and take my chances." I verbally spoke to Emil, but my eyes addressed Dante. I didn't get the reaction I suspected. He continued to stare at her without even an eye flutter in my direction.

"I know this, Phenice." His tone was harsh as he turned to Dante.

Without being addressed, Dante knew he was looking at him and requir-ing his audience. He turned and looked at Emil.

"I am on your side, Emil. I see no problems with having a human around."

By this time, he was gazing at Alina again, as if she were a cloudless night sky. "Plus, I get the sense she has power about her. She isn't quite human, but she is not a vampire either." He could feel her change. Good or bad, the deed was done.

"She is meant to be with me. She feeds me." This received Dante's full attention as his head snapped in my direction.

"But she is alive," he gasped.

"Yes. I healed her," I replied.

"Healed her…how? We don't heal people. We bring death, Phenice. Just death," he whispered. I could hear the sadness in his soft, accented voice. I knew he had offered death to many, both as a human and as a vampire. He was clearly still torturing himself for it.

"I have the power of the elements, and with them I can give life. Emil saw Alina's fate. She is meant to give me life, and I am to replace what I take. It makes her more powerful, more than human, but not a vampire."

I got the feeling he understood my words, but still didn't completely comprehend the power I held. He changed the subject.

"Emil, Phenice simply disappearing isn't good enough. We must create a paper trail of her death," Dante whispered.

"I agree." Emil began to rub his beard.

"What do you mean?" I questioned.

"We need to submit a missing person's report and follow it with an obituary within the next few weeks. You can be 'cremated,' so it appears to the world you really did die, Phenice." Emil was looking at the wall, refusing to look at me. This felt so final, like something I couldn't come back from. I understood their motives; it was reasonable, even if I didn't like it.

"Guys, I have no idea how to fake my death in that manner," was all I could mutter. I was at a point of no return, but I didn't see another way.

"The caste can handle this part while you tie up the details involving your home, business, and the university. It makes more sense for us to do this part anyway," Dante spoke to Emil and me, yet he continued to watch Alina the entire time.

"Okay. I'll leave you two to figure out those details, if that's okay. I really don't want to help plan my 'funeral,' if that is all right." I stood. Emil grabbed my hand, giving it a gentle squeeze followed by a delicate kiss atop it, all while he glanced up at me under his lashes. I felt my knees go weak. The power he held over me was simply not fair. I squeezed his hand back in appreciation. He dropped my hand with a seductive smile on his lips. He knew the effect he had on me.

With our conversation over and my mind dipping into the gutter, conjuring up images of what that mouth could do to my body, I decided it was wise to check on Alina. I left the living room thinking I would find her still in the dining room, but she wasn't there. It was a great opportunity to practice using my new senses. I stood where I was and inhaled. Within a split second, I knew she was in the hearth room, and she had started a fire in the fireplace. It was late, and she needed to sleep, so I left her there. I looked down at the piece of paper on the table, and as I thought, she had gotten all the numbers she would need for the morning before she went to lie down. She was amazing.

I turned to go back to the living room. Dante and Emil were talking about Alina and me. I walked back in the room anyway, my mood lighter because I now had a plan.

"Hey, did anyone ever tell you two how rude it is to talk about someone while she can hear you?" I mused.

They grew still and silent. I wanted to laugh at them, but they were way too serious. It took all the fun out of my joke. Honestly, I didn't think they could go anywhere within the house and have a private conversation with my new and improved hearing.

"What's so dire? Alina and I will take care of everything tomorrow. We have a plan for my 'death.' What's left to worry about?" I probed.

"Dante believes Alina will not be welcomed. Even as the master of our caste, I may not get them to accept this situation without a challenge to you or myself," Emil responded.

"Then I'll stay here," I stated flatly, making it clear this was a subject I would not budge on.

"Phenice, I fear that is unwise." Dante was being patient with me.

"Then what other choice do I have? Do you have a shed we can sleep in?" I snickered, trying not to get upset again. I was determined to stay in a good mood for the moment. Dangerous circumstances be damned.

They mumbled something extremely quiet to each other. I had been wrong about my hearing because I didn't catch a single word.

Emil smiled and said, "That's wonderful."

Dante retorted with, "Thank Phenice. It was her idea."

So maybe it was the shed for us after all. Me and my big mouth.

Chapter 24

CUSTOS

Dante and Emil stayed in the living room sharing their should-be secrets; I knew they were talking about me. I was only half-successful at tuning them out. I heard bits and pieces of their conversation but not enough to comprehend. Since I was utterly lost in the discussion, and quite frankly, I didn't want to be part of it, I decided to head to bed.

I wasn't tired even though I should've been beat. Considering it was now one in the morning. I had been up for over twenty-four hours and had a very eventful day. I wondered why I wasn't exhausted. I should be incoherent by now, not feeling as if I had just awoken, fully rested and ready to go. It was becoming more obvious a lot about my life was changing.

Brushing that thought aside, I walked into the hearth room to check on Alina. She was fast asleep, lying on the sofa with a fire roaring in the hearth. The room was peaceful. I was going to miss this room. The French doors looked out over the rose garden that served as my backyard. Even with the doors closed tight, I could smell the inviting scent of the roses wafting in. It was sweet and delicate. I could see the petals bathing in the moonlight.

I wasn't cold, but out of habit I grabbed a blanket from the cedar chest behind the sofa. I curled up in the large oversized chair close to the fire, wrapping myself up tightly. It should've been hot sitting that close with the fire at its peak, but since I transitioned, I found I always felt perfectly comfortable. Vampires apparently didn't feel cold or hot. The loss of something so mundane made a bit of sadness creep in.

I closed my eyes, no longer hearing the guys after choosing to tune them out. Instead, the sounds of the fire popping and snapping rhythmically filled my ears. I was devoured by the power the fire held as the flames consumed the logs within the hearth. There was a sense I could call the fire to me. The fire was part of me, part of my soul. The sounds were soothing. I felt deep within myself the ability to wield the flames as I desired. A sweet, sinister smile spread across my lips and lit up my face. I wasn't power hungry, only learning to embrace what I had become. I knew right then, sitting in that soft, comfortable chair, bathing in the warmth and power of the flames I would be okay, maybe even better than that.

I had lost so much in my life. The last week was so unbelievable in its extremes, it was hard to hold everything in my mind. Yet as I felt the power stirring inside my body, I felt truly hopeful and eager. Maybe for the first time since I was attacked.

I snuggled in under my blanket, letting the element of fire warm and cheer me. As a vampire, I should fear the flames, but I knew they would not burn me. Instead, they danced along my skin and swam within my mind, teaching me what I was meant to be. The fire held me, called to me, and I loved its popping lullaby.

The sky was bright and glorious, as flawless as a painting, but it was real, colored in hues of periwinkle and cornflower. The sun passed filtered rays of creamy yellow light around the large puffy white clouds dotting the perfect sky. No signs of rain anywhere. Not a touch of gray as far as the eye could see.

I was pleased with my new life. To be honest, I was surprised at the freedom I felt. I was happy as I walked through the grassy plains surrounded by the climbing mossy green forest. I could see the ferns tucked away, nestled in their canopy deep within the trees.

A gentle breeze blew throughout the land and petted everything in sight. My hair caressed my face, and the grass danced across my outstretched hands, tickling my palms. The sun warmed my skin like delicate kisses from your favorite lover. This time was exactly what I needed.

As I walked slowly through the plains, I realized I was being watched. I turned my eyes skyward and saw a falcon in flight much lower than normal. The bird's essence was unusual; it felt too large to be contained within the small body of the falcon, and it was radiating too much power for just one of Mother Nature's creatures. I continued to walk forward with my eyes on the falcon. As I reached for the elements, I sensed the air moving differently around this bird. It made more room than was needed for its frame and size.

I stopped and watched. The falcon noticed my attention on him. He turned around and flew in my direction. Once he was close, he began his descent with such speed he became a blur. As he reached the earth, the falcon transformed from bird to man. The landing was lovely and flawless. The transformation was magic. I had no other way to describe what I witnessed. He stood ten feet from me now.

Fear crept up in my gut. Then the voices of the Fates chimed within my head.

Trust him, Phenice. He has been sent to you, for your protection.

As fast as they entered my mind, they were gone.

There I stood in the middle of the rolling grasses, staring at this beautiful man with his honey-brown skin and glowing gold eyes. His dark groomed beard hugged his sharp jawline matching his rich black hair, full of sweeping golden-white highlights that hung past his shoulders; a half top knot sat atop his head with a braid hanging just behind each of his ears. Both ears were pierced, adorned with dangling gold earrings in the shape of the Egyptian Ankh. He was a sight standing there at about six and a half feet, dressed in white.

We gazed at each other, speechless for what felt like forever. He felt familiar, as if I had always known him, but I didn't recognize him. He slowly stepped closer to me. His power washed all around him like a shield. I could feel he was a force of great and otherworldly power. His power was scary, but it also inspired awe within me. I remained frozen in place gazing at this shifter.

He continued to approach me without saying a word. As a matter of fact, he wasn't making any noise at all. I had learned to listen for the rustling of clothing because with vampires, that might be all the warning you got of their approach. I strained my ears, trying to hear something. No sound came from his feet moving in the grass or from his body passing through it. I saw the grass moving. I saw his clothing manipulated by his movements, but he generated absolutely no noise. How was that possible?

When he was about five feet from me, he finally spoke. "Hello, Phenice. My name is Custos. I have been sent to you as your guardian." His voice was soft yet firm. It echoed with ancient power. He was indeed otherworldly. That was why he didn't make any noise. He wasn't really a part of this world. I was curious if he was in this world or only projecting himself.

"What are you meant to guard me from?" I inquired, intrigued and wondering who I needed protection from. I hadn't had anyone trying to find me. All my enemies thought me dead.

"I am the protector of the righteous. You are now my charge." He bowed but maintained eye contact.

"The righteous? I am a vampire, Custos. There is nothing righteous about that," I stated with some humor, not with any resentment. It was just how I felt.

"You are wrong. You will change this world. I am here to help lead you along your path, so you may accomplish all you are meant to, to help you become who you are meant to be," he stated in a singsong voice, which was a complete contrast to his physical appearance. His tone was gentle, but his body screamed "don't fuck with me."

"What are you?" I asked, hoping I didn't sound rude.

"I am the Slaughterer of Damned Souls. I punish the wicked and assist the righteous placed in my charge. At this moment that would be you," he replied with a longing in his eyes I didn't understand.

"Okay," I whispered. Even though I didn't feel any clearer about who or what he was. "May I ask for more clarification about what you are without being completely inappropriate?" I questioned, not wanting to offend him but curious all the same.

I had never encountered someone who felt the way he did. Here but not here. So powerful I wanted to kneel at his feet and give him all my unconditional love. He was divine in some way. The pull to worship him made that abundantly clear.

"I am an immortal, as you are, but not a vampire. There are many other creatures in the universe besides vampires and humans. For lack of a better way to explain my existence, I am a demonic god meant to walk the mortal planes among the many universes, protecting the virtuous and damning the ones so evil they have begun to tip the balance within the cosmos. For as long as the Powers see fit, you are my charge. I will lead you where you are meant to be. Trust me, and don't forget me."

Before I could speak another word, he transformed back into a falcon and took flight. Within the blink of an eye, he was gone. I was back in the hearth room, staring into the fireplace.

———∞∞∞———

Chapter 25

HUNTED

I awoke or maybe came back to consciousness. I don't think I had been sleeping. Something was different about what I was shown. It was unexplainable but important. I glanced around trying to reorient myself. I was still snuggled up in the chair. Alina was still asleep on the sofa. The clock on the mantle read 6:11 a.m. I was right; it was different. Time had passed during the vision, making it more dreamlike. Though I would not call it a dream, it wasn't a vision either. It felt like it had happened, like a visitation, or I had been pulled somewhere for the meeting. The Fates had sent me a message to trust Custos, and somehow he had come to me, or I went to him. I had a strange feeling I would be meeting Custos in the flesh very soon.

I was curious about the "leading me" part of the conversation. I didn't understand the wicked and righteous speech, but I decided having a soul slaughtered didn't sound like a good thing. It sounded painful and very permanent. Therefore, I was happy to be placed on the good list instead of the naughty. I wanted to completely avoid the slaughtering of my soul if possible.

Shit. How had my world become so confusing so fast? A snicker fell from my lips. I'd gotten exactly what I had asked for, a new beginning. A mental note for the future: be more specific next time.

I felt more like the old me. The me before the nightmares had started and the resurgence of the PTSD symptoms. I had more control over my emotions and how much control they had over me. I sighed in relief. I was going to embrace this and try my damnedest to be open-minded.

It was time to get moving. When I entered the living room, I was surprised to feel disappointed upon discovering Emil gone. Dante had left as well. On the coffee table was a note.

Phenice,
Sorry to leave without saying goodbye, but you seemed to be in a trance. I couldn't arouse you. I assumed the Fates had a hold on you. Please let me know what they have shown you.

Dante and I have left to meet the caste. We are making arrangements for your and Alina's arrival. Plus planning your "funeral."

I hope your day goes as planned. Call if you need anything, and please be safe.

With love,
Emil

I smiled. I was falling way too fast for this man. I sensed the morbid humor we shared as he mocked about planning my "funeral." The absurdity of having to plan your own funeral to disappear was nothing but hilarious. The years in health care and working with some of the darkest emotions and the pain people worked desperately to overcome had left me with a twisted, morbid sense of humor; it felt necessary to prevent burnout, which was high in my profession.

I held the note in my hands, lost in his long flowing script, which was not what I had expected from a ruggedly handsome vampire. Next to the letter was a business card with his name and number, nothing else. It was simple, elegant, and to the point, much like the man himself. I folded up the letter and grabbed the card, putting both in the back pocket of my jeans.

I stood looking around my house, realizing how different everything was going to be. I craved stability for obvious reasons. I loved routines and predictability. As a human I started every day with a shower then a cup of tea. Why change that now? This would be easier on me if I held on to as much of my routine as I could. I didn't see a reason to change myself completely simply because I was now a vampire.

I turned toward the stairs just as an intense pain tore through my gut, forcing me to double over. Shit, I was hungry again. How often would I need to burden Alina?

I turned around, going to the kitchen to put on the kettle. I slowly headed to the hearth room, toward Alina, noticing the growing weight of my infinity necklace. The necklace weighed the same; it was my conscience and guilt weighing on me and racking my heart. I was about to use the small knife hanging from my neck to cut my best friend open so I could drink her down like she was an ice-cold beer on a scorching midsummer day. My stomach churned with hunger and self-loathing. I tried to swallow the loathing and shame down. I could feel the fear of being this dependent and vulnerable on another person. I needed her in a way I'd never needed anyone. This was my life now, and no amount of self-hatred would change what my new body needed.

I stood still, giving myself a moment to prepare. I took a deep breath and felt the world flood into me. It didn't overwhelm me this time; it felt like a gift. Acknowledging that this life wasn't all bad gifted me with some acceptance. I would take it, even if it was only a fraction. One step at a time was all I could ask of myself. It gave me the strength to walk into the room with Alina.

Alina laid there peacefully. I kneeled in front of the sofa and brushed a few rogue ringlets from her face. It was enough to wake her. She smiled at me. Not saying a single word, she stretched out her right arm. I was so grateful for her kindness, for how thoughtful and loving she was. This was hard enough for me, and she was making it so easy. Loving warmth filled my heart. She was the sister I never had. I would die for her if I had to.

I pulled on the infinity pendant and out came the tiny blade. I called on my spirit and sent it to her. Alina began to shimmer with a soft lavender and gold glow. She sighed slightly, a sound of contentment. I knew she wouldn't feel any pain.

I made the cut in the soft pale tissue at the bend of her arm while supporting her elbow. Before the blood could escape, my mouth was over the wound, and I drank deeply.

Warmth washed through me. Alina moaned. I would've been more uncomfortable if it was from pain, but I could taste her joy. My own pleasure was pulsing through me, crawling up and out of me, spreading over her in sheets of bliss.

With this feeding being private and not overshadowed by my terror of hurting her, I could feel the exchange between us. She was feeding me, helping to sustain this new life, but she was feeding from me as well. I could sense my immortality wrapping around her. Whatever made a vampire immortal was passing to her, making her immortal as well. Our arrangement was not one sided. I could sense I was giving as much as I was taking, and as long as she fed me, she would live forever. In an instant, the guilt, shame, and self-loathing fell away. I hadn't even considered a life without Alina since becoming a vampire. Without this arrangement she would grow old and die and ultimately leave me. It was completely worth it. I would be vulnerable if it meant she would never have to leave me.

As I finished, I called on the needed elements to heal her. Before I even pulled my mouth away, her flesh was intact. I could sense her blood replenished. I was getting good at using these new powers much faster than I anticipated.

Alina sat up.

"Wow! Phenice, that was amazing. I didn't notice any pain, just power, and it felt good," she gushed. "I'm hungry." She finished as she stood up, stretching.

I was happy she didn't mind feeding me, and I felt better about it now too. Plus, anything was better than killing for my food. I was hoping as time went on this wouldn't be such an emotional roller coaster. I am sure a time would come when this was simply part of our daily routine. My heart longed for that day.

We both walked to the kitchen. She started to make breakfast, while I made tea. I sat at the table sipping my tea and thought about trying to eat some solid food. In an instant I became extremely nauseous. I guess that meant I was on a strict liquid diet for all eternity.

I wondered if that would get boring.

"Huh." I breathed.

"Did you say something?" Alina responded.

"Oh, sorry. No, I was thinking," I replied.

"About?" Alina questioned as she brought her food to the table and sat down cutting into her over-easy eggs.

Watching her eat made me a little sick. I snickered. "About whether or not I will ever be able to eat solid food again, and if being on a liquid diet would get dull."

"That would be something to ask Emil. Speaking of, where are they?" she inquired.

"They are preparing for our arrival. We will call them when we are done today. I don't mean to be rude, but watching you eat is making me want to puke. I don't think I physically can, but the nausea is uncomfortable. I'm going to go take a shower," I told Alina as I stood to leave.

"Sorry, Phenice," she said while chuckling around a full mouth. I got up with my teacup to leave.

I smiled and laughed along with her. "Oh, Alina, please don't be. If you can handle me drinking from you, I can handle a little nausea," I joked with her.

She smiled and nodded as she spoke. "You know I want to make this transition easy on you, right?" All laughter gone.

"Alina, you have no idea how much easier you have made this for me, and I don't think I could ever verbalize how grateful I am for you," I replied, meaning every word.

She stood up, walked over to me, and hugged me. I hugged her back tightly. She pulled away looking up at me. "I want this too, remember that. Now, go shower. I'll be here."

My bedroom was still a mess, but if I was going to rent out my house, I would have to hire movers, so why not a cleaning service too?

"No big deal," I said aloud to myself. Even though starting over felt like a big deal, I would get over it. There was no choice in the matter; I had to.

I grabbed some clothes and went to the bathroom. I walked in and reflexively locked the door. I've always felt physically vulnerable in the shower. The image of one of my father's friends letting himself into the bathroom when I was a teenager tried to surface. It was a painful memory, one I had worked on for years in therapy, a memory proving just how much my father failed to protect me. When the PTSD flashbacks would happen, I could feel the whispers of his unwanted touch upon my body. I'd fought him as hard as I could, yet nothing gave me the strength to fight off a grown man from taking what he wanted. It was probably the event that sealed me leaving my father's house a few short months later when I got my driver's license. I quickly shoved it down with a shiver, locking him in a steel box, hopefully never to be seen again. Some memories belonged locked away forever. He was one of them.

The bathroom was a large white room, which always looked pristine. The tile spread along the floor and up the walls in a smooth sheet of porcelain paleness. A border danced around the room about two feet from the nine-foot ceiling, also in white, but it stood out in a rose texture, no color, but beautiful all the same, as each rose popped out in ceramic bliss. It screamed order and tidiness. I found myself chuckling under my breath at the concept of anything being tidy with the mess I was currently in.

The pedestal sink and built-in claw-foot tub were also white porcelain, bright and brilliant, not a spot on them. They were decorated with soft-brushed nickel fixtures and piping. The showerhead hung down over the tub. It provided an inside rain shower when turned on. I walked over and turned the hot knob on full blast, and for good measure, I slightly turned on the cold knob. Water poured down into the tub, and the sound of water splashing happily echoed throughout the room. I grabbed the white lily–embossed shower curtain and pulled it in place around the tub along its rubbed nickel rod along the ceiling.

Turning back to put my clean clothes on the dressing stand next to the sink, I saw my reflection in the built-in full-length mirror. The clothes fell from my frozen hands. I couldn't believe the woman staring back at me. If I could call her a woman. I tested it. I waved. I jumped up and down. I opened and closed my mouth. I turned completely around. The woman in the mirror mimicked every single movement. Of course, she would. This felt insane. No matter how foreign she looked, I was staring back at myself, totally in shock.

She had wavy, gold hair hanging long, longer than I remembered, down beside her perfect porcelain face, complete with rosy cheeks, full garnet lips, and gleaming bright vortexing sage and gold eyes. She was sexy. I couldn't believe that was my image. I was majestic, flawless, and stunning. How could I change so much and so fast?

I continued to stare at the strange woman in the mirror as I undressed. The room was beginning to fill with steam, making the mirror fog. Thank goodness for small blessings. I found peace in the loss of my appearance. Seeing my reflection had brought back some of the panic I had felt when I first awoke from my transformation. On my way to the shower, I cracked the window overlooking my rose garden to let out some heat. Once I made it to the shower, I climbed in.

The embrace of the water washed away a lot of the turbulent emotions from looking in the mirror. I could feel the elements rolling over my skin: water, fire, earth, and air all there to heal my hurts. I let them fill me with happiness. I let the scent of the roses in my garden embrace me. I lost myself in the joy they provided.

Alina knocked on the door.

"Phenice, are you okay?" she asked.

"Of course I am. Why?" I yelled back. I was so happy, why wouldn't I be okay? I could hear the peace in my voice. Feel it ringing throughout my entire body all the way to my toes. It was probably radiating from me in tidal waves. So why would she think something was wrong with me?

"You've been in the bathroom for an hour and a half."

Holy shit! How had I lost so much time?

"I have made the appointments. I also left a message with Dr. Postmere's assistant." Alina paused. She was waiting for an answer. I could smell her. She was still outside the door.

"I'm sorry, Alina. I didn't mean to stay in here this long. I'll be right out, and we can leave." My reply was hasty.

I rushed to turn off the water. That's what I get for installing a supersized water heater. There was also a feeling my power over fire kept the water temperature where I wanted it. This shift in my world could have benefits I was beginning to recognize and fall in love with.

I stepped out and dried off. I slid into my panties, ripped jeans, and socks, followed by my favorite soft, crisscrossed, open-back, lavender-cream cashmere sweater. The sweater covered my infinity necklace as it hung gracefully over my heart. It had been the only thing I hadn't taken off for my shower. I didn't even realize it until now. Funny how it had already become that much a part of me. I finished dressing by putting on laced-up brown-suede wedged ankle boots. With the small heel, they made me at least five foot ten. I had dressed appropriately for the weather, even though I could've worn shorts and a tank. It was going to take time getting used to the constant physical comfort, never feeling hot or cold again. It seemed an odd thing to miss.

I grabbed a pair of gold earrings then started on my hair. All I needed was some hair cream so it would air dry faster without becoming frizzy, and I was done. No makeup needed anymore. I honestly didn't like it; I always found putting makeup on relaxing, fun, and…human. Oh well, who am I to complain about ridiculously full and dark lashes and naturally blushed cheeks? Today, it was a good thing. I had left Alina waiting while she worked hard to fix my life.

When I stepped out, I saw Alina had already showered and changed using my guest bathroom.

"Where did you get the clothes?" I knew they weren't mine. She was too short to fit in my jeans.

"When I talked with Emil last Friday, I started carrying a bag in my car. I didn't know when I wouldn't be able to go home," she answered.

Her response hit me hard. This was happening to her too. Her life was getting flipped upside down right along with me. She was doing it because she loved me. Our destinies were intertwined for some reason.

"Sorry I was in there so long. I got lost in the shower. It was relaxing," I expressed.

"You've been through a lot," she stated with a chuckle, compassion apparent on her face.

"You have too. How are you feeling? Are you okay?" I asked. She was giving up so much for this.

"I feel great. Better than ever actually. Really, I feel stronger after this feeding than I did yesterday," she informed me.

I wanted to know more about the big picture. Her having to probably leave school, giving up her dreams and career because of the cascading path we now found ourselves on. I didn't like being in the dark about the future. I longed for answers. I craved a plan.

Even though I didn't want to be in the dark about what happened next, it made me uncomfortable to dig deeper with her. Honestly, I didn't know how to ask. I found it hard to look at her. Guilt started to worm its was back up inside of me. I was using my best friend as food, and she found it wonderful. It felt like she was throwing her life away for me. How do you address that with someone? I found myself speechless.

"Phenice, please don't get weird about this. It's fine. I'm okay. And you're not the only one gaining from what we are doing." She stepped closer, trying to convince me.

I wanted to yell at her: *We* are not doing anything! I am the bloodsucker, and you are the fucking victim! I'm destroying your life! Everything you ever wanted will be gone because of me.

Then realization hit me hard, like I had run smack into a steel wall. I wanted to push her away, like I did with everyone. I was sabotaging this relationship like I always did. That was my modus operandi.

Instead I replied, "Okay, I'll try, but it's hard. You're my best friend, and I feel like I've crossed a line." No shit. The line had been blown to smithereens.

"Phenice, listen to me. I can feel you, and I know you are hiding your feelings from me. That's fine, hide, but this is necessary for you and for me. You think you're being selfish, feeding from me. Well so am I. I won't be expelled from your life. I need the strength you give me so I can live in your world. I won't survive any other way. You are all I have, damn it. You need me, and I need you. So things have changed, and this is how it is going to be. Tough shit! Get over it and stop feeling sorry for yourself because if you're honest, I mean truly honest, your guilt is about you not me. Guilt is a selfish emotion that makes us do stupid shit and nothing more. Both of our lives are forever changed. I'm good with it because I choose you. Okay?" Fire burned bright in her eyes. She was breathing hard. I don't think she took a single breath during her rant. She was pissed. "I get to choose what is right for me—what I want. Not you."

"Damn, Alina, I forgot how dangerous a doctoral student in psychology could be." I smiled at her. She was right. No one gets to make choices for someone else. To love someone means giving them the freedom to make their own decisions and supporting them even if we are scared.

She broke out of her anger and smiled back. I needed to let it go. This was why I loved her. Why I needed her. She would always call me on my shit, and she would love me no matter how ridiculous I could be.

"Sorry. You're right. I'm done feeling sorry for myself, at least for now." I winked at her. "Are you ready to go?" I asked with my smile still in place.

"Yeah, I don't want to be late. I should drive. I think it would be best if we left your truck in your driveway and not move it again," she stated.

"Speaking of my truck, I should sell it too. It will draw attention to me since they know it." I loved my truck since it was the only thing I had left of my mother, but with all the changes I needed something that blended in. Not a rare, custom pickup.

"Phenice, you cannot sell your mom's truck. Let's store it or something. For now, just leave it in the driveway, and we will figure something out. Maybe Dante or Emil will have a suggestion." I hoped Alina was right. In my heart I didn't want to let it go. It felt like letting my mom go, again. That truck was my last thread to her.

The bank appointment went smoothly. The papers would be finalized within a few days. We arranged for Alina to pick them up. The appointment with Jeffery was about the same, simple and to the point. He would draw up all the contracts and put Alina as property manager. After creating a new and totally random email address, he and I agreed to communicate via email and only if completely necessary. Jeffery was to go through Alina as much as possible.

Dr. Postmere had called Alina back and agreed to meet her off campus at 2:30 p.m. While we waited, Alina got some lunch.

"Phenice, I will start to contact your patients tomorrow and refer them to other psychiatrists and therapists. I got a list from Dr. Postmere's assistant." She was talking between bites and drinks.

"Thank you. I believe it would be best if I don't have contact with anyone. Emil has made the queen sound very dangerous. I need to be careful. I don't want anyone to get hurt because of me," I replied to her while I drifted off.

I got lost in the possibilities of the patients in my life getting hurt because of their association with me. That thought felt horrible. I didn't think I would be able to handle anyone getting hurt, or worse dying, because of me. I had tuned Alina out, lost in my thoughts. As soon as I realized it, I tried to figure out what she had said.

"You should be careful."

I don't think she noticed I was lost in thought.

After lunch we went and canceled my cell phone. Alina opened a second line on her plan and gave it to me. I now had a new number and no account to be traced. It was time to meet Dr. Postmere.

Alina pulled up to the coffee shop at 2:24 p.m. and dropped me off. The plan was for her to park and wait a few minutes before she came in and sat at a distant table.

When I walked in, Dr. Postmere was already there. He was sitting at a table in the back corner, drinking coffee. He picked a table so he could people watch. He wanted to observe. As a psychologist, he was always the observer. It was something we shared, to always be watching how humans interact. I found it fascinating, and from the look in his eyes, I knew he was a kindred spirit. There was a fire, a joy simply to be taking in the life around him.

He looked right at me. I expected him to smile or wave me over, but instead he glanced at me then away. I froze midstep. He didn't recognize me. A part of my heart broke. This man was a mentor, a surrogate father, and someone who had helped me rebuild my life when I came to Oregon. I didn't recognize myself when I looked in the mirror, so why was it so painful to have Bruce not recognize me? I stepped to the counter with my eyes still on him and all my attention tuned to my surroundings, awaiting any danger. I ordered a tea latte.

Once I had my tea, I walked toward Dr. Postmere, feeling different in my body. Not like a human, not anymore. I wasn't walking; I was gliding along the ground. I could feel everyone. I could sense them in a palpable way. I heard them breathing. Their heartbeats created a percussion throughout the small space. I could also feel what they were made of, what power they possessed inside. I could sense whether they were good or wicked, or on the fence teetering, waiting to be tipped over one way or the other.

That sense brought up Custos and what he said in the dream when I met him. I was bathing through their essences. It was an invasion to say the least. I didn't mean to assault them like that, but I had no control. I understood now why I needed training. A fire lit in my belly, igniting an eagerness to learn how to avoid swimming through people.

Dr. Postmere looked at me when I stopped in front of him.

"May I help you?" he asked.

Right then I felt Alina walk in. My core was tugging me toward her, drawing me in her direction. I knew without looking she was walking to the counter to get a drink. Then I heard her voice. It was so familiar. It felt like home to me, so inviting. Enticing. Her words wrapped around me like a rich velvet blanket with the promise of safety and security. I blinked, trying to focus. I came back to Dr. Postmere.

He sat there staring at me with soft, delicate, pale-blue eyes. He seemed so harmless with such a small stature of only five foot five and a very thin build for a man. His natural dark skin had very few wrinkles; the years had been kind to him, and the only thing giving away his age was the receding silver white hair.

He really had no idea who I was.

"It's me, Dr. Postmere. Dr. Jones. I asked Alina to arrange this meeting for me so I could talk to you," I said.

His eyes widened in disbelief, and he rose to his feet. "Phenice?"

"Yes." He wrapped me up in a hug then stepped back in confusion. "May I sit?"

It's hard to believe, I know. I'm still adjusting, I mocked in my head.

"Yes, of course. I'm sorry," he blundered, swinging his arm toward the seat across from where he had been sitting, gesturing for me to sit.

Once we were both seated, his confusion was obvious. Without meaning to, I pushed my power outward to soothe him. I saw him shimmer slightly with a gold dusty glow. Then the gold sunk deep into his skin and disappeared. Slightly panicked, I wondered if anyone else could see it. With a quick glance around, it was clear only I saw it. That didn't stop my paranoia.

"You don't recognize me?" I inquired.

"I do now. I'm sorry, you looked different at first," he replied.

I knew he was being polite and kind as always. I don't think he would know me if my power wasn't embracing him. My energy must've made me feel familiar. It hadn't been intentional, but instinctual. Again, another reason to start training as soon as possible.

"What is it you need to discuss?" he questioned.

Now that I was here, I realized I hadn't prepared myself for what I was going to say. What should I tell him? I sat and stared into his pale-blue eyes and decided to tell a small version of the truth as I had done with Alina initially.

"I need to disappear for a while. Something horrible happened to me last week, the evening after we talked, and I nearly died. If the people who hurt me realize I'm alive and able to talk, they may come after me. So I want to leave." Once I said it, I realized how scary it sounded. It was too much and too late. I felt fear bubbling up within him. I petted him with my energy and pushed his fears and anxieties away. He relaxed quickly.

"What did they do? Can't you go to the police?" he asked the expected questions.

"The police can't help me. As far as what happened, I don't really want to talk about it. I was almost murdered and the people—" I used the word loosely "believe they were successful. I need them to continue thinking so."

His face dropped in disbelief. "Phenice, dear god, are you okay?" he gasped.

"Yes, but I need some time off, and you can't tell anyone where I went or that I spoke with you," I commanded. As soon as I said it, I knew he wouldn't have a choice. He wouldn't be able to talk to anyone. My words bound him somehow.

"Whatever you need, of course just tell me," he responded, completely oblivious to the loss of his free will.

I would have to talk to Emil about my new powers of persuasion, or should I say, powers of vampire compulsion. Clearly that part of vampire lore was true. Looking into his eyes, I could see he was lost to me. I didn't mean to do it, but I had complete control of him. It started with wanting to comfort him, and it ended with me taking his free will. It was an evil thing to do. I instantly decided it was a necessary evil that may save his life in the end. The morality lines were getting blurry.

"I need to take a sabbatical, please." The *please* wasn't necessary, only polite.

"Sure. It will be done. Do me a favor and take care of yourself, Phenice.

You can have as much time as you need." Even though I had control of him, I felt his sincerity, his general concern for my well-being. He'd always been invested in me.

"Thank you," I said.

"You're welcome." He smiled.

I sat and stared at him, while he held his peaceful smile in place. He felt more like a puppet than a person at that point. I had overdone it without meaning to, and it was starting to freak me out. I didn't know what to do. I had never wanted to do anything like this to someone, and especially not to him.

"Dr. Postmere, I want you to forget meeting me today. Just put in my request and forget all about me until I come to you again."

He nodded.

I stood with tears creeping up and walked away, taking my crazy vampire powers with me. It felt all wrong, but with every step away from him, I could sense him returning to himself, whole and intact. He would do what I asked, case closed on my position at the university. He sat there finishing his coffee, a hollowness grew in my heart as I wondered if I would ever see him again. My old life was now void. I was walking away from everything I knew. I made eye contact with Alina. Well, almost everything.

She stood and walked out the door. I turned to follow her, but from a far corner in the coffee shop, I felt a deep, corrupt darkness trying to hide. The hair on my arms rose as goosebumps prickled over my flesh. Terror seized my heart. I spun and there sat the female vampire with creamy ivory skin, silky black hair, and eyes to match from the night of the ritual. She was beautiful and downright wicked. I gaped at her. She smiled at me.

Damn it! I rushed outside.

I felt her follow me, like a wave of heat swallowing me whole. Once she knew I had seen her, there was no more hiding; the game was on. She pressed her power out for me to taste. She crept down my throat in a gagging rapture of pain and rage. She wanted to kill me, and I could feel it throughout my entire body that she could. She tasted rotten, like death and decay coated in joy. She would kill me slowly, and her laughter would overwhelm her as she did it. She would take great pleasure in my suffering as she murdered me. I wanted a place to hide, a place to run, but I had nothing. All I could do was save as many as I could. I knew she would spare no one to get me. I had to get away from people.

I focused hard. I needed to see if I could feel any of the others from that horrible night. After a moment I knew she was alone. So either I was too scared, or she had come by herself. I prayed none of the other Hunters were here.

Alina was waiting next to her car. I hurried past her. She was about to call out to me, but I gave her the slightest acknowledgment by barely shaking my head side to side. I was relieved when she took the hint. She lifted her phone with an aloof expression on her face. To everyone, she would look like someone lost in her phone and completely oblivious to the world around her. Perfect!

I continued to glide down the sidewalk with overhanging trees. Their leaves were turning rich hues of red, orange, and yellow due to fall approaching. They left most of the walkways and alleys shaded.

Alleys, shit. That's what I needed to keep her from the crowds of people! I turned down the next alleyway. Once I was halfway down the alley, I turned to face her. She had followed me. I hadn't stopped choking on her power since I saw her in the coffee shop.

"Why are you here?" I thought I knew why. Either she was going to kill me, which was what she wanted to do, or she was going to take me to her queen.

"You know why. I must collect what belongs to the queen." Her eyes began to glow with the lilt of her voice. She was going to enjoy "collecting me," as she put it. I had a feeling I wasn't. She could make this one of the worst experiences of my life.

"Are you alone?" I asked.

"For now." She smirked.

That was good, I guessed, but I didn't know why. What was I going to do? She felt old and powerful. Then I felt him. He felt the same as he did in my *dream*, larger than life and powerful. Too much power to be contained in any one being. I didn't look for him, but I could feel him flying high in the sky. I continued to keep my attention on the dark, deadly beauty in front of me.

"Who are you?" I asked, trying to stall.

"Emma is my name, but to you, I am your maker, child. You will come with me," she barked at me.

Before I could protest, Custos dove from the sky with such swiftness that if you were not looking for him, you would not have seen him. Emma didn't, thankfully. It left me speechless. The man materialized behind Emma without a sound. Again, the only word I could think to describe what I had witnessed was magic—raw, powerful, and unearthly magic.

Then as he made eye contact with me, I knew what to say.

"Emma, I will not be going anywhere with you. You're wicked, and I'm not." I didn't understand the concept of wickedness, but I knew it was true. Something about Emma felt wrong, broken, and corrupt.

She was about to offer a rebuttal, but Custos reached up with his huge hands. They outsized her beautiful face by at least three times. With such grace he gently wrapped his hands around her head, interlacing his fingers in front of her now-frightened face. With a delicate upward thrust, he popped her head off like popping the flower top from a dandelion. Her body continued to stand there, headless, facing me as before. Custos slowly lowered the severed and fear-struck head to the ground by its long, silky ebony hair, which now had traces of sticky red blood glimmering by the slight rays of sun passing through the tall surrounding trees and buildings.

With his hands free, he grabbed her standing and still alive body by the arms, pinning them to her sides, making her immobile, even though fear had already left her motionless. He bent his mouth down to the cavernous hole between her shoulders where her head once was and opened his mouth wider than any being should be able to and began to drink. "Drink" was probably the wrong word.

A light swam around them. The light started off as a dark, almost-midnight wine shimmer. The more he drank, the lighter it appeared. Her power poured into him as he drank her life force. Blood was life for all creatures, and Custos was drinking all of hers down. As he drank her, the body dropped to its knees, and he rode it down.

It was hard to look away, but I looked down to see Emma's face, to see the expression on the decapitated head, and I couldn't think of a word to describe the terror on her face, nor the pain. Tears ran down her face, and her mouth was stretched out in a soundless scream, for it had been severed from her vocal cords. She couldn't even express her horror and pain. All she had left were tears. All I could think was, *Good. The bitch showed me no mercy and would've rejoiced in my death and pain. Why should she get any?*

My eyes went back to Custos as he was finishing. The light around Emma's body was fading to nothing and swirling around him only. He opened his mouth wide, and the light dove inside him. He closed his mouth and swallowed, hard and audible.

He let go of her body. She was facing me, kneeling. She was still alive and powerless; her body had turned a deathly shade of gray. Emma's decapitated head was still crying soundlessly next to her body. Custos was not done. His white linen clothing was covered in her blood, running fresh and bright down his chest. His massive hands were also stained with her life. He glowed, basking in her power.

He bowed his head and pressed his hands together in prayer. Then when he looked up, his gold eyes were glowing bright like a beacon in the night. His honey-brown skin was humming with a great energy. Heat radiated down the alley, so hot it was almost unbearable. Then with a wave of his hands, Emma burst into flames.

I stood and watched as the flames danced over her clothes and body. Her clothes lit in an instant, but her skin rebelled against the flames. It seemed to take forever. If she had been able to move or if she had had her powers, she might've been able to stop it, but she kneeled there, beheaded. The flames kissed and petted her flesh. I could see the agony in her eyes. It was torture. Finally, she caught fire. In an instant, she turned to ash.

I looked away from the pile of ash that was once Emma to Custos. He took a deep breath. With his exhale, a great gust of cold wind came roaring through the alley. His black-and-white highlighted hair danced on the wind. The wind picked up Emma's ashes in tiny tornados numbering in the thousands and whipped her out of sight. I watched as her ash swirled in all directions and flew away. Emma was no more.

I turned back to Custos. He was spotless. He was the picture of purity and everything wholesome. Even his hands were clean and untainted. He pressed his hands together in front of his heart and bowed to me, eyes still gazing at me.

"The wicked has been dispatched, and you are safe for now. May I take my leave?" he requested as he lifted his head and dropped his hands to his sides.

"What?" I whispered, frozen in place.

"May I depart?" he replied.

"Why did you have to drink her?" I knew he wasn't a vampire.

"To take her powers. It makes her unable to fight and gives me her memories. It is necessary. I am the Slaughterer of Damned Souls," he stated matter of factly.

"Why did you need her memories?" I questioned.

"Much power is in the memories, Phenice. For one, I know she came alone to look for you, to see if you were alive. The queen is not positive you are. This is good news," he said.

"Thank you for saving me." I didn't know what else to say.

"I don't need thanks. It is my duty. You will find out, Phenice, you are more than you think. You are more to me than you may ever know. It has been my honor to protect you," he said, bowing his head to me. I thought I heard a hint of longing, but I was unsure. It vanished as fast as it appeared, making me think it was imagined.

"So, my dream was true? You are my guardian?" They were questions not statements.

"I know of no dream. I only know of you, and yes, I am your guardian," he informed me.

I wanted to explain my dream, but before I could continue our conversation, a beautifully large falcon was standing in front of me. The underbelly was dressed in white feathers and all down his back were honey-brown feathers, exactly like Custos's skin. Staring back at me from above his sharp beak were the most gorgeous and mesmerizing golden eyes I had ever seen.

I hadn't seen him transform. The man was simply gone, and in his place was the falcon. Before I could take a single step, he took flight and was gone.

I felt like I should've been disgusted by what I had seen, but instead I felt safe, protected, and cared for. Lost in a world of serenity, I tried to find my way back to Alina. Before I could take three steps out of the alley, she came running for me, scared and panicked. And of course, why wouldn't she be?

"Are you okay? What happened?" She was gasping for air. Obviously she had sprinted the whole way here.

They were good questions. What could I say? How could I even begin to explain what I had witnessed?

Chapter 26

FAIRY TALE DRIVE

I stared at her as she gawked at me with her eyes desperately pleading for answers. I was still in shock, and I found myself at a loss for words. Instead, I reached out and grabbed her hand. I let my peace spread over her. She calmed instantaneously. With her hand still in mine, I guided her back toward the coffee shop. She remained silent until we were in the car and I was no longer touching her.

"Phenice, please say something. You're scaring the shit out of me." I could feel her fear.

Her pulse was thudding like thunder booming in the small confines of the car. With each beat I felt a slight vibration rippling from her, and as the predator I now was, I found it enticing.

I should've been scared for many reasons: being hunted, beholding Custos as he murdered Emma, and now wanting to devour Alina due to her fear. However, all I felt was peace. I found that strange and unnerving. The emotion didn't match the events.

"I'm okay" was all I could manage. She wasn't buying it because even to me, my voice was a soft whisper that was barely audible.

She started the car and pulled out from the parking spot. I didn't know where she was going. I wondered if she even knew. She was driving toward the north side of town, and if she kept driving, the road would dead-end into trees. Finally, she pulled into a lot and stopped.

"I can see you are *okay*, in the sense of the word that you are alive, but what I want to know is what the hell happened. When you walked past me, you looked like you had seen a ghost." She was angry now, and "ghost" wasn't too far from the truth.

I never thought I would see that face again, even though I committed it to memory hoping one day I would get my chance. At what? Revenge? As I sifted through my feelings, it was clear revenge was what I wanted for what Emma had done.

As I thought more about that horrible night, I started to awaken from the trance. I was still peaceful, almost euphoric, but not as catatonic as before. If I was honest, I was happy, almost to the point of baleful laughter. Still confused by my inappropriate emotions, I decided to tell Alina what happened.

"There was a woman following me, with ivory skin, ebony hair, and eyes to match. She was beautiful. Did you see her?" I asked.

"Yes, but I didn't realize she was tailing you," Alina stated, her fear still present.

"She was a vampire, and not just any vampire, but one of my makers. She was there when I was attacked nine days ago." I watched as my declaration turned to understanding and surprise crept across her face.

"Holy fuckin' shit! We gotta get the hell outta here. Phenice, they are coming for you. She knows. Where is she now?" Alina went to put the car in gear, straight terror etched across her face. Her heart was beating frantically.

I reached over and touched her hand. It was hard to control myself. I could feel an animal rampaging within me wanting to hunt, to consume, to be satisfied, yet my soul wanted to console and comfort her. I promised myself right then to always let my soul guide me unless I needed to fight for survival. Then I would unleash the animal within. In an instant, the lioness within me let out a low rumbling hum and quieted, and through my touch, I was able to send peace to Alina to calm her down.

She looked at me. She could feel what I was doing, and she smiled.

"Thank you. I needed that," she mused.

"You're welcome. Plus there is nothing to fear now. She's dead," I informed her.

"How?" I witnessed the shock in her eyes. She knew I wasn't a warrior. Not yet, but I intended to become one, especially now. I recognized how necessary it was. She knew I couldn't have killed Emma.

"Honestly you wouldn't believe me if I told you."

She stared at me, puzzled, but I didn't let go of her. I asked her to trust me in my head, and I sent that message through my touch. She smiled again and nodded.

"You tell me when you're ready. I think we'd both be surprised what I'd believe anymore," she stated with a smirk.

I let out a soft chuckle then responded, "You and me both."

We both laughed lightly for a moment.

She was right. So much had changed in such a small amount of time. Two weeks ago, I would've fainted in that alley. Instead, I welcomed Emma's death. I didn't want her to have a second of mercy. Honestly, I enjoyed it. I didn't know how I felt about the glee within me from Emma's death. I now felt a darkness that had never been there before, or maybe it had always been there, and I was only now embracing it. With time I hoped I would learn more about the animal within. I prayed not to lose myself to it.

I reached in my bag and grabbed my phone. It was time to call Emil. I knew I couldn't go home, not now. Thankfully he answered on the first ring.

"I hope you're ready for us because the hunting party has arrived." After I said it, I wished I could take it back and be more tactful because if vampires could have a myocardial infarction, Emil would have died.

"Are you there? Emil?" I waited. I pulled the phone away from my ear and watched the time of the call tick by. I knew we were still connected. "Emil?" I asked again.

He had to still be on the phone, obviously. I almost laughed. I recognized how ridiculous it was for me to find hilarity in the situation. My new life and the experiences of the last nine days had left me with even more of a morbid and twisted sense of humor. I needed to get a grip for everyone else's sake. If I didn't get some control, I would appear cruel, but really the emotional whip-lash was kicking my ass.

"Emil?" Nothing. Silence filled my phone. I waited. Finally he spoke.

"Are you okay?" His voice was hoarse and dry.

I felt bad. "I'm safe for now. She only sent one vampire, and she is dead."

"What? How?" he questioned in disbelief. Everyone assumed I couldn't take care of myself. Can't I just be a badass? I laughed to myself. I was the furthest thing from a badass. They had every right to question me on this. Now if we were discussing conquering a fiction series, then I was your slayer.

I cleared my throat, trying to make sure my voice didn't hold any of the sarcasm and odd humor I felt. "I'll explain everything when we meet. It will be easier if I tell everyone at the same time, so I don't have to repeat myself."

Emil paused for a moment, probably wanting to insist I tell him everything right then. However, he was able to accept that I was alive. "Makes sense, and Phenice, get your arse here now. I am texting you the location," he ordered and hung up. I ignored the excitement I felt being ordered around by this man.

I hung up. I opened the text with the meeting location, showing it to Alina, even though I didn't understand. We were meeting in the middle of nowhere, at a dead-end road.

Alina started to drive. I had gone oddly tranquil from the adventures of the day. Not just Emma, but what I had done to Bruce, Dr. Postmere.

We stopped right at the forest's edge, and there was Dante leaning against a tree almost completely hidden, but I saw him clearly, every single feature. Emil climbed out of his Aston Martin as we pulled up, an intense look of worry painted across his features. It was an emotion I never wanted to see him express again. Sadness filled me. I was sorry I had put that look on his enchanted face.

Alina stopped and was out of the car, walking toward Emil before I had moved. It wasn't that she was fast. I was completely out of it, and I knew I couldn't leave him waiting any longer. I forced myself out of the car and met everyone at the forest edge.

"Why have us meet here, Emil?" I didn't understand why we were in the middle of nowhere.

Dante answered, "This is the start of our driveway."

"Where?" Alina was turning around with her arms outstretched and looking while she spoke. I couldn't help but glance around myself.

"It's a hidden portal created by Amora, a member of our caste. Only if you know of its existence can you find it." Emil looked worried. "We must hurry to make sure no one can follow us. For a brief second, the glamour is broken as we enter, and the world can see the portal and the road beyond. We need to leave before anyone can follow you here."

"I will drive you two as we follow Emil. Let's get in the car now." Dante didn't say anything more. He was gliding toward Alina's car, and Emil had vanished, already in his Aston Martin, the engine purring and ready to go.

Alina and I were standing there like lost children. She turned and ran. In my mind I thought, *Run*, but that isn't what happened. I was in the car waiting on her before she had made it two steps. I thought, *Run to the car*, and I appeared in the car. I felt a rush of wind over my face, then I was in the car. I looked at Dante in the driver's seat. He nodded and grinned as if what I did was normal and he was happy to see it.

Alina was in the back seat now without a single word of protest to Dante driving her car. Had we been in my truck, I would've had something to say, but we weren't. So I sat back and looked straight ahead, wondering what the hell was about to happen. Enough weird shit had already happened today.

Emil backed up and turned his car to face the tree line. Dante was right on his bumper. A second later a paved path was exposed in front of his car. It was right out of a fairy-tale book. Emil shot down the road with Dante tight on his ass.

It was amazing. I watched the trees vanish from in front of the Aston Martin. Emil should've been hitting them, wrecking his car, but instead they transformed into a smoothly paved road for us to speed along. I turned in my seat to look behind me. As soon as Alina's Honda passed over the path, the trees shot back into place, reaching high into the sky. They were back where they belonged. The portal was apparently closed again.

We were hidden, trapped amid the thick ferns in the moss-covered forest. The pavement wound up and down and through the massive trees. I knew we had driven miles, but at the speed we were traveling, it had only taken minutes. We were so far away from any reality I had ever known.

Moments later a huge house appeared. As we got closer and began to slow, I realized calling it a castle wouldn't be an overstatement. We came to a stop right in front of a pair of massive wooden doors.

We climbed out of the car. Emil walked up to us from the garage.

"Phenice, tell me what happened." His eyes filled with clouds of silver. He was trying to control his power; I could feel it.

I knew I had to tell him, but how much? Should I tell him about Custos? I knew I couldn't tell them I killed Emma. I wasn't capable.

"Phenice, please. I can't help if I don't know what is happening." I felt him wanting to make me talk. He wondered if he could, but he was refusing to control me. I didn't know why I was able to read him so well, maybe the soulmate connection, but I decided I would tell him the complete truth. Besides, what else was there? I wasn't going to lie to him.

So I started with feeling the dark, evil energy trying to hide in the back corner of the coffee shop only to discover it was Emma. I explained who she was. I wanted to tell him why I led her down the alley, but the truth was I didn't have a good answer other than instinct. The introduction of Custos, my guardian, was next. I went back to my dream from early this morning, so they would understand why I had trusted him. I didn't even leave out the brutal details of Emma's death.

"Shit!" was the first response I got, and it was from Alina.

Emil studied the ground for a while, and Dante was staring at me so intensely I wanted to look away, but I didn't.

"I have heard of such a creature, but we had always been led to believe it was a myth, a boogeyman of sorts," Dante said with his eyes fixed on mine.

"He is not a creature, Dante, no more than we are. He is a god, an immortal demonic god," I replied. I was offended he had called Custos a "creature," but I didn't understand my defensiveness.

"You can't just take his word for it, Phenice." Emil reached for my hand, and I pulled away from him.

"If you were listening, I knew of him from a dream, a prophetic dream, I guess. So I'm not taking his word for it. I am taking the word of the Fates. Are you saying they are not to be trusted?" I snipped.

I felt the heat rising from within. Emil and Dante struggled to hold their ground. I was burning them with my anger, and they wanted to get away from it, from me. Good! I was happy to watch them struggle and fear me a little.

"Phenice, it's okay, honey." Alina was the only one unaffected by my fire.

The sound of her voice reminded me who I was. She brought me back to myself, to who I wanted to be. I instantly felt remorse. I had wanted to burn them where they stood.

I blinked. Then looked into Emil's eyes. "Sorry. I'm sorry." I swallowed my anger.

"Phenice, you're right. Dante and I will not say another word. I'm grateful Custos was there. Without him, I wouldn't have you now." His eyes flooded with waves of amethyst hues as he stifled his anger and power, exactly as I had. It made me wonder what my eyes looked like moments ago.

In a passive tone, Dante spoke: "We should go inside, if you are ready."

"As long as we are settled about Custos, I am." I knew he was my guardian. I felt a strong connection to him although I didn't completely understand it. I knew I would defend him against anyone. Even Emil. I found that fact strange but true.

"We are, Phenice. I apologize." Dante bowed slightly, gesturing his apology. Though it was clear he was an amazing warrior, he also seemed to be a bit of a peacekeeper as well. I was starting to really like Dante.

Chapter 27

THE CHALLENGE

We passed through the massive doors and into the foyer. The ceiling must've been twenty-five feet tall with a gorgeous bronze and amber chandelier hanging from the ceiling. It filled the entire space as if the walls had been sculpted around the radiating lights. To the right was a hand-carved spiral staircase climbing up to the second floor of the house. The foyer seemed vast and endless. My eyes scanned the room, trying to familiarize myself with the space.

Emil continued to walk forward, leading us through to the heart of the room. Once we made it all the way to the back, I noticed we could go left or right. Emil chose left. As I followed, a feeling of being caged crept up. I felt trapped. Emil was in front of us, and Dante brought up the rear. I didn't like feeling cornered as if they were trying to block my escape. My muscles tensed. The urge to flee was overwhelming. This sensation to run was an old, learned pattern from years of abuse. The symptoms of PTSD rising. My body was attempting to take over. It screamed loudly to me, yelling danger was near. Even though every impulse was howling at me to save myself from some unknown disaster, I continued to follow him anyway. We stopped in a room roughly the size of the entire ground floor of my house. It was a sitting room with a massive hearth.

As the sounds of the crackling fire hit my ears, the tension began to melt away. I let my power stretch out and caress the warmth of the flames. I was discovering fire was a part of me now. As if it was in every fiber of my being. Like my soul danced with flames. It called to me, wanting my attention, and

I happily gave it. I was grateful for the temporary distraction. It helped me focus. Once I was more at ease, I allowed myself to glance around the room.

One wall was constructed of nothing but glass. Beyond the glass was a dense, lush forest wrapped in the darkness the setting sun had left behind. Regardless, I was able to make out every leaf, twig, and blade of foliage on the ferns without straining. I even found the Willamette River meandering through the trees. My new eyesight was a sensation worth marveling at, but it paled in comparison to the call of the elements. Being surrounded by so much nature left me swimming in the music of the world. The elements swarmed around me, caressing my flesh, while calling to my spirit. Without intention, my power awoke, causing my core to shimmer. It was an answer to the surrounding atmosphere. I closed my eyes, fully surrendering to the embrace, to the breath of life all around me. An involuntary smile tugged at my lips. Joy slid through me.

Emil gently wrapped his hand around mine, bringing me out of my trance. My attention came back to the vampires in the room. They were all staring at me. I knew they had seen my soul shimmering, and as a result, I felt more vulnerable than when I had first walked into the room. I let my eyes absorb the others, realizing I was going to have to greet them using my newly acquired vampire customs. They were going to test my strength. My hackles rose with the decision to test them in return.

It was obvious everyone was at a loss. I was the first new vampire to join their ranks since they had fled from their queen. Instead of being comforted by the fact this was new to everyone here, I felt like an outsider. They had fled and learned to survive together, while relying on each other for centuries, making them a family of sorts. I had never felt more like on outcast in all my life.

I looked at them one by one, hoping my instincts would guide me. I knew the first vampire I greeted shouldn't have been the one I found the most intimidating, but what I saw in his steel-blue eyes was a kindness the rest were lacking. I knew he was the oldest, older than Emil. He had a quality about him. It reminded me of the earth. As if he had always existed somehow, since the beginning of time. He was extremely powerful. There was also something about his power that felt familiar and safe. I was drawn to him, similar to how I was drawn to the elements.

I took a step toward the mountain of a man, close to seven feet tall. He had long hair, so blond it was almost white, weaved into intricate braids. I caught a glimpse of black markings, unlike any tattoos I had ever seen, creeping along his neck and around his wrists. He was ruggedly handsome. My instincts had made my decision. I walked the rest of the way toward him with confidence. His confusion by my choice was clear on his face. He and I both were amazed that I would be aggressive enough to greet him first, but I saw acceptance in him and possibly friendship.

"I accept you, Aidan." I knew the man before me was Aidan from a vision. I could sense his energy swirling around him. He was happy I was here, and he understood why I needed Alina. He found her brave and respected her for her courage.

He laughed. It was a warm laugh. The impact of his energy had felt like when you turned on the heater in a cold car to knock out the chill. He smelled like wood smoke and clean pine. I found it pleasing and safe. I smiled in return.

"I accept you as well, Phenice. I am glad to finally meet you. This is Alina, I'm guessing." He gestured toward where she was standing safely by Dante's side.

"Yes." My smile widened, thankful he was making a point to the others.

"Hello, Alina. Welcome." He extended his hand, a human gesture.

It was clear Aidan had been exposed to human society and was used to trying to blend in. He was comfortable with her being here. Tension I didn't know I was still holding released. No part of him wanted to tear out her throat. Aidan was showing the caste he supported us. He supported Alina. I instantly liked him.

Alina left Dante's side and walked up, confident. It wasn't an act. You would never have guessed she was the only human in a room full of vampires. Good for her.

She took Aidan's hand and shook it with her normal firm shake as she stated, "Thank you, Aidan. It's nice to meet you and put a face to the name. Emil and Dante have spoken kindly of you."

"Liars, really. Don't trust them." Aidan laughed, as did Alina. I was grateful he was trying to ease the awkwardness with humor.

Dante walked over to stand with Aidan and Alina. It was as if the room was now segregated into two groups: those for me and those against me (or Alina). I knew Alina was safe with them, which freed me up to greet the next vampire.

My eyes landed on the only other man in the room, Avery. With my boots on, he wasn't much taller than me, maybe six feet. He had gorgeous, wavy brown hair. He kept it off the collar of his shirt but wore it on the longer side. His eyes were a warm shade of chocolate, and they pulsed with power. His skin glowed with a bronze light that seemed to ripple right under the surface of his tanned, flawless flesh.

I watched as he observed everything and everyone with a neutral energy, leaving his expression stoic. Though powerful and obviously intelligent, I sensed he would not give Alina and me trouble. I felt he would do what he must to make Emil happy and keep peace in the caste even if that meant accepting me, and my baggage (meaning Alina).

I stepped to him next. "I accept you, Avery." My voice was firm yet gentle as I maintained eye contact.

"And I you, Phenice," he replied flatly, as he slightly bowed his head, keeping his eyes locked on mine.

I should've been offended by his expressionless demeanor, but I had a feeling he was always dry and matter of fact in all situations. And honestly I didn't care either way, not at that moment. He could like me or not, but it was still one more vampire on team Phenice.

There were only two vampires left, the only other women in the room. Amora and Eden sat on one of the sofas together. They were the picture of ease and comfort. I studied them for a moment. They both were pretty, with dark, creamy skin and rich, chocolate hair. The texture of their hair differed though. One had thick, straight hair, and the other had curly hair. The one with curly hair had high cheekbones set in a heart-shaped face with amber-pink eyes. Her aura was lovely, like a moonlit meadow filled with glowing white flowers swaying in the night's breeze. She had to be Amora. Her power was love. She could make anyone fall recklessly in love with her, causing extreme devotion, and if she wished it, their destruction as well.

Therefore, the woman beside her with thick, straight locks and gray eyes rimmed in bright blue was Eden. Her cheekbones were less prominent in her smaller oval face. Eden's aura was pure bliss and happiness. I could feel laughter tap-dancing all around her.

It was clear, even in their differences, they had been born as twins in their last human experience. I stood there looking between the two of them, trying to decide who to greet. I felt intense love and joy for both. I called on my powers to read their energies, and in an instant, I discovered they were working together to fight me. The truth was there was no love or joy for me. Their auras were tainted with hate and resentment for both Alina and me.

Anger welled up from my gut. They started using powers on me before challenging me, making both a threat. I took a step closer to them. Emil was suddenly by my side with his hand on my forearm, pulling me back. I turned to him and shook my head side to side. This damsel didn't want, nor need, rescuing, and I was not in distress. I was pissed.

In a blink he let go and receded a few strides. I could read everyone in the room like words on a page. They were all apprehensive, preparing themselves for what was about to happen.

As if he could read my thoughts, Emil yelled, "No!"

"Silence, Emil," I snarled while instinctually pushing power toward him.

My lioness lifted her head and roared. From my lips a growl flew as I spoke. "I challenge you both."

Before I could even finish, I felt their power intensify. I wanted to go to them. My body pulled me involuntarily forward as my mind screamed no. The elements came to life around the room as I mentally protested. The air began to form a vortex. I focused my attention on Amora and Eden, and air followed, encasing them in the eye of my storm.

I called to earth in a roar, "Hold them."

Roots sprang up from the floor, wrapping around them, trapping them in my prison.

I heard water smashing against the glass wall from the river. I looked deep into Amora and Eden. They were scared. Their fear pleased and encouraged me. My skin began to glow bright orange, like the sun. Fire ignited in my hands. The flames from the hearth danced across the floor, encircling the sofa where the two women were chained by earth and air, and now they were ringed by fire.

"All I have to do is ask for air to depart, and you both will burn," I spoke in a husky whisper. I felt the fire burning in my irises.

"Phenice, you don't know what Amora has done for you, for you and Alina," Emil spoke in a rushed whisper.

I called on my Pythian powers to reach inside of Amora. I didn't care what she had done for me, but I was curious about her motives. I plowed through her brain to find what I wanted. She flopped and seized. She stopped once I pulled back out of her head.

"Emil, she did it because you are her master and she must." It's what I saw in her mind.

"You can't know that." Emil was upset, but I didn't care.

My hands became larger orbs of fire. I lifted them skyward, ready to pull air back and douse them in flames.

"I accept defeat, Phenice! I am no challenge to you!" Amora screamed. She looked past me to Emil. "Yes, Emil, she can know my motives. She is Pythia. She skipped through my brain freely, and I didn't even stand a chance of stopping her." With her confession, I pulled the elements away from her only, leaving Eden encased and chained, ready to finish what I started.

If I didn't do this now, I feared what they would do to Alina.

Amora slid from the sofa and kneeled before me. "Phenice, my life is yours to take if you wish."

I didn't respond. I left her on her knees, forehead to the floor, as I turned my attention back to Eden. My fingers twitched slightly, tightening the roots around Eden, causing a whimper to escape her mouth. I couldn't suffocate her, but I could crush her. She wouldn't die, but it would hurt like hell. It was apparent Eden's whimper was a verbal betrayal that infuriated her, but she remained reticent. I pulled my hand back a millimeter, and air dissipated. Instantly, the flames rose high around her, forming a tighter circle.

"Please, Eden!" Amora screamed without lifting her nose.

"I submit," Eden gasped, clearly not wanting to, but something about Amora's plea made her give in.

I believe she would've let me kill her before showing such weakness.

Somehow the love she held for her sister caused her to swallow her pride and submit.

"Your will is mine, and my life is yours." Eden dropped her head, trying to bow beyond the abilities the roots gave her.

I sent all the elements back where they belonged with only a thought. It was like nothing had happened. No burned floor, nothing out of place… nothing. Almost like an illusion. It was fascinating. Eden slid from the sofa and crouched beside Amora.

My mouth opened, and an unearthly roar poured out. My lioness wanted a kill. She was pissed her hunt didn't end in blood. My skin grew brighter, shedding light into the room so bright everyone but me shielded their eyes. As fast as it came on, it went out.

Emil walked up, gently taking my hand. With his free hand, he placed his fingertips under my chin, slowly tipping my head up so I could look at him. He kissed the tip of my nose and dropped his forehead to mine.

"My love, your eyes are still burning." He smirked.

"Sorry," I whispered, closing my eyes and swallowing my fire. I opened them again. "Better?" I asked.

He bent forward, putting his lips to my ear and whispered. "Yes, and no. The fire is gone, but in truth I found it sexy. I hope to see that look under different circumstances soon." He pulled back, looking at me with a devilish smile stretched across his mouth. I couldn't help but return it.

Once I was back to normal, no power leaking out of my being, I turned to Amora and Eden. "I'm not going to kill either of you. You can get up." I tried to stay neutral as I spoke, but there was a mild snarl underlying my speech. I'm sure every vampire in the room heard it.

They stood, neither of them raising their heads enough to meet my gaze.

"How about this instead…we start over, and you two give Alina and me a chance?" I recommended. It sounded like a question, but everyone in attendance knew it was an order.

Their heads snapped up simultaneously, shock on their faces.

"I don't want, nor do I need, any more enemies." I gave a small smile as they nodded in agreement.

It was the truth, I wanted to get along with everyone in Emil's caste. For better or worse, they were his family. We didn't need to be friends, but I didn't want petty prejudices causing drama. I had sympathy for why they did what they did, but regardless, it would never happen again. I would keep Alina safe, no matter what. For her, I would kill anyone and everyone. Until that moment I didn't know I had it in me to kill anyone, but there was a point I was going to burn them, and I wouldn't have cared. For Alina, I would burn the world to ash.

With the battle over, the tension had drained from the room almost as if nothing had happened. The only difference was Amora and Eden kept a safe, cowering distance from Alina and me. I wondered if I should feel bad about this dynamic, them fearing me. I dug down inside, and the only answer I found was that I didn't give a shit. Not to sound childish, but they started it, and I knew now I would make sure I would finish it. I felt proud of myself. I felt safe, like she and I might make it in this new world filled with ghosts and goblins.

We all sat down. Amora and Eden kept a faux safe distance. Easy conversation started to fill the room. Even Avery joined in, losing some of his flat emotional affect. I believe I saw him think about smiling once, which caused a smile of my own.

The conversations lasted hours. We discussed things of importance, like what to do next, how to avoid the queen and her Hunters, and how to get my truck here, which Aidan offered to do in the morning. Emil agreed with Alina; he wasn't going to let me sell it once he discovered it belonged to my dead mother.

In the end, the talk was causal. We were trying to get to know each other. I found myself feeling at ease, almost normal again, but it took effort to maintain because as soon as I realized how easy it was, I would chastise myself. Shouldn't I be loathing what I had become? Did I know how to be kind to myself? It was starting to seem like I didn't understand the first thing about radical self-acceptance, and becoming a vampire was bringing out my worst inner critic. At the heart of it, I truly might be a masochist. If I really wanted this new life to work, I was going to have to get out of my own way first.

Chapter 28

THE QUEEN ANNE

Everyone was talking. I heard the sounds but not the words. I left the conversation a while ago. I stood at the wall of glass looking out at the darkened sky filled with millions of bright, vibrant stars radiating in the night. It was a clear evening; not a single cloud tainted the black sky. Even the gibbous moon failed to conquer the darkness from consuming all it touched.

Part of me felt as if I should be bothered or afraid by the all-consuming blackness, but my skin hummed with joy. The darkness was my time now. Peace poured over my bones like hot wax coating me, protecting me. I was something different now, and I was beginning to embrace it.

My reverie was spoiled by Emil's reflection in the glass as he approached. Not that the sight of him could spoil much. He was strikingly beautiful, so handsome he didn't look real. As if the best filter ever made enhanced everything about him. There was nothing on earth as lovely as he was. My soul ached for him. I felt myself reaching for him even though I physically didn't move. A deep part of me pulled toward him like two magnets snapping together.

He walked without making any noise until he stood almost directly behind me and slightly to my left. I could see his shape staring at my reflection as I was gazing at his. As if it had a life of its own, seduction rose like an invisible sheet, then cascaded down upon us, wrapping us tightly. It was vast and sweet to the palate.

He slowly and very gracefully took his right arm and wrapped it around my waist. Then with a quick movement, he pulled my body to him. I didn't stumble, but I remained stiff where I stood, afraid to give in to him, to lose control. His palm was on my belly. He was so warm. It was clear he had fed recently because I felt his slow pulse coursing through him, strong and steady. The sound of his heart swarmed around me, leaving me dizzy and intoxicated. I took a deep breath out of habit, hoping to calm myself. Instead, the scent of rosewood and musk chased by a hint of lavender rode into my lungs. His scent caressed me, luring me to collapse into this man.

Now drowning in his scent and lost in his heart's rhythm, I had no choice; I submitted. My body went limp in his arm, and my head fell back to his chest, but I never took my eyes from his reflection. He was grinning at me, a sexy, seductive grin.

He leaned his sweet and luscious ruby lips down to my left ear, and as he parted his lips to speak, the faint aroma of mint and citrus whipped around my face. I almost turned and tackled him right there, but I had enough sense left to remember we had an audience. So I let him speak. I prayed I was sober enough to hear what he had to say. I was drunk on him.

"My love, I have a gift for you, something to show you when you are ready." He was smirking at me. He knew and felt the impact he had on me. I didn't care, all I could think was, *He is my gift.*

I managed a nod to the reflection of my Emil; calling him mine felt so right. I was afraid of what I would say if I tried anything more. I leered into the glass, seeing his gorgeous eyes staring through me, a rich royal purple. I loved his eyes. I found myself lost, more lost than I would care to admit.

He was leading me out of the room when I smelled Alina. I snapped out of my trance and back to our reality.

"Emil, what about Alina?" I was not about to leave her in a room with a caste of vampires who I didn't trust to keep her safe. They hadn't wanted her here.

"Please, don't worry. Dante has vowed to keep her safe, upon his life. He will lead her to you later. I promise." He gripped my hand and gave it a slight squeeze of reassurance.

That squeeze wasn't enough. I glanced over to Dante. He nodded at me.

"Promise, mistress," he said as he finished his nod. He had heard my concern and Emil's reassurance. I knew I could trust him and Aidan.

I gave a weak smile, then I mouthed, "Thank you."

Emil began to lead me from the room again when I processed what Dante had said. I was left wondering why he called me "mistress."

We walked down a long corridor to a gorgeous kitchen. Emil continued to pull me gently by the hand, not really giving me enough time to look around. We passed through a large parlor and out into the enormous garage. Again, his pace didn't grant me the chance to gawk at how many cars were lined up in the concrete car lot. He paused briefly to open a door; within an instant we were out amid the great darkness.

I couldn't take it anymore. "Emil, where are we going?"

"You'll see." It was obvious from the joyous grin on his face he wasn't going to tell me. He loved the suspense I felt way too much, and I loved seeing him lit up with so much delight. Therefore, I didn't ask again. I allowed him the game of leading me.

The Emil I had grown to know as a patient was always worried and overcome with fear for his soulmate and the seriousness of his role in her life or lack thereof. Seeing him so free and light was a blessing, one I didn't intend to chase away with too many questions. Now that I knew I was his soulmate, I wanted to give him happiness. It was clear he had not experienced much joy in his very long life, and that saddened me a great deal. He deserved so much more out of life. I wanted to change his life for the better.

"How far is our walk?" I asked.

"About two miles. Would you like to walk or run?" He smiled.

I thought about it momentarily. If we ran, I would find out within seconds where he was taking me, but if we walked, I would be able to enjoy being with him. And this was the first time outside of my office he and I had been alone since I completed my transition. My enlightenment made my answer easy.

"Walking is fine. It will give us time to talk." I also wanted to experience some normalcy. Being turned into a vampire had been traumatic—shit, the last few hours, for that matter, had been straight out of a supernatural horror novel. I needed some time to decompress.

"I would prefer to delay the surprise anyway." He was smiling. It was almost evil. I liked it. He was enjoying himself, relaxing. Something I had a feeling he didn't do very often. I could feel the burdens he carried; I hoped he would share himself completely with me someday.

I simply smiled in return, allowing myself to get lost in the darkness and how it felt to be wrapped in it. I was surprised how the night had a life force. It felt feminine to me. There was a heartbeat to the darkness, a breath, a very distinctive ebb and flow. I felt her emotions, and now she was happy to have two of her children embraced in her arms. I wondered if Emil felt her the way I did, or was it my powers?

"Emil, um…" I paused trying to decide how to talk about what I was experiencing.

"Yes?" he questioned.

"Do you feel the darkness? It's like she is a person…a mother?" I probed.

"Yes, we all do to some extent. It is different for each of us. Some feel it more intensely than others. I have a notion it will be stronger for you due to your power of the elements. The ritual used to turn a human into a vampire requires all the elements and the night. Our souls are tied to our bodies through the elements and the darkness. So other than our makers, I think the darkness and Mother Nature have the next strongest claims on us," he said in a soft singsong voice.

It made sense. I still wanted to find out more about the transformation and this ritual because I didn't understand how it worked. Emil had given me some insight, and I could have probed further, but in that moment, I was content to leave it be. I wanted to soak in the love I felt right then, from him and from the darkness.

I walked beside him, perfectly at ease. I was lost in the feel of his hand holding mine. Touching him sent tiny electric pulses from my hand through the rest of my body. It was the most physical pleasure I had ever felt.

After some time though, I had another question I didn't want to put off.

"Emil, why did Dante call me 'mistress'?" I asked, looking over toward his face.

"You caught that, did you?" He stared at the ground and his smile slipped slightly, but it didn't vanish.

"Yes. What does it mean?" I inquired.

"I have a feeling you will be hearing it a lot now." He looked over at me quickly, making eye contact for only a split second before his irises darted back out to our path. It was long enough for me to see the silver bleeding back into his eyes. Magic and shielding were taking back over in place of love. I preferred his eyes purple. I was discovering his eye color gave away how he felt. Purple was a sign he was happy or at ease.

"Why?" I wanted to understand, but I didn't. I knew nothing about the caste or its hierarchy.

"The truth is your display of power at the house was a small showcase of what you are probably capable of, and still you made ancient vampires submit to you. You could've burned the house down around you, including all of us, but you controlled it very well for how new you are. That is unheard of. Most new vampires are almost feral. And your power will only get stronger with age and training," he answered.

I couldn't imagine my powers being stronger than that, but I felt he was right. Still, he hadn't given me a direct answer regarding Dante's "mistress" comment.

"Why the title 'mistress' though?"

"It means, my love, Dante accepted you as his equal when at your home, but when he called you 'mistress,' he was letting you and the others know he now accepts you as his dominant, just as Eden and Amora have." He held tight to my hand.

"But I didn't challenge him," I reminded him.

"You didn't have to. He knows his place and is willing and happy to take it. We are a functional caste, Phenice, not a violent one. We want peace."

His face was so tranquil.

"Then if I am mistress, that makes you what? My master?" I interrogated. I couldn't help the slight tone of indignation in my voice.

"No, my love." He chortled. "For now, we are equals. You are the mistress to my master. Besides, in no way do I want to challenge you." He hooted. It made me smile to hear him so unrestricted. I reached out and put my other hand on top of his, now holding his hand in both of mine.

The silence overtook us again, as we walked down a thin dirt path lined with tall ferns and mountainous trees covered in moss. The forest was dotted with uprooted trees caused by lightening, heavy winds, or maybe just old age. They rested across the forest bed, and they, too, were moss covered. Everything was an intense eye-popping shade of green, even in the darkness. It felt like being on a foreign planet. It was one of the many things I had always loved about Oregon. It felt prehistoric. Now with the new enhanced senses, everything was even more vibrant. The life force of all the trees and plants was palpable.

I heard water following as it made its way to the ocean, so peaceful and happy. The water sung a song for only me to hear. After the transformation I hated being able to hear such things, and now I regretted that I had lived all my life until now with such a void. It felt wasteful to have never heard the earth's music. In that moment, I didn't feel alone. It was maybe the first time in my whole life.

The sky was lost in the canopy of the treetops cascading overhead, protecting us from the moonlight. They provided us with even more of the night's darkness, letting her cloak us in rich blackness. I felt at home with her. I felt safe. Tears began to fall from my eyes, dancing one by one down my cheeks like delicate waterfalls on my skin. Each drop was a celebration of love. Out of nowhere my skin began to glow with a warm amber shine like the embers of a fire. Emil stopped and turned to me. Eyes wide, mouth open, and speechless. I didn't know what I had done, but I knew I felt good, and I didn't want it to go away.

I wanted to ask him what was wrong, but in that instant, he smiled and hugged me.

"I have never seen one of us glow in the darkness. All vampires have a slight ember essence in the sun due to being bound by fire, but I have never seen one shine with internal light. It is a blessing. You are a goddess, Phenice." He beamed at me.

"What do you mean?" I requested.

"Again, we are connected to the elements. Our slight sheen comes from fire. Avery believes this is why fire can kill us, but only wind scatters our ashes." Images of Emma's demise flashed before my eyes.

"No one has ever returned from the flames. The way you controlled the fire in the house, letting it caress your skin, and yet you didn't burn, well it must mean you have a much stronger tie to fire beyond a simple elemental connection and beyond your power to wield it. Aidan is a fire burner as well, but he has never glowed with the embers of the flame like you do, and he can only allow it to touch his skin due to the ancient runes etched deep in his flesh."

That must be why I felt a tie to Aidan. Our powers were calling to each other. And that explained the tattoos I noticed crawling over his skin. I couldn't wait to learn more about them.

I listened to everything Emil said, but at that moment I didn't know how to process everything. There were so many puzzle pieces, and this was all so foreign. It wasn't hard for me to feel lost.

"Why do you think I started to glow?" I asked. It was the only question that came to mind.

"I don't know. What were you thinking of?" he asked.

"I was thinking how I felt safe in the darkness. I was amazed it was the safest I've ever felt. I guess I feel safe being a vampire and belonging to the night. I honestly believed my life was over when I found out what I was. Yet now I find myself happier than I ever felt as a human." As I spoke the words aloud, I let them sink in. With the penetration, acceptance started to root. I was starting to accept myself.

He laughed a deep warm chuckle while wrapping his arms around me. Pulled close to him, I looked into his eyes, and he leaned down to press his sweet crimson lips to mine in a delicate, chaste kiss. I began to glow a little brighter, and his laughter began again with his lips next to mine.

"By the way…not wanting to ruin the moment because I very much like having my hands on you, but we have arrived. Would you like to see your surprise?" He was still smiling.

"Yes, please."

He reached a soft hand to my face and turned it toward the dense forest.

There was nothing but trees. I looked back at him in puzzlement. I went to speak. He rested his fingertips on my lips and shook his head side to side. He pointed forward. He turned me to pull my back against his warm chest. Wrapped in his embrace, his lips dropped down next to my ear, sending shivers from the side of my neck all the way to my toes. With my toes curling, I did as he asked and looked back to the trees.

"I tell you of this place, the home we conjured within these woods for you to inhabit. May the veil be lifted for your eyes to see," he intoned with a simple soft rumble that snaked into my ear and wrapped around my soul.

I was about to turn to him with another protest. Just as my head turned from the forest, something appeared in my peripheral vision. I whipped my head back around, afraid to miss it. There stood an amazing house where the forest had once been.

It wasn't just any house, but the perfect house. I couldn't have asked for a more beautiful home in all my life. Emil had infused so many of the things I loved about my house yet made them better in the one standing before me. It was a balanced and artfully blended sculpture of architecture, filled with the eccentric style of Queen Anne and the fancifulness of the Italianate.

"Hmm," I whispered, lost for words because no one had ever done anything so kind for me. I honestly didn't know how to respond to being cared for in this way. I froze.

I felt Emil go rigid behind me and not in a good way. I thought maybe he craved more of a response. Shit, he deserved more. How do you show emotions you were never taught how to express? I had always had a hard time expressing myself. Anger I could do. Detachment, I'm your gal. But this—receiving love and kindness—I was a deer caught in headlights. Completely and utterly lost. I stood there, stoic. The interesting question was whether it was because I was a vampire, or was I emotionally fucked when I was human? I was leaning toward the latter.

Emil hadn't released me, though the embrace was more awkward. I had dropped my head in shame and confusion. He wrapped the tips of his thumb and forefinger around my chin and lifted my head. I dropped my head back to his shoulder and looked up into his eyes. His eyes were richly purple, and the black night paled in comparison to the enchantment of him. Instantly I was lost. He relaxed into me and smiled. He nodded toward the house. I had forgotten all about it with one simple glance from him. I had forgotten all about the structure that had appeared out of thin air in the middle of the forest. I only wanted to look at him, but I did as he silently asked. I turned back to the Victorian beauty.

As I looked, I noticed roses surrounded the house. It was completely encased by them. I then took a voluntary breath, and the smell was rich and sweet, so cleansing and blissful. They smelled different now as a vampire. It was as if I could scent each individual petal. I felt their softness in my hands from the aroma wafting in the air.

I found tears starting to build in my lower lids. I let my eyes drift slowly over the roses and slide, tear filled, to the house. Though I now realized *estate* was a better word. The beauty of this gift filled me. The tears escaped the cage of my eyes, falling freely down my cheeks in a silent, much-needed cry. My knees weakened as the enormity of this loving gift slammed into my heart. Emil held me tightly, refusing to let me fall or break our embrace.

I wanted to say thank you, but it wasn't good enough. It would sound worthless, empty. He gave me a home, a house. A sensation in my gut tore at me. Emil was the first man to take care of me, to love me enough to provide for me, to want to keep me safe. This truth made my tears come faster.

All the years of work and struggle, pain and fear, loneliness and sadness came crashing down on me. A wrecked shriek crawled up my throat and escaped my lips. No matter how desperate I was to hold it together, to be strong, with that one sound, I snapped.

I had never truly dealt with any of it. The death of my mother. The abandonment and abuse of my father. The growing up so fucking fast that it cost me my innocence. The fight to survive. The desperate need to make something worthy of my life. The gaping hole right through my core. All these years going through the motions thinking I had conquered all of it came crashing down, shattering all my illusions. The tears kept falling.

The worst part was Emil was a witness to one of the most embarrassing moments of my life. I loathed letting anyone see my tears. Since becoming a vampire, I had cried more than I had in my whole life. The ironic and hilarious part was, along with these tears, this catastrophic breaking of my soul was probably the healthiest thing I'd ever done. All my internal walls came crashing down right there in his arms.

After some time, the tears began to slow. I steadied myself and looked up at him. My eyes should've been red, tear stained, and swollen, but I could feel they weren't. My body no longer reacted as it did before. Once more I found a reason to be thankful I was a vampire.

Emil delicately lifted one hand from around my body and brushed my cheeks, wiping away the evidence of my mental collapse. His eyes were so attentive to every stroke his fingers made across my flesh. "Whoever put that hurt in your eyes—in your heart—doesn't deserve you. They never did. I make this vow to you: even if it takes every day for the rest of eternity, I will vanquish the pain I see in your eyes and replace it with infinite love."

Looking into his mesmerizing eyes, I found myself lost and in awe to have found the one person who might be able to do exactly what he just vowed. This monstrous angel of a man was going to be my salvation. The irony of being rescued by a vampire was not lost on me.

I found my voice while gazing into his eyes, and instead of thanking him, or acknowledging the most beautiful and kind words anyone had ever said to me, I softly murmured, "This isn't a shed."

His laugh erupted out of him as he pulled me up into his arms and sat on the ground, resting me in his lap. He pulled me to him, rocking and kissing me on the forehead, then my eyes, flowing down to my cheeks, and lastly his lips found mine. His kiss was possessive and sweet all at the same time. His arms held me like he would never let me go, like he would watch the world burn if it meant he could have me. I shouldn't be so selfish, but I needed what he was offering me. I, too, would watch the world wither and die if I got to be with him. I would forsake all others to hold this man in my arms forever. He ended the kiss with a hand locked in my hair so he could forcefully tip my head back a bit farther.

He leaned down next to my ear and hummed, "My lady, I would never be such a cad to only provide the love of all my lifetimes with a shed."

The sound of his voice in my ear and his breath upon my skin had the power to undo me. Without thinking I mumbled, "Emil, you shouldn't have done this. It's too much. I can't…"

"Phenice, fucking shut up, right now." He tugged my head back a bit more and stared straight through me. "I have spent over half a millennium without you, knowing you existed but never finding you. Waiting for you… finding you and thinking I couldn't have you. Then believing I lost you almost undid me. Trust me, this was simple. You lost a home you loved, and I love you. I am not asking permission. I will do this for you, and you will accept it. It's done. Understand?" He broke the trance I was in by pulling me tighter into his embrace. He was gentle yet aggressive; his voice was commanding. He placed a sweet, soft, tender kiss on my lips. His blend of sweetness and commanding confidence was perfect, and it left me undone in all the best ways.

Even if some old part of me wanted to be stubborn and ridiculously independent, I was finding Emil's dominant protectiveness undid me in the most tantalizing ways. I found my body melting into his embrace. I surrendered to him. I wanted this powerful man to hold and protect me. For the first time, I trusted someone would protect me, and I was going to let him.

The second I decided to trust him, to let him protect me, old thought patterns fought their way in to my mind. Somewhere in my core, I couldn't believe I deserved to be taken care of. Life had taught me the opposite. Emil was offering blind, unconditional love, and I didn't know how to trust love.

It wasn't Emil I didn't trust. I felt in my soul I could. No, it was love. Love left—it broke you in ways nothing else could. In irreparable ways.

I watched my father's love for my mother obliterate him when she died. Even though I never met the funny, laid-back Weylyn Jones I heard he was. I did get a front-row seat to the destruction of his soul due to her absence. My entire childhood was filled with moments of his demise. Sadly, he took me right along with him.

Through all of it, I loved him anyway, and what did that love do for me? The truth was simple. My heart was broken. Repairable? That was still to be discovered. After the last couple months of nightmares, brutally dying, transforming, sucking Alina into this world with me, losing the life I built, finding my soulmate, dealing with immense powers—really all of it had left me more broken. And confused. Could I be saved from my distant and near past?

Fear seeped deep into my bones. Was I as broken and fucked as my father? Was I simply repeating the family pattern of pain and destruction? A cold sweat blossomed on my skin.

Emil's sweet voice filled my ears, tugging me out of my internal torment. "Phenice, come back to me, love. Whatever or whomever is invading your thoughts isn't here. I've got you. Let me take care of you through this."

I came back out of the past and into my present, wrapped in the arms of the most handsome and generous man I had ever met. As I released the stream of tormenting thoughts and feelings, a conflicting realization came over me.

How odd was it that I would call finding love and a place of belonging "despair"? I couldn't help feeling like all of this was shrouded in doom. I felt this impending gloom hanging over me, waiting to eat me whole.

I let my eyes trace their way up Emil. I found his godlike face gazing down at me. His mirth was slipping because of me. I wouldn't allow that to happen. Maybe I didn't deserve this, but he did.

"Of course. I'm sorry. I'm still in shock or maybe simply overwhelmed. Thank you so much. No one has ever taken care of me. It's all a little much." I gave him honesty without telling him where I had allowed my mind to drift as I kissed him again.

I wanted to be honest with him. At a young age, I had developed this ability to tell just enough truth while still hiding the scary stuff. It kept me from feeling vulnerable and kept people at a distance, which left me utterly alone. Alina had been the only one ever to call me on my shit. I felt an ache starting in my heart. I wanted to let Emil in, but the thought of exposing myself in such a way left me riddled with crippling fear. So in the moment, I decided to be a coward for a bit longer. Maybe soon I would be strong enough to let him love me and to fully love him in return.

I stood and stared at the slate path. It stretched out in wondrous smoky shades of gray, the red clays of the earth and the beautiful oranges only autumn could bring. Even in the darkness, the stone carried my eyes forward. I was amazed how the stone shone in the blackness. Every twenty feet or so, the walkway had a step up framed with a black wrought-iron archway, covered with thick and rich star jasmine vinery. Each tiny five-point flower popped out like a shining star against the luscious greenery of the Oregon forest.

There must have been fifteen acres surrounding the house. Most of it was manicured gardens. The path twisted through the property, giving me a tour of all the beauty I would be surrounded by every day. The more I walked, the less I missed my house in town. I knew that had been his purpose. I smiled knowing he had done all this to help me cope. It was way too much and a marvelous gesture, one I was so grateful for.

I knew Emil had picked each flower. Flowers had meaning. How long had he been watching me? I loved flower gardens. It was probably safe to say they were my happy place. Well, gardens and taking hikes through the woods. And here he had given me both happily coupled together, guiding me to my new home.

We walked under archways of the dainty white flowers over and over. White jasmine was a symbol of attachment. With each archway we walked beneath, his smile grew, as if he were getting away with something. His joy was adorable, and the fact he couldn't hide it was precious. I loved being the cause of his loss of control. Emil didn't seem like a person who lost control often or smiled and laughed much. I had a hard time understanding why doing something for me pleased him so.

As we got closer to the house, I saw it was bordered with creeping juniper evergreens mixed with strikingly tall spiraling evergreens. Spread out at their bases, as if to keep them warm and tucked in, were tiny, bright-red, ground-covering rose bushes. Waves of cherry-colored petals carried the green plants as if they were floating on a sea of blood. Part of me thought I should find this disturbing, but I enjoyed the irony of it. Blood had a new meaning for me. It no longer signified injury or death, but life. I needed others' blood to live. In particular, Alina's. It was a surprise how fast I was growing okay with that fact.

My eyes scanned over the rose petals, while I listened to their chimes ringing sweetly. I took my time letting the music of the surrounding nature serenade me. With each new note, my eyes would try to find the source. I heard a low bass vibrating richly. It was a pitch my ears had never heard. Mesmerized, my attention swept to the emerald, sky-reaching evergreens. With so much life calling on my newfound connection with the elements, I would've forgotten about the house, had Emil not put the evergreens right where he had. Their placement was perfect because as I lost myself listening to the low, soothing beats, my eyes drifted up right to the front door of my new home. That's when I remembered why I was here. A bigger smile etched across my face, and Emil laughed at me.

"What?" I was a bit breathless due to my perma-grin.

"Nothing, love, I just knew the plants and flowers would give you peace. I didn't know they would put you in a trance. I'm happy to see you relaxed, or I guess 'sedated' would be more accurate." He sniggered and then continued, "I never in my wildest dreams thought you would forget about the house."

"Hey, I didn't forget. I was only admiring the…view." It was worth a try, but it only made him laugh harder.

"Come on, I want to show you the rest." He reached for my hand. I was more than happy to take his. As I took his hand, my own laughter crawled out of my throat and danced over my lips. The sound of my cheer echoed in the darkness, reminding me I didn't laugh enough either, and we both should laugh more. I hoped we could be that for each other.

He led me the rest of the way up the stairs to the porch with a very gentle pull of the hand. Slowly he wrapped his long, strong arms around me in a tight embrace. Even though I was tallish for a woman, I fit perfectly into him. I leaned in, giving myself over to him and the laughter. I let him hug and pet me as the roars of joy continued. The laughter felt good. Sadly, it didn't stop me from feeling overwhelmed by all that had happened. It wasn't only the pain but the happiness too. I wanted to cry because I was happy. I had never felt so content in all my life. It felt pathetic, like until this moment, my whole life had been wasted. It was sad to learn I had never really felt anything close to real joy, and that made me want to weep. I was also excited to find out what would happen. I felt hope like never before. True, I wasn't happy with every-thing, but it seemed there was more good than bad in this new life.

"You shouldn't have" was all I managed before I felt like I had no more breath to speak. A moment of grief struck when it occurred to me that my heart should be racing with excitement, my breath should be quick in antici-pation, and my cheeks should be flushed red. I longed for the involuntary re-actions that meant I was human. I missed the sensations. I let the longing slip away as fast as it came. I knew I would get used to my new body soon enough, and I might be happier for it. I turned my head up to gaze at Emil.

Emil ran a strong hand over my cheeks, first the left, then the right, as if he were wiping away tears. It was clear, even though I wasn't crying or having a physical reaction, he knew what I was going through. It was nice not having to explain everything; he just knew. I smiled at him.

He spoke to me in a soft, gentle whisper. "Phenice, this house is your new home. I would've happily welcomed you into my caste, to stay at the manor with the others, with me. Sadly, some didn't want Alina there. I could've forced it, but I prefer to rule in peace. I didn't want there to be any resentment, for you or her, or for them. What I never imagined was you gaining as much control over your powers as you have. I didn't fathom you becoming mistress to most in the caste this soon, or I wouldn't have placed you so far from me."

"So take it back," I said, looking into his eyes. I said it more because I didn't feel worthy of his gift, not because I was ready to live with him; I wasn't ready to live with anyone. Honestly, I needed the distance. I needed it so I could adjust. I had never lived with anyone in my adult life. Especially a man.

"This isn't up for discussion, Phenice. It is my gift to you, one I am happy to give. It will help you adjust, and it didn't cost me anything. Please, just say yes." The way the word *please* fell from his lips made me want to give him anything he asked of me. It also felt like he could read my mind, and it wasn't the first time. He knew I needed space. I am sure this wouldn't be the last time he knew what I needed before I even did. What was a woman supposed to do with that?

"It doesn't look cheap," I replied because it was the easiest thing to place emphasis on.

"It is real, Phenice, as real as any house you have ever seen, but it is magic," he said petting my cheeks again, but with both hands this time. His left hand came toward my mouth as he used his thumb to caress my bottom lip.

I stood lost in his touch. I was finding it hard to speak as he teased my lip. It caused a fire to erupt between my thighs. I let out a breathy laugh. Pleased that some involuntary physical responses survived the transformation. Who needed to blush anyway?

It took me a few minutes to think past the reaction he was causing me before I could speak.

"Okay," I purred. "I accept." I grinned at him, knowing his touch would cause me to surrender to anything he could ever want from me. I may not feel worthy, but he thought I was, and that was more than enough for now.

"Could you do me a favor though?" I asked.

"Yes, of course. What would you have of me?" he whispered next to my ear after dropping his lips next to it.

I shuddered. I lost my request for a moment. When I recalled what I was going to ask, it came out husky and broken as I stumbled over the words. "Please, uh, please…stop calling it a house. You could, um, fit ten of my houses…in there," I managed to slur.

He only smiled and nodded. He then continued to explain how the magic worked. "Dante and I came up with the design. We could both tell from your home you loved the Victorian style. We tried to cater both the inside and outside to your likings. I knew you loved roses, and with your new elemental powers, the gardens will be tranquil, calming in times of need. After it was all mapped out, we gave the design to Amora, and she conjured it into reality."

"She conjured this? How?" I knew the shock had to show on my face.

"Magic. She is an enchantress. She can take a picture or a concept in her mind and turn it into life, or reality if you will. She uses portals and the power of manifestation. It is one of the reasons the queen made her. The main reason, really, but the queen did find use for her other gifts. Her powers to control, manipulate, and create love were used for evil deeds by the queen. Amora hated her for what she made her do. Amora truly has a kind heart. Her powers cut both ways, you see. She has never been able to make someone love her absolutely without loving them to some extent in return, causing her to feel the pain of everyone she was made to destroy. With each conquest the queen sent her on, Amora lost a piece of herself, a piece of her soul. That is how I knew she would help us escape. Had she not agreed, we would all still be at the queen's mercy. It was her blindness to love that gave Amora the advantage. The queen has never understood love for the gift and the curse it can be."

"How did Amora use love against her?" I was enraptured by the story. I found myself hanging on every word as Emil continued to pet the features on my face. It was like he was trying to make up for lost time. I didn't mind at all.

"That is a long story for another day. Let me take you to see your new home…mistress." He chortled as he called me "mistress."

"Are you submitting?" I smiled.

"No. Unless you have something else in mind." His eyes stormed full of silver, and my mind flashed to images of him tied down so I could have my way with him. I shook my head. He was still talking, and I missed it all.

"You are the mistress of this *estate* though, and you are mistress to my master, for now anyway." He laughed slightly as he kissed my forehead. It was like he knew exactly what images his words conjured in my mind. He released his hold on me. I finally looked around at the classic Queen Anne porch where we now stood, and I couldn't help but smile. I already loved it.

There were bay windows popping out of the structure here and there. Turrets adorned the top level, along with at least a half dozen balconies. I had a cupola on the east side of the house, my own *little* watchtower. It was my belvedere. Something told me from the size of the house, it wouldn't be little at all.

I looked west down the porch. It had the illusion of endlessness. I turned my gaze to the east, and it felt the same. I was enthralled. I couldn't wait to explore its bounty, but for now I had to give in to Emil and his wishes. I turned to face the large front doors. There, meeting my gawking eyes, were two massive doors. Within the hand-carved wooden frames, a design of leaded art glass depicted the glory of the goddess Hestia. A ring of fire burned all around her in every shade of red, orange, and yellow imaginable. Her hair cascaded throughout both doors, each strand was a flame all its own, licking at her flesh and gown. She was the Greek goddess of home and hearth, meant to protect all within. She was known to induce potent ease and serenity. She was able to manipulate architecture—which I found humor in having her image on the front doors of a magically created home. She was also known for manipulating order. What a wonderful way to be greeted every time I came home. I felt peace knowing she would be watching over Alina and me. I stood frozen as I tried to take her in.

Emil noticed. "I thought it would be a lovely reminder of who you are, of where you have been. She is part of you, tied to the Eudora within."

I didn't know what to say. I stood staring at Hestia and nodded my head, hoping he understood how grateful I was.

"It's open. You can go in." As simple as that, Emil had told me to enter my new home.

I felt as though I should've been shaking with nerves, but I was as steady as a rock. I reached for the bronze knob that I only found because it was where it belonged. It blended in among the rich chocolate door with its beautiful hand-carved flames. Once I felt the cold metal in my hand, I turned it to the left, and with a small click, the door released. I pushed the door open and entered my home for the first time.

At once the house spoke to me. Welcoming me home like the comfort of a warm fire on a cold winter's night, while I snuggled under my favorite quilt, reading a great book with a hot cup of tea. I sensed Hestia had truly blessed this place. I let the feeling take me over, and I couldn't help but smile as a warm breeze danced around me, bringing a slight giggle from my lips. Without meaning to, I brought fire to me. I looked down, and I was glowing again. I studied my body. I had tiny flames dancing under my flesh. I gasped once I understood what I was seeing. I turned to Emil for an explanation.

Emil had taken a small step back. Was he nervous?

"I won't burn you." I told him. I knew I had enough control over the fire within. I would only burn someone if it were my true intention.

He reached out, staring at my hand. When he placed his hand in mine, I let the flames travel safely into his flesh. His head snapped up leering into my eyes.

Surprised, he spoke. "I feel it. The heat feels wonderful. It reminds me of being human. To feel the heat of life flowing through my body." He continued to stare at me in awe. I loved the look in his eyes. I loved it even more knowing I was the one who put it there.

I held on to his hand and turned my attention back to the details of the house. I was standing in the foyer on oak wood floors in a deep shade of chocolate. The ceiling stretched three floors high and was outlined with thick, strong wooden beams. I tried to take it all in. We stood there holding hands while my eyes floated down from the ceiling to the second floor's exposed catwalk guarded by a hand-carved oak railing in the same chocolate. The railing reached out far and then curved around, forming two staircases leading down to the entry, right to where I was standing. At the base of each staircase was a colossal wooden pillar encasing a beautiful bronze lamp that lit the foyer in a fiery glow. The light lit the area under the open walkway, revealing there was much more to the room than just the two curved staircases.

Once I could manage, I blinked and asked Emil the first thing that came to my mind. "Why are there two staircases?"

"There is the main house straight ahead under the walkway, including the kitchen and the dining, family, living, and hearth rooms. There is a space for entertaining, a library, a study, and multiple bathrooms. On the second floor, off the back of the walkway between the two staircases, you have several guest rooms. The staircase to the left leads to the west wing and Alina's part of the house. The staircase to the right leads to the east wing and your part of the house." He gestured with his free hand as he explained.

I couldn't help but laugh.

"What?" He said in response to my outburst. He was from another place and time. He didn't understand why I found this absurd.

"Emil, houses don't need wings. How can Alina and I possibly utilize all this space?" I stated.

Once he understood, he explained. "Five hundred years ago, people spent most of their time at home, only traveling away maybe a few times a year."

Looking at it in his context made more sense. To prevent cabin fever, it would help to have many places to travel to feel like you were somewhere different every day.

"I think *houses* have changed drastically over the last five hundred years, Emil. They are much smaller now, as I am sure you have noticed. That being said, I love it. As long as I don't have to clean it." I laughed.

He smiled in return. "I understand we are from different times, but we never know what the future holds. You may need the space at some point. And the nice thing about this conjured home—it never needs cleaning. Hestia manipulates order…remember? The goddess's power will keep the place clean."

I busted out laughing, again. "Now I love it more!" I traded his hand for wrapping my arms around him. I pushed my flames through him where our bodies touched. He quivered in response.

He leaned down and kissed my lips, then pulled away too soon as he said, "Do you want to explore the rest?"

My mind immediately thought about exploring the rest of him, but I knew he meant the house.

"Yes, I do." I beamed, still thinking of exploring his body.

I think he realized my mind was in the gutter when he asked with a smirk on his face, "What would you like to see first?"

He was wondering if I would be bold enough to say *you*, but I wasn't. Instead, I said, "How about we start small?"

"Would you like to see the east wing, your part of the house? Then when you feel more up to it, you can go exploring on your own," he inquired.

I felt like an open book because I was sure my bedroom would be in this east wing. Butterflies took over my stomach at the thought of Emil naked in a bed. I shivered slightly trying to shake that thought out of my head.

It was obvious he wanted to make my transition as easy as possible. He wanted me to be okay with being a vampire. I knew he felt responsible, even though it was fated and out of his control. There was nothing he could've done, but here he was, trying to fix it, trying to ease my pain. The anticipation filled his eyes, the eagerness to wash away all my pain swarmed around him like a hurricane about to pull him under and drown him. I realized in that moment I needed to save him from himself. If I didn't, he was going to lose himself in an unnecessary task. I didn't need him to take care of me, at least not in the ways he felt he needed to. All I wanted from him was, well, *him*. I could handle everything else.

"Emil, I would like very much to see my part of the house. Actually, it would be lovely." And that was the truth.

His face lit with a small smile as he leaned closer to me and placed a light kiss on my lips. His mouth parted slightly, enough to permit his hot breath to flood into me. Fervor ran up through me from between my legs, making me feel as if I might burn alive right there.

He pulled away, untangling himself from me. "Welcome home," he said as he went to close the door.

Chapter 29

PASSION

We had walked up the right staircase to the east wing. At the top we turned right and passed through a pair of glass French doors. The doors led to a richly decorated sitting room. The furniture and art matched the era that inspired the home, Victorian. Three of the walls were lined with bookshelves, ready for me to fill. The sofas and chairs were covered with a soft monochrome floral print, in shades of whites, creams, and muted gold tones. All the walls were painted a vibrant buttercream except the south wall, which included windows from ceiling to floor. The windows overlooked the view of the east gardens. Hanging at both ends of the wall of glass were long, thick antique-white drapes with a meandering crimson-paisley print. They would provide privacy and darkness when pulled.

The massive fireplace was the focal point, with a hand-carved wooden mantel climbing to the ceiling. A fire was already dancing in the hearth. The room was tranquil. I could see myself sitting in here for hours, daydreaming or reading. The space felt relaxing and cozy. He and Dante had done an amazing job. They had taken my small hearth room off my kitchen and magnified it, creating a room grander than my imagination would have had been able to manifest. I already saw myself in the space. It would feel like home in no time.

"It's beautiful."

Emil smiled as I grabbed his hand.

"Thank you."

"There is so much more," he said. "What would you like to see?"

"My bedroom. It has always been a sanctuary for me, no matter where I have lived. I would like to see it more than any other room, please," I told him. As a child my bedroom was my one true escape. Still to this day, when life was hard, that was the room I would always retreat to.

"Of course." Without another word we moved through the sitting room and into a corridor. There were doors to the left, but I didn't know what they were. I would explore some other time.

At the end of the corridor was a set of engraved double wooden doors. Emil stopped and waved me past him with a sweep of his hand and a slight bow of his head. The small grin on his face couldn't be missed. He was excited to share this with me. I did as he gestured and stepped past him. I grabbed both knobs and turned, pushing them open.

My reaction couldn't be contained. My jaw dropped. Followed by a shit-eating grin that must've consumed my whole face. My elation had to be obvious. I couldn't contain it, and for Emil's sake, I didn't want to.

The ceiling had to be at least sixteen feet tall and had the same thick, dark crown molding as the rest of the house. The walls were painted a deep red, deeper than the red in my old bedroom. I loved it. There was a fire blazing in the hearth in here as well. Just like the other hearth, the mantel climbed all the way to the ceiling. The difference was this one wasn't only wood. It was adorned with wrought-iron inlay, molded to look like vining roses climbing the wood all the way to the ceiling. It had to be some of the most stunning artwork I had ever seen anywhere, and he had placed it in my bedroom. Love bloomed in my heart. I knew without a doubt I had loved this man since the beginning of time.

Forcing myself to continue to take in the room, I turned in a slow circle. Large bay windows sat on both the south and north sides of the room, giving me a view of both the garden in front of the house and the river that ran behind the house. I couldn't believe it. I walked about halfway into my new bedroom so I could get a better look, and that's when I saw the door to the southeast corner.

"Emil, where does that door lead?" I thought I knew, but I wanted him to tell me.

"That door leads to your cupola, my love." I was so excited.

I knew from up there I would be able to see the entire grounds. I could only imagine how beautiful it was going to be.

He sensed my happiness and walked toward me. "You also have a pair of French doors off your bathroom that leads to a wraparound balcony, providing you with a view of the north, east, and south sides of your estate, my love."

I laughed, loudly and abruptly. Emil was pleased by my response, and as much as I wanted to contain myself, it wasn't possible.

I continued my slow circle, trying to see everything. The bed was a huge four-poster with a set of small steps leading up to the bed. The room was absolutely perfect. I turned back so I was facing the fire, lost in my astonishment, trying to find the words to tell him how much I loved it all.

I was about to attempt an expression of my extreme emotions when Emil came up behind me. He wrapped his arms around my body, pressing his chest and abdomen into my back. Everything stopped. My body became still and motionless. The sound of the fire cracking in the hearth vanished. All that was left was him. The color had drained from the room, leaving it black and white, dead, and meaningless, compared to the warmth and emotion radiating from the embrace holding me where I stood.

Musk, rosewood, and lavender filled me. I sighed, losing control. I turned in his arms and lifted my eyes to his. His eyes were lit midnight purple. Lust filled me. I'm sure it was motivated by love, but in that moment, lust poured through me. It had been so long since I had been with anyone.

His lips parted, not for speech but in anticipation. He scented me, and his heart quickened briefly then stopped again. The sound of its rhythm excited me. I felt alive.

A thought told me I should wait. Too much had changed too fast. There was so much I had learned about my new existence. So much I still needed to learn. I didn't think I could handle all of it, but as I stood there in his arms, feeling him, the excitement and the passion raging within me, I challenged my inner restraint. I had nearly died. I was in hiding because I was being hunted. I was feeding from my best friend. And my whole world had been flipped upside down. What was I waiting for exactly? I was only torturing myself. Feeling unworthy.

Fuck waiting.

I jumped in the air, wrapping my long legs around his strong, lean torso. His face was between my hands, and the feeling of his silky cashmere beard sent electric shocks up my arms. His eyes went wide briefly before they filled with so much need. Even though my movements were quick and animalistic, when I pressed my lips to his, the kiss was soft and gentle, warm and wet. He tasted divine.

He held me tight to him but with so much care as if I were fragile. He caressed my back as he walked us toward the middle of the room. I continued to kiss and taste him. The more familiar I became with his smell and taste, the more I craved him. What had started off as gentle led to deep, uncontrollable passion. I nearly climbed inside of him as my tongue explored his mouth. My hands slid through his thick hair.

He took a step up, then another, followed by two more. I realized he was climbing the stairs leading to the bed. I didn't protest; instead I heard my internal monologue screaming, *Oh, yes please*, as a moan escaped my mouth and invaded his.

I had anticipated him kneeling once he reached the bed, but instead he walked up on the mattress with me in his arms, standing tall with me wrapped around him. He kept one arm wrapped tightly around me, bracing me, while the other slid under my sweater in one fluid motion. Like magic, my top was gone, in the blink of an eye. Chills ran through me as I rested topless in his embrace, exposed to him. He paused.

"My love, is this what you want?"

A smile crossed my lips, seductive and eager as I said, "If you even think of stopping, I'll have to kill you."

That brought laughter from deep within him. His rumble vibrated across my sex, making me ache for him more. He threw me on the bed. I landed with a bounce on the soft, luxurious mattress. I was elated to have the first feel of my new bed be from love and passion and not simply sleep. This was so different from my old life; I didn't feel alone. My smile grew from this connection, from his laughter, and from love for my new life.

Emil kneeled between my legs. His strong hands working on my boots, socks, jeans, and panties. It only took him seconds to remove what had taken me minutes to put on that morning. I was lying before him, naked. He was fully dressed. I longed to see and touch him.

If I had still been human, my mouth would have been dry. I would be short of breath out of fear and self-consciousness. Since I wasn't, I was calm and eager as I waited for him.

I was lost in my passion, lust rushing through my veins. I smiled up at him for many reasons. One, because I knew I loved him. Two, I was grateful to be a vampire. The realization shocked the hell out of me. It gave me confidence to lie there and allow him to view me naked, leaving me unembarrassed. I felt free in a way I never had.

"Phenice, my love, you are truly a vision." He couldn't help but stare at me, a devilish smile on his lips.

I had waited long enough. I wanted to see him. "Thank you, Emil. I think I could say the same about you, but the simple fact is, my sweet, you are still dressed," I stated with a suggestive smile.

"Oh, don't worry. I won't be for long. I am not going to be able to wait much longer before I devour every luscious inch of you." His sinister expression made me open my legs farther wanting to be taken.

Exposing and offering myself to him brought a growl from his mouth. The sound made my insides throb to be touched, for release. I could feel myself growing wet looking at him fully clothed. The way he looked at me made my body ache in the most delicious ways.

My eyes danced over his tall, sculpted frame as he stood up from between my legs slowly. His boots were gone. I didn't know when he took them off, and I didn't care. I was busy peering into his eyes, daring him to devour me.

I could feel my spirit at my core warming, growing bright with my love and desire for him. I could see it with my eyes, glowing with a brilliant white shimmer deep within my core. It swirled within me, consuming all my body. It wanted out.

I kept my attention on him as he continued to stare deep within me. Emil unbuttoned his midnight-black shirt and tossed it to the floor, giving me the first glimpse of his chest and abdomen. My spirit began to pulse with light, and I knew now it was reacting to my love and passion for this man. He was strong and well defined. His muscles were thick, sculpted, and corded. He was breathtaking. Exactly how you would expect a god to look. His hands fell toward his jeans. Automatically, I sat up to help him. I wanted to touch him.

He stopped me by waving at me as though I was being naughty. "You, my goddess, must stay as you are."

I fell back. "As you wish." I wanted to touch—true—but I could wait because watching him was a blissful torture I could learn to crave.

My body grew hotter and more eager with each movement he made. It had been so long, so, so long. I felt like I was coming undone. The truth was I had only had sex a few times in my whole life. I had never been comfortable being close to someone like this. I wondered why I wasn't nervous or scared due to my inexperience. Maybe I had avoided intimacy because some part of me was waiting for him. Maybe I didn't have any fear or reservations because I was made for this man as he was made for me. Instead, I felt happy, relaxed, and ready to do anything with this stunning creature before me.

Emil stepped out of his jeans. He was now naked and completely exposed to me. Flames of energy from my spirit went dancing across my skin in a clear crystalline white. Emil smiled.

"Watching your joy and desire burn within your skin might be the most perfect thing I have ever seen. And it might be the death of me." He growled.

He dropped to his hands and knees and crawled around me. I was the prey to his predator. The lioness in me hated it—she wanted to pounce on him—but the woman in me loved it. I wanted my soulmate to devour me. He stopped, hovering over my face, and then lowered slowly to kiss me deep and hard. His mouth was so hot and moist. I had to touch him. I reached up and ran my hand through his long, thick mahogany hair. He let out a moan, and it echoed down my throat. Hungry for more, I pulled him to me. It was something more than kissing. I could feel our souls wrapping around each other, merging. The white light from within me started to pour into his mouth and deep within his being.

Moments later he tugged away, drunk with laughter. Still on his knees, he straddled my waist, resting the hardness of his shaft on my navel, making my back arch so high I thought my spine would snap. He caressed both hands down the sides of my face, pausing to trace my lips with a finger. There was fire and love in his fingertips. Everywhere he touched me left orange flames dancing above my skin, licking his flesh. I had never felt anything like it.

I never took my eyes from his. I was amazed at how deep and dark they had turned. The color was so rich, such a dark plum they almost appeared black. His hands continued to make a path of warmth on my body, leaving my face and traveling to my neck until they were on my breasts. There, he paused to play with me, pinching each nipple lightly. I gasped and moaned. Had his strong legs not been pinning me down, I might have tried to crawl away from the intense pleasure. He leaned forward pressing himself harder into my belly, causing wet heat to drip down my thighs.

I could smell him. My head spun. His scent was rich and warm, intoxicating. I wasn't used to smell being something with so much power, so seductive. I started breathing in and out. I had to smell him. His arousal added a touch of spice to his normal heady and alluring scent. He was scenting me too. I briefly wondered what I smelled like to him, and how I smelled differently now that I was dripping wet with need.

Emil lowered himself down and placed his mouth to my skin, starting at my neck. Chills ran throughout my body. He chuckled and growled with pleasure. He slowly worked his way down to my breasts; another moan poured from my mouth. It felt like breathing fire. I lost it. He had to hold me down, not forcefully but just enough so he could taste me. I wiggled and cried out while he feasted on the flesh I was offering. He tasted all he could with his ruby blood-filled lips and wet, skilled tongue.

He nibbled, sucked, and bit all along my breasts and nipples, all while wet fire continued to drop between my folds and down my thighs. I never knew anything could feel this good and torturous at the same time. He tasted all my body, working his way down my navel, only to skip over the apex screaming to be touched and licked. He dropped down to my legs and started kissing and licking up and down the length of them.

When I couldn't take it anymore, I begged. "Please, Emil. For fuck's sake… I need more of you, *now*. This is torture. *Please*," I cried with unbridled need.

I saw the twisted glimmer of joy in his eyes when his head popped up from my legs, thanks to my desperate pleading. I didn't care as long as it worked. He crawled up to me stopping at my knees.

"Please what, my love?" He was having so much fun. Passion filled the room.

I smiled. "I need you. I want you. Please," I whispered because my moans of pleasure had left my voice strained.

He reached out with his hands, spreading my legs. Then slowly ran a couple of his fingers up one of my thighs, sliding through the collected wetness he had inspired. Smiling, he brought them to his mouth and sucked my juices from them. His eyes fluttered closed momentarily. When his eyes snapped open again, the darkness was swirling with silver storm clouds. His desire poured from him in waves of heat.

"I must taste you fully, Phenice. Then you can have all of me." His voice was low and husky, more of a growl, filled with need.

Before I could beg or protest, Emil grabbed my thighs, spreading them wide, completely exposing the most vulnerable part of my body. In an instant he was flat on his stomach between my legs, running his tongue up each thigh cleaning up the mess he inspired to run down my legs.

I cried with desperation. I was ready to yank his head to where I needed him most. I started to plead again, right as his mouth came down and buried deep between my folds. Instantly he was licking and sucking up my wetness like a man starved. As he pulled my nerve bundle into his mouth, I screamed in ecstasy.

My orgasm was explosive. I could feel myself filling his mouth as he greedily drank every drop of me down. I wanted to beg for mercy. It felt so good it was nearly painful. I would've never reached this point without all the tortuous touch he started with.

My body jerked and convulsed with each flick of his tongue. When I thought I couldn't burn any hotter, Emil slipped two long, strong fingers deep inside me as a deep groan rumbled from his throat vibrating along my center. Another orgasm swallowed me whole. He curled his fingertips up and pumped them steadily into my body in rhythm with the licks and flicks of his tongue. I couldn't help myself as I pushed my body down on his fingers and ground down against his mouth. Finally, a scream so loud tore from my lips, I thought my lungs would rupture.

On my way down from my orgasmic high, I fell limply back into the bed, unable to move. Emil lifted his body up to take me in. His face was gleaming with the evidence of my pleasure. It coated his lips and beard. I took the whole man in as he licked his lips then wiped his chin. His eyes were twin pools of burning lust and desire. I let my eyes slip down his body, and once they feasted on the hard length of him, the burning desire erupted within me again.

I was going to combust if he didn't let me have him. As if he could read my mind, he slid up my body, nestling his hips between my thighs. With his eyes locked on mine, he slid his cock slowly yet fully, all the way in me, in one gentle, penetrating thrust.

Stars swam in my vision from the impact of how full I felt. My breath caught. He wrapped his arms around me, nuzzling his mouth next to my ear.

"Are you okay, my dove?" The rumble of his voice sent shivers down my spine. And him calling me dove meant something, but I was so high I couldn't recall.

"I am so beyond okay, Emil. Please, don't stop," I pleaded breathlessly.

"Anything for you, my dove…always," he whispered, as he started to slide in and out of my wetness, slowly at first.

My body opened more fully to him with each passing stroke. My walls grew wetter and more eager. I needed more. I could feel another release coming.

We were tangled up in each other. Emil began to pick up speed, and the moans, whimpers, and cries poured as helplessly from my mouth as the wetness dripped from between my folds coating him.

Sensing I was close due to my body starting to quiver and my whimpers growing louder, Emil's rhythm picked up. He went even deeper and faster. He began to moan as the sounds of his pelvis slapping mine filled the room.

"Fuck…Phenice, you are the death and rebirth of me." His voice was raspy with desire.

As if he couldn't help himself anymore, he lifted his upper body over me, grabbed my legs and pulled them over the tops of his hips, changing the angle. I was staring into his eyes when he wrapped his big hands around my hips and started slamming my pelvis down in time with his forward thrust.

I screamed from the intensity of the pleasure and pressure. I felt as if I was going to explode from the magnitude of sensations invading all of me. He moaned as he picked up his pace. I felt another climax begin to build deep inside my body. Then a light exploded from my core, encasing us both in what looked like starlight. White flames sprang up, dancing from my skin to his. As soon as the white flame ignited us both, Emil lost his steady rhythm. He became desperate. Within seconds we exploded in pleasure together, sending the starlight and white flames out from our bodies to engulf the entire room.

In a blink the flames slammed back into us with a flash of light, and then they disappeared.

Emil fell to the bed beside me, slowly sliding out of my body. He scooped me up in his arms and laid me on his chest. I could hear both of our hearts pounding, and our breathing was labored from the force of our ecstasy. I wondered how long our bodies would hold on to this human reaction.

Laughter erupted from Emil's lips. "Phenice, I have been longing for you. I waited for you, my dove. You are mine, my mate, and the other half of my soul." He ran his hand through my hair with so much love and longing.

I felt it too. I also remembered where I had heard "dove" before. Xenres had called Eudora his dove. My heart lit up. They were reunited through us. I hoped it created peace somewhere in the universe. I prayed our story would have a better ending this time.

Whatever had happened with the starlight and the white flames had tied us together. It had melded us into a completed whole in some way I didn't understand. I didn't know if I would ever understand what happened or if it would ever happen again, but I felt something click into place. He was mine. I was his. He was my mate. The other half of my soul. And he would always keep me tethered.

"I know, Emil. I felt it too. I feel you here." I placed my hand above my heart. "As if you make me whole. You are what I have been missing."

He pulled me closer and rubbed his fingers up and down my back while I tried not to sabotage the most perfect moment of my life.

We were lying there holding each other, and damn we were messy. To be honest, probably the messiest I had ever been. I loved it. I wanted him again, and from the feel of him against me, he felt the same. I prayed for many more nights like this one.

Right as I was about to initiate round two, I started to feel dizzy. Vertigo slammed into me fast. I knew instantly I needed blood.

The infinity necklace, my first gift from Emil, was the only thing I was still wearing. I was so close to his neck. His heart was still beating from our lovemaking. I could hear the slow steady beat of it. I could feel the strong, bounding pulse thrusting under his beautiful skin. It was his blood I wanted. As far as I knew, he wouldn't sustain life for me, but it felt right. I played with the pendent hanging close to my breasts, and I slowly slipped the small knife from its gold sheath. Without hesitation I slammed it straight into his jugular.

I felt his shock as I put my mouth over his wounded neck and drank from him for the first time.

I came upon a bonfire. I could see Emil and his caste, Custos and Alina, in a clearing surrounded by a deep, dense green forest. I could smell the moss. Their sadness wafted in the air, consuming the darkness, as the wind carried their grief into the world. I knew their pain would infect everyone that breeze would touch. It made me sad to know how many would grow with despair and not have an answer for their pain. I wanted to know what had caused so much pain among the ones I cared for.

As I focused on the vision, I saw Emil and Custos weren't among the grieving. Custos stood stoic. Emil was brooding and angry, but it wasn't grief. Something else plagued his mind and thoughts. He was encased in a physical darkness, darker than the moonless night; I kept losing sight of him as the shadows swarmed and wafted around his body, ready to swallow him. Even lost in the eerie shadows, he seemed hopeful for something the others could not see. I wanted to know what was going on.

I stopped looking at the people and began to look around. They had gathered in a circle around the bonfire. Off to the side was a pile of herbs, timber, and something else I couldn't make out. It reminded me of the ritual I witnessed as I relived my past life as the wise woman. Right in front of Custos and Emil was an urn filled with a moderate amount of ash. Fear pricked my heart.

"Phenice, what the hell!" Emil screamed.

Emil was bleeding badly. I placed my hand over the wound and called earth and water to me. Then I panicked for a moment. Would this work on a vampire like it had with Alina? Before the doubt could even fully blossom in my mind, my spirit lit up in a soothing light, providing peace. I knew his wound was gone and his blood replenished.

"Oh…" He was staring at me, more like staring into me.

"I'm sorry. It felt like the right thing to do." I panicked. I didn't know what else to say.

I was afraid I had hurt him both physically and emotionally. I'd crossed a boundary I shouldn't have. I didn't ask permission. I just took, reflexively. Would he ever forgive me? I was scared he would never forgive me.

"Did you see?" That wasn't what I expected him to say.

"See what?" I asked.

"I saw us standing around a pile of ash. Did you see it too?" He seemed anxious, but not mad.

"Yes, I saw it, but I have no clue what it means." I felt calmer since he didn't seem mad. Was he excited?

"You shared my power through drinking my blood; you became a Fate Seer." He informed me. I didn't know what to do. I couldn't read how he was feeling.

"Permanently?" I forced myself to keep talking. I didn't want more power to control.

"I don't think so. I believe it only lasted during the exchange. I'm sorry for my shock. No one knew it was possible. We never drink from our own kind. It does not keep us alive. What did you feel? How did you know to drink my blood?" I relaxed a bit, knowing I didn't have more power to manage, and he seemed intrigued now, curious.

"I didn't. I had no clue what it would do. Honestly, it felt…right, I guess." I wish I could've told him more, but I really didn't know anymore. At least I didn't think I did. However, something inside of me radiated with knowledge. It was in there somewhere, but for whatever reason, I couldn't touch it. "Whose fate was it? Do you know?"

"I don't know. I usually control the visions, meaning I get to navigate them. That is how I figure out the answers I need or whatever I am seeking. In this situation you were in control of where we went and what we picked out of the vision," he said.

"So we have no idea what we just saw?" I felt like I had missed something huge, something extremely important. Why else would I have gone to that exact moment. It had to be an answer to something. Or a clue to something I needed to understand.

"As far as the vision goes, my dove, it wouldn't have come to us without you, but I don't know how to decipher it. The knowledge of sharing powers is new. No one, to my knowledge, can know what that will mean." His face grew sad and worried toward the end.

"Why? What has you worried, Emil?" I asked, hating his expression.

"If the queen finds out about this, she will be even more deadly than she is now. This is something we can never let happen. She cannot know. This sharing of power may be isolated to you, and if it is, she will want you even more." His eyes grew stormy silver as they wandered off to some distant place. He stayed with me physically, but his mind ventured off. I wondered if he was lost to some painful part of his past, inflicted by this queen, or if he jumped into a vision, seeking answers.

The conversation died. I knew I had lost him to his thoughts, but his arms stayed tight around me, holding me as if he would never let me go. I was grateful for his protectiveness and happy to take comfort in his arms.

So much time had passed. Dawn was approaching. I could feel it, even though I could not yet see it with my eyes. The sun didn't bother me, but still some kind of warning was sounding within me to let me know the large star would be upon me soon.

"So you can heal anyone, it appears." It had been so long since he had said anything that he almost startled me. I had heard him, but I didn't quite listen to what he had said, so I had to think before I could answer.

"Dove, are you okay?" He ran his fingertips down my face, stopping at my chin so he could turn my head to look at him. Once I could see his eyes, dark purple swirling with lavender, I felt happiness run through me.

"I'm sorry, Emil, I didn't catch what you asked." I gave a shy smile, but he returned it with one so lovely that mine grew to match his.

"I was commenting on the fact it appears you can heal both humans and vampires. It's an amazing gift," he informed me.

"I guess I can. I didn't think it would be any different though. Vampires are alive, the same as humans. So why could I not heal them?" I asked.

"It is true, I guess. I just don't feel we deserve such a gift. It felt amazing. I can't even begin to explain it to you." He avowed.

"Alina has said the same thing to me every time. I've had a hard time believing her." I sighed. "It might be my guilt getting in the way."

"You should believe her and let the guilt go. I know why it makes Alina stronger, having experienced it now. You have so much power. You give a small piece of it to the ones you heal. If you had any doubt left about the dynamic of your bond, your relationship, and how it has changed, please let me tell you I am sure she does not suffer." He kept slowly caressing my face and running his fingers through my hair as he spoke. It relaxed me.

I was happy to have him tell me I wasn't causing Alina harm. She has been insisting the same. Maybe it was time I started to believe the ones around me instead of the nagging voice in my head telling me I was no good. That voice was present before I became a vampire. It had been a constant companion who sounded like the voice of my father, if I was honest with myself.

"I feel slightly buzzed still from it. I don't remember the last time I felt anything like this. As a vampire we can't get drunk or high. Alcohol and drugs have no effect on us, but you, Phenice, you are something completely good and different." A slight laugh accompanied his low, rumbling voice.

"Please, Emil, can we talk about something else? I already feel like a freak, and this is not helping." I was feeling uncomfortable for the first time since we came to my room.

It wasn't from the amazing sex or the fact we were both still completely naked and tangled up together. It was because I had stabbed him in the neck, drank his blood, and mind raped him, and though he was initially shocked, he loved it. Emil loving it was the most disturbing part. Disturbing yet interesting. Stabbing my soulmate didn't bother me as much as him liking it. So which of us was more fucked up?

Silence filled the room. It lasted for so long I began to worry I had hurt his feelings. When he spoke, I knew differently.

"Do you know how long I have been waiting, longing to touch you? How hard it has been?" He was holding me tight. I buried my head into his chest and inhaled, scenting him. He was like nothing I had ever known in my entire life. He filled my senses. I exhaled so happily in love, and his scent left behind the taste of lavender honey on my tongue.

I thought about his question before I said a word. I couldn't imagine what he had gone through. I've only waited hours to be here with him like this. He had been waiting months, possibly longer.

I looked up at him and replied. "I don't think I could've been as close to you as you were to me, knowing what you knew, and not have done anything about it. You are so much stronger than me. You went too many months denying yourself this. I only waited hours. I wouldn't have made it." I saw pain growing within him; I could feel it. The bond between us was strengthening.

"Try centuries, Phenice. I remember Eudora, my *dove*. I have carried her with me. The memory of her and that lifetime. Of other lifetimes when our paths crossed. Of what it felt like to have my soul united with another. I longed for it. For the peace of it. Then one day, I passed you. I felt a part of my soul within you. It made me let down my guard, and like water through a broken dam, your future, your destiny, at least pieces of it, came flooding into me." He paused. I caught how he kept calling me dove so I would know he felt the same for me in this lifetime as he did in our past lives. I melted a little every time he said it. He mentioned other lifetimes as well. Did I have lives I didn't relive during the transformation?

"I came to your office simply to talk to you. I became a patient to be near you, to smell you, to hear your voice. I wanted you so fucking bad. My soul burned and ached for you."

Tears started to build in my lower lids.

"I began to follow you so I could protect you from this world, even though I knew maybe if you were like me, a vampire, we could be together, but I didn't want any of this for you. I failed you." The last part was a whisper filled with so much anguish.

"I tortured myself being so close to the one person I so desperately wanted but knew I could never have. You were my sanctuary and my hell. Don't get me wrong, every freaking second was worth it. I would do it for the rest of this cursed life. If I never got to have you, I would've taken that pain forever. I would have taken a life of hell with you in it, rather than a life of nothing… because before you that was what I felt. Absolutely nothing." His voice was rough and torn from his pain.

My tears had silently slid down my face.

"Emil, stop. Shhh." I climbed on top of him, gently grabbing his face between my hands, forcing him to look at me. "The torture is over. You weren't meant to prevent this, any of this. The Fates themselves told me it was meant for me. It's my destiny. You know you can't change that; no one can. The Divine wanted it. I no longer need to be your hell. I don't ever want to be that for you ever again. Let me be your sanctuary. Always." I wanted, needed him to hear me.

"I didn't want this life for you, not for my love, not for my dove." He pulled me closer and buried his face in my hair. "Even if it meant forever without you, I would've surrendered my soul and paid in pain to save you. Dove, this world is cruel. It will try to break you. It will try to ruin you."

I leaned down and kissed him to comfort him and also to silence him. There was no use hashing over something we had no power over, and we couldn't change it.

Though I didn't want whatever the Fates had in store for me, I knew there was no avoiding it. I would go where I must, even if I went reluctantly. I only prayed one day, hopefully sooner rather than later, I would find the courage to face my destiny with bravery.

We lay there in each other's arms. I let him grieve the loss of my human life. I grieved with him. The longer I thought about it, I was grateful to have him. I felt confused why he didn't feel the same. We had eternity together, and shouldn't that make him happy?

"Why, Emil?" I tried not to take it personally. I knew it was about life as a vampire and not me. Nonetheless, it hurt to feel like he didn't want me. It was a painful reminder of days past. Of never truly being wanted by anyone.

"This life, Phenice, it consumes. It devours the goodness inside. It's difficult and painful, bloody even. And the blood of this life should never taint someone like you." He was running his hand through my hair as if to calm me, but he was the one upset.

"I believe we can be exposed to great horrors in life, even as a human; the world was nasty. Yet most of us find a way to survive. We can be strong enough not to be broken by tragedy. I believe through the struggle, there is the ability to learn kindness, love, and joy. I'm not going to let this life, this world, break or soil me, Emil. That's a promise," I whispered to him.

"I hope so." His voice was strained.

"Trust me." I pulled myself higher than him on the bed and wrapped his naked body up in my own. I held him close to me, hoping he could feel the truth in my words the way I did.

I chose to give him proof because I knew I could. I called on the Pythia inside. I closed my eyes and called her name, *Eudora*. We were one and the same, but she still had her own identity. I wanted to honor her life, to respect what she once was. She had earned the right to be remembered and cherished for her courage in her short lifetime.

She came to me. I saw her standing before my closed eyelids with her nutmeg skin; long, dark, wavy hair; and radiant chestnut eyes. Those eyes were all for me, staring straight into me, asking what I needed from her. So I asked, not out loud, but within my own head.

Will this life, this world, taint or break me?

She showed me no images, no scenes as if I were watching a movie. She gave me only knowledge. She smiled at me, then I was filled with the knowledge that I would change. I would be different, stronger, more powerful, but never tainted and definitely not broken. I smiled back at her.

I used my newly discovered Eudorian energy and pushed out the knowledge to Emil.

I opened my eyes to find him lying motionless within my arms. His worry had taken him away from me. His dread was wafting from him in waves.

I let my energy sweep out of me. It swirled around him in a beautiful, sparkling iridescent mist. I watched as the mist turned to a reddish tangerine dust and settled down on his skin. On contact it began to seep into him and vanish deep into his body. He shivered; his body grew hot. His eyes opened. He found me above him still holding on to him. I watched as his eyes widened and transformed from lilac to storm clouds of silver as he became drunk with my power.

I held him in silence letting the knowledge take hold of him.

"You have gotten very strong. Very quickly. I didn't even feel you coming, and I should have." His voice sounded different, deeper, if that was possible. It was also whisper quiet.

I said the only thing I could think of. "I'm sorry. I just wanted you to know."

"Don't be sorry, dove. I want you powerful. I need you powerful. I'm simply amazed." He paused. "Thank you for showing me."

I knew he felt better. I didn't say anything. I slid down in my new jumbo bed until my head was next to his chest, and we were tangled back up in the bed linens. He took my hair into his hands so he could run his long delicate fingers through my locks. He would twist pieces around his fingers, intertwining my hair with his hand. Every once in a while, he would take a tuft up to his nose and inhale. Every time he did, these chills ran down my spine. He had his other arm underneath me, holding me tightly to him, and I knew he wasn't going to let go for some time. I was fine with his plan to stay put. As a matter of fact, my plan was to stay right here in this moment forever.

Chapter 30

RECALL

I walked through an open prairie surrounded by Oregon's rich, mossy evergreen forests close to the location of my estate. I was lost in my thoughts. I was happy. This time, this moment belonged to me. I didn't get much time by myself, and I was grateful for every chance I got. As a human I had always been alone. As a vampire I rarely received any solitude. After everything I had been through, the loss of my privacy was the biggest adjustment.

Months had passed with the caste. Winter had come and gone. Spring was here, and I was enjoying the cool, breezy weather. Time stood still with Emil, as if we were forever locked in our first night together. He demanded to stay uninvolved with my training as much as possible. He wanted to be my lover, not my teacher, and never my master. On a psychological level, it was a wise decision. We were close, and I had fallen completely and madly in love with him. I hoped it would always be so easy.

We did discuss vampire history at times, and he helped me control and fine-tune my powers, but it was always casual and fun. My training consisted of time with Avery, who was a physician and scholar. From my understanding Avery had been born, then made, in the 1600s. Emil had said he was close to the eldest daughter of Galileo and had studied with Galileo after she had died, which I found mind-blowing. I still didn't understand what *close* meant, nor did I know if his studies were when he was human or a vampire, and I didn't have the courage to ask about either situation. Avery was withdrawn and quiet. I understood wanting to have your solitude to maintain your sanity.

What I did know was he had dedicated his immortality to the understanding of vampires and how they differed from humans. He had mountains of books and scrolls dedicated to every subject imaginable. He covered religion and science, and how they pertained to the world of vampires. I loved listening to his theories and the philosophy of our kind. Avery was always excited as he taught me all he knew. It was the only time I saw the man emote. I couldn't help but let his exuberance infect me. The nerd inside of me loved getting lost among the books and scrolls. The smell of the pages gave away how old they were, and it made me feel as if I were being let in on an ancient secret, which I was. A whole world existed that no one knew about, and I found that thrilling, to say the least.

I had shared my dream of Sadeh with him, which I now knew was a vision of what was to come and who was after me. The queen may have forgotten her name over the years, now preferring Lourdes, but it didn't change who or what she was. In my mind she would always be Sadeh because she was not my queen. It was a relief to finally understand the Egyptian queen who had haunted my sleep for so many months. It gave me some closure to make the connections.

One day as I began to describe my reoccurring dream, Avery leaped up from his chair, vanishing into the stacks of the massive library. I kept telling the tale because I knew he could still hear me. Within seconds he returned clutching a thick, old brown tome. I continued retelling the dream as Avery sat making documentation on the thin parchment pages within the tome. His hand moved so fast it blurred. I glanced at the pages, expecting his writing to resemble chicken scratch, but it was far from that. The page was covered in beautiful flowing script. I didn't ask what the book was. It was clear to me it was a log of all he could find about vampires.

After we finished Avery thanked me over and over. I had never seen him show so much emotion. He had never found any information about the original creation of vampires, and finally this small piece of knowledge pleased him immensely.

Avery spent countless hours over the past months filling me in on the histories. The vampire world was bloody, as Emil had warned. It was filled with battles for power with vampires and humans, surprisingly. Many vampires had banded together to overturn the queen, and not one lived to tell the tale. That was why the caste had fled and hid from the queen. They wanted to be free of her, but they also wanted to live. As much as Emil hated what he was, he feared the nothingness awaiting him if he died the True Death even more. I had learned the definition of the True Death for a vampire; it was the inability to be reincarnated again. It was the true loss of our soul's immortality. Though no one can ever really know what happens to vampires after they die, they've discovered not a single human who had been turned recalling a past life as a vampire; therefore, Avery had deduced once a vampire dies, they cannot be reborn, as human or otherwise. The real question remained: Where did the soul of a vampire go after the True Death? This could not be understood.

I learned the queen had started wars with humans to take their lands, and sometimes simply out of boredom. I was shocked to hear how many wars I had learned about in school didn't start as our history books stated. Avery had spoken of the wars with a hint of sadness in his tone. I don't believe he was aware it was there, but it was very apparent to me. I believe his sadness came from the fact humans never stood a chance against an army of vampires, no matter how many soldiers they had.

As the months passed, I noticed a knot growing within me. I knew our world didn't have to be this way, and just because it was our history didn't mean it had to be our future. I felt determined about this. I didn't understand why, but I knew it could be different. I wanted it to be different. Part of me knew someday it would be, but the how was still a mystery.

On my days away from Avery, I trained with Amora and Eden on calling my powers. We worked with the elements to see what I was capable of. We also worked on calling the Eudorian energy, which is what everyone was calling my ability to summon the past and future. I felt it was right to name this ability after its rightful owner. It had been her gift, and now she handed it to me. I was grateful to her for carrying such burdens during her lifetime.

As time went on, my abilities increased. I was good at calling on Eudora. I learned to focus on what I wanted to see, and more than half the time, I was successful. I knew someday I would be able to every time.

We had discovered one day in training I could control what others were able to see, giving me the ability to create illusions. Aidan was elated when I told him of this new ability. He said it had great potential as a weapon. Once I had control of it, I would be able to use it against my enemies, as I had by accident against Eden. As excited as the men were about my progression, I could tell both women feared me. As I grew stronger, so did their fear. I had only practiced with them for about a month before my powers were so overwhelming for them they refused to come near me.

I felt a sense of loss, but I couldn't control how they felt regarding me, so I had to let this go and keep moving forward. Emil was about to order them to continue, but I didn't want to use force. I had already changed the dynamic of the caste, and I didn't want to give them any more reasons to hate or fear me. Admittedly, my first reaction was sadness and rejection, but something kept nagging at me, pushing me forward with a sense of desperation. I couldn't let emotions slow me down; there was something critically important waiting in my near future.

When I started to practice with Aidan and Dante, I realized they could teach me much more, and much faster. They were stronger, and they found my powers exciting instead of terrorizing, which was encouraging. It did make me wonder what had been done to Amora and Eden while they were in the queen's keep. I wondered if they simply feared me because I was a strong female and somehow I reminded them of her. I hoped this dynamic would resolve with time as they got to know me better.

As I walked through the prairie thinking of time past, the wind blew warm across the land. It caressed my skin like a lover's fingers. It made me miss Emil, but I'd see him soon enough. I needed to be alone for a while. I found the field tranquil and quiet. After living alone for so long, these past months had been a challenge at times.

The warm breeze continued pulling my thoughts back to Aidan and Dante. They had taught me how to use my powers more completely. In the beginning I was able to commune with all the elements, and when I was emotionally charged, I'd pull the elements from my environment and use them. I feared I might not be able to stop what I started if the emotions were too strong. I had gotten lucky the night I had challenged Amora and Eden. I was fortunate I had not killed them by accident.

Being pyrokinetic, Aidan was able to teach me how to manifest fire, not simply pull it from the environment. Once it made sense how to do it with fire, the rest of the elements became easy. Now I could start a fire, make the wind blow to spread it, then call a rain shower to extinguish it, and finally call on the earth to regrow the scorched grass and flowers.

I felt like a version of Mother Nature. I could make it snow on a warm day, create rain and small tornados, and pull flowers from the earth. I could focus the elements on one person or many at a time. The first time I created snow, Aidan stood under it with his eyes closed, outstretching his hands, allowing the snow to fall onto his flesh. With each melting flake, his smile grew. I had watched as his tattoos danced under his flesh. I hadn't worked up the courage to ask him about them; one day I would. I did however ask him why he enjoyed my snow, and he told me it reminded him of being human. He divulged my manifested snow had more life to it than real snow, allowing it to penetrate his skin, leaving him slightly chilled, a feeling he hadn't felt since his transformation. I loved providing him with this mild enjoyment. None of my creations lasted very long, but with each day of practice, I improved.

I knew it might take years to produce anything of magnitude, if I ever could, but I found great pleasure in nurturing my powers. I also discovered I needed less blood from Alina the more I worked with the elements. They gave me sustenance, and I found it easier to leave Alina be. She still gained the benefits of our connection, and I felt more at ease not requiring as much from her. It felt like a healthier balance.

Aidan and Dante had worked to turn me into a warrior. They had trained me using many different styles. I had learned tae kwon do, aikido, judo, along with other fighting styles from history, considering they had been warriors for centuries. Boxing and kickboxing had also been on the training rotation. They believed the more forms I knew, the better I would be at defending myself. It would give me the advantage of mixing styles against any opponent, and since I had absolutely no experience, I followed their lead. A few times a week, we did weapons training as well. I improved each time, but not nearly as fast as I had with my powers.

When they introduced me to kendo, I learned I was best with two swords. My weapons of choice became the *daisho*, the katana, and the shorter *wakizashi.* My spirit preferred these weapons, at least for now. I didn't understand how a spirit could pick a weapon, but Dante says I must fight with what my soul tells me to. So I continued to take my training seriously, and I have gotten good enough to beat Aidan on occasion. I believe that's because he prefers a heavy axe, and I have agility and speed on my side; part of me thought he let me beat him to provide encouragement—it had worked. I have yet to beat Dante at anything, and I don't think I ever will. I am happy to have a goal to aspire to.

I never would've thought I could do any of these things, but after months of training, I was morphing into a real warrior. I have days I cannot remember what my life used to feel like. In the beginning I mourned the loss of the lonely woman I was, but now I saw so little of her in me, it was almost as if she were a figment of my imagination. I guessed time could heal everything because this was the happiest I ever remember being.

The part of my training I still found myself resisting was taking on the role of a leader. Aidan and Dante spend time teaching me war tactics and how to command a group of warriors without having them fight me for dominance. There wasn't much mercy involved with that type of training. I felt like I lost a small piece of my remaining morality each time. So some days I completely refused.

Part of me knew I couldn't avoid it forever. It was that nagging voice telling me this was part of my destiny. Someday I would have to lead, even if I didn't want to, but that day wasn't today. Hence the procrastination—or "denial" may have been a more appropriate word. Even though I had accepted so much about who I was and this new life, I still found myself resistant to the idea I had great purpose and was meant to change the world.

I continued to walk out into the vast nothingness of the tall grass as the wind blew warm and powerful, making the blades dance and sway to a rhythm of worship as my essence walked through. The earth and air sang to me. I hummed along in thanks, complacent with my existence. I felt strong and powerful, but I still had a sense my power was more in control of me and not the other way around. I knew something was missing because even with all the energy raging through me, I still felt fragile in some way. There was more, some puzzle piece yet to be placed or discovered. I knew only time or the Fates could fill in the gaps I felt were missing. Nonetheless, I contented myself with my present, knowing my story had truly just begun.

There was nothing in sight apart from the surrounding mossy, fern-filled forest bordering the rolling grassy plains of the prairie. I straightened my arms ever so slightly at my sides, letting the feathery tops of the grass tickle my palms as I walked through the knee-high field. The sun kissed the earth, making her warm and happy. I heard her giggle with joy, and I felt pleased and peaceful.

Suddenly, the periwinkle sky vanished. All was black and bleak. I didn't struggle. A vision was coming. The taste of blood was the first to appear to my senses, rich, warm, and thick. It ran down my throat. It was familiar, not the sensation of the drink, but the taste. Then the images flashed before my eyes. My makers came to me. I was tasting some of them again, but not all of them.

I would never forget how they tasted. Their blood, forever present in my veins, gave me this life, and for that, they would always be with me. While human, they tasted stale and metallic, but now they were sweet and enticing, like honeysuckle. Once you smell honeysuckle on the air, your mouth waters for it, for its sweetness, and that was what happened to me.

I searched through the blood in my mouth. Emma wasn't there—she was ash, dead and gone—but I could taste three of the others. They were delightful. I singled them out one by one, and as I did, the vision came on in full force.

Chapter 31

DAMNED SOULS

The streets of Eugene had waved goodbye to winter. The temperature increased, and spring was fast approaching. Small, delicate buds popped out on the limbs of the town's trees. The people were pleased to be out enjoying the sun-filled sky while it lasted. No mist fell from the sky this day to shower them, but sadly there was more to worry about then the next rainfall. While they were walking the beautiful town and sipping their teas and coffees, stopping by cafés for lunch, they were being hunted.

Eugene had residential vampires, but none like these. The three of them roamed the streets, unique in their abilities to torture and maim. They were here to collect a missing vampire, and from the looks on their faces, they were going to have fun doing it.

Flashes of victims danced before each of their eyes, a movie screen to view the horror each had inflicted since their arrival. It was gruesome; they were killing more than needed to survive, and some were only mutilated and murdered, not food at all. Their body count was well into the double digits, but no one would ever know what had happened to their prey. They had incinerated their corpses and scattered the ashes, not leaving a trail. No bodies equals no murders; therefore, no one would be looking until long after they were gone. The humans would be looking for the missing, not the dead, and never for dust in the wind.

With their tracks covered from the fun they had, they got down to business. They were headed to their destination. Their package was the newly made vampire, Phenice. Her office was closed. She hadn't been seen at the university where she taught. In her human world, she had vanished; there had even been a funeral for her about two weeks after they had attempted to turn her. Most of the people they questioned about her were murdered as well; they couldn't leave a path pointing to them. They couldn't find her assistant, and they found that odd. Since nothing else had turned up, they were heading for her home, hoping to find a trail. If she had truly survived the transformation, she had completely disappeared without a trace.

Briant, Heath, and Abagail glided up the street to Phenice's house. Emma, one of their own, had been sent on this same task and had never been seen again. The queen believed her dead, which is why she believed Phenice was alive and transformed. So here they were on a fool's errand. At least they believed that to be the case.

Abagail knew the queen was punishing them for their error during the ritual. Had they succeeded that night, she wouldn't have spent two months in Hell's Hollow being dismantled, having her bones set, waiting for her to heal only to be torn apart again. She feared what would happen if she failed again. Chills danced over her skin at the thought. She shivered even though vampires don't chill. She chose to have as much fun as she could while here in Eugene, for it could be her last chance. She spied on the townspeople, waiting to see if someone caught her eye. She was picking her lobster from the tank.

Her long, wavy auburn hair caressed her back in rhythm with her swaying walk, as her feet made no noise. Her face was flawless with peach skin and hazel eyes. The thoughts of her torture no longer plagued her beauty. She was simply a cunning monster and nothing else.

Beside her walked Briant, dwarfing her not because she was small—quite the opposite—but because he was just a giant man. He appeared to be miles away as he smiled to himself. The sun bounced off his white-streaked hair, so blond it lacked color, the same as his skin. The only color was his pink-tinged cheeks. Make no mistake, he was awe inspiring; men and women both noticed him, and he knew it too. It kept his victims willing. People gladly gave their lives to him, but he still loved the hunt. He kept human lovers, pets if you will, and once he was finished with them, he gave them pleasant deaths. He took pride in watching them die with smiles upon their faces, but there was still a part of him that was savage, and for that, he hunted.

Heath was a completely different story. He walked ahead of the other two. He was always on the hunt because in all his immortal years, he had never gained control of his bloodlust. The queen usually killed her children who were unable to master their thirst; they were a liability. But she hadn't been able to part with Heath. He was special to her.

He was an unusual-looking man, tall and stalwart with flaming red hair hanging in ringlets to his shoulders and eyes layered in rings of gray, smoke, and black. They were complete darkness. A hollowness meant to consume anyone, not with beauty but with utter hatred.

He was the first to speak.

"You two need to stay focused. I will not burn for this." It was a whisper, but still his words filled the air with rage and rattled the bones of anyone near, including Briant and Abagail.

It was clear why the queen kept Heath; he was vile and able to taint those around him with so much hatred he could tip the scales, making a good person wicked. She would have seen him as a most valuable treasure. He was the polar opposite of Amora. Where she invoked love, Heath could devour a soul in rage, fury, and violence. He could cause a complete collapse of a person, society, or organization with little to no effort. He was the apocalypse made flesh.

The house turned up nothing. They had no trail, no proof of transformation. It appeared Phenice was no more, and this is what they were going to tell the queen. Abagail was hopeful she would believe them. Briant was debating going rogue. Heath, well he knew better. She may spare him because of what he could do, but the others would be scarified, a warning for all to see: you don't fail the queen.

They agreed to hunt before they returned to France.

They slithered down the dark, chilly sidewalks of Eugene, lurking as they blended into the shadows from the trees and buildings. It felt as if spring was no more and winter had returned. It was simply the abandonment of the sun. Tonight, they would go unnoticed until they wished otherwise. Darkness held them in her midnight embrace like a lover, concealing even the whitest hair on Briant's head.

A group of late diners flowed out into the night from a fine restaurant, full and pleased, as they loudly laughed from too many glasses of wine. They hugged and said their goodbyes, some with kisses on the lips, some on the cheeks, and only a few handshakes.

A stunning brunette with long, straight hair waved as she departed. Her smile slipped as the last bit of laughter rolled over her lips. Once it was gone, the only sound filling the night was her black three-inch heels clicking the cement of the sidewalk as she strolled away.

Briant's smile grew larger as she grew nearer, knowing her life was growing shorter with every step. This was the moment he was fantasizing about earlier today. He picked her out when they arrived in town a few days ago. He had been following her since. He wanted to play. To the others she was simply food, but to him she was so much more. He could smell the sweetness pumping from her heart and exactly how much of a delicacy she would be. She was meant to last. He knew the secrets to make a human last. You tie them down, give them intravenous fluids, and force them to eat, while you enjoy their body as well as their life. You make them last as long as possible. You break them before you kill them. If only he could take her home, the things he could do to her. He wanted to make this one last a very long time. The others didn't understand. Heath wanted pain; he saw no pleasure in this life. And Abagail, well, she was as shallow as they came.

Briant debated on taking his newfound toy somewhere here in Eugene and never going back to the queen. She was an abomination in his eyes. And as the grin curved over his face, revealing his decision, a realization hit him. The others were gone.

He had become so lost in his thoughts, so dedicated to the life of the predator and his daydreams of torture, he hadn't realized tonight he was the prey.

Two large honey-brown hands reached for Briant, grabbing his head and encasing his entire face, covering his mouth before he could even gasp his astonishment. In reaction Briant thrashed his hands up, wrapping them around his captor's white linen-covered forearms, desperate to break free. No amount of strength would break this hold. Briant's frantic eyes roamed over his chest, up his neck and to his face. It had been a long time since Briant had met a man bigger than him, but as he found the face of his attacker, his body ran cold and limp. He accepted his fate as he peered into shining gold eyes. He had been deemed wicked, and he knew no one could defeat Custos, the Slaughterer of Damned Souls.

Custos towered over his prisoner. Briant was the last to pay this night, marked for coming to claim his charge, Phenice. It would mean his death, as it had for Heath and Abagail, who had died so quickly and quietly no one noticed. The night was cold. A slight breeze blew down the abandoned street. Most of Custos's hair blended in with the darkness. The night cloaked his warm honeyed skin, helping to hide his duty of death and damning of this soul. The only parts truly visible were his glowing gold eyes and his wavy white highlights blowing around his face.

With no effort, Custos gave a slight upward tug as Briant closed his eyes. The sound was inhuman. The loud snapping, popping, and ripping of muscle and flesh filled the street, followed by a short silence. Briant's head thudded to the pavement, and Custos began the Drink of Damned Souls. His mouth expanded and stretched, making it large enough to engulf the gaping wound and devour Briant's life force. The gulping noise started, and a warm burgundy light chased away the cold night air. It shimmered, swarmed, and crackled around Briant's alive yet decapitated body. They were encased in a light that departed Briant and entered Custos. It slowly decreased in brightness, color, and warmth. Once the chill returned to the night and Briant had no blood left, the light flowed from the space around them and down inside of Custos through his mouth. Briant's knees buckled, and Custos released him, letting him fall to the pavement next to his head.

Covered and stained with blood, Custos steepled his hands in prayer as his mouth moved in a silent chant. Moments later, Briant's body and head combusted. He showed no fear, no pain; he was a warrior until the end. The flames licked at him, not burning but taunting and teasing. Offering him death. A promise of what they could do, but only if he begged for it, and right as his eyes flew open in panic, his flesh began to melt and peel, exposing the muscle and bone that lay beneath. Seconds later, he was reduced to ash.

Still chanting, having paid no attention to Briant's anguish, Custos waved his hands skyward and thousands of tiny tornados made their descent, attacking the ash and carrying it away.

The grassy prairie returned as I slipped out of the vision. The taste of blood in my mouth turned to ash. I spit to get rid of it, but it wouldn't leave. It wanted to linger. Custos had devoured all three of their souls. I knew now only two of my makers remained. The names of the two remaining came to me at that moment as if I had always known them. Dover and Lecter. Chills ran through my body.

Chapter 32

THE BIRTH

Back in the present, I was surrounded by the sky in shades of periwinkle and cornflower, spotted with cottony white clouds. The sun warmed my face. Even with this peaceful place surrounding me, I was chilled with fear.

"Why show me this? I am at peace with my new life. As you wanted. The life you gave me. Revenge is not something I seek any longer." My voice was weak, a whisper so meek I almost didn't hear myself. And apparently neither did the Fates. They didn't answer.

Why show them to me? Why show me the monsters they were? The people they had murdered because of me. Dr. Postmere popped up in my mind while sadness cracked my heart. I didn't know if he was murdered simply for knowing me, for caring for me. Was he one of the people they spoke to? Is he dead?

All my peace and contentment had been replaced with dread over a simple vision. I was still being hunted. I wondered if I was safe here with the caste. Were they safe being so close to me? What about Alina? They had been looking for her. My being here put all of them in danger. So many people died while they looked for me. Grief and anger warred inside me.

Yet my fear was winning, telling me to turn around, to seek safety with Emil. Something pulled me forward, compelling me to finish my walk. Since I came to live here, I made this trip daily. To visit a young cherry tree, which oddly grew out of place toward the back of the prairie. I loved it. I claimed it as mine the moment I laid eyes on it. It was young and starting anew in this world, same as me.

Once, I had lain dying my mortal end under an arthritic cherry tree. Now this young, healthy tree grew in a place it didn't belong, and as I built a life here among the caste, I still didn't feel like I belonged either. I had days when I felt more in common with the old broken tree in the Owen Rose Garden and this young sapling carelessly abandoned in the middle of nowhere. The sapling was thriving but didn't belong here. I felt a deep oneness with both trees. It was as if they symbolized both sides of who I was, broken and barely held together while also carefree and strong regardless of the environment. It comforted me, knowing I could be both. I didn't have to be perfect.

As I sauntered, I was focusing on the clouds floating across the sky. I slammed into a metaphysical wall, hard as steel. I stumbled and staggered, trying to maintain my balance, but it was a losing battle. I finally fell flat on my back with a clear view of the sky. I saw him gliding through the sky in falcon form. I knew it was Custos, for he always took up more space in the surrounding air than a true bird would need. I tried to blink, to get a better look at him, but when I went to open my eyes, my world was gone.

The hospital was cold and sterile. The strong smell of disinfectant filled the air, covering human death, an attempt to wipe clean the constant mortal decay, which always tainted its hallways. It was a stinging smell, one that made your eyes water and nose run. It provided a strong sense memory, one never to be forgotten, not after this moment.

Time had turned back. The decor was outdated, as were the people. The hospital lacked the comforts of the world today, hard chairs and stiff beds. Everything was bland, white, and cold. The nurses walked the units in all white. They appeared to be identical drones going through their duties without any emotion. The only way to tell them apart was that the women came in different shapes and sizes with different color hair and eyes. It was creepy how they, too, appeared sterile, impersonal, and irrelevant. They were not what I was here for.

The birthing unit came into view. This was where the story began, as well as the pain.

The door to birthing room nine opened. It was cool inside, but a sense of warmth rushed out. It was the sweetness of happiness. Inside was Weylyn Jones, perched next to the bed of his wife, Brianna, who was holding their tiny newborn baby Phenice so tenderly in her motherly arms.

Weylyn was a tall man with sandy hair and blue eyes so light they almost lacked color. He was handsome, and it was obvious he was a gentle man as he stood smiling, his face showing signs of recent tears. Joy radiated from him as he took in the sight of all he loved, his wife and his daughter. This was everything to him. Gazing down at his family, he vowed his life was complete. He knew he could want for nothing more, not ever.

Brianna reached for his hand. He happily gave it, running his free hand through her labor-messed blond locks. She was beautiful, even after so much physical work. Her long, straight, blond hair framed her gorgeous oval face. Her green eyes gleamed brightly at Weylyn through the fatigue.

Their love filled the room. It was intoxicating, an overwhelming feeling. They sat talking in the slightest of whispers, giggling often, as they watched Phenice, who was staring and listening to her new world in amazement. They stared at her with the same bewilderment.

Hours passed. When night fell, Weylyn went home to shower and bring some clothes back for Brianna to wear home. Her labor had been early and unexpected. He didn't want her to wear her labor-stained attire home the next day. While he was gone, his world would change.

Brianna slept soundly in her bed, a slight smile curving her lips skyward. Phenice was tucked away in a bassinet next to her bed. She hadn't allowed her to be taken to the nursery for the night.

Power swelled, filling the hallway. It crept toward its destination: room nine.

The queen glided into the room without making any noise. The door didn't creak or groan, not even a footstep was heard. She slid farther into the room and was trailed by three others: Heath with his fiery hair, Emma decked out in ebony including her cloaking hair—a stark contrast to the decor—and Lecter, who always appeared bored and ready to move on to the next task.

Silently the queen motioned out her orders. Emma moved to the left of the bed, Heath to the right, and Lecter stood at her side. With a feathery wave of her hand, death came to room nine.

Brianna found her arms and legs pinned as she opened her eyes, horror freezing her face. She looked instantly at Phenice. Her baby was fine, for now. Emma and Heath had her locked down by her arms. Lecter had grabbed her legs and pulled them apart. He held her steady, molded in that position for as long as he wanted. She couldn't even wiggle.

She tried to scream, desperate for help, but all remained silent until the queen giggled at Brianna's attempt, pleased with herself. The queen levitated, moving over Lecter and placing herself down in front of him, between Brianna's legs. Brianna eyes widened as she became completely still.

"At first, Brianna, my love, I wanted you. You are so powerful," the queen said as she petted Brianna's legs, whose skin pricked with gooseflesh.

"You radiate the gifts of the gods. I wanted you to be my mightiest weapon, but when I came to claim you…" She smiled, and it lit her face up with villainous joy. "I felt her." She lifted an arm in slow motion sweeping it over Brianna, while extending a long index finger toward the bassinet.

Her eyes were glowing black as her evil spilled out, poisoning all it touched. It was as if the devil had claimed Phenice. She watched as Brianna cried and begged soundlessly, fighting to move without shifting an inch. The queen loved Brianna's pain.

"I felt her growing in your mortal womb, and she put you to shame. She doesn't just radiate the gifts of the gods; she commands them. So you see, I choose her; therefore you must die. Our Phenice can have only one mother, only one Creator. I will give her life and make her strong. I will give her what you cannot." She purred.

Before the last word fell from her perfectly formed mouth, she plunged her right hand between Brianna's legs deep inside her, tearing internal flesh as she dug. After finding what she wanted, she closed her hand tightly and tugged, severing Brianna's uterine artery. Massive amounts of blood began to pulse out around the queen's still-inserted arm.

Brianna tried to scream. She yelled *no* over and over, shaking her head weakly back and forth. Not a word was heard.

The queen removed her arm. "Taste, my children, but leave enough to make it look a natural death."

Emma and Heath gave up their posts holding down her arms. Brianna was dying fast. She was so weak, there was no longer any need to restrain her. Lecter simply stepped back to the wall. He reclined, watching the scene.

The two vampires had their heads between Brianna's legs, drinking as her life drained away. The room filled with a metallic stench. The vampires gave death a form, a shape, and it grew. The queen didn't join. She simply watched and enjoyed the mess she had created, slowly licking blood from her fingers as if it were frosting left after eating a cupcake.

Lecter focused in on Brianna's face, tears silently rolling down her cheeks. She reached for Phenice as her life was leached from her. Her eyes were screaming *no*, even though her mouth couldn't. A smile gradually began to play across Lecter's lips. He no longer looked bored. Death was his only joy, his only reprieve from his eternal life. Power began to pulse from him. He was feeding. Brianna's fears, the fight to live, it was food for him, not her blood. He drank his victims, of course, but he wanted power more. He wanted their pain.

The queen spoke low and stern. "Emma, Heath, enough. Let her die on her own."

They stopped. Bloodlust consumed them, but their fear of their queen was greater.

"Lecter," she said his name, but it was a command.

He didn't move. He wanted to stay and watch the end. He wanted to see the lights go out.

She walked up to him. He didn't wince as she got right up to his ear. "I know—my darkness, my agony—you could make her suffer for days, gaining strength from her, but this was not my purpose. Release her now."

He glared at her, pissed. It may not be her purpose, but it was his. They exchanged a look, a test of wills, and Lecter lost. He always lost. He fell in line because he didn't have another option. He obeyed his queen, and he would pay for his minor defiance. He didn't care.

Like ghosts, the vampires vanished as quietly and as quickly as they arrived.

"*No!*" Brianna screamed, crying and gasping as she tried to make her way to Phenice.

Footsteps echoed through the hallway. Two nurses ran into the room, but by the time they entered, Brianna was dead, lying on the floor, both hands outstretched toward her baby, and her lifeless eyes locked on the motherless newborn.

I gasped. Air stung my lungs. My eyes were burning. The light was too bright. My face was drenched with tears.

The sky returned to blue overhead, as bright as ever. The vision was over. I sat up, and there was Custos, sitting at my feet in a cross-legged position with his head in his hands, some of his hair falling forward to cover part of his face.

"I'm so sorry, Phenice," he said. His voice was flat, but it was clear he was genuinely sorry for my pain. He looked up at me. His eyes were filled with tears. I was stunned to see the demonic god crying because of my pain.

I attempted to wipe away my own tears, but I was unsuccessful because I was still sobbing. Images of my life flashed before my eyes. My father, broken and beaten down from grief. He was not the same man from the vision. That man was so full of life, love, and joy. That man *loved* me. He *wanted* me.

How different would my life have been had that venomous bitch stayed out of my world? If my mother hadn't been *murdered*?

I would have been loved. I would've had a family full of love and kindness, not abuse and neglect. She took everything from me. Every moment of pain and suffering started with that one moment. That one life-altering interference from her. She changed the whole trajectory of my life from my infancy.

Images of the Egyptian queen popped into my mind. I thought she had been haunting my dreams for mere months before she attacked me. The truth was she had been haunting and tormenting me my whole fucking life. She murdered my mom. She stole her from me in some sick, twisted game of power.

I found my voice. "You knew she didn't die giving birth to me? You knew she was murdered?" My voice was flat and weak. I was surprised when he answered, shocked he heard or understood me.

"I have always known. I know all deeds deemed wicked," he breathed.

"I want Lecter dead." Anger filled me.

"Yes." He replied with a nod.

"I want *her* dead, Custos," I whispered.

"That is the plan," he replied.

"I want to do it myself. You can't help. You can't do it for me." My voice was low and steady, thick with determination.

"Again, that is the plan," he repeated, holding eye contact.

I figured he would fight me. Tell me no, but he didn't.

"Whose plan?" I asked.

"The Fates, Phenice. I am here to take you to her, if you are ready." He held out a hand.

"You mean prepared?" I knew I wasn't prepared. Not physically, not mentally, and I didn't have my powers mastered, not even close.

"No, I mean ready to punish the wicked," he said.

I thought about it, and it didn't take long. I wanted her dead and gone from this fucking world.

"Yes, Custos. I am." I took his hand.

Chapter 33

LA ROQUE SAINT-CHISTOPHE

I stood in front of him, letting the last of my tears fall as great determination took me over. Custos's eyes held a glint of pain in them. It might have been remorse or sadness, but in an instant, my sight was pulled away from his golden eyes to the wings escaping from his back.

They were colossal, and he stretched them high above his seven-foot muscular frame. I stood there stunned. My jaw was unhinged as I stared, gawking at the once man, now angelic-looking demonic god standing before me. I knew he was truly not of this world. He was heavenly, a heavenly creation to be worshiped, to be feared, to be respected and followed. My heart was beating faster than normal when looking upon him. I had never seen him in this form. I had only been blessed with his falcon and his human shapes. They were both beautiful, but this hybrid was so much more. His skin was still the same rich honey, his eyes continued to burn brightly gold set in his chiseled face, with his wavy black-and-white highlighted hair framing it perfectly as it hung to his shoulders, his gold Ankh earrings resting on his braids. The white linen clothes that have become his signature for me hung from his body so cleanly. With all his inhuman beauty, I still couldn't turn my bewilderment away from the wings encasing him.

As if simply floating behind him were two massive, iridescent, golden-auburn and ebony-and-white wings. He spread them high above and out along the sides of him. He was a large man before, but now I knew he was indestructible. His energy finally made sense to me. This was why he took up so much air. His energy was enormous, otherworldly. He didn't belong, at least not here, but neither did I.

I felt small, fragile, and unworthy.

"Phenice, are you okay?" he questioned.

"I...I...it's just...you're striking, Custos," I sputtered, and he was.

"Thank you. Most have never seen this form, but if I am to have you travel with me, it is the only way." He stared at me so intently, so passionately. It was with love.

"Is this your true form?" I knew the answer, but I had to hear it for myself.

"Yes," he replied stoically.

He never gave me long descriptions, but they were honest, short and sweet. I saw value in him not sugarcoating anything. This had to be his true form. A falcon, while powerful, was beneath his power, a wonderful way to travel without bringing suspicion. It was simply a disguise, as was the human form. A way to try and have a normal life, I was sure. When you were a demonic god, you must want for more than only punishing the wicked.

I decided to ask him someday.

He pulled me from my wondering and back to the task.

"Are you ready?"

I wanted to tell Emil. I wanted to run to him. To tell him what I was doing, but I knew he wouldn't want me to. He would do anything and everything to stop me. So I didn't get to say goodbye. I just had to leave. It felt right to go. Now was the time.

I nodded to Custos. I was afraid if I opened my mouth, I would say more than a simple yes. I would reason. I would rationalize. Ultimately, I would back out. So with a simple nod, I sealed my decision.

With the tip of my head, Custos stepped forward, and even though I'm not short, he dwarfed me. I felt safe as he wrapped me up tight in his arms. He was my guardian, after all. He was here to protect me, always.

In an instant I heard the whooshing and beating of his wings. We were off the ground and soaring in the air. The prairie vanished, as did my young cherry tree. Oregon was gone too. The wind rushed by. His wings were so immense and strong it took him so little effort to move us through the sky.

I rested my head to his chest and let my cheek absorb the heat radiating from his body. His warmth was soothing, comforting. I felt as if part of me was home in his arms. He felt familiar, as if I had been here before. Maybe not in his arms, but somewhere he had been. Possibly in the place he truly existed. As if pieces of him made sense to me. It was so peaceful and relaxing. The vibration of his flight was a lullaby to me, a sweet song I had heard before.

Within a few minutes, his actions changed. He took his massive wings and cocooned me. My heart quickened for a moment as we floated in midair completely in silence. Then he slanted his body toward the earth and dove. I wanted to scream, but I calmed myself. I trusted him. He would keep me safe. We traveled at immense speed, but there was no wind, no noise, no light, absolutely nothing, a complete vacuum. I tensed, waiting to hit the ground. I knew it wouldn't kill me, but that didn't mean it wouldn't fucking hurt.

Then I heard Custos speak. "Phenice, open your eyes."

I didn't want to. I was still waiting for impact. I didn't want to see it coming.

"Please, don't fear and open your eyes. Trust in me." He was calm. His voice was sweet and reassuring.

I did as he asked.

There I stood on solid ground, staring at Custos in human form.

"What happened?" I gasped.

"A portal, Phenice. I used a portal," he informed me.

With that I let my eyes leave his handsome face and looked around to see where he had taken me. It was picturesque and serene.

I stood in the night as the midnight sky encased me. The brilliant light of the half-moon and its twinkling stars bathed the earth. Their light allowed me to stare at the cliff of limestone climbing about three hundred feet. Bright-green trees popped out of the rock like shining emeralds, beacons in the night sky. I could see all the alcoves and crannies within the cliff. There had to be hundreds of chambers, caverns, and terraces within the massive stretch of rock. I scanned the length of the cliff, and it had to be over three thousand feet long. I turned in a circle, in total awe of my surroundings. This place was ancient. Behind me was a beautiful river. I had heard the water singing to me, calling out, wanting my attention. I knew it was larger years ago. It had once filled this valley, but now it gently coursed through the land only mildly content to still exist.

"Where are we, Custos? Where have you brought me?" I needed a name for this place. It hummed of so many lives come and gone. It held so much earthly power.

"We are in France, in the Vézère Valley. The high cliffs are the La Roque Saint-Chistophe, and that is the Vézère River. This is where the vampire Lordes has settled. It has been her domain for the last century. It is where you must go, Phenice, to claim your destiny." Custos stopped talking and simply started walking forward toward the cliffs and away from the river. I followed.

This place called to me. Something here felt familiar. We crossed a road man had paved at the base of the wonderful cliffs. I trailed closely behind my guardian. Suddenly pinned to my spot, I was forced to stiffly stop. I felt Aidan. He was the familiar claim I had to this place. His essence was calling to me.

I could sense his blood. His human blood screamed up from the earth. I kneeled in the grass and placed my hand to the cool terrain. Images flashed through my brain, snapshots of his life. I saw his boat leave a large ship and navigate up the river during the night. They had planned to steal from the people living in the towns here. That was when she stole him. She took him from that dark night. There was no moon in the sky since it was easier to sneak in without being seen, but he didn't see her either. He fought all the way to this point where I kneeled in the grass and listened to his screams, feeling the power of his blood. He fought all six of them even with the rods piercing his body. They nearly killed him. He wanted to get away. He wasn't willing to die. I saw her eyes burn with anticipation to have him. She was so thrilled about her new toy, and that was exactly what he was to her.

I left the vision of Aidan's mortal end. I petted the soil, which had his life etched in it. Tears came to my eyes for his pain, and for his life. I briefly grieved for him.

Custos put his hand on my shoulder, and I jumped. I should've felt him coming. I should've sensed him there, but I was lost in Aidan's pain.

"I'm sorry." His hand slipped from me.

"No, I'm sorry. I lost myself in a vision," I said.

"Of Aidan?" he questioned.

"Yes," I murmured. Of course, he would know. He knew us all.

"She was proud to 'tame that beast,' as she says. He is quite the warrior," he replied.

"Yes, I know he is. I'm lucky to have him as a friend, to have him on my side," I said with gratitude shining in my eyes, replacing my tears.

"That you are." Custos grabbed my hand. "Come." He led me to a ladder.

After feeling Aidan's death, I wanted to avenge him as well. I could not even begin to understand the lives she had ruined in over four thousand years. She had to be stopped, somehow. Though I needed to stop her, now that I was here, I started to feel panic rise. What could I possibly do against a monster like her? I was only me.

"Custos, what is the plan? I can't do this on my own." The fear and panic crawled over my skin, through my mouth, and down into my gut. It infected me completely. If I could still tremble in fear, I would've been shaking so hard my bones would break. I wanted my heart to pound beyond the quick initial beats. My heart would always quicken briefly, then return to its near-absent pace. I wanted my palms to sweat, but I was the picture of cool. It gave me no release for how I was truly feeling. In becoming a vampire, I lost most, if not all, bodily reactions to my emotions. I still felt them all deep inside, and I missed the visceral responses that made me human. Those reactions made me feel alive, and without them, something vital was simply gone.

When Custos responded to me, I snapped out of my internal rant. "It's not my place to tell."

"Why am I here, really?" I asked. It seemed about more than my revenge.

"To punish the wicked. To fulfill your destiny," he responded.

"But she has an army, and there is only me," I stated, wondering what I could possibly do to remove her from this world.

"Have faith, Phenice, and ascend," he demanded and pointed to the ladder.

You will understand once you have walked the path. We cannot tell you unless you have the faith to embrace the destiny chosen for you. The destiny once upon a time you agreed to accept. The Fates whispered in my mind.

I did as they said. I had faith. I was surprised when Custos followed behind me. I had no idea what was going to happen, but this was clearly a key part in fulfilling my destiny. Even without the Fates murmuring in my mind and Custos's encouragement, I could feel it in my soul.

It didn't stop the dread from invading me with each new rung I grabbed on the ladder as I ascended. Yet the closer I got to the top, the more determined I felt.

Once I reached the top of the ladder, I walked onto the terrace and into a cavern. The cavern led to a larger chamber. I walked in blind, knowing I was taking a leap of faith, and as I stepped into the lion's den, my eyes landed on Lecter, the Queen's Agony, one of my makers.

Chapter 34

ABOMINATION

I should've panicked, but Lecter was the one who showed surprise. I stood there and stared him down with Custos at my side. I was no longer scared or nervous. I found myself gazing at death without a care. I didn't even blink. The silence was intense, deafening. I waited for him to attack, for him to say something or for his expression to change, but nothing.

After a while I gave in. "I'm here to see Sadeh. She murdered my mother, as you well know." I kept it short and unemotional.

I sounded as if I didn't care, and the truth was I didn't feel much more than a sweet, blissful numbness. I briefly wondered why I was so calm, but Lecter quickly recaptured my attention.

His eyes widened slightly, but he remained silent. After a moment he replied with the smallest nod. He turned on his heels and led the way.

We passed hordes of vampires on the way. No one said a word, not to me or about me as I passed. I would've heard the whispers of gossip. It was odd. Everyone seemed to be in shock, frozen due to my sudden voluntary appearance. I had an urge to speak to Custos, but they would hear anything I said, so I held my tongue.

Lecter led us through tunnels, which made way to antechambers and larger caverns. They had somehow taken this ancient cave system and turned it into habitable cozy spaces. Finally, once we were deep into the earth, we reached our destination. A knot grew in my throat and my heart quickened, but only for a fraction of a second. In a blink the numbness returned, causing me to stand without a care. Why did I feel so indifferent and emotionless?

You are on the path—where you belong—at the time you are meant to be there. The Fates whispered in my mind.

With the reassurance of the Fates, the curiosity about my indifference vanished. I may not understand why this was the time to confront Sadeh, but clearly it was necessary for whatever was to happen next. I felt confident as my attention fell on the woman in front of me.

There she sat dressed in gold and crimson, radiating power and emulating the mortal Egyptian queen she once was. As we came farther into the great chamber, her head slowly turned, giving me her full attention. Her black eyes filled with mischievous joy.

"Oh, it can't be," she whispered through her evil smile and rose to her feet.

She was taller and thinner than me. She looked fragile, but I wasn't fool enough to believe it. She was a dark beauty, intoxicating to gaze upon, but her eyes—they were pure evil. I could see the curse of the heavens etched within. Looking into her eyes felt like falling into hell itself, as if they could burn your soul to dust.

I closed my eyes to get a sense of her. I could sense the curse wrapped throughout her whole being, but I felt something more morbid. She tasted of rust, rot, and pus. The room began to tilt as dizziness engulfed me. Her smell filled my nose, so strong of mold and rotting flesh, and nausea rolled up from my gut. I could hear the screams of all the innocents she had murdered, as their begging and pleading swarmed around her and filled my ears. I felt their pain. I wanted to cry for them. To scream for them. To avenge them. The only sound louder than the shrieking was her evil laugh as she ended their existence.

I turned my hands out toward her to feel her. She was full of seeping wounds and covered in scales. With my eyes still closed, I focused on seeing her not as how she wanted to be seen but as her true cursed self. There before me stood a monster, reptilian in appearance and zombielike. As she walked toward me, she left puddles of fluid behind, drainage from her many wounds. She wasn't beautiful; she was an abomination, but only I could see her true form. Pure evil had tainted her, and it danced all around her. The curse had made her. It marked every molecule. I could sense it, but she made herself evil. This monster is not what the heavens had intended. Her hatred was all consuming, and she had morphed into something different. She was two separate beasts. What my physical eyes could see was the vampire the heavens created, and what my metaphysical eye could see was the monster Sadeh had been when she cursed the heavens while still human.

She took two steps closer. I held out my hand.

"Stop, Sadeh!" I commanded, interestingly confident. I opened my eyes, and the monster had been replaced with the dark beauty I was positive everyone else saw.

"By whose name do you call me? That is *not* mine!"

Clearly her human name pissed her off. It was a small victory, and I took joy in it.

"It has always been your name. Or has it been so long you have forgotten?" I chided.

"I forget nothing! My name is Lourdes, but you will call me queen! I am your Creator!" Her eyes grew even darker if it were possible. I could see a storm brewing. Bad for me. *Oh well*, I thought, *this is the path I have set on.*

"You must have forgotten because Sadeh was your human name, remember? The one—"

"You will call me queen, or you will die!"

Yeah, I had pissed her off. Yeah, it was bad for me because I would never call her queen.

"Let me tell you a story I know, then you can kill me. Once upon a time, there was an Egyptian queen named Sadeh. Sound familiar?"

Her eyes grew wide in disbelief. I paused, but she didn't stop me.

"Well, long story short, she wanted to be a mother, but the heavens didn't deem her fit. So after the fourth attempt, she cursed them. And in return they cursed her back. Now here you stand. The part that pisses me off the most though, Sadeh, is when you decided you would come into *my* mother's hospital room and take her from *me*. So the only other name you will ever hear me call you other than your worthless human name is *murderer*!" I screamed the last.

The storm had come.

"I gave you life, you ungrateful bitch!" She closed the distance between us.

I whispered back to her, "No, my mother, Brianna Jones, who you murdered, gave me life. You just altered it, you fucking monster." My tone was a growl as I finished.

"Without me you would be nothing. You will join me. You will call me your queen and accept me as your Creator, or you will accept the same fate as your human whore mother," she was whispering in my ear, and as she called my mother a whore, she placed a sweet dewy kiss on my earlobe.

I shifted and leaned in next to her ear, attempting not to choke on her stench as I replied.

"Sadeh, let me rot, or kill me and be done with it…because if you don't, I will make sure to take you out of this world. I will never—you hear me?— *never* accept you as anything other than the ash I will make of you." I returned the soft dewy kiss on her rotting earlobe. As gross as it was, it had the effect I was going for. I felt satisfied.

She stepped away from me and laughed. It made my bones ache and my skin crawl, but I felt no fear.

"Is this your final decision?" she inquired, looking me up and down as she regained her composure.

"Yes," I rebuked. Short and sweet.

"Wonderful! Let the agony begin. Take her to Hell's Hollow, then we will see if her mind can be persuaded." She laughed.

My heart sank. Flames erupted in the blackness of Sadeh's eyes. I said nothing as Dover and Lecter descended upon me. I didn't run or fight, I didn't plead. I stood staring at her burning eyes with their lust for the pain I would soon suffer by her order, and I felt remorse. I couldn't explain it. I had come here to destroy her, but sorrow filled me.

She stole my childhood, my mother, and even my father indirectly. She took away my human life, and as I stood there flanked by her men, my makers, I felt sorry for *her*. I knew through my gifts that at some point in her existence, she had been good, kind, even loving, but now because of the monster she had created within herself, she needed to die.

"Take her! What are you waiting for? I want this thing away from me. She stinks of morality! Torture it out of her, then we will see who she serves!" she bellowed.

"Yes, my queen." In unison they bowed to her while holding me immobile in their grasps. I wasn't going anywhere. I knew that now.

"Skip the simple tortures. I want her broken. Tear her down. Rip it out of her! I want a beast when you are done. I will worry about taming *it* later." She smiled at me.

"Yes, my queen," they replied in unison as they bowed again.

How pathetic.

I was escorted out of the large chamber. I knew I should've been horrified, but Sadeh's fear filled the room. She was scared of me, of my remaining morality, the part of me she deemed a human quality. Of my kindness and compassion. She must have felt my sympathy for her. She must have seen the remorse I felt for her, and it petrified the ancient vampire. I smiled at my diminutive victory because I knew deep down within myself, it was the only one I was getting. As they led me to Hell's Hollow, I realized Custos was gone.

⬤⬤⬤

Chapter 35

HELL'S HOLLOW

Custos had left me. He led me to her and left without my noticing. I should've blamed him for leading me to the lion's den, but I couldn't. I was supposed to be here. The Fates had made that clear, and even if I didn't understand why or what was to be gained, I felt it in my soul this was the next step toward accepting my destiny. Destiny wasn't about understanding; it was about accepting the journey, even if it felt like it was tearing you apart. I was pretty sure I was about to get torn apart in ways that would change me forever.

I was led in silence, held tight by both men, even though I didn't fight. I had no intention of doing so. They were not going to disappoint their queen. If I were them, I would do the same. She was not one to piss off, and I had done just that.

It felt like we walked forever. I paid no attention to where we were going. I thought of no escape and no survival. I was peaceful, a smile on my face. I should've been panicking, but for seven months, I had feared that losing my humanity meant I had lost my morality. I believed I was a monster, a demon, or pure evil, but when I saw her fear of my compassion for something like her, I had an epiphany: I was still me, and I would only be a monster if I chose to be. I was right where I was meant to be. I would endure.

As I was led through the maze of tunnels to their version of hell, I vowed no matter the tortures they bestowed on me, I would never be her beast. I would never be a monster. I would choose death first. I had come a long way from my day at Devil's Churn…I no longer wanted to die, but Sadeh had left me with no other option. So death it would be. This was an interesting path the Fates had set me on. I was confused: How could this lead me to a bigger destiny? All I felt lingering in my future was my inevitable death.

I was ripped from my thoughts and torn back to my reality as Dover relinquished my left arm to Lecter, who locked them both tightly behind me. In front of me stood a thick iron door with no window to see in, or out for that matter. The hall smelled of dirt and death, and it was mind-numbingly silent. Dover inserted a key, and the sound of it sliding in vibrated off the rock with great intensity. He turned the key, and a bolt slid to unlock the massive door. The sound was crushingly loud as it echoed down the endless tunnels we had paced. Instantly I felt alone and hollow.

"Welcome to hell, Phenice," I muttered.

Lecter pushed me through the door Dover had opened, and I couldn't help but gasp. The large room was covered in blood, new and ancient. The stench of pain smacked me in the face. I could sense death, some recent, but most of it was etched in the rock, years old. Centuries' worth of agony and demise vibrated in the stale air. Dover closed and locked the door behind us, causing a repeat of the agonizing sounds. It might as well be the sounds of a guillotine because I knew I wasn't leaving that room alive.

I was alone with them. Finally, my body showed some response to the terror I felt. My heart sped up and slowed repeatedly. I didn't care about controlling it, but I focused on my vow. No matter what, I would never be hers.

Dover walked to the middle of the room; Lecter followed with me in tow. For the first time, I fought. It was involuntary as fear started to bubble up from my gut. Lecter laughed and picked me up as if I were a doll, a mere plaything, and to him I was.

There, in the center of the room, Dover removed my boots and cuffed my ankles to the stone floor with shackles. The floor was cold, not that it bothered me physically, but I didn't like the feel of death touching my feet. I looked up and saw the chains dangling from the ceiling of the cavern. I fought without saying a word, no screaming or crying, just pure struggle. Lecter pulled one arm out from behind my back as if I were his posable little doll and lifted it skyward. Not that there was a sky in here, only midnight blackness lit by firepits. Dover took that arm and locked it into a ceiling shackle. Lecter then repeated the same with the other arm as I continued to fight. The sounds of the shackles clicking into place sealed my fate; I wasn't going anywhere. I was at their mercy.

Something told me they knew no mercy. I was helpless as I hung suspended. Lecter circled me laughing. I closed my eyes and attempted to focus on something else, anything, but when the first whip struck my back, my eyes popped open, and I screamed.

Nothing in life could prepare a person for that kind of pain. The leather snapped, fabric tore, and skin shredded. I didn't want to scream, but it was too much. Too much, too fast. I wasn't ready. I was never going to be ready for pain like that. Who could be?

So I made peace with the need for the release of my pain. I betrayed myself and cried out. It hurt so badly. The sound of my flesh being torn from my body filled my ears. I wanted to brace myself for the next blow, but there was Lecter with a cat-o'-nine-tails standing in front of me, his arm skyward. I started to cry before it even demolished my breasts and stomach a second later. A moment later Dover struck my back again with his leather whip.

The cracking and snapping sounds filled my ears as they echoed off the stone. The ripping of my skin was so fast, I could barely hear the tearing of flesh that went with the pain, but I heard the blood dripping to the cavern rock at my feet where it began to pool. I heard my blood fly off the whips and splatter on the surrounding walls as they were raised high in the air to strike again. Tears ran down my face. The salt stung the gaping wounds growing all over my body.

They tore my arms, legs, back, and torso apart. Not even my face had been left untouched. I was being skinned alive, so weak I hung limply from my restrained arms. Lecter took a deep breath in then moaned. I wanted his bliss due to my suffering not to bother me, but the way he stared at me made me want to die. His eyes were worse than the pain. I knew he was the Queen's Agony, and he was making the pain worse. That was his power. He could make it hurt so much worse than feed off the growing agony he summoned.

My tears turned into screams. The pain was so unbearable I couldn't even form a coherent thought. As time passed my screams died to whimpers. Eventually, mercy found me when my world faded to black.

⊶⊷

When I woke, I was staring at a table with leather cuffs for wrists and ankle re-straints. Apparently, the rack was my next punishment. Since I couldn't make my eyes focus, I was unable to tell if my torturers were present.

I jumped when Lecter spoke. "All you must do is give in, submit, and I won't put you on my table. Oh, Phenice, the things we do there." The last statement was a seductive purr, a promise of pain for me and deep pleasure for him.

He scared me. Lecter's voice crawled down my torn skin and made my spine hurt. My blood had dried over my body, which meant I had been out for a while. I tried to squirm away from his voice, but the pain made me stay put.

"If you surrender, it's over. I'll have mercy on you." He walked closer to me. "But honestly, I want you to be stubborn. I want to play with you. I want to tear you apart. I want to hear you scream again…and again…and again. You see, this is my happy place." He patted my head. "I'll leave you to think about it." He leaned in and licked the dried blood from my face.

I shivered involuntarily. Traitor, my body was betraying me again. I took back my wish for visceral reactions. I didn't want to show these bastards a single bit of my true feelings.

He locked the door as he left. I heard the bolt click home, followed by an echo throughout the room. I closed my eyes. I wanted to cry, but instead I saw my spirit shimmering deep within me. Without thinking, I called water to fill me and earth to heal my flesh.

The veins within my body started to coarse with blood as my heart pounded, forcing it to circulate and restore my life. It was so loud, it was deafening. My tattered body began to fuse back together, mending itself as if an imaginary seamstress stood over me. The quick knitting of my flesh was an unnerving sensation. I felt whole again, no longer dismantled. No tears came. Instead, I smiled. I found comfort in the song of the earth and water that filled me, and I allowed myself to get lost in the melody.

Have strength, sister—trust in the journey. The Fates whispered sweetly in my mind. A chill went through my body. I knew they were trying to lend me strength, but their words brought understanding—the worse was still to come.

It wasn't long before Lecter and Dover returned.

"What the fuck?" Dover ran his hands over my exposed body, searching for my absent wounds. He tore away the small slivers of clothing that were left behind by the whips, leaving me completely exposed. He only found clean and perfect skin underneath. "We heal fast, but we ripped you apart. This should've taken days, not hours, to rebuild."

"She doesn't have any marks. No signs of being touched." Lecter petted my hair after pacing around me to examine my pristine skin. His mouth came close to my ear again, and he locked his fingers in my hair and tugged my head back sharply.

"Goody," he whispered into my ear. "We get to try harder to break you. I'm so happy you see things my way, dolly." He kissed my neck below my ear slowly and seductively. Had he been my lover, it would've made me wet, but instead I wanted to crawl out of my skin as I tugged away from him.

With my hair still tied up in Lecter's hand, Dover released my ankles from the floor shackles and held me tight. Lecter finally let go of my hair to release my wrists. He paced around, ready to devour me. He didn't watch his hands as he removed my cuffs. Instead, he stared right through me. I didn't look away or flinch; I smiled at him.

While I was tightly in the embrace of both men, they transported me to the rack and latched me in.

Round two.

I lay bound on a wooden rack as Dover turned a crank. I heard the metal notch clicking into place. They were planning to conquer my body slowly, one loud *click* at a time. The sound bounced off the rock walls.

Click…click…*click*.

I was being slowly pulled apart. The pain radiated throughout my entire body, but unlike before I made sure I didn't cry or scream. I closed my eyes, calling my spirit to me, and endured. I could feel Lecter gazing down at me, willing me into agony, trying to summon my pain. He wanted me to cry for him. He ached for me to beg as Dover continued to separate my extremities from my body, but I didn't wince. I wouldn't, not this time. I held tight to the spirit shining bright in my core. They could break this body, but they couldn't break *me*. They couldn't have my soul.

The ripping noise filled the air as my muscles were torn from the bone. I wanted it to stop, but I wouldn't be a monster. Part of me was stubborn enough to let it go on because I would never give these bastards the satisfaction of hearing me cry ever again.

So it continued.

Loud shattering sounds followed the shredding of muscles as my cartilage and ligaments snapped. The joints of my body were pulled apart with thunderous, shrill cracking sounds, followed by a nauseating sucking and popping, leaving them dislocated and ripped from their sockets. Pain roared through me. My pain craved to be released. I needed to scream. Anything to help cope, but I could've yelled until my lungs bled for air, and it wouldn't have helped. Nothing about this was bearable. I wished for death, but they would never make it so easy. The only thing left to focus on was my sense of pride for remaining silent this time and knowing this was the path forward.

Dover continued his crank, turning it one notch at a time.

Click…click…*click*.

My body responded.

Snap…pop…crack.

The blood-curdling noises filled the air, echoing off the rock that was now my prison, my hell.

I never screamed, cried out, or shed a single tear. I refused to give them a fucking thing. Instead, I embraced the pain until the darkness came for me again.

⸺⸺

I woke to an empty chamber, still almost pulled apart, pain engulfing all my senses. Once I realized I was alone, I let it out.

"Oh, please. Oh, please, no. Make it stop!"

Without thought, I healed myself. Everything mended: bones, joints, ligaments, cartilage, muscle, and even the skin that had torn. Instantly, I was pain-free. I sighed in relief. The tears stopped. The knowledge hit me like a freaking train: I was still strapped to the rack with the crank rotated to pull me apart.

In a flash, I was torn rapidly apart. I relived the last hours of torture. The pulling, tearing, and shredding of my tissues, along with the snapping and destruction of my bones.

"*Fuck!*" I howled, long and painfully. My lungs burned. My wails echoed off the rock walls, bouncing back at me to mock me with the horror of my own self-inflicted pain. I had become my own torturer. Tears ran down my face. I prayed to pass out from the agony. I wanted it to kill me. I wanted—needed—mercy but received none.

I felt blood pouring out of the fresh wounds I had created. I wriggled slightly and cried out. All my joints had been separated, including my spine. I had been pulled and ripped apart. I cried and moaned until all I had left were sad, pathetic whimpers. I hated myself for it, but still I didn't pass out.

I froze as I heard Dover and Lecter coming. I immediately stifled my pitiful whining, praying they heard none of it. I heard them outside the door arguing.

Lecter roared at Dover. "Do as you have been fucking ordered and stop being a little bitch!"

"I can't do this anymore, Lecter. Just kill me. I won't do it," Dover raged back.

"Oh, I would never offer you anything so simple. I will keep you in my chamber for the rest of your eternal life if you defy this order. Do…you… understand?" Lecter growled.

Silence fell. After what felt like forever, I heard the bolt in the steel door slide. I plastered on a pain-free, stoic face for them to admire. That was all they would get from me.

All courage and fiery determination were back at the sound of the door scraping opening and being locked tight behind them. Some of the pain strangely faded. I felt a slight pinch of joy spark in my heart. It surprised me. It felt masochistic, but I would take anything other than pain and allowing them to gain a victory over me. Though after the conversation I'd overheard, Lecter seemed to be the only one enjoying himself.

"She looks worse than we left her," Dover stated. He sounded sad, defeated. His demeanor was dark and tortured. It was clear something had changed outside these walls while I was inflicting pain upon myself, something bigger than the conversation I had heard.

"I think she looks perfect." Lecter smiled down at me, eyes glowing with hunger. He leaned down so close to my ear I could feel his hot breath caress the side of my face. Chills danced up my spine as he whispered, "I will break you." It was a promise.

I said nothing. I simply stared impassively at the rock ceiling, giving him no reaction.

Dover went toward my feet as Lecter paced around me, showing me his toy for this round of torture, a medium-sized knife that glinted from the dim light in the cavern. A loud click echoed throughout the room. Pain radiated through my hips and legs as Dover spread them apart by moving the wooden planks they were bound to.

I was now lying flat on my back with my broken legs parted wide. Dover stood between them staring toward me, but somehow through me. His eyes were vacant, hollow, as if he were elsewhere. What happened to him? I wondered. He was a ghost. Whatever happened to him in the time I laid passed out in my hell broke him. Or maybe he had already been broken.

Worry crawled through me. My blood chilled. I was cold for the first time since I had been turned into a vampire. I knew what was coming. This wouldn't be the first time something like this happened to me. I remember my father's friend coming into our dingy bathroom and taking what he had wanted from me when I had forgotten to lock the door. I never wanted that to happen again; I would take death instead.

Lecter gained my attention as he started to use his razor-sharp toy. He slowly dragged the tip across my skin causing a slight tickle, a promise of pain to come. I didn't recoil. No, instead I held my blank stare in place. It was clear my lack of expression pissed Lecter off. With his next tracing, he dug the knife deeper, cutting my skin into strips. He followed the carving by digging his fingertips in. He began to pinch my flesh.

Understanding came soon enough to brace myself. He smiled at me as he ripped the section of flesh from my body and threw it to the floor with a smack. The pain was unspeakable. The sound made my blood curdle. He was literally going to skin me alive.

I reached down inside, focusing on my spirit, hoping to find the courage to endure. I wished I could force myself to pass out again. Yet I managed to remain stoic as he continued. I focused on the gold glimmering starlight bright inside. I tried so hard to see only the light so I could block everything else out.

The queen had ordered them to strip me of everything. My freedom. My sanity. And most of all, she wanted my morality. She wanted them to break me, to convert me into a beast, a monster. They were trying to carve out my soul. I saw the lust in Lecter's eyes. He was longing for the moment I snapped and gave in, the moment I threw away everything to make it stop.

Fuck him and his queen.

They couldn't fucking have me! I would overcome anything. Even death. Regardless of what the caste believed, my death couldn't be the end. I felt it shining bright in my soul. There was a greater purpose, even if I couldn't see or understand it yet.

Just a little longer, child. We are here with you. The Fates sang to me.

A tear slid down my cheek. I was grateful to not be alone. I took a deep breath. I could smell my freshly spilt blood mingling with the stale blood from my earlier tortures. I lay naked and completely exposed. Lecter continued to carve the flesh from my body, but the movement between my legs quickly caught all my attention.

Dover was still between my legs, but now he was stripping down. Once he was completely exposed, I knew what would happen. It was going to hurt, physically and emotionally. Every bone was broken, and he was still going to take me against my will. This was clearly what he had been ordered to do.

Lecter noticed that Dover had my attention. He couldn't allow that. He cleared his throat to make me look up at him again. He stood there with his knife in hand, staring at me. I bravely or naively stared back. I didn't want to look away, for fear of what he was about to do, but I wouldn't dare let him know it was terror I was feeling. I let mockery sink into my eyes. I leered so long I forgot about Dover, until he entered me. Pain tore through me. Wind pulled into my lungs, and I whimpered slightly until I caught myself.

He was thrusting in and out as hard as he could, and still I gave Lecter my undivided attention. His torture was one I thought I could live with. I was mostly numb, but the sound of hearing my bones slushing, slipping, and sliding around within me from the impact of his pelvis hitting mine caused nausea to rise from my gut.

The pain really was gone; my nerve endings must have been destroyed. Now the torture was all mental. I couldn't think of a word to describe what I was feeling because it was beyond despair or agony. I was slipping into a deep, dark hole of utter hopelessness. Don't get me wrong, I was grateful for the dark. Happy to no longer be able to feel anything. It gave me a sense the end was close.

"The queen said to break you. You are broken, so submit and it will be over, Phenice." Dover snapped me out of my darkness. His words were breathless, and he was near tears. It wasn't a torment; he was pleading with me so he could stop for himself.

I risked a glance at him, and there, written all over his face, was the desire to be done with me. He didn't find pleasure in raping me. He was doing as the queen ordered, or he would be her next victim in Hell's Hollow. It was obvious; she had broken him so long ago, once upon a time, when he had been in my place. I wondered who had raped him. It was clear on his face; someone had violated him in similar ways. He was so beaten and broken. I felt only sadness for him.

"No," I whispered. I wouldn't be a monster.

He shook his head and continued, with sadness. A single tear slid down his cheek as he looked away from me and toward the wall. I couldn't feel my body anymore. I was physically shutting down.

I closed my eyes to the den of terror. Instead, I pictured the life I had in Oregon. I thought of Emil and our love. I got lost in the memories we had created in such a short time. They were the most amazing memories in my life. I was grateful to find love and sad to lose it. I took comfort knowing I'd been blessed to have found love at all. Maybe he and I were star-crossed lovers, soulmates designed only to find each other briefly, to love fiercely, then be torn apart, again and again. It seemed cruel but not as cruel as never loving at all.

I tried to hold on to the image of Emil's face as long as I could. Sadly, blinding pain pulled me back from my daydreams. A sharp, shooting pain burned across my abdomen. I screamed out. I couldn't help it. I wanted to be brave, but I had lost my concentration by letting my mind roam to happier thoughts. I tried to look down but had to settle with rolling my eyes toward the pain because my neck no longer worked. Dover was standing to the side of me with a haunted look, lost a million miles away. I wasn't the only one checking out to hold it together.

Lecter had taken his knife and stuck it in my gut. With a smile proudly on his face, he dragged his blade from right to left across my belly. That, I couldn't ignore.

"*Shit!*" I screamed it as loud as I could. Fuck it, let him be satisfied with himself. Let him have his agony. He had sliced my stomach open. It burned as my blood poured out and down my side to paint the rack and cavern floor. Dover reflexively took several steps back.

Lecter turned his attention to the other man.

"Focus, Dover. You know what will happen if you don't." He finished with a gleam in his eye.

It was clear Lecter had no problem putting Dover on his table after he was done with me. From Dover's flinch, I knew he'd already broken Dover time and time again.

Dover walked away and returned with a modern, stainless steel surgical table. He made eye contact with me briefly. In his eyes I could see deep, heart-breaking remorse and self-hatred. I had missed it in the beginning, when he was whipping me, because he had been standing behind me. Dover was nothing more than a broken Stockholm syndrome victim, held by his captive. The queen who stole his life probably killed the people he loved and broke him using the same type of techniques I had gone through. In truth we weren't much different. He had just broken under the pressure. Seeing him gave me strength to carry on to whatever came next. I never wanted to see the look in his eyes reflected back at me in a mirror. I was determined to be stronger than that.

He pushed the metal table up next to Lecter. Lecter sat his knife down with a loud, echoing clang, then clapped Dover on the back with his blood-soaked hand. Dover jumped at the macabre gesture of a job well done. Unlike

Dover, Lecter was thriving. He was in his happy place following the orders the queen had given him. Cringing, Dover finally walked away to lean against the stone wall, his eyes locked on the floor.

With his full attention back on me, Lecter took both hands and slid his fingers into the wound he had created.

"No, no," I whispered. "No, no, no, no, no! *Stop*!" I yelled.

He paused with his hands inserted in my gut. "Do you submit, dolly?" he hummed.

Fuck no, I thought. I sighed, closed my eyes, then whispered, "No."

"I must continue then, lovie," he purred as he began to slowly pull out my insides and place them on the table next to me. The pain and sounds were too much.

A tear rolled down my cheek. My show of weakness lit a fire under Lecter. Not able to restrain himself a second longer, he violently ripped open my gut, nearly tearing me in half. Overwhelming gratitude filled me as total darkness claimed me. The room vanished.

Chapter 36

CHOICE

When I woke, I was no longer in the chamber known as Hell's Hollow. I was outside. It was night, and the moon was full, making it bright. I was naked and covered in black soot. Exposed in the bright moonlight, I was stretched between two tall white marble columns tethered by long chains latched to my wrists and ankles. I glanced around and noticed I was in the center of an outdoor arena. As my eyes began to focus, the surroundings became clearer. There were thousands of vampires, all staring at me. I continued to scan the arena. Directly in front of me sat a throne with three chairs to the left and four to the right.

My vision was still blurry, but things slowly started to sharpen. The first face I was able to make out was Custos. My heart pounded in my chest briefly as excitement and relief filled me. He was standing close to the throne and its empty chairs. A sense of calm washed over me as I stared into his eyes.

Vampires came out into the night to fill the empty seven chairs around the throne. Two of them were Dover and Lecter. I was startled when, in unison, everyone stood and kneeled. Sadeh came gliding out of the surrounding cliffs.

Once she sat on the throne, all the vampires sat back down.

"Phenice, Lecter says you would not submit in Hell's Hollow. What say you here, in front of your queen, your counsel, and your people? Do you deny us all?" She glared through me instead of looking at me.

I stared at her. Here I was chained at her mercy, and she acted as if she was giving me a choice. As if I were free to walk away. I would not be a monster. She couldn't have me. My only option for freedom was with my death. I knew it now. That was the whole purpose. This was the moment I had been led to. I glanced at Custos. The look in his eyes confirmed everything I felt. Eudora had once chosen death over imprisonment, and now I found myself in a very familiar situation. I had already lived this experience. I knew I could do it again.

You choose wisely, Phenice. Have faith. The Fates chimed in my mind.

With my voice strong but quiet, I spoke up. "Sadeh, you are not *my* queen, and even though these people are my kind, they are not *my* people. They do not make the same choices I make. I will not join you, and you will not own me. You can't have me. I'm not for sale, not at any price, and not for any pain, not even death."

"You disrespect your queen! Be cautious in what you say; mere words will justify death!" she shouted loud and clear, her tone commanding.

"Then I choose death. For you have given me no choice. You are *not* my queen! Nor anyone's, for that matter. You are a curse to this world. You are nothing more than an abomination. A mistake. A fucking plague of damnation and ruination!" I found the strength to make my voice firm and clear.

"Death it is, even though it saddens me, Phenice." She smiled as she said it.

"So be it," I responded.

With a nod from their queen, Dover and Lecter stood and walked quickly to me. So quickly I lost them for a moment due to my weakened state. Then, once again, the pain took over. It shot through my back along my spine.

I gasped, swallowing my screams. I would not squeal for her.

It burned as my blood ran hot down my naked body. With their knives they worked with fast and skilled hands. I could feel precise cuts being made, but that didn't make them hurt any less. They paused, giving me a moment of relief, but it was followed by my skin being torn from my body. Pain flared again; light flashed in front of my eyes. I thought I might pass out and darkness would be my mistress of mercy.

I prayed for the darkness, but I remained conscious and painfully aware. I felt their busy fingers digging deep into my back. Then the popping and snapping started. My gut tied in knots, nausea rose in waves up my throat, but I swallowed it. I wouldn't give that bitch anything else. Not today, not ever!

I was sweating. The fresh air helped. I made myself breathe through my mouth. I didn't want the smell of my blood to be my last memory.

They pulled my ribs away from my spine one by one, giving me wings and exposing my lungs and other organs for them to play with. I started to go blissfully numb. I was thankful. Once they were done, I was left a boney-winged vampire for all to see. They paused.

"Let this be a warning to all. Phenice dies here tonight for her moral righteousness, for the heart in her chest which consumes her. It's a weakness, one I will not tolerate. As a result, I am taking it from her. Whether she would've submitted or not, she is worthless as long as that *thing* beats in her chest." She turned her cold, icy stare on me. "Your death means nothing to me." She spat.

Then with no warning, Lecter reached into my opened back, putting his hands around my heart, and pulled.

In an instant I was cold. I felt numb, dead, even though I wasn't. I was hollow. Just a shell of existence, truly a living corpse. If I ever wondered before if being a vampire made me less than I was as a human, that moment answered every question I ever had on the subject. The transformation didn't take anything from me. It didn't make me a monster or broken. It didn't even make me not human. I had simply become *more*, and now it was all being taken away. Ripped out by the hands of a true monster, ordered by an apocalyptic beast.

Lost in the dread consuming me, I hadn't noticed Dover setting the fire. The flames began to dance around my feet. I was happy for the warmth. I welcomed it after the blistering coldness had begun to eat away from the absence of my heart. I felt the fire screaming out to me, wanting me to call it. I probably could have done something to stop it. I might have been able to call the flames to me, to set them all on fire, but the coldness was turning into a gaping dark void consuming my chest. All desire to carry on was crushed. There was an icy gloom hardening my earthly vessel.

I lifted my head slightly. I saw Sadeh holding my heart in her hand. How she got it, I didn't know. She licked my blood from it, tasting her victory. She took pleasure in my defeat, in my death, but I didn't care. She hadn't really beaten me. I would die untainted by her evil. I would leave this world whole. I was proud she had not broken me. I continued to stare at her through the fire. I wasn't afraid.

It took a while for my flesh to catch fire. I expected it to hurt, but after the torture in Hell's Hollow, it was more of a tickle as it caressed up my body, burning me to ash. I was happy to be dying. My only regret was not saying goodbye to Emil.

I closed my eyes, holding the image of Emil's face. He would be the last thing I saw, while I let the flames have me. I felt a thud and knew Sadeh had thrown my heart into the flames. She wanted all of me to burn and with my heart ash at my feet, death truly was my only choice.

The heat consumed me. It poured over me. The last thing I remembered was being engulfed by the scorching blaze as it tickled and licked me. Then, nothing.

EPILOGUE

I wasn't supposed to have an afterlife. Death was supposed to be the end for a vampire. My soul was bound to that body for all eternity, and there it was ash. Yet my soul floated up and away, and I still existed in some form. I was not defeated, but my body was no more.

I watched as Custos shifted into his falcon form. What a beautiful creature he was in any form. With amazing speed, he flew toward the columns and the ash of my remains. Once there he circled around and around my cinders, creating an incredible tornado that lifted what was left of my earthly self into the air. Then he vanished.

To be continued…

"New beginnings are often disguised as painful endings."
Lao Tzu

Connect with Me!

https://linktr.ee/maddieroseandry

Desperate for more of Phenice and Emil?
And can't wait for book two? I've got you!

Below is a special spicy after dark bonus scene.

Mortal End—After Dark: Predator & Prey

Deep in the dungeons of a hidden castle, soulmates collide in a necessary battle for survival. When one turns predator, will the other submit, and be prey? Find out in this After Dark bonus scene.

Content Guidance

- This Bonus Scene contains sexually explicit content, and an image considered NSFW (if you select the one with the image).
- Now is your chance to turn back 😉
- No… you're going for it? Well have fun—I know I did while writing it!!! 👻 🖤

Mortal End—Predator & Prey (with image)
https://BookHip.com/XBPVTLP

Mortal End—Predator & Prey (no image)
https://BookHip.com/DRMKGWL

ACKNOWLEDGMENTS

This may be harder to write than the book you just finished. Firstly I want to thank my husband, Matt, for so many things, but mainly for loving me just as I am and for supporting me through this incredible journey. Without him no one would get to read *Mortal End*. Matt is my soulmate. I am glad life threw us together.

To my young daughters (well, not so young anymore) for understanding what it means to follow your dreams, for being patient with me while I put in the long hours to give *birth* to this story. It has meant so much to finally publish a book I finished before they were even born (2009, to be exact). I decided to be a mom for years while this novel sat on the *shelf.* I am proud of the amazing people all of my children are becoming, and I am so grateful to spend my days with them. I am grateful for the support my sons have given me through this process too. My children are etched on my soul, and I couldn't image life without any of them.

To my fur babies, for their presence and company during my long writing sessions. Their unconditional love has kept me going on the long, hard days, as has the food my husband brings to me because I often get so caught up in writing I forget to eat (seriously I do).

I want to thank my amazing staff at our medical practice for everything they do to keep things running smoothly so I may make time to write and follow my dreams while still being able to see the patients who rely on me. Also thank you, ladies, for believing in me. I love you beyond words.

To my best friend, Heather, I appreciate every push you have given me along the way. I don't know how much longer this would have taken me without your support and love. You have forever been my soul sister and forever will be. I love you.

To Olaf, thank you for the encouragement to drop my sails and let the wind carry me—it has been an adventure, and with your support the waves have been delightful.

To Bret and Christine, you both are the ultimate cheerleaders and support system. Thank you for supporting all of our family—we love you both and are forever humbled by your presence.

To all of my family—I love you and thank you for believing in me. It truly means more than words can express.

To the team at Elite Authors and Smith Publicity, thank you for answering every one of my questions—they were vast, and you all were patient and amazing.

To Jenelle Hovde, artist extraordinaire, thank you from the bottom of my heart for bringing my characters to life through your awe-inspiring talent. Your patience with me was beyond precious—words truly are not good enough for how much I appreciate you.

And finally, to my high school English teacher who believed in me and fought for me when no one else would. Mrs. Claire Schaffer, you didn't see a statistic; you saw a smart, hurt, and struggling young woman—one you refused to let fall through the cracks. Your acts of kindness and love most definitely changed the trajectory of my life. For that I will forever be thankful and inspired by you. My deepest gratitude to you!

Until Next Time,

ABOUT THE AUTHOR

Maddie Rose Andry is a licensed nurse in private practice as a certified relationship and trauma specialist.

Mortal End: An Opera of Cursed and Fated Vampires is her debut novel.

Maddie is the founder of Gothic Medicine, where she merges her two worlds—her therapeutic knowledge and the power of fiction. Healing can happen through storytelling, which was an original purpose of classic gothic literature. Our realities are shaped by the stories we hear and tell ourselves; reading increases our empathy and compassion for ourselves and others.

Through her fiction, Maddie encourages readers to connect with themselves as they embark on otherworldly journeys that reflect real-life traumas and obstacles and explore how to overcome, heal, and thrive.

Maddie is a wife and a mother to two daughters and three stepsons, two goldendoodles, and two Maine Coon cats.

She resides in beautiful Bloomington, Indiana. She loves books, tea, yoga, and everything cozy.

Website: www.maddieroseandry.com
Instagram: @authormaddieroseandry